Kelly Black
STRETCH Island
2004

O9-BUC-792

7⁵⁰

32 CADILLACS

By Joe Gores

NOVELS

A Time of Predators (1969)
Interface (1974)
Hammett (1975)
Come Morning (1986)
Wolf Time (1989)

DKA FILE NOVELS

Dead Skip (1972)
Final Notice (1973)
Gone, No Forwarding (1978)
32 Cadillacs (1992)

NONFICTION

Marine Salvage (1971)

ANTHOLOGIES

Honolulu, Port of Call (1974)
Tricks and Treats (1976)
  (with Bill Pronzini)

SCREENPLAYS

Interface (1974)
Hammett (1977–78)
Paper Crimes (1978)
Paradise Road (1978)
Fallen Angel (1980)
Cover Story (1984–85)
  (with Kevin Wade)
Come Morning (1986)
Run Cunning (1987)
Gangbusters (1989–90)

TELEPLAYS

Golden Gate Memorial (1978)
  (four-hour miniseries)
High Risk (1985)
  (with Brian Garfield)
"Blind Chess" (B. L. Stryker, 1989)

EPISODIC TV (1974–92)

Kojak	Remington Steele
Eischied	Scene of the Crime
Kate Loves a Mystery	Eye to Eye
The Gangster Chronicles	Helltown
Strike Force	T. J. Hooker
Magnum, P.I.	Mike Hammer
Columbo	

32 CADILLACS

JOE GORES

THE MYSTERIOUS PRESS
New York • Tokyo • Sweden
Published by Warner Books

 A Time Warner Company

Copyright © 1992 by Joe Gores
All rights reserved.

 Mysterious Press books are published by
Warner Books, Inc., 1271 Avenue of the Americas, New York, NY 10020.

A Time Warner Company

Printed in the United States of America

First printing: December 1992

10 9 8 7 6 5 4 3 2

Library of Congress Cataloging in Publication Data

Gores, Joe, 1937–
    32 cadillacs / Joe Gores.
        p.   cm.
    ISBN 0-89296-298-4
    I. Title.   II. Title: Thirty-two cadillacs.
PS3557.7 .O75A614   1992
813'.54—dc20
                                                        91-51183
                                                           CIP

This book is for

My beloved Dori

Who helped me snatch a Cadillac from
Mafia hitman Jimmy "The Weasel" Fratianno
on our first date

"Please don't talk," said the nun. "It's dangerous for you to talk, you're very seriously ill."

"Not so seriously as you're well. How don't you enjoy life, mother. I should laugh all round my neck at this very minute if my shirt wasn't a bit on the tight side."

"It would be better for you to pray."

"Same thing, mother."

Joyce Cary
The Horse's Mouth

Every man is as Heaven made him, and
sometimes a great deal worse.

Miguel de Cervantes
Don Quixote

JUST SO YOU KNOW

I offer the usual disclaimer: the characters, events, and places in this novel are totally fictional, products of the author's lively imagination. Now, having said that:

Once upon a time a band of Gypsies really did rip off thirty-two cars from a large San Francisco Bay Area bank in a single day. During the next months David Kikkert & Associates, hired to recover them, grabbed twenty-nine of the thirty-two all over the U.S.A. (including Hawaii) and in Mexico.

Here's where, in *32 Cadillacs,* the currency of truth becomes funny money, for not every repo in the novel took place while tracking down these Gypsies during a twenty-six-day time frame. Some were "stretched" a bit, others were from elsewhere in my dozen years as a legal car thief, but all really happened—even Lake Shore Drive in Chicago and the Lovellis in Nebraska.

Although my stance toward the *rom* during my detective career was strictly adversarial, my Gypsy lore in *32 Cadillacs* is as honest as research and experience can make it, as are their scams, cons, and grifts. And I have tried to make my fictional Gypsies realistic— and fun—without sentimentalizing them. If you sentimentalize Gypsies, you run the risk of ending up with a car that won't run, a roof that won't stop the rain, or a driveway that comes up on the sole of your shoe.

On that note: our society becomes ever more bland, ever more afraid of countless pressure groups poised to scream foul if their particular toe gets stepped on. In *32 Cadillacs* they can find a lot to scream about. But to sanitize the tough and lively world I am writing of would be to make its people mere hollow reeds, the novel itself an exercise in futility.

The amount you can withdraw from a bank account without federal scrutiny is *under* $10,000, so actually my Gypsies should be moving $9,999.99 around during their bank scam. It was just a lot less cumbersome to make it an even 10K.

Bizarre as they might seem, the shenanigans at the Giggling Marlin in Cabo San Lucas are a real, nightly occurrence.

Finally, I want to round up the usual suspects:

First, foremost, and always, Dori—beloved wife, best friend, peerless editor, critic, greatest support—who bled a lot over this book and lent it her own invaluable Gypsy research.

My agents, Henry Morrison and Danny Baror, poked and prodded and threatened and cajoled and never lost faith.

Otto and Carolyn Penzler, early enthusiasts when they *were* Mysterious Press, and Bill Malloy, who continued their enthusiasm after he took over as editor in chief of Mysterious.

Martin Cruz Smith shared his research from *Gypsy in Amber* and *Canto for a Gypsy;* his lovely wife, Em, did the same with the notebooks and diaries from her remarkable clergyman grandfather's lifelong involvement with the Gypsies.

Inspector Victor Rykoff, SFPD Bunco, is not anything at all like Dirty Harry Harrigan; and no one like Stan Groner was ever remotely involved in the Great Gypsy Hunt.

Don Westlake found these tales amusing over a long Mohonk weekend, and later, during a train ride in Spain, suggested sharing a chapter of this book with one of his own (it turned up in his Dortmunder classic, *Drowned Hopes*).

Finally, the real guys and gals of the once-real DKA:

Dave Kikkert (R.I.P.)
Hiroko Ono (R.I.P.)
Ronile Lahti

32 Cadillacs

Maurice James O'Brien
Floyd Ryan
Ken Warner
Isadore "Izzy" Martinez
and
the Me I was then
Gang, I couldn't spin all these tall tales without you.

Joe Gores
San Anselmo
April, 1992

32 CADILLACS

SIX MONTHS BEFORE

At 5:04:09 P.M. on a Tuesday, October 17, Daniel Kearny Associates' narrow high-shouldered old charcoal Victorian at 760 Golden Gate Avenue . . . *fell over.*

Seven-point-two on the Richter scale. That's all it took.

In the Gay '90s the old building had been a high-class bawdy house for San Francisco's movers and shakers, and Dan Kearny had just gotten Landmark status for it by shaming the City into honoring these fallen women among its other heroes—madmen, tarnished athletes, dishonest cops, corrupt politicians.

But what the State of California had been unable to do in ten years of trying, the San Andreas fault, after gulping downtown Santa Cruz a hundred miles south, accomplished with a discreet belch. Only because DKA had closed early for the World Series was no one hurt during those seventeen violent seconds in which 760 was gone, gone to dust, its memories with it.

Which left the DKA Head Office (Branch Offices in All Major California Cities) abruptly located Nowhere. Yet Giselle Marc, DKA's office manager, when surveying the tipsy splintered remains the next morning, sighed as much for the ghosts of scented ladies and boar-eyed power brokers as for DKA's current plight.

1

"The damnedest finest ruins," she murmured, echoing San Francisco's epitaph after the Big One in '06.

Giselle, who combined an M.A. in history with her own P.I. license, was an exquisite racehorse blonde with bedroom eyes that masked boardroom brains. Brains discovered to their sorrow by many of DKA's cockier adversaries just moments before the hammer fell on them.

"I wish Richter had gotten flattened himself, before he invented the damn scale," Dan Kearny growled.

Kearny was a flint-faced 52, with icy grey eyes and a cement-mixer jaw, his thinning curly hair getting frosty around the edges. His nose obviously once had met an object harder than itself moving very rapidly in the opposite direction.

"What good would that have done, Dan'l? Somebody else just would have come up with a measurement for seismic activity."

"Seven-point-two on the Smith scale?" He chuckled for the first time in two days. "Well, what the hell, the place had gotten too small for us, anyway."

Which was true. The upstairs clerical offices had been a rabbit warren of tiny rooms crowded with too many people and too much equipment, and Kearny and the field men had been crammed into mouseholes in an under-the-building garage with room left over for only a repo or two. For over a decade DKA had leased storage lots all over town for the cars it had repossessed.

"I wonder if the phones still work?" Kearny muttered.

They didn't. But those down at 340 Eleventh Street did. Years before, when the state first started trying to get the old Victorian condemned for a Social Services parking lot, Kearny had bought a disused laundry South of Market as a backup site, and had been desultorily remodeling it a weekend at a time ever since. Now, suddenly, that old laundry was the New Jerusalem.

*   *   *

As Kearny and Giselle talked, by honest, genuine, sheer chance, a man calling himself Karl Klenhard and his wife of over fifty years, calling herself Margarete, were waiting for the light at a corner in Steubenville ("Where the Tall Corn Grows"), Iowa. Steubenville—not to be confused with the much more nifty Steubenville in Ohio—was county seat for 9,581 souls and several hundred square

2

miles of rich alluvial flatland below the bluffs of the Mighty Mississippi.

Steubenville had been settled in the late 1800s by farmers from
Trier, Prussia; in those early days, paddlewheel steamers plying
the river offered tempting access to markets for their produce.
But times change, markets shift, prices rise and fall, and with the
Midwest farm crunch Steubenville had become Stupidville to those
unfortunate enough to still live there.

Karl did not look stupid, but he did fit right in with the local
populace: his Santa Claus smile, great walrus mustache, and gold
watch chain glinting across a benevolent expanse of belly all suggested the retired German burgher. As for Margarete, her plump
bosom, high color, and twinkly eyes above glowing apple cheeks
made her look like a ceramic cookie jar. Only the cigarette smouldering between the first two fingers of her right hand hinted at
anything other than classic *Hausfrau*.

Here's where chance comes in: as they waited at the light, an
elderly Eldorado with those majestic '50s tailfins stretching out
forever behind it rolled by them. Karl leaned jauntily on his ornate
gold-headed cane and gave Margarete a nostalgic little pat on the
fanny in honor of other tailfins in other times.

"Remember the pink nineteen fifty-eight Caddy convertible we
rode to my coronation? Ah, darling, what times we had!"

"Yes, my dumpling," said Margarete with shining eyes. Then a
hint of sadness crossed her face. "We're getting old, *Liebchen*. It
makes one think of retirement."

The light had changed. They started slowly across the intersection, two loving old people arm in arm.

"Retirement." Karl's voice savored the word, but his eyes had
taken on a speculative gleam. "Nineteen fifty-eight." He smiled a
beatific smile. "The year I became King."

CHAPTER ONE

T. S. Eliot once remarked that April is the cruellest month. But on this Tuesday the 17th, six months to the day after the Bay Area's devastating temblor, April did not seem cruel at all.

Oh, there were the usual traumas: breakdowns on BART, too many homeless on the streets, a tanker grounded in the bay, water rationing in place for this sixth straight drought year despite the miracle March rains. But the IRS beast had gotten its human sacrifice for another season; most of the quake damage had been repaired or swept out of sight; and the A's—if not the Giants—looked in top early-season form.

And remodeling was finished at 340 Eleventh Street. In the first of two (count 'em, two!) huge open ground-floor offices—each larger than the entire setup had been at 760 Golden Gate—were the skip-tracers and clerical staff. And Dan Kearny himself, strategically placed to slip out the back door if a process server stormed the front.

In the other ground-floor office were the CB, the fax, and the computer. Here also, under Giselle's watchful eye, were the teenage girls who earned after-school money churning out skip and legal letters on the old but serviceable automatic typewriters.

Upstairs were actual *offices* for the field agents—with desks and chairs and phones and even typewriters for one-fingering reports.

And out in back was storage for *twenty* cars.

So, with **DANIEL KEARNY ASSOCIATES** backward on the glass of the door in fresh paint, DKA was again ready to find people who had defaulted, defrauded, or embezzled, and to wrest away their purloined assets for return to its clients. Clients who, unfortunately, were not the sultry blondes and devious tycoons of fiction. They were, rather, much more mundane banks, bonding companies, financial institutions, and insurance conglomerates.

On this bright spring day, typewriters clacked, phones clamored, exhaust fumes wafted in from the storage yard where someone was gunning a repo. At Jane Goldson's reception desk a big hard-looking man with a tough jaw and lank, close-trimmed brown hair had written KEN WARREN on an employment application and was trying to add to that. Jane kept rolling the conversational ball at him, which he kept not rolling back.

"How did you say you found us, Mr. . . . um . . ."

Warren chewed on his pencil eraser in morose silence.

"If you've never done this sort of thing before, actually, it is rather difficult to . . . er . . ."

Warren laboriously filled in another line on the app. His scowl could have blistered paint. Sliding back her chair, Jane gave him a brilliant smile and some equally brilliant thigh.

"Perhaps you'd best speak with Mr. Kearny directly . . ."

Daunted by the application form, Warren was unaware of smile, thigh, or remark. Okay, sure, applying in writing was better than trying to explain himself verbally; but even so, most of what he did best really couldn't be put down on paper.

Kearny's left hand was shaking a Marlboro from his pack as Jane came up to his desk; his right continued its creative bookkeeping on the rather thin stack of billing before him. Cash flow, cash flow—relocating had cost a mint, and clients, waiting to see if they'd survive it, had been hesitant. A minor irritant was the cleaning service—it was lousy.

Jane moved her head slightly toward the man scowling over the clipboard at the far end of the office. Kearny raised heavy interrogative brows at her through his first wisp of carcinogens.

6

"So?"

"Actually, Mr. K, he just wandered in off the street," Jane said in her tart cockney accent. "But . . ."

"So what's the gag?" Even in a slow month they always had room for a good repoman. "Let him fill in the app and—"

"So maybe you'd best hear for yourself, hadn't you?"

Summoned down the office, the big man looked okay to Kearny. Better than okay, in fact. Hard-faced, moved well . . . of course in a 3:00 A.M. alley a lot of self-styled tough dudes had tiny balls. Kearny stood up and stuck out his hand. He'd hear what the big guy had to say.

The big guy said, "GnYm Kgen Gwarren."

Oh.

*   *   *

Those same six months since the San Francisco quake did not seem to have been so kind to Karl Klenhard back there in Stupidville. No longer did his gold watch chain stretch taut across a splendid belly. It sagged. No longer did he stride. He shuffled. No longer did he use his gold-headed cane with a *boulevardier* flair, but as one dependent upon its support.

Margarete held his free arm protectively as she guided him into the town's largest department store. He was being loud, querulous, and rambling in a newly acquired old-man's voice.

"But we gotta get her somethin' today!" Close to tears. *"It's our own little granddaughter we're talkin' about here . . ."*

Margarete said placatingly, "I saw a lovely little pinafore just her size on the lower level, *Liebchen . . ."*

She had to let go of his arm so Karl could grasp the moving handrail of the down escalator at the same time that he stepped on one of its moving stairs. His hand missed, his foot missed. With a loud cry, Karl took a terrifying headlong tumble, arms and legs windmilling, cane flying, falling down . . . down . . . down . . .

Thud! Crash! Crunch!

Margarete, screaming and wringing work-roughened hands, looked down the escalator to her septuagenarian husband crumpled at its foot. Karl lay in an unnatural position, his only movement the flapping of one hand as each stair passed beneath it. Horrified clerks were dashing about, the manager was coming from his office at a dead run, the floor man was already calling for an ambulance on his cordless phone.

*   *   *

In San Francisco, her office manager duties being post-move slow, Giselle Marc was on the street. She'd gotten her driver's license just before the quake—on her 32nd birthday, yet!—and since then had been doing all the field work she could squeeze in. More valuable to DKA at her desk, perhaps, but she *loved* it out here. And she was good at it.

Well, maybe she didn't *always* love it. Maybelle Pernod, fat, black, and 61, should have been home bouncing grandchildren on her knee. Instead, after a week of skip-tracing, Giselle had found her sweating off the pounds over a pressing machine in a dry-cleaning plant on Third Street's 4600 block. They had to shout to hear each other over the *hiss-s-s-swhoosh* of the pressers, sweat stippling their faces and running down between their breasts as they faced each other through clouds of steam.

At issue was a 1991 Continental that was two payments down.

"Woman, Ah *cain't* give up ma car!"

"You *have* to, Maybelle. We've got no current residence address on you—"

"Hain't rightly settled into my new place yet—"

"Maybelle, you don't have a new place. No res add, casual labor here at the cleaner's, your third payment comes delinquent the end of the week—"

Maybelle's dark eyes gleamed stubbornly in her ebony face. She stuck out an ample lower lip. "Hain't gonna give up ma car."

Giselle held up the coil wire she had taken from beneath the hood of the Connie before entering the plant.

"That isn't the question here, Maybelle. I thought maybe you'd want to remove your personal possessions before it goes."

"But that car . . . I don't got that car, I don't got . . ."

Big fat tears rolled down Maybelle's big fat cheeks like rain down a windowpane. Giselle had to stiffen up before she got all soggy, as Larry Ballard sometimes did with hard-luck women.

"Maybelle, the car is history. Do you want your personal property or not?"

8

Maybelle swiped a catcher's-mitt hand across her eyes and gave Giselle the keys. "Honey, you jes leave all that stuff in that Connie. Maybelle get her car back, you jes wait an see."

*   *   *

Within hours, like concentric rings of wavelets from a stone tossed into a pond, word about Karl Klenhard's plunge down the escalator began going out from the Midwest to the *rom* scattered around the country. Officially, Gypsies do not exist in the United States; in reality, as many as two million of them from four "nations" and some sixty different tribes roam the land unrecorded and un-checked by an indifferent bureaucracy.

The King is down, went the word. The King is injured . . . the King is *badly* injured . . . the King (only whisper this) *may not recover . . .*

The strongest candidates for his crown were both working out of San Francisco. One was a woman known to the *rom* as Yana, and to the straight, *gadjo*, non-Gypsy world as Madame Miseria. The other was Rudolph Marino, who right now looked not like a Gypsy but like a Sicilian who had gotten his MBA from Harvard and had aced the bar exam on his way to Mouthpiece for the Mob.

Marino's gleaming black razor-cut was thick and lustrous, the planes of his swarthy face piratical. His pearl-grey suit, ghosted out of a Rodeo Drive clothiers in that oldest of gags, a suitcase with a snap-up bottom, was worth $1,200; his maroon silk foulard wore a *faux* ruby stickpin as big as his thumb.

As he sauntered up to Reception at the venerably luxurious St. Mark Hotel, where California Street starts its swoop from Nob Hill down to the financial district, he covertly sized up the check-in clerk. She wore a name tag that said MARLA and she was tall and blond and businesslike; but he saw the little click in her eyes when they met his. Useful. Perhaps very useful. Already he was fitting her into his plan.

"May I help you, Mr. . . ."

"Grimaldi," said Marino. He caressed her face with black eyes, limpid yet with cold depths that made *gadje* girls go weak at the knees. He laid a Goldcard on the desktop. "Angelo Grimaldi from New York. I have a reservation. A suite."

Her fingers flew over the keyboard. The screen scrolled its reservation arcana. "Here it is, Mr. Grimaldi." Their eyes met again. She fumbled getting the registration blank on the desktop before him. "I hope you will enjoy your stay with us."

He let his eyes widen very slightly. He tapped a finger on the face of her telephone to show he had memorized her extension.

"I am sure that I will, *cara.*"

He stalked away, followed onto the elevator by one of the Mark's ancient bellmen burdened with Louis Vuitton luggage picked up by a Florida tribe from a Worth Avenue shoppe torched in an insurance scam. To Marla the Check-in Clerk he seemed a leopard on the loose among the flocks of tourists—mostly name-tagged, camera-laden Japanese. She made a small noise in her throat, then jerked herself erect, reddening at her own X-rated thoughts.

In the elevator, Marino was also occupied with his thoughts, and indeed she was part of them. But not as she might have wished. Women, though useful and capable of giving great pleasure, were unclean. Especially *gadje* women. He would use her, nothing more, during the three weeks before the real Grimaldi returned from the Maine woods to find his Manhattan apartment rifled and his credit cards stolen. Three weeks.

Time enough. Marino's elaborate scam on the hotel's management would be his greatest coup to date.

*   *   *

On the far side of Russian Hill, Larry Ballard and Patrick Michael O'Bannon—O'B to the troops at DKA—were getting into the elevator at the Montana, a high-rise co-op overlooking bowl-shaped Aquatic Park from the foot of Polk Street. The site had been zoned low-rise until certain of the City's key officials had found their Christmas stockings stuffed with—miracle of miracles!—foreign vacations and new cars and fur coats for their wives. Subsequently—another miracle!—the Montana Development Corporation had been granted the supposedly impossible building code variances it sought.

"Just your typical San Francisco success story," O'B was explaining to Ballard as they rode up in the elevator.

Larry didn't answer. He was getting his fierce expression in place for Pietro Uvaldi, a piece of cake who lived the good life at the

Montana with his latest poopsie. Unfortunately, Pietro had fallen behind on the payments for his $83,500 Mercedes 500SL sports convertible.

Ballard considered him a piece of cake because Pietro was an interior decorator—nudge, nudge, wink, wink—while Ballard was blatantly hetero and unwittingly macho, eight years a manhunter, a shade under six feet tall, 180 pounds, with sun-bleached blond hair and a hawk nose and killer blue eyes and a hard-won brown belt in karate.

He flipped the coin O'B had handed him. O'B called it in the air. "Tails."

The coin's reverse glinted in the elevator's plush carpet.

"Two out of three," said Ballard quickly.

O'B merely shook his head and pocketed his coin without revealing that it had tails on both sides. While not Ballard's physical equal—slight, 50 years old, with a leathery freckled drinker's face and greying red hair—O'B was wily as a Market Street hustler, fast-talking as a southern tent preacher. Some quarter-century before he had broken in on credit jewelry, the world's toughest repo work: you can't pop the ignition on a diamond wedding set and drive it away from the curb.

"Sorry, Larry me lad. *I* get to drive the Mercedes and *you* get to make out the condition report and file the police report."

They left the elevator at the twelfth floor. O'B rang Pietro's bell and straightened his tie and let his face relax into its world-weary expression; Ballard's fierce expression was already in place. But the door was opened by a six-foot-six 240-pound man wearing pink spiked hair and black leather underwear with chrome studs. His biceps were like grapefruit.

Certainly not Pietro the defaulting decorator. Perchance his poopsie? But hey, no sweat: to O'B and Ballard, those stalwart repomen, interior decorators and those who slept with them *all* ate a lot of quiche.

A voice in the background called, "Freddi, who is it?"

"Two guys to see you."

"How exciting! Show them in, darling, show them in."

Ballard and O'B already were filling the antechamber with their collective bulk, mean and world-weary expressions in place. As expected, fearsome Freddi (*Freddi?*) faded away without challenge.

11

Pietro, small, precise, barefoot, wore a silk *smoking* of an incredible green paisley and looked as if he might have danced a mean Lambada during its fifteen minutes of fame.

"From the bank," grated O'B.

"About the Mercedes," snarled Ballard.

"You . . . want . . . to take . . . my . . . Mercedes?"

"As in two payments down," sneered Ballard, flexing.

"The keys." O'B held out an inexorable palm.

Pietro got a glazed look in his eyes. His color suddenly matched that of his paisley jacket. He crossed to the coat closet where his topcoat was hanging, the perspiration of distress etching his bare soles on the polished hardwood floor.

O'B turned to grin at Ballard. The keys would be in the topcoat pocket. An easy repo. The old mouth-breather routine got to this sort of creampuff every time.

Pietro turned back with a 12-gauge double-barreled shotgun he'd taken from behind the topcoat. Ballard's mouth fell open. O'B's riot of freckles was suddenly very prominent against the pallor replacing his ruddy drinker's complexion.

"Wait a minute," he said, the extended hand now palm-out like a traffic cop's.

Pietro broke open the shotgun with a jerk of his stubby square-nailed hands. Clear lacquer glinted on the nails.

Ballard said, "You don't have to—"

Pietro rammed a double-O shell up the shotgun's nose. Ballard's and O'B's eyes met. The whites showed all the way around, like those of spooked horses. Each hoped to see the other miraculously transformed into James Bond lounging against the door frame, silenced 9mm Walther PPK in hand. Neither did.

They began in unison, "We can work something ou—"

Pietro rammed another double-O up the shotgun's other nostril. He slammed the gun shut with the clap of doom.

Taking the twelve flights to the ground floor, O'B and Ballard didn't bother with the elevator. They barely used the stairs.

*   *   *

Over in North Beach, last night's stale beer and cigarettes still fouled the air of the Pink Flesh, a topless bar somehow surviving Broadway's Carol Doda days. On a minuscule stage an overage

12

blonde in an underage costume lackadaisically bumped-and-ground to the canned music. No one, not even herself, paid the slightest heed to her gyrations. Most of the customers were Chinese, but behind the stick was a tough-faced Italian who sprinkled salt in beer glasses, scrubbed them, sloshed them around in hot sudsy water, and put them upside down to drain.

Once upon a time, Chinatown and Italian North Beach happily had shunted bilingual insults at each other across Broadway from Columbus Ave all the way to the Tunnel. In those halcyon days, Broadway was a knife-cut between the racial entities. But the topless '70s weakened the strong Italian presence, and the open-armed '80s brought a vast influx of legal and illegal Hong Kong FOBs— Fresh off the Boats—into Chinatown. So many Chinese immigrants spilled across Broadway that for a time it looked as if the Italians would disappear from North Beach.

But everything that goes around comes around, as they say, and in the tight-ass '90s, legal and illegal *Italian* immigrants began flooding back in, shouldering aside the Chinese, replacing the Italian families that had fled to the suburbs.

Hence the Pink Flesh: Italian ownership, Chinese clientele, suspended between cultures. And, being topless, as anachronistic as a VW van wearing peace symbols and psychedelic colors.

Among the customers dotting the stick like adolescent acne was one who was neither Italian nor Chinese: a swarthy gent who that week called himself Ramon Ristik. He might have been a Roosian, a French or Turk or Proosian—but he was in fact a Gypsy. Brother of that Yana (a.k.a. Madame Miseria) who was in line for possible succession to the damaged King's throne.

Ristik was trying to read the palm of one Theodore Winston White III, a slender half-drunk blond chap descended from Marin County's rarefied heights for a day in the fleshpots.

"You don't understand," Teddy said, rescuing his hand from Ristik with drunken gravity. "There is nothing you can tell me. *Nothing.* Never knew my mother, never knew my father . . ."

"Yezz, yezz, I know," buzzed Ristik in uninterested gutturals, reaching again for the hand. "Izz most difficult."

Teddy again pulled it away. "I was adopted right after I was born. Never knew 'em. My parents. But I've always felt . . . there was something hanging over me . . ."

"Fate," said Ristik. "Yezz. Izz bad. Izz very bad. That izz why I must . . ."

He finally succeeded in snaring Teddy's hand. He turned it palm-up on the bartop. He stared at it. Teddy didn't want to be interested, but the very intensity of Ristik's attention was like a focused burning glass. Ristik emitted a low moan.

Teddy demanded, despite himself, "What is it? What . . ."

But Ristik had dropped Teddy's hand as if it were the monkey's severed paw, capable of scuttling off around the bartop all by itself. His buzzing sibilants were gone.

"My God, man! You're too heavy for me, I can't handle it!"

"What do you see? What—"

"This is a job requires my sister!" Ristik exclaimed hoarsely. "She's the only one strong enough to deal with this!"

"Deal with *what?*" Teddy looked about to burst into tears.

Ristik leaped to his feet, clasped Teddy briefly and fiercely to his bosom, sorrow and terror in his face.

"The curse!" he hissed. "You've been *cursed!*"

Then he rushed out, thrusting aside the threadbare plush curtain over the open doorway and letting in a stream of dusty sunlight to impale Teddy's hand palm-up on the bar. Teddy jerked the hand away, scattered paper money across the stick, and ran out, yelling, after Ristik.

CHAPTER TWO

Margarete Klenhard sat beside the Emergency Room Admitting Desk in Steubenville General Hospital, answering questions. Two of her answers were even true—the man calling himself Karl had indeed been born, and he was indeed her husband. He had, in fact, paid a $500 bride price for her over half a century before, back in the days when a dollar had meant something.

Hovering over her chair like a parent at a first recital was a large man with an extra chin and bullet eyes and a fringe of greying hair around a bald pate. Manager of the largest department store in Stupidville, he hoped that by paying Karl's medical bills he could avert a lawsuit for negligence in the matter of the escalator—and thus avoid skyrocketing his liability rates through the roof.

"Name of patient?"

"Karl Klenhard." Margarete's accent was heavy as a Black Forest cake. Her hands mauled the cheap handbag in her lap.

The nurse typed. "Date of birth?"

"My Karl is in Prussia born on the twenty-eighth of June, nineteen hundred and fourteen—the very day that the Archduke Ferdinand is in Sarajevo assassinated to start the Great War."

"Yes, I see," said the nurse, typing. She had a round red face and didn't see at all: she was of that age which thought Desert Storm had been the Great War. "U.S. citizen?"

"*Ja*. Naturalized. On the boat in nineteen twenty-five to New York City he comes. To the Statue of Liberty."

"Religion?"

"We are Lutheran, of course," said a scandalized Margarete.

"Emergency notification?"

"Me. Margarete Klenhard." Her real name was Lulu Zlachi, as Karl's was Staley Zlachi, but what's in a name? She laid a hand on her heart. "For more than fifty years I am his wife."

"Insurance?"

"We have none. We are poor folk. We—"

"No insurance." Typing. "That's going to be a prob—"

The department store manager cut in hurriedly, "Ah, the store will be . . . ah . . . handling monetary matters in, um . . ."

On the floor above, Staley was being rolled into the X-ray room on a blanket-covered gurney. Two husky orderlies in green gowns carefully took hold of the ends of the sheet on which he lay and slid Staley onto the cold metal table. The X-ray machine hulked over him like some obscene metal vulture. At the move, he cried out.

The hovering nurse made a distressed sound in her throat.

"We have to turn him on his side." To Staley she said, unwillingly, "Sir, can you—"

Staley only groaned. The orderlies gingerly began to turn him. He shrieked with the pain and fainted just as Lulu burst through the door. The nurse grabbed her to keep her from throwing herself upon her husband's silent form like a dishonored Roman upon his sword. Lulu could only stand there, weeping copious tears and mauling her purse, as the vulture lowered its electronically charged beak to Staley's ashen flesh.

*　　*　　*

In San Francisco, Bart Heslip got out of his DKA company car because Sarah Walinski had just pulled her year-old Dodge Charger up across the sidewalk on the other side of the narrow Richmond District street. Sarah had beautiful taffy hair but was built like a bridge piling and had a face like a firedoor, with rivets for eyes. Since she was a skip out of New Jersey with the Charger, and had skipped again after running a previous repoman off with an axe, Heslip had a REPO ON SIGHT order for her car.

He was not afraid of playing hatchet-tag with Sarah: he'd won thirty-nine out of forty pro fights before deciding ten years before, then age 24, that he would never be middleweight champeen a de woild. At least not without having his brains scrambled into instant Alzheimer's.

So he'd traded his boxing gloves for a set of repo tools. Man-hunting for DKA gave him the same exhilaration and challenge he'd formerly gotten in the ring: out in the field it was still one-on-one, you against him. Or her. May the best person win.

One sack of groceries was out of the backseat and Sarah was reaching for the second to take into her rented half of the pastel stucco duplex row house when Heslip spoke cheerily to her back. "Sarah, I'm sorry but I have to take your car."

She whirled to glare at him. "How the goddam hell'd you find me, you goddam bleep-bleep-bleep-bleep nigger?"

Heslip was indeed black; plum black, in fact, with kinky hair and a thin mustache and the trained fighter's wide bunchy shoulders and natural physical arrogance. He'd been called all the bleep-bleep words before, by men who'd subsequently taken nourishment through a straw; but you couldn't bust a woman's chops, not even if she outweighed you by fifty pounds.

He said only, "You know how it is with us darkies, Sarah. We always out dere on dat street jivin' away, yessiree ma'am."

Jiving indeed. He'd already won, because he'd slipped into the driver's seat while she'd been bleeping away. Thus—unlike his timid-souled predecessor—he had control of the situation *before* it got out of hand. The keys were in the ignition and the engine was running. This would be the easiest grab of the month.

"Oh, take the goddam thing! Just lemme get the rest of my goddam groceries outta the goddam backseat . . ."

A charmer. Heslip drummed the steering wheel with patient fingers, then finally started to twist around in the seat.

"Sarah, if you need help with—"

The three-pound can of coffee, slammed lustily against the side of his head like a hurled rock, split his scalp as if it were a ripe apple. The blow knocked him right out of the car. Through double vision and dripping blood (*drip* grind, he thought confusedly), he

17

saw 200-pound Sarah slither into the front seat like a sea lion going into the water off Seal Rock. He thought he heard shrieking tires, dreamed he smelled burning rubber . . .

They were taking the twelfth stitch in Bart Heslip's scalp before he woke up again, flat on his back at SF General.

* * *

Lying naked on his back in the sex-rumpled bed, watching Marla the Check-in Clerk dress by the soft light from the bathroom, Rudolph Marino congratulated himself. His questions, apparently casual but as skillful as his lovemaking, had obliquely confirmed that his plan for the hotel would work.

Marla caught his eyes and gave him a slow, sensual smile as she squirmed into her pantyhose.

"That New York jet-lag didn't slow you down any, Angie . . ."

He pursed his lips in a little kissing motion. "Who could be anything but tireless with such beauty to spur him on?"

He had called her at the reception desk directly after checking into his suite. She had met him in the Garnet Room for a drink on her meal break, and that had led to this. He hadn't known whether she would be useful or not. She had been.

"From the moment I saw you, *cara,* I had to possess you."

She sat down on the edge of the bed, kissed him again, long and passionately. It was she who finally came up for air.

"I *knew* I was going to regret getting dressed so fast."

"There are other times, *cara,*" he said.

Cara. Darling. One of the dozen words he knew in Italian.

He let her kiss him once more, was out of bed as the door closed behind her, calling Housekeeping for a maid to bring fresh sheets, flushing the condom, jumping into the shower for a needle spray first hot as a chili pepper, then cold as a kidney stone.

Gadje women were unclean.

But useful.

He got dressed in front of the 5:00 P.M. news, becoming alert at the item about the President's forthcoming visit to San Francisco. That visit was why Marino was here, checked into this particular hotel. Yes! He went out to find a payphone from which to make his phony bomb threat in the phony Arab gutturals.

He returned to word of their fallen King.

*   *   *

Meanwhile, the smell of hot grease was, like Banquo's ghost, following Trinidad Morales up the trash-cluttered stairs over a 24th Street *taqueria* in the Mission District. Morales was 35, heavy-set, with small precise hands and feet and sly brown eyes and broad white teeth, a front one glinting with gold when he unclamped his thick lips from around his habitual cheap cigar.

Trin had quit DKA almost six years ago—"quit" was his euphemism for getting his butt booted into the street by Dan Kearny— had gotten himself his own P.I. license, and had opened an office down here off Mission in the Spanish-speaking end of town. On the door he had put:

TRINIDAD MORALES
CONFIDENTIAL INVESTIGATIONS
Cool—Careful—Confidential—Discreet

No more skip-tracing and repos for Trin Morales. Divorce work. Insurance frauds. Electronic snooping. Betrayed wives ready to get even for their husbands' infidelities by clocking a little motel time of their own with the investigator who'd wised 'em up to them cheatin' hearts. People who had said too much on a bugged phone willing to cross a brown palm with silver for discreet silences. The meaty stuff with the perks on the side.

It hadn't quite worked out that way. Puffing his way to the top of the stairs, Morales found his landlord, an Anglo with a face like a toothache, installing a new lock on his office door. A lock for which Trin would not have a key.

"Hey, what the hell you think you're doin', man?"

"I don't think, I *know*, beaner."

Trin started after him, then stopped abruptly with his hands surrendering their fists for placating palms: the landlord's heavy screwdriver was not being held the way screwdrivers are held to drive screws. Trin's gold filling glinted in a wide disarming grin as genuine as junk bonds.

"Whoa, man, there's some mistake here."

"An' you made it." The toothache put the screwdriver in its

toolbox, clanked it shut, strutted past Trin. "You can get your stuff back when you come up with the back rent—beaner."

Trin bounced rapid-fire Spanish curses off the landlord's heedless back, then sighed and got out his picks and started working on the new lock. Might as well clean out the office; he wouldn't be back. And since he'd just lost an argument with Pac Bell over *their* cut-off service, he might as well rip off their rental phone and sell that while he was at it.

And then maybe swallow his pride and ask that *chingada* Dan Kearny for his old job back as a DKA field agent. He could use Kearny's phone and company car and gasoline charge to work his own cases on the side. If he could get any cases on his own. If Kearny'd have him back.

* * * *

MADAME MISERIA
KNOWS ALL . . . SEES ALL . . . TELLS ALL . . .
No Secret Too DEEP . . . No Future Too BLEAK . . .
MADAME MISERIA Can Help <u>YOU</u>

A panting Theodore Winston White III caught up with Ramon Ristik outside the street door of Madame Miseria's palm-reading emporium on Romolo Place, one of the narrow one-block alleys leading up the side of Telegraph Hill from Broadway. It was so steep the sidewalk had stairs cut into it. The door had a seamed human palm in gilt paint facing out from inside the glass.

Teddy puffed, "I saw you . . . turning the corner down . . . on Broadway . . ."

Ristik, who'd made a point to be seen, paused for a moment, then shrugged as if submitting to fate and briefly and almost formally clasped Teddy to his bosom again, as in the bar. He stepped back.

"I cannot handle the weight of whatever future Madame Miseria might uncover," he said in a low voice, "so I must leave you alone with her. You will not have to tell her why you have come . . . she will feel the emanations . . ."

The fog had rolled in, the air was raw; it was starting to sober Teddy up, refocusing his paranoia, making him remember fanciful tales about Gypsy fortune-tellers.

"Listen, maybe I'd better come back tomor—"

But Ristik was already herding him up narrow, ill-lit interior stairs toward Yana's *ofica*. Teddy covertly and belatedly checked that his wallet with his money and I.D. was still in his suit coat pocket. It was. Ristik indeed had lifted it when he had embraced Teddy in the bar, and had telephoned Yana a *précis* of its contents; but then he had returned it intact during their second brief embrace just moments before.

Incense, a mere thought at the street door, became heavier, thicker, almost palpable as they ascended. When they were four steps from the second-floor landing, the heavy drapes were swept aside, squealing on their runners, to disclose a dramatically backlit woman in bright clothes staring down at them.

"Quickly," she said. "There is not much time to move through the aperture to infinity my brother opened when he looked at your palm."

"Listen, I don't think I want to . . ."

But she already was drawing him through the curtain, the rounded swell of her breast momentarily firm against his arm, her thigh fleetingly hot against his through the filmy layers of floor-length parrot-colored silk. Raven hair, a truly beautiful oval face somehow stern despite small, full-lipped mouth and short nose. Liquid black eyes seemed to look right through him. Not yet 30, she had all the wisdom of the ages in her face.

"Do not talk, please."

"But—"

"Please."

She led him down a narrow drape-lined hallway lit by lamps with dangling crystal shades that tinkled with their passage, around two or three corners, abruptly into a room where blood-red plush drapes masked the four walls and soaked up sound. The only light seemed to come from the glowing cantaloupe-size crystal ball waiting for Yana's *duikkerin* on a three-foot-square table covered all the way to the floor with black plush.

On other tables pushed back against the draperies were museum-quality Greek Orthodox icons next to ceramic figures won at carnival midways. Bottles of holy water and glowing colored votive candles enshrined a faded phrenologist's chart. Draped around the neck of a cheap fat grinning Chinatown Buddha was a Catholic rosary, with amber beads exquisitely hand-carved in Poland and a heavy amber crucifix backed with antique silver. The unseen incense was making Teddy giddy.

"Please to sit," said Madame Miseria. Teddy sat. She sat down opposite him, the crystal ball between them. "Your hands. On the table. Palms up."

She put soft hands in his, gripped him tightly. Her underlit, slightly lowered head seemed suddenly suspended in midair, severed from her body. As she stared into the crystal, points of light began to glow in her eyes, grew, as if from apertures in the pupils themselves.

The eyes widened in shock. A low moan escaped her, exactly like Ristik's in the bar. She began to thrash. Alarmed, Teddy tried to pull away; but now those soft hands were steel clamps around his wrists. Her head whipped from side to side, spittle flying from her lips. She let go of him, leaped to her feet: her eyes rolled up into her head and she fell straight backward to land on the thick floral carpet with a thud.

Teddy started around the table toward her. One of the curtains was thrown aside. Ristik stormed in. They dropped to their knees on either side of her.

"What did you do to her? What have you done?"

"I didn't do anyth—"

Ristik leaned across her to grab the lapels of Teddy's jacket and begin shaking him hysterically.

"*What have you done to her? She has never before—*"

Her eyelids fluttered; her eyes opened, became sentient.

"Ramon—it is all right. He did nothing. It was just the . . . the power of . . . the vision that . . . I have seen . . ."

They got her back into her chair. She gestured weakly.

"Sit down. We will go on."

Ristik said, "No, I don't want you to—"

"We *must* go on. Leave us." Despite her weakness, when speaking to her brother her manner was somehow imperious.

"But if the vision should again overwhelm—"

"Leave us."

Ristik hesitated, then left. Teddy shifted uneasily in his seat. His dread and foreboding were back a hundredfold.

"In the crystal I have seen many things, confusing things, frightening things, Theodore Winston White."

"The Third," added Teddy automatically, then blurted out, *"How did you know my name?"*

"The crystal."

This was no Gypsy trick! He hadn't given Ristik his name at the bar! But she had taken his hands again, her palms were warm, moist; her touch, her eyes burning into his across the table, her words, all had a muted sexual fervor.

"You are in grave danger."

"Danger?"

"From the past."

"But I don't know anything about my past! Not my *real* past. My parents—"

"Put you up for adoption the day you were born. The Whites made you their legal heir. Yes. I know. But your blood parents still live inside you. Their fate is your fate unless . . ." She sprang up. Her eyes were fearful. *"No!* I cannot go on. Not without the protection of the candles."

"But you have to tell me—"

"No. It is too dangerous." She sank back down as if exhausted. "It is fifty dollars for the reading. You can pay my brother. If you insist upon a candle reading, it can be done . . . but it is dangerous for both of us . . ." Her eyes were dull with dread. "I hope that you do not return for it. Some things are best not known. Good night."

"No, wait! Madame Miseria, please! I . . . I must know . . ."

But she was gone through one of the plush walls.

When the downstairs door closed behind the reluctant Teddy, Ristik found his sister at the kitchen stove, switching off the gas flame under the frying pan full of smouldering incense that had filled the *ofica* with its heavy cloying odor. He gave her half the $50, pocketed the rest.

"You should have hooked him hard, tonight, Yana! We could have gotten a couple of hundred bucks—"

"He will be back. We will take him through a candle reading . . . no, two . . . a poisoned egg . . . a cemetery dig . . ."

"How do you know he'll be back? How do you know he has that kind of dough? Like I told you on the phone, I just cut into him in the Pink Flesh, I thought—"

"You said on the phone that he lives in Marin County. You said that all his credit cards were Goldcards. And a poor man would not reflexively insist on being called Theodore Winston White *the Third*." She tapped him on the arm. "Go over to Tiburon tonight, Ramon, learn what you can. He will be back."

Just then the phone rang. With word about their fallen King.

CHAPTER THREE

Word was: Staley the King was perhaps *dying!*

Word was: Staley had told his wife, Lulu, that if worse came to worst, he wanted an encampment in Steubenville to choose his successor before he went. Word was: he wanted to be buried in a perfectly restored pink 1958 Cadillac convertible like the one he'd driven to his coronation thirty-four years before . . .

Today such a vehicle would run you, oh, say, $46,000 and change on the open market. If you could even find one. Of course no Gypsy in the entire history of the world has ever bought *anything* on the open market.

Buying is for the *gadje*.

Buying is for when you can get what you want no other way.

Buying, in short, is a sucker's game. And no *rom*, ever, believes he is a sucker. For dealing with the straight world, the *gadjo* world, the non-Gypsy motto is: *Gadje gadje, si lai ame Rom san*—outsiders are only outsiders, but we are *the rom*.

In other words, Do them before they do you.

*   *   *

Dan Kearny, at his desk long after office hours, was trying to clear the meager post-quake billing so he could meet payroll at the end of the month. He paused, frowning, at an employment app with the name KEN WARREN on it, then remembered the big guy talked like Donald Duck with a cold—*GnYm Kgen Gwarren*—and filed the application in the wastebasket.

"Good," said a rich and oily voice from behind him. "That means you got room on the roster for me."

Trin Morales moved forward on small, almost delicate feet to plunk down his considerable bulk in the hardback chair beside Kearny's desk.

"Trin. How's tricks?"

The chair creaked in protest as Morales stretched to drop one of his business cards on the desk and shake a cigarette from Kearny's pack. He lit up and blew out the match and dropped it on the floor. Neither man had offered to shake hands.

"Never better."

"That's why you're coming around looking for work."

Morales shrugged with Latin expressiveness. "Slow month."

"What I hear," said Kearny, "is that you got locked out and had your phone jerked for nonpayment." He turned the business card over with blunt fingers. Trin's unlisted home phone number was scrawled on the back in pencil. "What I hear is that the Bureau of Collection and Investigative Services up in Sacto might pull your license for unethical conduct."

"Just like they tried to pull yours a few years back," sneered Morales, then added defensively, "you ever catch me with my hand in your pocket when I was working for DKA?"

"*Catch* you? No. You're a damned good investigator, Morales, I'll give you that, but you're trouble. I dumped you for trying to get into that Latina girl's pants, Maria something, Maria Navarro, that was it. Threatening to have her kids taken away from her if she didn't put out for you . . ."

"Aw, hell, Kearny, I was just clowning around—"

"Larry Ballard didn't think so." The two field men had come to blows over Maria. Kearny went on, "Put it this way, Trin . . ." A quick flick of his fingers scaled the card into the wastebasket on top of Ken Warren's employment app. "Don't call me—I'll call you."

The disgruntled Morales departed in a swirl of Mexican epithets, and Keary went in search of other game. Such a grand start was too good to pass up. He found Giselle outside under one of the anti-theft spotlights set at strategic intervals around the perimeter of the storage lot, itemizing the personal property in Maybelle Pernod's Lincoln. Neither thought it strange that the other was there long after office hours.

Hey, wait a *minute. In* Maybelle's Lincoln?

The invariable DKA procedure was to *remove* all the personal property from the repossessed vehicle, right down to an opened box of Kleenex, itemize it, box it, and lock the box in a labeled storage bin. Giselle was leaving it in the Continental.

"Why aren't you boxing that property?" snapped Kearny.

"Because Maybelle told me she would be redeeming the car in a few days." Kearny opened his mouth to interrupt, but Giselle held up an imperious palm. She had the same stubborn look on her face that Larry Ballard got when enmeshed personally with some subject's plight. "Dan, she's a fat old black woman who's never had anything remotely resembling this car before. God knows why the dealer put the loan through or the bank approved it in the first place, but—"

"Box that stuff," he ordered. "Label it. You know damn well she's never going to come up with fifteen hundred clams to redeem this boat. She's better off without it, anyway."

"I know nothing of the sort," said Giselle acidly.

"Grow up." Kearny indicated the blankets swirled messily across the backseat of the car. "Can't you see she's been sleeping in this thing?"

"Of course she has! Why do you think she needs it back?"

"So we can repo it again, and run up even more charges on her?" He nodded in mock admiration. "Now I get your drift."

"Dammit, Dan, you know that isn't . . ."

But Kearny was gone. He took a final turn through the ground-floor offices, savoring the lingering smell of fresh paint and his delicate filleting of Giselle, then climbed the narrow stairs beyond the partition behind his desk. At the top, a typewriter was clacking unevenly. He went around the counter and through the gate to the unused reception area. Light spilled from two open doorways down the hall.

In the first of the field men's offices he found Bart Heslip typing reports. The left side of Bart's lower lip stuck out so far he looked like a bigmouth bass with a hook in its jaw. The left side of his head was shaved and had a bulky white oblong around it. His left eye was narrowed and bloodshot.

"TKO in the first?" suggested Kearny.

Heslip's lip came out even farther. Then he suddenly broke down and started the high hee-hee-hee laughter that went with his detachable black field hand *patois*.

"Lawdy Lawdy, Marse Dan'l, when she done bash me wif dat coffee can, Ah thought Ah was goin' deef, Ah mos surely did." He dropped the dialect, said darkly, "I went right back out there from the hospital, but she'd cleared out. The front door was standing wide open when I got there. The place was stripped."

"Put her on the Skip List."

"Hell no!" exclaimed Heslip. "Nobody's gonna grab *that* car by accident! I want this . . . *lady* myself!"

The Skip List itemized by license number those subjects who had skipped from their known addresses with their cars. It was distributed to all the field agents weekly, and every now and then somebody searching for a different vehicle actually would get lucky and bust one off it.

Kearny paused in the open doorway. "Put her on the Skip List. And where's Ballard?"

"Staked out at the Montana waiting for what's-his-face—"

"Uvaldi."

"Yeah. Him. Larry's gonna clean his clock—"

"Why didn't he do that the first time around?"

"The man had a loaded shotgun, Dan . . ."

But Kearny, having brought joy into yet another humdrum life, was already on his way out. In the final cubicle at the end of the hall he found flame-haired O'Bannon working on his biweekly expense-account masterpiece. Kearny immediately stabbed an angry forefinger at one of the items.

"What's that twenty-five bucks for?"

"Driver for that Crowe repo over in North Oakland. That's misdemeanor-murder land, I wasn't gonna get out of there if—"

"What's this twenty-five bucks for?"

"Confidential informant on the Mollenkopf dead skip."

28

"Confidential informant my butt! Boozing it up in some ginmill, you mean, and trying to make me pay for—"

"But Great White Father!" O'B was only virtue, his blue eyes innocent of all guile. "If I hadn't found out he was sleeping with his brother's wife in Marysville, we'd never—"

"You think I'm gonna pay that thing as is, you're nuts."

These skirmishes over the O'Bannon Inflated Expense Account had been going on during all the years since Kearny had broken off from Walter's Auto Detectives to form DKA.

"Giselle's crying in her beer over some poor old black washer-woman sleeping in her car—"

"Dan—"

"A *ninety-one Continental,* no less, but Giselle—"

"Dan'l—"

"Another woman does in Heslip with a can of coffee—"

"*Daniel!*"

"And you and Ballard let a gay hairdresser weighs ninety-eight pounds kick sand in your faces—"

"*MR. KEARNY!*"

He paused for breath. "What, dammit?"

"Wanna go get a beer?"

"Huh? Oh. Yeah. Okay. Sure."

*　　*　　*

Ramon Ristik, bottle of beer in hand, called the meeting to order. A dozen *rom* crowded the room where, a few hours before, the education of Theodore Winston White III had begun. This was not quite a *kris*—that council of elders who act almost as judges or a governing body for the *rom* on important occasions—but it was a serious meeting of the leaders of two *kumpanias.* So no children ran through the room, pulling food off plates and trying to drink from wine or beer glasses.

The heavy drapes were gone, so the room was half again as large, open all the way to the four walls. The trap underneath the crystal table for the complicated special effects (such as the tiny halogen bulb that bounced light through the crystal ball into Yana's eyes to make them glow during readings) now was covered with a tattered rag rug.

The table itself, like the others in the room, was heaped with food: meat-stuffed cabbage, pancakes called *boliki*, sesame-flavored yogurt with cucumber rounds and tomato wedges to dip, eggplant cubes to be eaten with black *pufe* bread. There were bananas and oranges and plums and grapes—and also candy bars and potato chips and Hostess Ho-Hos and Twinkies. Six-packs of beer, soft drinks, jugs of red wine. Since the telephone call about the King, Yana had been scheming, and generosity, even calculated generosity, got high marks among the Gypsies.

Ristik opened their gathering with the traditional "By your leave, *Romale*, assembled men of consequence, we must discuss the news which has come to us." His dark eyes roved the assemblage. "The King has beckoned. We must respond."

In the old country, or even in the old days in America, such discussions would have been limited to men only, and would have gone for hours, each speaker orating in abstract, proverbial, and convoluted ways rather than convey a direct statement directly. But times had changed.

"Going back to Iowa now will be very expensive," said Josef Adamo bluntly. He was an excessively fat Gypsy whose specialty was posing as a road-paving contractor. "The season is just beginning here in the West . . ."

Immaculata Bimbai, an expert at fainting in jewelry stores, said, "But necessary. From this room will come our new King."

All eyes swiveled to Rudolph Marino. The mob lawyer look was gone. Now he was totally *rom*, his razor-cut mussed and swirled into curls that gleamed in the overhead light. He ate a chicken drumstick with greasy hands he kept wiping on the tails of his flamingo-pink silk shirt. He nodded and smiled acceptance of their assumption that he would be the new King.

"Yes," he said, "a new King will surely be chosen."

But Wasso Tomeshti, whose scam was TV wholesaling, spoke in heavy gutturals from the other side of the room. "Or Queen."

All eyes swiveled again. To Yana this time. She looked as she had when fleecing Teddy White of his fifty bucks: like every *gadjo*'s idea of what a Gypsy fortune-teller looked like. She also smiled. At Rudolph. It was a smile on which to sharpen razor blades.

"Yes," she said softly, "or Queen."

"It is for the King to decide who will succeed him," snapped Marino.

"Which he can do without someone trying to seduce his judgment."

"*That* is a woman's trick."

Somehow, Marino invested "woman" with all the nightsweat qualities of succubus. And somehow, though they had been on opposite sides of the room, he and Yana were now in the center, almost chest-to-chest, glaring at one another.

"Or of a woman-man."

Marino raised a hand as if to strike her; then the tension went out of him and he laughed and stepped back.

"We know who wants to wear the biggest balls in this room."

"And we know who doesn't wear them," she said sweetly.

There was a small wave of indrawn breaths, shuffling feet; traditionally, no Gypsy woman would talk to a man that way. But Yana was not traditional, even though she honored the old values: she had been careful to pass in front of no man getting to the center of the room, for instance, and had made sure the hem of her skirt had touched no male hand in passing. Such taboo acts would have forced a ritual cleansing of the man involved, and could have gotten Yana ostracized from her Gypsy society.

On the other hand, in the last few years, against all advice, she had learned how to read and write. Here, beyond the standard Gypsy paranoia about opening the closed *rom* society, the taboos were only monetary—a child in school studying could not be out scrounging money from the *gadje*.

Ristik, meanwhile, had grabbed back control of the meeting.

"You both gotta agree, this is a decision for the King. We got two *rom* nationalities here, of equal standing because one is Kalderasha, the King's nation, and the other Muchwaya, the nation of his wife, Lulu." The two other true *rom* nations, Tsurana and Lowara, were not represented in the room. "Fighting each other will not help. Whoever becomes the new *Baro Rom*—Big Guy—it is to our advantage that it be someone from these *kumpanias*."

"Yes, one of us," echoed Sonia Lovari, who, though past 30, still passed as a Native American teenager soliciting donations for American Indian causes.

"So we must go back in style—"

"We must make the most impressive gifts to the King—"

"Which means," said Yana, "a nineteen fifty-eight pink Cadillac convertible for him to be buried in."

"Yes!" thundered hulking, barrel-chested Nanoosh Tsatshimo (bogus gold and silver electroplating). "If we can find one—"

"*I* will find it," said Yana.

So, Marino thought, she obviously knows *where* to find it. He obviously didn't. Since whoever brought back such a cherry '58 pink ragtop as a gift to the dying King would have the inside track to be his successor, let Yana get the car—and then let her try to keep it until she could give it to the King . . .

"Meanwhile," he said, "I have the plan that will let us all go back to Iowa in the proper style. Yana will not share her knowledge of the pink convertible with me, but I will share my idea with *her*." He swept a bow to her side of the room. "With *all* of you . . ."

Two hours later the Gypsies, laughing with delight at his plan, went their various ways, some to con, others to drink, more to gamble—a standard Gypsy downfall—and Ristik over to Tiburon to paw through Teddy White's garbage for personal clues his sister might use in the upcoming candle reading.

Alone with Yana, Marino slowly paced the room, gesturing with another half-eaten chicken leg. Yana sat at the table, placid at last, not turning her head, following him only with her eyes as he walked and talked.

"Remember when we were children, Yana . . ."

"Always fighting."

"But always together."

Her eyes softened for a moment. "Yes," she said softly, "always together."

He stopped behind her chair. He put his hands on her shoulders. He leaned down so his face was touching her hair. He breathed in her heady scent. "Betrothed to each other by our families when you were seven and I was fifteen—"

"But then *you* screwed it up."

"Perhaps. Anyway, now we would be unbeatable together."

The softness disappeared. She drew stiffly away. Stood. Began pacing herself.

"You know that I am married."

32

"To Ephrem Poteet, a man who beats you when he is with you but who has been away for over two years."

She shrugged. "I hope in prison, may he rot there. But anyway, Ramon is all I need to run my business."

"Ramon is your brother." He tried to put his arms around her. "Can a brother take the place of a strong man in your bed?"

She pulled away angrily. Her voice was scornful.

"Since we are children this is who you are! Always trying to control me! With sex! With your games! Always scheming! Always planning! Always wanting to be *Baro Rom*—"

"Me?" He raised his shoulders and spread his hands in a pained shrug. "Who is planning to take the Cadillac back for the King to get into his good graces?"

"Who knows where to find such a Cadillac?"

He nodded, conceding the point. His own face hardened. He spoke in Romany to her for the first time that night.

"All right. We will talk of this again, when you have more sense to speak." He started for the door, paused. Now he spoke again in English. "I have a scam running and I need a few more days to bring it off."

She was silent for a moment; then she too smiled. Many men would kill to have such a smile bestowed on them; quite a few *gadje* men had died financially because of it. Before they hit the road back to Iowa, she intended Theodore Winston White III to be another.

"All right, Rudolph. I too have an . . . operation running that needs more time. But . . . we begin now . . ."

"Good!" he exclaimed, laughing. "I will start opening the bank accounts and finding the offices for the phone rooms . . ."

She didn't say that ripping off a certain 1958 pink Eldorado convertible from the *gadjo* who had it was another strong reason she wanted a delay in returning to the Midwest. He didn't say that ripping off the same convertible from her was his strongest reason for agreeing to such a delay.

CHAPTER FOUR

Rudolph Marino strode into the main branch of California Citizens Bank at One Embarcadero Center (*Now Open Nine to Five Every Weekday to Serve You Better!*) just as the doors swung wide for the start of the business week. Studious glasses dulled the fire in his eyes. His curls were muted and tastefully greyed at the temples. He looked as straight as Ted Turner.

Since a man was handling New Accounts, Marino scanned the other bank officers behind the metal and Formica railing. He chose a pretty, early-40s, round-faced woman with pouty lips. She wore floral perfume and pink-tinted glasses that magnified her eyes into a slightly surprised expression. She did not wear a wedding band. Her nameplate said HELEN WOODING.

"Ms. Wooding," said Marino as he sat down across the desk from her, "I hope that I offer no offense when I say that you have very beautiful eyes."

The beautiful eyes crinkled behind their tinted lenses. The ample bosom swelled beneath its white frothy blouse. It did not swell with indignation. "You've just made my week."

His head was slightly inclined and his face held considered pleasure, as if he were a connoisseur tasting vintage wine.

34

"Western Wisconsin, am I not right?"

"Red Wing, Minnesota, just across the river. But how—"

"The accent. When I was a kid I used to spend summers at my uncle's summer place in the Wisconsin Dells."

Actually, he'd been a roughie with a carny traveling the Midwest county fair circuit. He shook himself like a man coming from a dream of childhood, and gave her a card. On it was ANGELO GRIMALDI in that sort of raised lettering that looks like engraving under casual examination. After his praise, the eyes behind the tinted lenses would be extremely casual.

"I am out here to your beautiful city from Manhattan seeking investment opportunities. Perhaps we can give our little yellow friends from across the sea"—he winked to emphasize the racial slur—"a bit of homegrown American competition."

"In the banking business we know just what you mean, Mr. Grimaldi. What sort of opportunities are you looking for?"

"Real estate."

The blue eyes glinted. "Since the quake, and with the recession, the Bay Area has tremendous bargains. If we can help with any suggestions . . ."

"I *knew* I picked the right bank," Marino exclaimed, lightly slapping her desk with delight. "Next week I would be honored to take you to lunch . . ."

Her hand moved slightly, as if wanting to touch her hair. She restrained it. She said, "I would like that very much."

"In the meantime . . ." From a thin glove-leather wallet he extracted two folded oblongs of paper, one pale green and the other pale pink. "I would like to open an account . . ."

The pink oblong was a certified check for $6,000, the green a certified check for $5,000, both payable to Blue Skye Enterprises. Helen Wooding's practiced eye registered they were drawn on New York banks Cal-Cit did business with, but her mind was on that lunch and not on the intricacies of finance.

"We can certainly do that for you, Mr. Grimal—"

"Please. Angelo." He flashed perfect teeth in a wide white grin. "B. L. Skye, the company founder, is from Wyoming, and he wanted *Big* Skye—but that title was too close to one that was already registered so he had to settle for Blue Skye."

They laughed over that one together, and went through the paperwork together. She gave him the temporary checkbook.

"Helen, queries about the balance in my account will be coming in. I'll be leasing a Cadillac, I like American quality, but I'd just as soon none of the dealers knew I'm shopping around with any of the others."

"On customer accounts we only furnish the balance as of four, five, or six figures, low, middle, or high range."

"Wonderful! And if I need to draw a few thousand in cash without prior notification . . ."

"A small branch bank might have trouble covering, but not here at San Francisco Main—so long as it is under ten thousand. Then we'd have the federal reporting requirement—"

He waved this away with a chuckle. "I'll just have to find deals with a downstroke that's under ten K . . ."

*　　*　　*

The fantastic pink beast squatted on its reinforced wooden riser as if it were a triceratops reconstructed in the days when paleontologists still put them together like lizards instead of rhinos. Overhead, around the perimeter of WONDERLY'S WONDERFUL WHEELS, long festoons of twisted gold foil shimmered and glinted and clacked in the hot desert wind. Flanking the antediluvian animal were twin posterboard signs:

RETURN TO THE HAPPY DAYS
OF THE FIFTIES

The monster was 18.03 feet long (on a 10.75-foot wheelbase) and weighed 2.66 tons. Beneath a gleaming hood as long as a Yugo crouched 310 horses, generated by 365 cubic high-pressure-cooled inches that had a 4.0 bore and a 3.63 stroke. Its tailfins were right off one of Wernher von Braun's rockets from those halcyon '50s when the Army still ran the space program. Doubled twin headlights (an industry first soon to become an industry standard) stared out from chromium eye sockets. Outthrust rubber-tipped metal tusks parenthesized the grille's toothy grin.

It seldom rains in Palm Springs, so the top on the 1958 Eldorado Biarritz convertible was lowered. Gawkers could check out the

36

power steering and power brakes (with auto-release parking brake), the cruise control, the two-speaker radio with automatic signal-seeking tuner, the leather interior, the automatic windows. The restorer had even gold-anodized the large "V" on the hood and the "Eldorado" lettering on the trunk lid to return them to their original satiny gold finish.

In this fossil-fuel-conscious age, the lot was crowded with much newer, smaller, more efficient vehicles—mostly trucks and vans and subcompacts. Poster-paint lettering across their windshields pimped their stylistic allures, but the '58 ragtop gas-guzzler was very definitely the star of the show.

Jeeter Pickett, an oily-faced, oily-haired, oily-mannered '50s used-car salesman reincarnated in living color, lay in wait for customers brought in by the convertible. Preferably dumb little blondes he could take out into the desert for a test drive that would leave their dusty heel prints all over the headliners. He hadn't nailed anybody in the old Caddy ragtop, not yet, but . . . But, oh *wow!*

Check out that sweet young thing just threading her way through the lesser cars toward it right now! Wearing five hundred bucks' worth of summer frock so carelessly it might have been $19.95 off the pipe at Mervyn's.

Pickett drifted across the lot to cut her off, ignoring the Fleetwood V-8 limo parked in the side street behind her. As he approached, he stared at her crotch. It was his belief that if you stared at a woman's crotch—*any* woman's crotch—when pitching her, you'd make your sale and make her as well.

Up close the girl was a thing of almost awesome beauty, with a shining blond Marilyn Monroe hairdo and a figure to match, but with startling dark brows and smouldering black eyes. *Great* tan. And with a mid-'50s innocence that sheathed, he was sure, a white-hot sensual core ready to be probed. Pickett could feel the probe against the front of his pants already.

Yeah! Or, in the spirit of the '50s, Hubba Hubba!

She looked at him with soft little-girl's eyes, she spoke to him in a soft little-girl's lisp (with a soft little hint of exotic accent) that made him touch the talisman packet of Trojans in his pants pocket. "I want to buy that nineteen fifty-eight Cadillac convertible."

"No, you don't, little darlin'," he beamed, "you want to buy this BMW Bavaria. Twelve thousand easy miles on her, belonged to a shut-in who only drove it to friends' funerals. Zero to sixty in seven-point-four seconds, comes factory-equipped with—"

She said in exactly the same tone as before, "I want to buy that nineteen fifty-eight Cadillac convertible."

"The BMW out of your price range?" He put his hand on her arm. "Well, little darlin', you have come to the right place."

She looked as if his hand were leaving a slime trail across her sleeve. Pickett and his hand ignored the look. Instead, they steered her toward an ancient paint-pitted Hyundai Excel that looked as if it had just been winched from a reservoir.

"Wonderful economy you want, wonderful economy you get! This little subcompact right here—"

She repeated patiently, "I want to buy that nineteen fifty-eight Cadillac convertible."

"Little darlin', that ragtop is just not for sale."

"Of course it's for sale. Everything is for sale."

Pickett began urging her toward a GM pickup truck with a camper shell fitted inside the bed, letting his knuckles brush the side of her breast as he did.

Staring at his hand, a swarthy Arab-looking man in a black chauffeur's uniform straightened up abruptly from the fender of the R/V. The Arab wore a black mustache eight inches from tip to tip; Pickett's breath stopped in his throat when the man flipped open a horn-handled flickknife as long as his mustache. The blade made the knife seven inches longer.

The girl repeated, now somehow with menace, "I want to buy that nineteen fifty-eight Cadillac convertible."

The Arab began cleaning his fingernails with his knife, but his eyes were honing themselves on Pickett's throat. Pickett's hand went limp on the blonde's arm. His probe prolapsed.

"Look, it . . . it's not for sale. Honest." He had started to sweat. His voice had lost its jocularly suggestive tone. He put up a hand to tug at his suddenly tight shirt collar and momentarily shield his throat from the chauffeur's knifeblade eyes. He found himself talking faster and faster in shorter and shorter sentences. "It's a loaner. From the guy. Who restored it. We just borrowed. It to drum. Up trade. He spent. Over. Three. Years. Just—"

"Give her a price," the chauffeur interrupted in a flat voice full of soft sibilants like Zachary Scott's in *The Mask of Dimitrios*. "She will pay it."

"But—"

"Give her a price."

"Our promo still has a week to run—"

Dead eyes, dead voice. "The price."

"Uh . . . sixty thousand?" Even filled with dread he couldn't help overstating it by fifteen grand. He added quickly, "But if the guy who restored it don't want to sell—"

"Then you will find a way to convince him," said the blonde.

She snapped her fingers. The chauffeur immediately flicked shut the knife and produced a checkbook. The checkbook was in a folder made of thin beaten sheets of what looked like solid gold. The girl opened it and began writing.

"Sixty thousand . . . to Wonderly's Wonderful Wheels . . ."

Pickett automatically said, "Ah, no no no. To, ah, Jeeter Pickett, but, ah . . . you can't . . . I can't . . . we can't . . ."

The switchblade eyes again laid the edge of their cold gaze against Pickett's throat. The woman ripped out the check as if it were Pickett's jugular. The check, for $60,000, was on creamy bond as thick as a money clip.

"Fine," she said, "that's settled, then."

Ten minutes later, pink slip denoting ownership in hand, she gave Pickett one momentary flash of golden thigh as she slid under the wheel of the pink monster. Then she was gone and he really looked at the check for the first time. It was drawn on the First National Bank of Bahrain, and by the name engraved on it he would never get to run his hand up that silken flesh.

Because the name was Turk or Moslem, or some damn thing. Her tan was not from the sun, but from the Levant. Opium traders, he bet. Her father made a lot of money importing heroin and married a blond American. His daughter spent the money under the protection of that life-taker with the mustache. Probably one of them eunuchs guarded the caliph's harem, with his balls cut off so he couldn't hump the merchandise.

Mean-looking mother. Course who wouldn't be mean with his things turned into Rocky Mountain oysters?

But some of Pickett's habitual jauntiness returned as he looked at the check one more time before folding it and putting it in his shirt pocket. No need to tell the restorer the selling price was sixty. Hell, the guy would be delighted to get $50,000 for his car. And no need to tell Wonderly, owner of Wonderful Wheels, anything at all. Jeeter Pickett would just keep the extra ten large for himself—camel jockeys were no match for a wheeler-dealer like him. Nossir.

*   *   *

Half a state north of Palm Springs, and twenty miles north of the Golden Gate Bridge, Rudolph Marino walked into the Cal-Cit Bank on the corner of Fourth and Court streets in downtown San Rafael. He paused just inside the door of the modern glass and concrete building to scan the officers behind their desks.

The woman handling New Accounts would have won by a nose at Golden Gate Fields; her face should have whinnied instead of spoken. But his practiced eye noted there was no bra under her conservative dark blouse and no wedding band on her mid-40s finger. Her nameplate said RITA FETHERTON. Up close, her perfume was an aggressive musk. Perfect.

Marino walked over to her desk and sat down and crossed his legs and looked deep into her eyes and smiled.

"Ms. Fetherton, I hope that I offer no offense when I say that you have very beautiful eyes . . ."

A thousand in this account, then the same at the Cal-Cit branch in downtown Oakland over in Alameda County, then the same at the Cal-Cit branch in downtown San Jose. That would complete the necessary loop of banks: the City, the North Bay, the East Bay, the Peninsula /South Bay. Tomorrow, phone rooms.

*   *   *

The blonde slid over, the chauffeur got behind the wheel of the pink Cadillac. The stolen credit card with which the Fleetwood limo had been rented wouldn't hit the lists until tomorrow, earliest. As the chauffeur pulled the ragtop out into traffic, the blonde took off her golden hair to become Yana.

"The *schvartzes* brag that if you could be black for just one Saturday night you'd never want to be white again."

40

"Huh?" The puzzled chauffeur was driving one-handed while stripping off his mustache to become her brother Ramon.

"So the *rom* should say that if you could run just one Gypsy scam you'd never want to be a *gadjo* again."

Then he understood. They both started to laugh.

"I'll drop you at the airport and drive this back up."

"Be sure and hide it when you get there," she said. "Rudolph will be watching for my return, intending to steal it, and I don't want to have to worry about him. Tonight is Teddy's first candle reading, I want that to be perfect. He's going to be my biggest score ever."

"Until you become Queen."

"Until I become Queen," she agreed.

And right now she was riding in the pink 1958 Caddy that would *assure* she would become Queen. Rudolph Marino was out of the running for royalty before the race had even begun. He just didn't know it yet.

CHAPTER FIVE

In Stupidville that same night, Staley Zlachi thrashed and turned in his semi-private hospital room (courtesy the department store down whose escalator he had fallen) and then began crying out as if in drugged sleep. The nurse peeked in, withdrew; Lulu was there to wipe his fevered brow with a corner of her shawl.

In San Francisco, Ristik hid the pink Cadillac, Yana held Teddy's first candle reading, Marino read the classifieds for storefront rentals, and Dan Kearny took Jeannie out to dinner. Without the glue of the kids living at home to hold it together, Kearny's marriage had begun leaking sawdust at the seams. Time for a little candlelight of his own, and wine, and romance.

But they squabbled at the restaurant.

They squabbled on the way home.

They squabbled in the bedroom.

Instead of romance, Dan Kearny got the couch in the spare room he'd converted into an office a few years back—never realizing that this office-in-the-home neatly epitomized a great deal of what was going wrong with his marriage.

*　　*　　*

42

O'B was also dining out with his wife that evening, also in search of domestic felicity: Bella was pissed because O'B's most recent night out with the boys had been three days long. Since Bella was as Italian as O'B was Irish, and loved her stuffed cannelloni the way he loved his double Bushmills with water back, O'B had thought, a little candlelight, a little Chianti at that new Italian family-style restaurant on Taraval, and later, in the bedroom, a little romance . . .

But they squabbled at the restaurant (it had a full bar).

They squabbled on the way home (O'B ran a red light).

They didn't squabble in the bedroom only because O'B, after observing sagely that he must have gotten some bad ice, passed out in the middle of getting undressed. Staring at her snoring spouse, Bella was more pissed than ever.

* * *

Giselle Marc was going out to dinner with a Brit (visiting prof of English lit at SF State) whom she'd recently taken to letting hold her hand while reciting poetry at her by candlelight—candlelight yet again!—in his Oxford accent. She felt so good she thought she just might let him finally seduce her.

You see, Maybelle had come in and redeemed her 1991 Connie, proving Dan Kearny wrong—which meant he was going to be, at least temporarily, a lot easier to work with. God knew where Maybelle had gotten the cash, but why look a gift horse in . . .

Oh-oh. Maybelle's Connie was parked near a fireplug on Turk Street. And around the corner on Divisadero, in front of a ribs joint, was all 250 pounds of Maybelle, poured into a tight cheap red satin dress slit up a thigh the size of a Clydesdale's. Vamping arthritically at anything male that strolled by, like Julia Roberts waiting for Richard Gere to show up. *Damn* the woman! And damn Dan Kearny, too: Giselle could already see the smirk on his face, already hear the laughter in his voice.

Then at the restaurant the Brit insulted her intelligence by trying to pass off Sonnet 116—"The Marriage of True Minds," that one, for God's sake!—as his own. It was all too much: she poured *fumé blanc* down the front of his trousers and stalked out yelling she couldn't abide an incontinent man.

*   *   *

Larry Ballard's evening began beautifully when Beverly Daniels, a pert little blonde with big blue eyes and a dancer's figure, picked him up in her yellow Nissan 280Z. He once had repossessed it from her, then had worked out a payment schedule so she could get it back. Beverly stood the same scant inch above five feet that Ballard stood below six, but somehow they fit together wondrous well on a horizontal plane. Which Ballard fully intended they should attain before the night was over.

Then everything went to hell. Blame it on Pietro Uvaldi, or maybe Dan Kearny—all *Ballard* did, after the movie and the pizza, was suggest they "swing by" the Montana . . .

"Don't you do this to me," said Beverly.

"Do what to you? All I said was—"

"I know what you said," she snapped savagely.

Beverly had some justification. Their first date had ended with her all alone in Ballard's car while members of a rock group called Full Moon Madness—whose Maserati Bora coupe Ballard had just snatched—tried to drag her out through the window without opening it first.

"This time isn't like that at all," he explained. "I even have a key for this one."

And he told her about Pietro Uvaldi, the wispy little decorator at the Montana with the $85,000 Mercedes. If they could get into the under-the-building garage, and the car was there, it would be a piece of cake. Of course Ballard didn't mention either the shotgun or Pietro's poopsie, Freddi of the cellophaned hair and leather underwear, so Beverly couldn't factor them into the equation until it was much too late.

A tenant was using his electronic door-opener when they arrived at the Montana; they swept into the garage on his rear bumper. He parked, they cruised, and there was the Mercedes, gleaming in a far corner like the Holy Grail!

"Just like you said—a piece of cake." Beverly secretly got off just a little on the excitement of stealing cars.

Ballard opened the door of the Mercedes with the key he'd gotten from the dealer, and did a somersault. He managed to hit the concrete floor in some sort of shoulder roll, cushioning the shock; but he was still dazed when he staggered to his feet to try and block Fearsome Freddi's second attack with a wobbly *shiko dachi* defensive stance, one hand at shoulder level in *shotei*, the other horizontal across his stomach in *nukite*.

Freddi didn't know from martial arts: he slammed his arms up inside Ballard's defense and smashed his head into Ballard's face. Luckily, Ballard ducked so their skulls met forehead-to-forehead, or he would have been a wasteland from ear to ear.

Undaunted, Freddi got in a rib-crushing front bear hug; Ballard countered by slamming his cupped palms against Freddi's ears. Freddi dropped him, screaming with the pain of almost ruptured drums. Ballard made a shambling run for the open door of Beverly's little yellow sports car, yelling as he went.

"GO GO GO GO GO!!!"

As he tumbled in and slammed the door, Beverly WENT WENT WENT WENT WENT—but not before the heel of Freddi's hand holed the windshield in a shower of plastic-coated safety glass. Trying to peer through the remaining opaque starburst, Beverly hit a post, ripping off the left front fender and bending the axle. She backed off and goosed it again, even more terrified than Ballard. The wheel was wobbling. By some miracle, another resident had just entered and the overhead steel mesh door was still clanking down as she zipped through.

Well, not quite zipped through. The reinforced lower edge of the descending door hooked under the front edge of the Z's roof just above the shattered windshield and stripped it back like opening a can of sardines.

Beverly kicked Ballard out of the car right there in front of the Montana and drove off in tears. He had to walk six blocks just to find a cab. When he finally staggered into the sanctuary of his apartment, with a blinding headache and a red welt the size of a bread plate on his forehead, he threw up all over the front-room rug from the effects of his concussion.

*　　*　　*

Only Bart Heslip, of DKA's minions, had a totally satisfactory evening. His forever lady, Corinne Jones, who was a warm golden brown to his plum black and had a Nefertiti profile right off an Egyptian wall painting, fixed him soul food while making big over his damaged face and stitched pate. Then she took him to bed for the sweetest loving this side of paradise.

All of this without ever once bringing up the old tiresome I-told-you-so subject of finding some other line of work.

CHAPTER SIX

Friday. Show time. Even though they had nine hours because the banks were open until 6:00 P.M. on Fridays, Marino could allow only one and a half hours for his people to work the dealers in each area. They had to do it all in one day to keep ahead of the bank's computers. He got the jump on his own part of the operation by strolling into the massive-pillared pseudo-Greco temple that housed Jack Olwen Cadillac on what was left of San Francisco's Auto Row just as the doors opened at 8:30.

"Ah, Mr. Grimaldi," exclaimed Sales Manager Danny McBain as he scurried up, "here for your limo?"

Marino grinned. "You said first thing Friday, so . . ."

"Ready and waiting for you."

Marino's Cadillac had been special-ordered from a limo-maker in Los Angeles to specifications he had gotten from a Gypsy in D.C. after a long hard barter. Of course it didn't really have the Kevlar armor-plating and polymer bulletproof windows of the real McCoy, but it *looked* like it did, which was all Marino deemed necessary for the St. Mark Hotel scam to work.

They crossed the display floor toward the finance office, past a husky, cement-dust-coated laborer, swarthy and vaguely middle-

European looking. His red satin warmup jacket had 49ERS WORLD CHAMPIONS across the back. He was kicking the tires of a Fleetwood coupe—one of those with the formal cabriolet roof.

"What's the sticker on this here baby?"

"Thirty-two-four base, Mr. Kaslov. Of course . . ."

"As she stands," said Kaslov gutturally. "No extras, nuttin' like that. I can swing eight down . . ."

McBain chuckled and said to the man he knew as Grimaldi, "They always kick the tires—as if that's going to tell them one damned thing about the quality of the car!"

Grimaldi chuckled also, in polite agreement. At three minutes to nine he drove the limo out into O'Farrell, one-way inbound, crossed Van Ness on the light, and was gone. Behind him he left a downstroke check for $9,800 drawn on the Blue Skye account in Cal-Cit Main at One Embarcadero Center. At that moment the check was good as gold; in ninety-three minutes it would be as good as, oh, say, the $8,000 check the artistically cement-dusted Kaslov would write on the same account at about the same time.

*　　*　　*

The San Francisco phone room was in a storefront on Turk, half a block short of what had once been and would again have been the Central Freeway's Gough Street on-ramp if they hadn't decided to tear down the earthquake-damaged skyway. Yana had refused the use of her *ofica* because she was working the Teddy White scam out of it, and didn't want the location compromised.

She and Ristik expected calls on seven cars. Three from Jack Olwen—Marino's phony paperwork on his limo scam had gone in earlier—two from Freeway Cadillac in Colma, two from Wilson Cadillac/Porsche/Audi Motor Car Company on Burlington's aptly named Cadillac Way. San Francisco, first of the day, was the linchpin of the operation: if it went well there, reasoned the surprisingly superstitious Gypsies, it would go well all over.

The first call came in at 8:53. Yana answered musically with the last four digits of the number.

"Three-four-six-two, good morning."

"Is this Acme Construction?"

"Yes, sir, it certainly is."

"This is Jack Olwen Cadillac on Van Ness—"

She interrupted with a delighted laugh.

"I bet Greg Kaslov is in there buying a car."

The caller paused for a moment. "Well, yes, he is, but . . ."

"It's all he and Joanna have been talking about for the last six months—getting their Fleetwood . . ."

"Well, they're finally doing it. I was calling to verify employment, but . . ."

She laughed again, not a care in the world. "Greg's been here for twenty-two years. He was the first man Mr. Arnold hired when he came back from Vietnam . . ."

The other phone rang while she was still pouring honey on Kaslov's head. Ristik picked up. There was no trace of Gypsy gutturals in his voice.

"Eight-oh-seven-six," he said. "Credit Department? Just a moment, I'll switch you."

Yana had just finished with Jack Olwen Cadillac. She stabbed the glowing 8076 extension button on her phone and said, "Trans-Universal Credit, how may I help you?"

She thumbed quickly through the stack of papers on the desk as she listened, plucked one out, scanned it.

"Yes, we are carrying the paper on Mr. Stokes's home in the three hundred block of Third Avenue . . ." She rattled the papers realistically near the phone. "Twelve years, excellent pay, has never missed a payment, has . . . um . . . No. Has never even paid a late penalty."

On the other phone, Ristik was saying, "Listen, I've known Sally Poluth my whole life. She's godmother to our kids . . . No, I didn't know she was buying a car, but with the insurance from Ritchie's death she sure as hell can afford one . . ."

* * *

By 10:30 A.M. Yana and Ristik had gotten the calls on all seven vehicles; they shut down the phone room just as Marino slid a withdrawal slip across the polished surface of a teller's window in Cal-Cit Main at One Embarcadero Plaza.

"I want to withdraw ten thousand in cash from my account."

"Ten thousand? Cash? That's—"

"Miss Wooding assured me there would be no problem."

Helen Wooding appeared as if on cue. With continental flair, Marino kissed the air a millimeter above her hand.

"What's the trouble here?" she demanded sharply of the teller. "Mr. Grimaldi's account certainly is good for the withdrawal and it meets the fed's ten thousand limit, so—"

"Right away, Miss Wooding." The girl was blushing. She started putting away her rubber stamps and locking up her drawers so she could go get that large an amount of cash.

"Trainees," said Helen in a voice deliberately loud enough for the departing teller to hear. She added with a coquettish laugh, "You should have come directly to me, Angelo."

"I didn't want to disturb you with such a trifle." His fine dark eyes lit up. "Since I hope to be settling here on a permanent basis, I have been looking for a house to buy as a company investment. And I have run across a marvelous bargain out in the . . ." he paused, grinning, "the Avenues, is that right? Off Sloat Boulevard? An old Italian gentleman who said I reminded him of his son . . ."

"The Avenues. Yes. South of the park is the Sunset. North of it is called the Richmond District."

"Sunset . . . Richmond . . . I'll remember."

The teller had returned. She counted out the cash, Marino put it in his slim attaché case, saying to Helen, "Maybe we can go see the property on Monday."

"Monday?"

He snapped shut the case. "Lunch—remember? And perhaps, since seeing the house will be a business activity for you, we could take the whole afternoon . . . perhaps spend the evening together . . ." He made subdued kissy-kiss noises with his lips. Helen Wooding actually blushed. "I'll call you Monday morning first thing . . ."

"Oh, yes," she said breathlessly. "Call me."

*　　*　　*

Forty-five minutes later, Marino deposited the $10,000 cash in the San Rafael Blue Skye account. He didn't invoke Rita Fetherton's assistance for the deposit as he would for the withdrawal; banks are delighted to see cash come in the door.

As he walked out, one of the two phones began ringing in a small office over an electronics store on lower Fourth just three blocks away. Immaculata Bimbai, who fainted in jewelry stores, spoke breathily into the mouthpiece.

"Five-four-nine-oh . . . Yes, this is Fashion Fabrics . . . Credit Department?" Immaculata, who was slim as a pencil and elegant as the diamonds she was always trying to steal, gave a sensual full-bellied laugh that suggested a woman with three chins and a milkshake in each hand. "Honey, I'm the whole ball of wax here. Owner, president, credit manager, sales manager . . ." Another pause. "Tibo Tene? Sure, Tibo's been our fabric buyer for, oh, hell, I can get the records, but over ten years, anyway . . ."

As she talked, the other phone began ringing. Josef Adamo, the fat bogus road-paving contractor, picked up.

"Three-seven-six-six."

Like San Francisco, the North Bay operation would account for eight Cadillacs, but was more spread out: the calls would be coming in from Corte Madera in Marin County; Vallejo in Solano; Petaluma, and Santa Rosa in Sonoma; Napa in Napa County (the wine country); and Ukiah in Mendocino, way up there in the redwoods.

At 1:00 P.M., Marino took the $10,000 in cash back *out* of the San Rafael account, and drove across the Richmond–San Rafael Bridge to deposit it in the East Bay account. At the same time, Immaculata and Josef closed down their San Rafael phone room and two other Gypsies opened theirs over a Greek *taverna* on Clay and Second near Oakland's Jack London Square.

The whole operation was completed down in San Jose just at 6:00 P.M. bank-close, exactly as planned.

*   *   *

The dealers' credit managers cleared their desks on Friday night, dropping all the paperwork, including the downstroke checks for the thirty-one Cadillacs, into their Out boxes to the four Cal-Cit Bank branches. But the bank's zone men, who handled conditional sales contracts on chattel mortgages generated by these auto dealers, didn't work Saturdays. As a result, the computer wouldn't be pushing any of those thirty-one down-payment checks through the accounts of origin until Monday morning.

Thus, on Sunday, the eve of destruction, Stan (the Man) Groner, efficient and ambitious president of Consumer Loans for the entire

California Citizens Bank system, still could have a wonderful evening eating popcorn and laughing at *America's Funniest Home Videos* (their bridge over troubled generational waters) with his 15-year-old daughter. Never for a moment did Stan suspect that starting that week, April would become the rottenest, lousiest, most stinking month of his entire life.

Because when Monday's computers started humming, down payments started popping in Cal-Cit Banks all over the Bay Area with a zest that would have made Orville Redenbacher and his wimpy grandson happy and proud. Stunned zone men started grabbing telephones and waving their arms and screaming. Stunned dealership finance managers started screaming back, turning white and dropping their phones and sometimes their pants.

Damage assessments started reaching Stan Groner's desk in Consumer Loans that same afternoon. He called for files. But it wasn't until early A.M. Thursday that the tally he'd come in early to get was complete. Then the stack of manila folders in the center of his desk, stinking of economic brimstone and glowing pinkly from the ghastly financial fires within, made him quickly reach for *his* phone.

CHAPTER SEVEN

Giselle Marc and Dan Kearny usually shared the day's first cup of coffee while going over the probable shape of DKA's day; but when the phone rang early on Thursday morning, their chat had degenerated into a verbal brawl because Kearny had asked whether Ballard was showing up for work yet.

"He's still home, Dan. Still has that lousy headache."

"From a concussion?" His voice was disbelieving. "I think he's on a toot." Kearny's slang was mired in the '40s. He added illogically, "And if it *is* a concussion, he got it falling down drunk in some barrel house. He's been working too many cases with O'B lately—try to bend an elbow with that guy and pretty soon you're dipping your beak in paint thinner."

"You should see the lump on Larry's forehead."

"All I see is his caseload getting fat without him doing anything about it. Hell, he's got four new assignments without twenty-four-hour first report, and sixteen others that—"

"I could pick up the slack on those unworked first-report cases," said Giselle quickly around her cup, as if muffling the words might keep Kearny from really hearing them.

"I need you here in the office. Besides, you've been acting so unprofessional lately that you can't keep up with the cases you've got."

"Just what is that supposed to mean?" she demanded coldly.

Kearny fired up a cigarette, watching her slyly past the smoke. "I hear your galfriend Maybelle is doing more than just *living* in the backseat of that Connie of hers."

Giselle dunked a doughnut in frosty silence. Her emotions were still tender from the scene with the Brit, and here was Kearny, just as she'd known he would, zeroing in on the very thing that had caused that painful rift in her personal life.

"She's on the hustle." When Giselle didn't dignify this with a reply, he added, "The Mary Magdalene lay. And eventually I gotta tell the bank about it."

Giselle stood up abruptly; she didn't want to think about Maybelle losing her car all over again, this time for good.

"I have to get to work," she said. Which is when the phone rang. Already on her feet, she snatched it up and snapped into it, "Daniel Kearny Associates."

"*Tellkearnyineedhimuphererightawaynohesitationsnoexcuses rightnowfiveminutesorimcallingholstromautorecoverybureau . . .*"

She picked out a word here and there from Stan Groner's long high scream of anguish, enough to know Kearny was wanted at the bank and wanted *now*.

She said, "I can't understand a thing you're saying, but I recognize your note of hysteria."

"*Goddammitgisellewereouthundredsthousandsmillions . . .*"

"I still can't understand you but we'll get on it right away," she said crisply, and hung up.

"Get right on what?" demanded Kearny. "Who was that?"

"Wrong number."

"*Wrong number?* I just heard you say that we'll . . ."

Giselle was already gone down the office with long, clean-limbed strides. She'd handle this one herself, and show Kearny just who the real professional was around here. She made an abrupt left turn through the sliding glass door to the back office that was her domain, then kept on going right out the back door and into the storage lot where her company car was parked.

Kearny morosely smoked another cigarette, stubbed it, took a slurp of coffee. Stone cold. The phone rang just as he reached for it to bitch at Giselle about the coffee, so he snatched it up to snarl at it. It snarled at him first.

"DAMMIT, KEARNY, WHY AREN'T YOU HERE YET?"

"Fine, Stan, thanks for asking. How's the family?"

"DAMMIT, I TOLD GISELLE I NEEDED YOUR BUTT HERE RIGHT—"

"*Giselle?* When?"

Some of the hysteria was fading from Groner's voice. He must have looked at his watch. "Well, maybe like only fifteen, twenty minutes ago, but this is . . . oh, here she is now . . ."

"Giselle? There?"

"At least *she* knows how to respond to a client . . ."

He was talking to an empty phone: Kearny was on his way.

What the *hell* did that woman think she was doing?

*   *   *

But Dan Kearny was too old a hand to let a bank man's panic panic him, so he parked in the usual lot and strolled across Battery to the glittering marble and glass monolith of One Embarcadero Center. It was one of those San Francisco spring mornings, clear and bright and crisp without a hint of fog, that make the gulls swoop and squawk raucously and dive-bomb passing pedestrians for handouts.

He wandered through the Consumer Loans Division, nodding to a man here and winking at a woman there, whatever her age and shape and marital status. It was ritual, like the bottle of decent bourbon each of them got, man and woman alike, at Christmastime. He knew that most of the women would have preferred a box of Sees chocolates, but candy didn't fit the DKA image. DKA was the rough-and-ready crew that took all the assignments the bank's men were scared of, closed out all the cases the other repo agencies struck out on. Kearny wanted the bank people to get a whiff of predator whenever DKA padded by.

The door with STANLEY GRONER—PRESIDENT—CON-SUMER LOANS DIVISION gold-leafed on its pebbled glass hissed shut behind him with a pneumatic sigh. Groner was a traditionalist: the dark-paneled room had sporting prints on the walls, heavy hardwood and leather furniture, art deco lamps. Only thing missing was a brass spittoon beside the antique oak desk.

"Here I am, Stan, now what . . ."

Groner, a normally placid and pleasant-faced man of 42, addicted to soft tweeds and knitted wool ties, was walking around his desk in tight circles. His arms were waving and his normally warm brown eyes were casting fell looks and foul toward the couch from behind his hornrims. Kearny took the ire to be directed neither at Giselle, sitting there rifling a manila folder, nor at her cigarette smouldering on the chrome smoking stand at her elbow. So Groner apparently was upset by the messy stack of files on the coffee table in front of Giselle.

Cigarette? Kearny thought belatedly. Damn! Giselle had started smoking again.

But he said only, "Files," and then added, "so?"

Giselle answered for Groner, excitement sparkling in her eyes like diamonds.

"Last Friday, Dan, the Bay Area's twenty Cadillac dealers, from Ukiah down to Salinas, wrote conditional sales contracts on thirty-one new Cadillacs. The works—Allantes, Broughams, De Villes, Fleetwoods, Eldorados, Sevilles, even a special-order stretch limo from Jack Olwen on Van Ness."

In a hushed voice, Kearny began, "You mean to tell me—"

"Yeah. Skips. All thirty-one of them. By these files, *dead* skips." In finance parlance, a "skip" is someone who has literally "skipped out"—usually with mortgaged property, such as a car, he has not yet paid for. A "dead" skip is one on whom there are no apparent live leads for finding him and bringing him back. "Eight financed through this office, eight through Cal-Cit San Rafael, eight through Oakland, seven through San Jose."

Kearny turned. "How'd you get onto it so quick, Stan?"

"The downs bounced," groaned Groner.

"All thirty-one of them?" Kearny was disbelieving.

"They were drawn on only four accounts," said Giselle. "One account at each branch."

"But . . . credit checks . . . reference and employment and residence verification . . ."

Groner's speaking voice was normally high-pitched; now it was pitched even higher, tumbling out excited words with fire-hose pressure and speed.

"Hell, Dan, you know the drill!" He was pacing again. "We make a big show of checking references, but it costs us a hundred bucks a head if we do a thorough credit check of all prospective car buyers. If we don't check anything out, and prorate the collection and repossession costs over *all* our auto contracts, it costs us *twenty* bucks a head. So we trust the dealers' credit managers to size the person up, make a few phone calls . . . But *this* . . ." He waved an unbelieving hand. "They hit every damn Caddy dealer in the Bay Area, *every one!*"

Giselle started to giggle. "Blue Skye Enterprises. All four accounts were in the name of—"

"*Blue Skye?*" Kearny had joined her at the coffee table to flick through the files. He looked up at Groner in amazement. "Come on, Stan, I know you don't pay your bank officers very much, but when a guy waltzes in and wants to open an account called *Blue Skye*—"

"What can I say? Apparently he looks like Omar Sharif in his *Doctor Zhivago* days, and went to women AVPs in each case. All four still swear he just *couldn't* have been conning them."

"I'd like to meet this guy," said Giselle thoughtfully.

Kearny was scanning the files as his computer brain was assessing, assimilating, relating with the bewildering speed of close to forty years—he'd ridden an old single-speed bike to his first repossession—of chasing deadbeats and absconders and embezzlers and outright thieves. He stiffened abruptly.

"Something?" Giselle asked with sharpened attention.

Groner was saying, "Cal-Cit Bank is out *one-point-three-two-five million dollars*, retail."

Kearny was saying, "The names."

Giselle checked the files again. She said in measured tones, "Oh . . . my . . . God . . ."

"*I need those cars back to keep my job!* I don't care what you do to get them, how many laws you have to break, what—"

"What it costs," inserted Kearny smoothly.

"I didn't say that." The *kvetcher* was magically transformed into the hard-nosed bank unit president again. "I can't go over a flat rate per car of—"

"No flat rate. Ten percent of gross value recovered for each vehicle, dealer cost, with expenses over and above—"

"*Ten percent!*" Groner clutched at his heart dramatically. "How can you even *suggest* doing that to me?" He turned to Giselle as if to display his bleeding heart. "How can he even suggest ten percent to me? *Me?* Plus expenses, yet?"

"How about eight percent?" asked Giselle sweetly.

Groner looked over at Kearny. He said, "I thought she was with you."

"So did I." Kearny grabbed Giselle's arm and hustled her into a corner of the room. "What're you trying to *do* to me?"

"Show you how it's done."

She pulled free, went back across the room as Stan the Man began judiciously, "Eight percent, that doesn't sound half—"

"Good enough," Giselle agreed briskly. "I agree. Eight percent wouldn't even cover field costs, let alone factoring in DKA's agency expenses—prorated office overhead, field equipment upkeep and replacement, licenses, salaries, the various insurances we have to—"

"*Overhead? Insurance?*" Groner had his hands up in front of him, the left one vertical, the right palm-down, bouncing against the left's stiffened fingertips. "Time out! Time out! You know the bank's policy is to pay *only* a fixed repo fee to cover that stuff, plus field time and expenses, not—"

"Not this time," said Giselle.

Kearny ventured, "Twelve-point-five would be—"

"Not nearly enough." To Groner she said, "I don't see us doing it for under twenty percent of gross recovery, Stan."

"*Twenty percent?*" shrieked Groner. "Not even Christ come down from His cross to find our cars would get twenty percent! Okay, *maybe*, just maybe, twelve and a half, but . . ."

Behind Groner's back, Kearny was signaling Giselle wildly to take it. She paid him no attention whatsoever.

"Seventeen-five-oh and a wonderful bargain, Stan."

He crossed his arms on his chest in a gesture of finality. "I'll have to go to Holstrom Auto Recovery Bureau if you won't take . . . fifteen percent. That's absolutely as far as I'll go."

"And all expenses."

"And all expenses."

"You've got a deal," said Kearny very quickly. He added, "We'll need keys for all the cars, tagged with vehicle I.D. numbers, model, and color . . ."

Groner nodded solemnly. He sighed.

"Why are you guys being so tough on this, Dan?"

Giselle said, "There's just nothing in here for us to go on—just the dope on the cars from the dealers. Every reference is phony. Jobs, home addresses, friends, credit information—*all* of it is phony."

"You don't know that, you just know that the downs bounced. Yet here you are, demanding guarantees . . ."

"We *do* know that." She glanced over at Kearny, who was silent, so she merely added, "Thirty-one Cadillacs, Stan."

"Even so." Groner had gone back behind the bastion of his desk. "There aren't going to be *that* many new Cadillacs around this town with the dealer stickers still on them to justify—"

"Around this town?" Kearny looked up from trying to close the leather straps on the bulging briefcase. "Uh-uh. Nope." He enlightened Groner with a single word. "Gypsies."

Stan Groner stared at him for a full thirty seconds before muttering, "Dammit, Dan, it *can't* be! I mean—"

"All thirty-one of them. Gyppos, working in concert."

After a long moment of assimilation, Groner slowly nodded in acceptance of this horror—Kearny was the expert. He put his head down on his arms as if he were very, very tired.

Anyone involved in big-ticket retail sales knew that giving credit to *one* Gypsy was exactly like burning the money. So what was giving $1.325 *million* credit to *thirty-one* Gypsies like?

CHAPTER EIGHT

A license to steal, that's what it's like. I gotta hand it to you, Giselle."

They were back at DKA, for some reason upstairs in the disused reception area from which the laundry's billing had once come, rather than down at Kearny's desk.

"Dan Kearny, if you try to put one of your fancy moves on Stan Groner after I as good as promised him—"

"We're gonna have to be thieves, and tricky ones, to walk away from this one without a bloody nose."

He spoke without his usual steamroller optimism. She had a sudden sinking feeling in her stomach. She had been delighted with herself at that unbelievable fifteen percent of recovered value. Why, if you took $25,000 as a median dealer cost per car, DKA would be paid $3,750 per recovery, plus expenses. Even when Kearny had pointed out they were talking about Gypsies here, she had just assumed the Great White Father would have a dozen ways to break the universal Gypsy solidarity against *gadje* attempts to pry information out of them. But now . . .

"Damn good car thieves, you mean?" she ventured hopefully.

"I don't know what I mean." Kearny was stone-faced as always, but after all these years she could read him as she could a case file report. "This is a lot of cars and a lot of Gypsies, Giselle. Or maybe I'm just getting old."

"How are things at home?" she asked, surprising even herself. She just didn't ask that kind of question of him.

He answered readily, if vaguely, "Spare-room couch."

Giselle knew and liked Jeanne, had often taken care of the kids when they were growing up. "Is . . . it anything I can . . ." He just shook his head. The moment had passed. She ventured, "Wh . . . what's our first move with the Gypsies?"

"You tell me."

In a small voice, she said, "Check out all those references they gave the dealers, even though we know they're false?"

"That's a start. Put the skip-tracers on it right away. Use the after-school girls, too—forget about the legal letters for the time being. The Gyppos might have slipped up somewhere and given us a crumb. You can coordinate that part of the investigation from here in the office while the field men—"

"No," said Giselle.

Kearny looked astounded, or as astounded as his tough, uninformative face could look. "No?"

"I want out in the field on this one. I'm the guy who went up there and—"

"You are, aren't you?"

"—nailed Stan's foot to the floor and—"

"You did, didn't you?"

"—got us fifteen percent, and so I expect to . . ." She ran down when she realized that Kearny wasn't arguing with her.

"Like I said, a license to steal." She had to admit, he gave credit where credit was due. Or blame. "Stan wasn't going to go over ten percent with me no matter what, because ten percent was the most I thought I could squeeze out of him. But he was in a panic and you were sore enough at me to believe you could get more—so you made *him* believe you could. Of course now we gotta find the cars . . ."

He stood, started pacing, abruptly sat down again.

"Call him, tell him we need a contract spelling out the terms exactly. They're desperate now, but if we start turning these babies they're going to think it's easy and start wanting to cut that recovery percentage fee."

"You're godfather of Stan's daughter, for Pete sake. He wouldn't try to—"

"Stan is just a unit president, he doesn't run the bank. So do it. And get a guarantee of exclusivity, too. If recovery is *slow*, we don't want some flunky VP to panic and start shoveling out these assignments to other agencies. We gotta hit the Gyppos hard and fast, get all we can before they realize we're after 'em—'cause once they do, they're gonna disappear into the woodwork." He was pacing again, thoughtfully. "We got that Gypsy informant with the letter drop down in L.A. . . ."

"The one calls himself Ephrem Poteet? He just wants to get back at other Gypsies he imagines have done something to him."

"Listen, at least one of our thirty-one is just *sure* to of stuck a finger in his eye sometime. Send him a list of all the cars—motor I.D. numbers, color, and model—plus the names they were purchased under. Send it fast mail, okay? Overnight. Tell him a . . . oh, a hundred bucks per recovery we make off his information— and stick in a fifty-buck bill to prime the pump. Then run some extra copies of Stan's list—"

"For our affiliates around the country?"

He shook his head, pulling down the corners of his mouth.

"Put this info into the hands of other agencies, and it'd be open season on every new Cadillac with paper plates between here and Key West. I want it in-shop only. Don't even memo our own branch offices on this one for the time being."

"Getting a little paranoid, aren't we, Dan'l?"

"Ever think how often paranoiacs are right?"

Well, yes, paranoia, come to think of it, was part of this business. An operating asset, as it were. Kearny's moment of hesitation, or introspection, or whatever it was, had passed; he was his old hard-driving self again. The lump suddenly was gone from the pit of her stomach. Kearny was on his feet.

"We'll use this office as command headquarters." He bent to smear out his butt, then banged his hand on one of the filing cabinets that had held the laundry's paperwork. It echoed hollowly. "Keep the case files in these babies, plug in some phones, bring up a computer terminal and one of the printers. Everything centralized so the field men can have easy access."

"Will all of the field men be on this, or—"

"No. Regular business is picking up again and some of our people will have to cover that." He looked at his watch. "I want you, O'B, Heslip, and Ballard here at five-thirty for a headbanger. Spaghetti feed afterward at the New Pisa . . ."

Surprising herself with a sudden rush of feminine emotion, Giselle began, "Dan, Larry's head is still—"

"*I want Ballard here if he has to come in carrying his head under his goddam arm, you got that?*"

"Yessir," she said immediately and meekly. Why push her luck? She'd gotten what she wanted: she was going to be out in the field playing with the big guys on this one.

*   *   *

"Why are we so sure they're Gyppos, Dan?" asked Heslip.

It was nearly 6:00 P.M. Giselle, O'B, Heslip, and Kearny were in the disused upstairs reception area for the headbanger. Ballard of the shiny red forehead was supposed to be on his way in. Kearny had announced they were going after a band of Gypsies and had outlined the scams used against the bank. Man, not just one or two Gyppos, but *thirty-one* of the mothers.

"Because of the names," said Giselle.

O'B was frowning. "Grimaldi isn't Gypsy, it's not even one of their usual phonies. Since he's the guy who set up the bank accounts—"

"But look at the others." Kearny was flipping through the list of names under which the Cadillacs had been conned out of the dealerships. "Gregory Kaslov. Kaslov is a Gypsy name. Stokes. Often a Gypsy pseudonym. Sally Poluth. Gypsy all the way. Tibo Tene? You can hear the tambourines. Yonkovich . . . Demetro . . . Petulengro . . . all Gyppo tribal names." He was flipping faster now, selecting pseudonyms the Gypsies habitually stole from the straight populace. "Hell, listen to these. Adams, Evans, Green, Miller, Mitchell, Steve, Stokes, Wells . . ."

Man, Heslip thought, this was *big*. No wonder Dan wanted Ballard there. Larry'd worked that Gypsy mitt-reader down in Palm Desert, who'd put that curse on him; and when the state had been trying to take away DKA's license, Larry'd gotten something going with that Gyppo crystal-ball gazer up in Santa Rosa . . .

A tall form at the head of the stairs said in a sepulchral voice, "Neither rain nor sleet nor dark of night—"

"I didn't know we was gonna do this in blackface."

"Whadda you mean 'we,' white man?"

Ballard's two blackened eyes were staring pointedly at the white bandage still around Heslip's head. Sooty calipers extended down on either side of Ballard's nose to the corners of his mouth. His forehead was just one large purple bruise.

"You look like you need a slice of watermelon," said Heslip judiciously.

"You're late," said Kearny coldly.

"Why am I here at all?" said Ballard cautiously.

"Gypsies," said Giselle without inflection.

When she'd called to tell Ballard there was a meeting he had to get to, she hadn't told him what it was for. She knew her Larry. Curiosity would bring him in like nothing else would.

"Thirty-one Gypsies," said Heslip.

"Aha," said Ballard. Something besides fatigue gleamed in his eyes. He took off his topcoat and tossed it on the desktop.

Kearny said, *"Thirty-one* Gyppos who conned the dealers out of thirty-one Cadillacs. All financed through Cal-Cit Bank."

Ballard sat down between Heslip and O'B. They all listened while Kearny sketched out what he had already told the others.

"I bet poor old Stan wishes he'd died in the quake," said Ballard. "How'd they work the downs?"

"A smooth and handsome guy looks like Omar Sharif in his movie-idol days shows up at Cal-Cit Main and approaches a woman AVP," said Kearny. "He's out from New York looking for investments, so he opens an eleven-thousand-dollar business account. Makes sure there'll be no trouble to make an unannounced ten-thousand-dollar cash withdrawal if he gets a good 'investment opportunity'—you with me so far?"

Ballard nodded. "Sure. Then, from what you tell me, he goes and opens three more accounts in three branch banks—"

"For a thousand each."

Somehow a drink had materialized in O'B's hand. "So last Friday people with ethnic names start going into the dealers and snapping up Caddies and making the downs with checks drawn on those Cal-Cit accounts. Starting in the City and then moving to Marin and then East Bay and then San Jose just at bank-close."

"Damn, that's clever," said Ballard admiringly.

"He closes the accounts out in order, too," said Heslip. "*After* the calls come in to confirm there's enough money in each account to cover the downs on the cars in that area, but *before* any checks can actually be presented for collection."

"Why doesn't the bank just charge 'em with felony fraud and get the cops involved?"

"He's too smart for that," said Kearny. "He doesn't *really* close out the accounts. He pulls ten grand—in cash—from Cal-Cit Main but he leaves a grand behind. Deposits the ten K in each account in turn; then, a couple of hours later, after the queries on the accounts' status have all come in, pulls it out again. Leaving the original thousand behind in each case."

"If somebody catches up with him," said Giselle, "he just says it was all a mistake, he got confused between accounts."

"Legally he can do that?" asked Ballard.

"Under California law, criminal intent can be assumed, and fraud charged, only if the account doesn't exist or has been closed prior to the presentation of the check."

Heslip's mind was momentarily drifting. It was at these conferences that he most keenly missed Kathy Onoda, dead at age 29 of a busted blood vessel in her head. CVA, they called it. Cardiovascular accident. Some accident. Icepick-slim Kathy, button-black eyes shining, classical Japanese features alight with excitement . . .

Him and her off in a corner giggling at each other's dirty jokes like a couple of schoolgirls . . . Neither one of them ever told off-color jokes to anyone else. It was like their little minority secret together, and . . .

Aw, dammit to hell, anyway.

Ballard was musing in an awed voice, "One-point-three-two-five million bucks!"

"Until this morning, when Stan finally collated all the contracts, the bank didn't know how bad they'd been stung. And until we told 'em, they didn't know it was Gypsies who'd hit them." Kearny slapped his palm on the files on the butt-scarred desktop. "These don't have a single name, address, credit reference, residence or work address that's genuine."

"But they *look* wonderful," said Giselle. "The dealer credit managers did everything right, made all the requisite background phone checks—work adds, home adds, personal refs, pay experience with other lenders. *Everything.* They all checked out. On paper and over the phone, pure as the driven snow."

"Like a certain Colonel Buford Sanders, USAF Retired," said Ballard slyly.

They looked at O'B and laughed. DKA had repo'd nine Caddies from the larcenous colonel before he took an insurance company for $275,000 in a fake injury accident scam. O'B went after him, but instead of proving the con, ended up being an affidavit eyewitness in support of the colonel's fraudulent claims.

"I'll still nail that guy one day," O'B muttered darkly.

"Maybe we ought to hire him," said Kearny.

"Why Cal-Cit Bank?" demanded Heslip.

Kearny stood stock-still for a moment.

"Damn good question, Bart."

Giselle added a note to the list on her shorthand pad. "Hmmm . . . yes . . . He could have gone to four *different* banks—going to branches of the same one made it a lot harder because he put himself in a time bind. He had to make the withdrawals and deposits in cash all in one day so the bank's in-house computer wouldn't catch up with him before bank-close. Why?"

"I'm still bothered by that non-Gypsy pseudonym for their main man," said O'B.

Heslip said, "Yeah, he'd have to have valid-looking I.D., just in case he got questioned on one of the ten-thousand-buck withdrawals—but why not use a familiar Gyppo pseudonym?"

"Maybe he already had the Grimaldi I.D. for some other scam he was working," said Kearny. "Giselle . . ."

She was already writing it in the notebook. Ballard, still catching up, asked, "How did they work the phones? It's a lot more sophisticated than pigeon drops or Jamaican switches."

"In each area," said Kearny, "all the purchasers used the same sets of phone numbers to confirm all false credit data and false personal and business references on the applications."

"Why four phone rooms? Why not just one?"

"They were working across area codes, and they'd want to keep everything local to help avoid raising suspicions."

"If you hustle cars for a living in the middle of a recession," said O'B cynically, "how suspicious are you gonna be when you're looking at the commission for a forty-K sale?"

Ballard: "Phone rooms—how do they help us?"

Heslip: "Somebody had to rent the rooms to them."

Giselle: "And Pac Bell had to put in the phones."

O'B: "All places to start."

Kearny stood up abruptly.

"Okay, that's enough for tonight. We've got a packet for each of you with all the information we've got so far, plus dupe keys and info on all the vehicles. Each of us runs down whatever leads he develops himself, but meanwhile check out any Caddy with paper plates that fits the description of any car on this list."

"How tough do we get?" asked Ballard.

"As tough as we have to."

Heslip muttered, "A felony a week if we need it or not."

"Current workloads?" asked Giselle.

"Turn 'em in tomorrow morning, reports current, for reassignment. I want to be able to get someone else out on them over the weekend so our regular billing doesn't suffer."

"Not Uvaldi," said Ballard hotly at the same time that Heslip exclaimed, with equal heat, "Not Walinski."

"Don't be a sap, Larry," said O'B. "Let somebody else get the next headache."

"Turn 'em in day after tomorrow," snapped Kearny. "*All* of 'em. From now on all *our* energies have to be focused on the Gyppos."

Ballard and Heslip exchanged looks that said: we got tomorrow to drop a rock on Uvaldi's Mercedes and Walinski's Charger. Kearny caught the look but said nothing. He wouldn't have wanted his men to feel any other way. Getting even was better than getting screwed without intercourse, every time.

On the other hand, they were going to have to move damned fast on the opposition. Being Gyppos, those guys wouldn't be standing still.

CHAPTER NINE

The black stretch Caddy whispered up Taylor to the blinking yellow light at California. Behind the wheel was Rudolph Marino in another $1,200 suit. Inbound traffic streamed across in front of him as he edged the limo farther up the steep incline. Ignoring a glaring old woman in a cloth coat who shook a fist at him, he violated the pedestrian walk to swing down California Street with his right blinker on.

Thirty-one brand-new Cadillacs—and no way the bank could ever find out who had them or where any of them were! The sheer brilliance of that scheme alone ensured him immortality in the legends of the *rom*. Plus this audacious hotel scam, another first; nobody could stop him from becoming King of the Gypsies.

But just in case, he would find the thirty-second Cadillac, the pink ragtop, and take it away from Yana to present as his own for the King to be buried in.

Cool shadow swept over the limo on the down-ramp to the St. Mark garage. After parking, he rode the escalator up to the lobby. Beyond the rest rooms and phone bank, he pushed open a door marked HOTEL EMPLOYEES ONLY; thanks to unwitting Marla the Check-in Clerk, he knew which of the four offices to enter and who to ask for.

A very decorative secretary wearing colored contacts and Obsession and a man-tailored blue pinstripe suit with enormous shoulders was putting the plastic cover on her computer when he came through the door. Wearing that perfume to work, she had to be sleeping with her boss.

"Angelo Grimaldi. One of your penthouse suites." Marino had chosen the end of business hours to heighten drama and tension. He pointed at her intercom, put into his voice the sort of steel his role demanded. "Harley Gunnarson. *Now.*"

"Sir, I'll have to call hotel security if you don't—"

"Ten days ago a terrorist death threat was phoned to this hotel. *Do you want that threat carried out?*"

Tense minutes later, Gunnarson, the St. Mark manager, opened his door to stand there frowning. He was a heavyweight mid-50s with thinning hair and piercing eyes and a hawk nose; the sort of man who looks soft and then beats you straight sets at handball.

"All right, Grimaldi. Come in and say your piece."

Marino sauntered past him, hoping that a penthouse suite at $900 a day carried enough weight for Gunnarson to run a check on him before calling the cops. It did: neither the big redheaded guy nor the little shrunken guy wore cop eyes.

Gunnarson gestured brusquely at the redhead, who had chiseled features and stupid blue eyes. His wide blue suit coat was unsuccessfully tailored to hide the gun under his arm.

"Shayne. Hotel Security."

Another gesture at the shrunken man, whose rounded dome had thinning strands of grey hair combed sideways across it in a vain attempt to hide its geodesic nakedness. For at least 75 of his 80 years he would have carried no hayseed in his pockets.

"Smathers. Corporate attorney. Now what the devil do—"

"Corporate doesn't cut it with me," said Marino.

He figured Smathers as the man with the moxie, but he had to be sure. The old man blinked bluejay eyes, bright and amoral and full of surprising mischief behind their rimless specs.

"Too old?" he demanded in a piping, birdlike voice. "No fire in the belly? No starch in the pecker?" His chuckle was bigger than he was. "Sonny, I was a Chicago D.A. busting scumbags like you before you were born."

"Christ, my mistake," said Marino with Grimaldi's tough New York inflection. He gently shook a tiny birdlike hand clawed by arthritis. "Maybe it's these other two clowns who should drift."

Smathers's smile drew a thousand fine creases in his aged face. "Now they're here, let's humor 'em and let 'em stay."

Marino shrugged, hooked a hip over a corner of Gunnarson's big messy desk. Yeah, Smathers was the Man.

Shayne rumbled, "We looked you up, wise guy."

"In the ten minutes since I knocked on Gunnarson's door?"

"Computers. Fax machines," snapped Gunnarson. "We found out that back in New York you're just some two-bit shyster, some sort of glorified corporate sharpshooter—"

"And that I'm on a fishing trip in the Maine woods where I can't be reached, right?" Marino clasped his hands around his knee in relaxed command, looked from face to face. "I gotta ask, do I look like the kind of guy goes fishing in Maine?"

Shayne said, "Why don't we just call the San Francisco cops and tell 'em we have the guy phoned in the bomb threat? We—"

"Better yet, call the Secret Service. They're the men who guard the President, right?"

Marino grinned into their sudden silence. Yeah! They *hadn't* reported the original bomb threat! Not to anyone! Report it and watch the Secret Service keep the President from coming anywhere near the St. Mark? Maybe keep him from coming anywhere near San Francisco? No way. A hotel man's P.R. nightmare.

"The threat was telephoned in by the Saladin," he said. "Iraqi fanatics whose name will appear on no Mideast terrorist flowchart but who have unlimited funding and a plan. Since the threat was for the future and wasn't repeated, you didn't report it to the feds. You could have. You should have. Now it's too late." He held up a hand. "No, I don't know the Saladin's plan, because nobody's paid me to know it. But if—"

"If?" Smathers's bluejay eyes gleamed. The smart ones were the easiest to fool; they conned themselves.

"If the hotel hires us, I'll learn it, and then my people will deal with the Saladin. *And* protect the hotel's name."

Gunnarson sneered, "Just who the hell are *your* people?"

This was the moment he was there for. He spoke mainly to Smathers and the little old man's wicked sense of conspiracy.

"Why, the Organization, of course. The Gangsters. The Mob. The Bad Guys. The Outfit. I'm Mouthpiece for the Mafia, get it?" Now he was all the Bronx. "We find these guys an' we smoke 'em for you—all for only seventy-five large."

Gunnarson, aghast, began, "We couldn't possibly—"

But Marino, with a wink at Smathers, was already leaving. Of course they'd need more persuading; but why have a stretch limo custom-made to the exact specifications of the President's own if not for a little extra persuading at the right time?

* * *

Yana, dressed in jeans and a pastel turtleneck, was getting ready for Teddy White's second candle reading. The first had been a great success; because of the strength of the curse, she'd had to use eighteen candles at $50 each. Tonight she would be burning another eighteen candles—this time at $100 each.

For her, preparing to cast out demons did not, as it did for a Catholic priest, involve confession and absolution, nor spiritual exercise to strengthen the soul and cleanse impurities from the psyche. Yana, before getting into her low-cut silver gown that shimmered like fish scales, merely reviewed again what Ramon had gleaned from Teddy's wallet and garbage.

Theodore Winston White III hadn't heard that Yuppiedom, that phenomenon of the '80s that had put Sharper Image on America's corporate map, was now considered *déclassé*. He still thought the one with the most toys wins.

So he drove an Alfa-Romeo Quadrifoglio Spider. He drove a Lexus LS400. When up in the snow, he drove a Toyota 4Runner equipped with mud and snow tires, all the luxury option packages, a ski rack, and a side pocket full of lift tickets for Squaw and Incline and the Village—even though he didn't know how to ski.

Receipts and prescriptions in the garbage, along with ads, Godiva chocolate wrappers, throwaways, coffee grounds (whole-bean fresh-ground French Roast/Guatemalan, of course), showed that:

Teddy worked out three days a week with a personal trainer, Linda Perry, at the World Gym in Kentfield, while wearing sweats with the legend *Live Well, Eat Right, Die Anyway* on them.

When not at the gym, Teddy wore Armani suits, Versace sportswear, custom-made dress shirts, Valentino ties, Dior underwear, Bally shoes.

Teddy belonged to the Mount Tam Racket Club and the Pacific Union Club and, through his late adoptive father, the Bohemian Club.

Teddy had credit cards from I Magnin's and Neiman Marcus, the American Express Goldcard, Gold MasterCard, and Visa Gold (three different lending institutions each), Tire Systems, Discover Card, the Pacific Bell phone card, the AT&T phone card, the Sprint phone card, and the MCI phone card.

Teddy had travel pass cards from Travel Access and Western Airlines (Travel Pass II) and American Airlines and Alaska Airlines and United Airlines. Hertz, Avis, and Budget, of course.

Not that he ever used any of them.

Teddy subscribed to *The New York Times* and *Time* and *Newsweek* and *The Wall Street Journal* and *National Review* and *Playboy* and *Penthouse* and *Skin Diver* and *Esquire* and *GQ* and *Spy*.

Not that he ever read any of them.

Teddy had check guarantee cards from seven different banks.

Not that any of them were much good. Between his monthly trust checks from the bank, he pretty much ran on empty.

Teddy also looked pale and was losing weight, and, most promising, had begun getting acupuncture treatments for a mild sciatica attack from a Chinese woman doctor named Wu.

And Teddy even now was on his way in for his second candle reading. Showing that Teddy, despite all the sophisticated trappings of his Yuppiedom, was a fool.

"He is here," said Ramon in low tones from the doorway.

"I'll get dressed. Keep him waiting in the hall."

Even that was carefully calculated. The hallway was dim, the incense overpowering. An opened window behind the plush drapes made it clammy and stirred the old-fashioned crystal lampshades into an incessant tinkling contrived to unnerve. Teddy was indeed unnerved: sitting in the half-dark, shivering and squeezing his hands, he jumped and twitched like a galvanized frog when Ristik suddenly appeared before him.

"Yana is now prepared to receive you."

The *boojo* room was stifling with incense and the waxy smoke of eighteen candles, as if hell itself breathed out contagions.

"You have come," said Yana in a deep voice almost not her own. Her eyes gleamed ferally. Tonight her lips were very red, overripe—slightly obscene fiuit ready to be bitten.

"I . . . yes, I . . . tonight you . . . you . . ."

"Sit."

Teddy sat down across the little table from her. The room was dim; there was no crystal ball. Yana took his hands; already there was familiarity in this action, the shared intimacy of trysting lovers, an implied security that made her necessary.

She shut her eyes. Her silver gown shimmered as her body began a sinuous, unnerving, snakelike undulation by candlelight. Sweat rolled down between her half-bared breasts. The incense made Teddy's head ache, made him want to lick away those rivulets of sweat, made him, for God sake, start to get an erection!

But then Yana cried out, *"Chi mai diklem ande viatsa!"* in a voice now definitely not her own. A voice deep, thick, guttural, almost male. *"Chuda. Che chorobia."*

Terror made him bold. He had to know. "What does it mean?" he demanded. "What are you saying to me?"

She was silent. Her body had stopped writhing. She seemed not even to breathe. Her eyes were open again. In the dim light the pupils subsumed the irises, leaving only obsidian buttons that stared at him without blinking, not even once.

"I see a snake. In your buttocks. Down the back of your leg. Beware. A yellow woman touches you." Her voice was male, throaty, threatening. Her face worked. "Needles. Beware."

"My sciatica," breathed Teddy. There was no way she could have known. She was indeed psychic. "My acupuncturist—"

"The yellow woman has made you sick."

Teddy'd had the flu twice since he had started with Madam Wu. He'd gotten prescriptions for it.

"She has caused you to be . . . *no!* The snake inside your body is *not* from her! But . . . the snake grows . . ."

There it was again. The snake. Her words terrified him. A snake. Inside him. Growing. "You mean canc . . ." He had difficulty with the word. *"Cancer?"*

"The same snake killed your mother."

He leaned forward, his fingers tight about her wrists. "My *real* mother died of cancer?"

73

"It is you who speaks of cancer. I speak of the snake." Obsidian eyes, reptile eyes, the *eyes* of a snake. Flat, black, unwinking, without pupils. "From beyond the grave your mother warns you." Her face, her eyes softened. "May she sleep well."

Teddy had always known, in his heart of hearts, that his *real* mother was dead. Now Madame Miseria had confirmed it.

"I am but a conduit. The spirit speaks through me. She says you have much money . . . that is not really yours."

"My *mother's* spirit? My *real* mother says that I . . ."

But Yana's head had fallen on her chest. Her fingers were lax in his. Her mouth had fallen open as if in profound sleep, but she was breathing rapidly, shallowly, like a person in great pain. She suddenly sprang straight up from her chair.

"*Mene!*" she cried, words she had memorized from the Old Testament she had loved when learning to read. "*Mene, Mene, Tekel, Upharsin!*"

She was staring over his head, her eyes wider than eyes could possibly be, popping out of a face now so congested it was almost purple. Teddy, no Bible scholar, whirled in dread expectation of seeing, not the words that Yahweh's moving finger had writ on Belshazzar's wall, but demons hulking behind him.

Nothing. No one. Just an empty room. He turned back. Yana had fallen back into her chair. She sprawled like a rag doll. She looked exhausted. Her voice was slow, dragging.

"The curse is in your body . . . the snake is growing there . . . because . . . when you were small . . . you wanted your foster parents dead . . . *you* created the snake . . . out of cursed money . . ."

"No!" cried Teddy. "I . . . I loved them, I . . ."

He went dumb. When they told him he was adopted, for a fleeting moment he'd wished them dead, to unsay the terrible knowledge of his real parents' rejection. Or had that death wish been so that he would be left their *money?* Could that insidious thought have lain in ambush within his mind down the years, exactly like a snake, finally growing into . . . *cancer?*

He began thickly, "How did you know that I—"

"Give me a dollar." She was brusque, almost cold. She snapped her fingers. "Quickly! We must test whether your money is cursed.

If the snake in your body indeed comes from your money, then perhaps there is a way . . . one way . . . to save you . . ."

"How? Save? How can? You? You *must* save—"

"The dollar."

As if mesmerized, he took out a dollar bill, started to hand it to Yana. She shook her head and pointed at the table.

"My touch would affect the power, make the curse more potent." Another gesture, this one to a point beyond him. "Through the curtain. Water. A bowl. Quickly."

Teddy tossed his dollar down and jumped from his chair, feeling the thick horrible ropelike snake in his buttocks and down his left leg as he ran limping across the room. Behind the curtain was a tiny alcove with a sink and a stack of ceramic bowls. He filled one from the tap, carried it back to Yana.

"Put it on the table. Put your dollar bill in it."

He picked up the dollar from the table and dropped it in the water. They sat on either side of the bowl, watching it. The water began to discolor. But not green from the dye in the money—which was supposed to be waterproof anyway. No. It was getting pink. Then red. Getting redder. Blood-red. His mother's blood. His own blood. In his money.

"Cursed," Yana said in a flat voice devoid of hope or pity; and Teddy knew he was going to be sick.

CHAPTER TEN

But she wouldn't allow him even that. Not right away.

"We have to be sure of the curse, we have to let the evil hatch," she told him at the head of the stairs. "When you get home, wrap a fresh egg in a sock and put it in a shoe . . ."

"A . . . shoe? But . . . what kind . . ."

"Any kind. Just leave it there. Also collect all the cash money you can and put it in a paper bag with the shoe and the egg and leave it. When I call you, bring both with you to me."

Only then was Teddy, shaking as if with fever, allowed to pay for the candles and go down to vomit out his horror at Madame Miseria's revelations into the slanting Romolo Place gutter.

* * *

As he was so engaged, Larry Ballard was leaving his two-room studio apartment on Lincoln Way with his case files and repo tools. On impulse he drove a dozen blocks west along the southern edge of Golden Gate Park to Jacques Daniel's.

Beverly had hung up on him five times since her car had gotten dinged up, which just wasn't fair. Look what had happened to *him*—without any insurance to cover it like she had, either.

Oh, man, he sure *hoped* she had insurance to cover it.

Bev and her partner, Jacques, had renamed the little neighborhood bar "Jacques Daniel's," swept out the local rummies, put in an espresso machine, hung ferns and fake Tiffany lamps, and started serving trendy drinks like Sex on the Beach. It was not a meat market, Beverly saw to that; rather, a place where neighborhood singles could mix and mingle. In the grand old tradition, they were about to sponsor a softball team.

Ballard stuck his bruised face and thatch of sun-whitened hair into the bar's blast of light and heat and noise. Hammer was hammering eardrums on C/D. Beverly and Jacques were behind the stick serving them up with both hands, but when Ballard pushed the door wider and stepped through, Bev exploded.

"*Out!*" she yelled over the noise.

"Aw, Bev, can't we talk about i—"

"*Out,* or I'll throw you out. Jacques."

Heads were turning, eyes were staring. Jacques sighed and took off his apron and dropped it on top of the beer cooler. Small, wiry, quick, balding, he once had been a diver with Cousteau. He and Ballard had SCUBA-dived together, they took karate from the same master—but he *was* Beverly's partner.

Ballard said placatingly, "Bev, it was an *accident.*"

"My beautiful car." Fire blazed in her eyes. Her lips were a thin enraged line. "Jacques. Do something."

Ballard began, "The insurance—"

"*Insurance?* The car is totaled. *Totaled!* I don't want insurance! I want my—"

Ballard lost it. "Why do you have to be such a sorehead? I mean, if the insurance'll buy you a new car—"

The blazing eyes were on Jacques now. "If you won't throw this bastard out of here . . ."

Jacques made little nodding, placating gestures toward her. He took Ballard's arm and spoke in his elongated Gallic vowels.

"Larree, better you to go . . ."

Ballard let himself be herded out. If he wanted to patch it up with Beverly, he couldn't fight her partner: he'd lose whichever of them ended up on his back in the gutter. Outside, with the doors swinging back and forth behind them, Jacques released his arm with a fatalistic French shrug.

"Larree, how can you reason with her *maintenant?* You should have telephoned first—"

"I did. Five times. She hung up each time."

He said illogically, "Just as I said. So there is no reasoning with her now. Maybe never, *hein?*" He added, with bourgeois practicality, "*Peut-être* this is the end. *Fin.*"

"Yeah. *Fin.* Shit." Ballard started rapidly away down the street, then turned back to add, "Pardon me, *merde,*" before going on again.

He drove right to the Montana, slid a tire iron up his jacket sleeve, and walked through the garage checking out the parked cars. No more Mr. Nice Guy for Larry Ballard.

No Mercedes for Larry Ballard, either. Twelfth floor, leaning on the doorbell for a timed two minutes. Nobody home. He printed CATCH YOU LATER in block letters on a business card that he stuck, bent, between doorknob and doorjamb.

Give the little toad something to think about.

For the rest of the night he sat in his car across the street from the garage entrance, dozing, listening to Live 105, The Rock of the Nineties, feeling blue about Beverly. She couldn't *seriously* have dumped him tonight, just like that, could she? In public and everything, just because her car . . .

Rising sun woke him. People were leaving for work; no trick at all to get inside for another walk-through before admitting he wasn't going to get the Mercedes. In two hours it would be assigned to someone else.

But as he drove away, he brightened: anybody who was going to get that car away from Pietro and his poopsie was going to have to be a better carhawk than Larry Ballard.

And Ballard had just enough ego to feel there weren't too many of them fellers around.

*   *   *

A few hours earlier, while Ballard dreamed of hypersteroid Freddies going out twelfth-story windows in leather underwear without benefit of parachutes, Bart Heslip drove south through San Francisco on the post-midnight-deserted James Lick Freeway. His white teeth gleamed in anticipation as he took the Silver Avenue off-ramp into the outer Mission.

Just after lunch he'd gotten a new lead on Sarah Walinski from the skip-tracers. Until she'd waved her magic axe at the other guy's head, Sarah had been a shift-worker at Bonnard Die-Cutting on Tennessee across from the site of the old Bethlehem Shipyards. Heslip had timed his arrival at Bonnard to chat in the noontime cafeteria with people who'd worked Sarah's shift. A Polish woman as old as water had beckoned him to her table.

"Hey, you. Ya want get hold Sarah Walinski? Hey, talk Mel Larson. A driver." She held up a hand with forefinger and index finger crossed. "Sarah and Mel like that . . ." She began moving her fingers in a shocking graphic rhythm and burst into raucous laughter. "Hey, that's Sarah on top."

After making sure Larson was out on his truck, Heslip used an insurance scam to learn from a bright-eyed personnel woman that Larson lived off Silver Ave, near the green postage stamp of Portola Playground. Tall skinny three-story wooden row-house that needed paint, ROOMS FOR RENT on the front door and a street-level one-car garage beneath. He checked through the dusty window. Empty. But fresh oil on the floor and junk shoved back against the walls showed a car was being parked in there.

The landlady had more chins than Chinatown, hawsers for ankles, and got more religion than a jackleg preacher when Heslip asked her about Sarah sleeping over.

"Oh my goodness, no! I keep a respectable house here . . ."

The Chicano who ran the little *madre y padre* down the street sang a different song. *Sí*, Sarah live in the white house needs paint. *Sí*, she lock up her car in that garage at night. *Y caramba,* she buy her liquor by the gallon.

Heslip did not turn in the new address at the office when he went back to DKA. He wouldn't do that until he'd gotten his final shot at Sarah himself: no tomorrow for him on this case. He tossed an old yellow Plymouth with only half a transmission on his towbar and, out at Larson's place, dumped it in front of the still-empty garage. He stuck a note hand-scrawled on cheap paper under the wiper arm: *im sorry wont run pleez dont call cops.*

Late tonight, when Sarah came back from whatever bar she was getting sloshed in, she would find the old Plymouth in front of her garage and, he hoped, being drunk and careless, would park the Charger in the street. From whence, Heslip thought as he drove through the night, he now would pluck it like an apple.

The Charger wasn't there. Nor on any adjacent street. He ended up down the block with a good view of the house, waiting for the bars to close. And sort of hoping that when she came, Larson would be with her, drunk and belligerent: he had begun to feel like hitting someone male, his own size or larger, several times very rapidly in the face.

Not to be. At sunup, as Larry Ballard drove morosely away from the Montana on the far side of town, Heslip was still sitting there, chilled and stiff and also empty-handed. No Sarah. No Charger. And at ten o'clock he would have to go back to the office and hand her file over to someone else.

Wait a sec! At 9:45 the landlady, shopping bag in hand, laboriously made her way down the front steps on her swollen ankles. She waddled obliquely across the street to his car, panting from such exertion. Heslip rolled down his window.

"Young man," she said, "I wish I'd told you the truth about that woman yesterday. She *has* been living with Mr. Larson, and she's a fat lazy slob who all she does is lay around and drink hard liquor and never change the sheets. And all they'd ever do after he got home from work was drink and fight up there in his room until all hours."

Noting the change of tenses, Heslip said, "Swell."

"Last night, along about ten o'clock, they had a terrible row an' she threw him down the stairs. Broke three of his ribs an' give him a concussion. Amb'lance come an' everything. Din't even go to the hospital with him—just packed up an' left. I seen you sittin' out here all last night and still here this morning, an' I just thought it was my Christ'an duty to tell you she was gone."

After she was gone. *After* he'd sat there all night.

"Even if you are a nigger."

Bart Heslip drove off cursing her, and himself for not slipping her a twenty yesterday, and for not being here last night at the right time, and Sarah, and the guy she'd thrown down the stairs, and most especially Dan Kearny for . . . well, just on general principles.

* * *

Kearny had sneaked into work early that Friday morning to upend the big metal barrels full of paper trash over a square of canvas laid out on the concrete floor—for once he was glad they were having so much trouble with their cleaning service. He was in before anybody else—especially Giselle—to look for Warren's app and Trin's business card. They should still be here, since the trash had been piling up for a couple weeks. No reason for Giselle to know he needed them after all, was there?

Forty minutes later he was still there, pawing away, when her voice made him leap and whirl as if stung by an asp hidden in the ejected paperwork. Giselle was holding up the elusive employment application and the wayward business card.

"Looking for these?"

He sighed and grunted his way to his feet and dusted off the knees of his trousers. "How'd you know I'd need 'em? When I tossed those, the Gypsies hadn't even hit the bank yet . . ."

"Woman's intuition."

"Yeah, sure." He eyed the offending papers as if they were cold-virus cultures. "A lying thieving conniving Mexican—"

"But a hell of an investigator."

"If you can control him. I seem to remember that nobody cheered louder than you when I fired him the first time."

Giselle shrugged. "Things change. Now we need him."

"And this other guy, Warren! Donald Duck on helium—"

"He doesn't have to talk, Dan'l. Not if he can grab cars. Maybe he's the greatest carhawk the world has ever seen."

"Yeah," said Kearny bitterly, "sure."

*   *   *

Something that sounded female and Latina and 15 max answered Trin Morales's phone at 11:00 A.M. Morales took the receiver out of the girl's hand to yell something short and Anglo-Saxon into it. The phone replied in Kearny's voice.

"Put your pants on and get your butt down here. Now."

*   *   *

Four hours later Ken Warren, also summoned by phone, wanted to give a great big YELL. Except nobody would have understood him, anyway. He wanted to yell because Kearny was showing him stuff right out of Auto Mechanics 101. And talking to him as if he had a mind defect instead of a speech defect.

"You put one alligator clip on the positive post of the battery, and the second one on the distributor . . ."

All right, Ken thought, *I know how to hotwire a car.*

Kearny showed him anyway. And then said, "These days we try to get key codes from the dealer and cut keys for the door locks. But if you don't have a key, this funny-looking thing here like a Buck Rogers raygun is a . . ."

I know how to use a lockgun to open door locks.

Kearny showed him anyway, and then said, "If you don't have a lockgun with you, this piece of thin strap steel can . . ."

I know how to go down alongside the window with a slim-jim and flip open door locks.

Kearny showed him anyway, and then said, "These days we use a lockpunch under the dash to . . ."

I know how to punch an ignition lock and substitute my own. I know how to hotwire under the dash. I know how to . . .

Kearny showed him all of it anyway. And then said, "Follow the instructions on the assignment sheet. If it's REPO ON SIGHT, just grab the car. But if it says to make contact first—"

"NgYe gho ntawk ta ghu man."

"Yeah, that's right." Kearny looked suddenly deflated, as if he had forgotten the extent of Warren's speech defect. " 'Gho ntawk ta ghu man.' That's very important—talking to the man if the case instructions tell you to. Most of our trouble with clients comes from field men who don't talk to the man."

He thrust the sheaf of field assignment sheets almost blindly back into Warren's hand, started to walk away slump-shouldered, then stopped and turned back. He sighed.

"One more thing. Two of those files are pretty salty. That guy Uvaldi—that's the Mercedes convertible—has a fag boyfriend who's six-six and two-forty and leaps tall buildings in a single bound. He—"

"Ngye *ndon'* gho ntawk ta ghu man."

Kearny looked surprised, as if a guy like Warren wasn't supposed to have a sense of humor. "Uhhh . . . that's right, Ken, you *don't* go talk to the man. You avoid the man like the plague. The other one you gotta watch out for is—"

"Ghu whooman."

Kearny thought, This guy talks funny but he sure ain't slow. All

82

he's had time to do is riffle through those files *once*, but he knows which cases I'm talking about. Could it be he might actually work out as a repoman?

Feeling almost hopeful, he said, "She busted Heslip's head with a can of coffee and Heslip is pretty nifty on his feet—won thirty-nine out of forty fights professionally before he—"

Warren went into a sudden fighter's crouch, bobbing and weaving, and threw a damned fast left hook/right uppercut combination at the chin of an imaginary opponent.

"Ngye ngsaw hym gnfigh ngleven nears ago."

"Ngsaw hym gnfigh." Kearny nodded as if pleased about something, and went back inside chuckling to himself. "Catchy."

That's when Ken Warren started to like Dan Kearny. Dan Kearny might talk to him like he was an idiot, but Dan Kearny laughed at him like he was a man. And left him on his own with a fistful of REPO ON SIGHT orders and a whole weekend to prove he *was* the greatest carhawk the world had ever known.

CHAPTER ELEVEN

When they had opened the turnstiles at Universal Studios Tours down in L.A. that same Friday morning, Ephrem Poteet had paid and queued up for the first of the long open-sided buses to the tour's backlot delights. It was just a week since the Great Cal-Cit Bank Massacre and already he had heard about it.

Poteet was late 30s and still handsome, sloe-eyed, well-built though starting to go paunchy. But by subtle alterations in his appearance, clothing, posture, and gait, he still could pass for any age between 25 and 50.

Today he was mid-40s, with a red bandana around his neck and a grey gunfighter's mustache and powdered hair to glint silver below a white wide-brimmed ten-gallon cowboy hat like Tom Mix wore in the Saturday morning serials long before his birth. He walked a little pigeon-toed in his cowboy boots, a bit bowlegged from aridin' that old cayuse on the lone pray-ree.

He was also sober—a small triumph not entirely his own, because his latest thirty-day stretch in the county slam had ended just last week. When he drank he got nasty, when he got nasty he beat his wife, when he beat his wife he got into bar scuffles, when he got into bar scuffles he got arrested and booked for Drunk &

Disorderly. He no longer had the wife, but he was still getting drunk, nasty, in scuffles, and arrested for D&D.

Poteet came to work at Universal Studios early most days during the peak April–September tourist season. Only after Labor Day, when the crowds had thinned and he would stand out as a regular despite his disguises, would it be too risky to continue.

Risky because Universal had no idea he worked there.

His first mark was an overweight red-faced woman with two noisy kids and a gaping purse. The bus stopped and everyone started crowding off for the earthquake special-effects show. While standing politely aside and speaking to her with a West Texas drawl, Poteet lifted his cowboy hat with one hand and her wallet with the other.

"First time y'all here, ma'am?"

"Yes. We're from Indiana. The kids are so excited . . ."

"Wal, don't let 'em get scairt—it's all jus' funnin'."

He sat behind her on the bleachers and, when the lights went down, slipped two $20s from the wallet. When the audience applauded the completion of the tour guide's opening spiel, he dropped the wallet back into the purse.

If the mark had only a bill or two, he took nothing at all. If the wallet was missed before he could return it, he merely dropped it on the floor. When it was found with money still inside, they were happy: at an amusement park with the kids, who knew how much actual cash they had left?

By early afternoon he'd made nearly $200, a very good day's score, when, from the queue for the next bus, he saw the door of one of the maintenance sheds was ajar. Awfully early in the season, but too good to pass up even though Universal would know a dip had been working the crowd that day. He would skip work for a week, let the pickpocket heat die down; the big score should make the interruption of steady income worth it.

He stepped casually over the low fence flanking the walkway and went through screening bushes into the shed. A minute later he emerged wearing a white knee-length smock with MAINTE-NANCE printed across the back. His ten-gallon hat had been replaced by a billed MAINTENANCE cap, pulled low to hide his greyed hair and shadow his eyes. His mustache was in his pocket.

"Pardon me, folks, could I get through?" Working his way clumsily up the line at the busiest food concession, a shoulder jostle here, a lurch there, a slip and a hand out to steady himself elsewhere. "Sorry, ma'am, something slippery there . . ."

All the time, dip, dip, dip—busy clever fingers darting into pockets and handbags as he moved along, sliding the take into the voluminous pockets of the maintenance smock. His mother had taken him to playgrounds to practice on other kids' mothers when he was too little to be arrested, so he had good hands.

At the head of the line he veered off to the side door, opened it, stuck his head and a $20 bill inside, reading the name of the nearest girl off the front of her smock as he did.

"Hey, Marie, can you give me two double cheeseburgers and two jumbo fries and two big Cokes? All in one big sack? We got a generator shorting out down by King Kong and I'm gonna be stuck there the rest of the day." She looked blank. "Charlie Bilton. We got our jobs the same day."

Marie didn't know him because they hadn't, of course, but now she *thought* she knew him. "Oh, sure. Hi, Charlie."

Her quick hands scooped up two bulky wrapped burgers and two fries and two Cokes, stuck them and napkins in a big bag with a bright logo on the side, took his money, gave him change.

"Thanks, Marie. See you later."

He worked quickly around the knoll, hitting three more concessions, then sheared off back to the shed. Inside, he dropped the food into a big green leaf bag but kept the paper sack—in it the wallets looked and smelled like hamburgers and fries. Off with smock and cap, mustache stuck hurriedly back on, aw-shucks-ma'am cowboy hat back in place, slip out of the shed.

This was the time of maximum exposure, when he still had the wallets on him. Usually, this kind of gig, you handed off to an accomplice. But he had no accomplice, he had to work alone, the rest of the goddamned Gypsies had seen to that. Just because, drunk, he'd ignore *marimays*—tribal taboos—relating to women. So now he was no longer welcome into anybody's *vitsa*.

Twenty minutes later, he was walking up toward the main gate past sound stages and bungalows with the names of current TV shows on them, past the Alfred Hitchcock Theatre, the editing building, then left into the newly refurbished commissary.

In the big echoing basement men's room he emptied the leathers of their money and credit cards, feeding the stripped and wiped wallets one by one into the tippy mouth of the trash bucket. He removed his mustache and ran wet fingers through his hair to blot out some grey, crushed his high-crowned cowboy hat into a nondescript oval under one arm. He emerged minus a dozen years and the cowboy's pigeon-toed bowlegged walk.

Out the main gate past the guard kiosk, across Lankershim to the Universal City branch post office. Check his P.O. box, then catch a bus down to LAX and sell the credit cards to a broker. Tomorrow they would be in play in New York, until the security nets got them on the stolen-card lists.

There was an Express Mail envelope from San Francisco in his box. At a table under the WANTED posters he pocketed the $50 bill it contained and read DKA's accompanying material. The *gadje* were offering *$100* for each hot tip that led to recovery of any of those San Francisco Cadillacs he'd already heard about.

He was sure his bitch wife, Yana, was involved in it. Yana, who wouldn't work like a good Gypsy wife to bring money home to her husband no matter how much he beat her. Yana, who taught herself to *read and write* like *no* good Gypsy woman should.

Since the *rom* chose to treat him as an outcast, the bastards, he would make them pay right along with her. He would spend his week off work from the studio tour to run with the *rom* once more, pick up a word here, a name there, then piece things together. Then he would make occasional calls to San Francisco and he would have his revenge—wonderful revenge, repeated revenge, filling as stolen eggs, sweet as wild honey.

Revenge at $100 an installment. Collect.

*   *   *

"To tell you the truth," said Alvin Crichton, M.D., chief of Neurosurgery at Steubenville General Hospital, "we don't have a clear X-ray picture of your husband's injuries yet."

"My Karl has been here days and days," said Lulu in her Margarete persona, "and you've had him up and down to that room with that big machine and made him lie on that cold table—"

"The X rays we have gotten don't really tell us anything."

They were in Zlachi's semi-private room on a beautiful spring day in Stupidville; the drapes were back and the shades up so the bright afternoon sunlight poured across the bed and dripped to the floor like honey. The other bed was unoccupied.

"Why don't they?"

Crichton had a big beak and was tall and lanky and slightly stooped, so in silhouette against the window he looked like a heron about to spear a fish with his nose.

"Because your husband won't lie still for the X rays."

"You keep puttin' him through all that pain," she snapped. "On the table, off the table—"

"That's why we'd like to run a few tests right here."

"Is it gonna hurt?" quavered Staley in his weak old-man's voice. "I gotta lotta pain even just lyin' here. I can stand that okay, but when I move—"

"I know, but it would be a great help in our diagnosis if we could localize the pain to find out *exactly* where it hurts."

If the patient had been younger, Crichton would have suspected some sort of scam, but this was a man pushing 80, with no insurance and a dozen witnesses to his terrible headlong tumble down the department-store escalator.

Mrs. Klenhard surprised him by patting her husband's arm.

"Karl, you gotta do what the doctor tells you."

"Whatever you say, Mama," he replied in a docile voice.

"Wonderful." Crichton rang for the nurse as he sat down on the empty bed and got out his pen. "Are you still having those bad headaches, Mr. Klenhard?"

"Alla time, Doc." He put a hand to his head. "They don't never go away."

"Not even with the medication?"

"Sometimes at night I kinda drift off . . . but otherwise . . ."

Crichton made cat scratches on the patient's chart. "And how about the vertigo?" Seeing the look on their faces, he amended, "Dizziness. Losing your balance when you stand?"

"Oh. Yeah. I gotta lean on Margarete when I gotta use the bathroom, Doc. Is very . . . makes me feel . . . *ashamed*, you know?"

The nurse came in, a sturdy freckle-faced girl with auburn hair and upturned nose. Crichton said he would like the patient to stand beside the bed for a few simple tests.

"Here we go," said the nurse cheerily. She drew back the covers and reached for Staley's feet. "We'll just—"

"No!" exclaimed Margarete. "He don't do it that way."

It was a major operation, with everyone helping, just to get Staley on his two feet beside the bed. Even then he wasn't upright; he was bent forward and pulled over to one side.

"That's fine!" exclaimed Crichton with dubious enthusiasm. "Now I would like you to stretch your arms out to your sides . . . yes . . . that's it . . . Now close your eyes and touch your nose with your forefinger . . ."

Staley tried with his left hand first. He fell over to his left. Margarete, expecting it, was quick to catch him.

"Gee, Mr. Doctor, I . . . I'm sorry . . ."

"You did just fine. Could you try the other hand?"

Staley tried with his right. And fell over left again.

"What's it mean he does that?" demanded Margarete in alarm.

"It suggests that the major injury is on your husband's left side." Crichton patted Staley's shoulder. "You're doing just fine, Mr. Klenhard. You game for another little test?"

This one was more daunting. Staley was to try to relax his body, and then bend gently forward at the waist as if to touch his right foot with his left hand.

He bent down a few inches. And shot erect, screaming.

Trying to reverse it, to touch his left foot with his right hand, Staley, pale and shaken, got down about a foot before he yelped and shot erect again with a hand to the small of his back. They got him carefully but quickly back into bed on his back, pale and shaken, with the covers still drawn down.

"Is that it?" he asked hopefully. Lulu was patting his face with her handkerchief. "I don't know if I can . . ."

"Just one more, then we'll give you something for the pain and leave you alone."

Lulu was fierce. "You gotta tell him what it is first."

"I'd like you to raise your left knee just a little, Mr. Klenhard, then straighten it out again . . ."

"Hey, that oughtta be easy!" exclaimed Staley with his first show of enthusiasm for the day.

He almost delightedly started to lift his left knee. And yelped in agony, jerking to his left. Lulu started forward protectively. The nurse stopped her. Staley was breathing quickly and shallowly. He finally relaxed, the lines of pain lessening on his face. He spoke apologetically.

"Guess I didn't do that so good, huh, Doc?"

"You did fine." Crichton made a little grimace of his own. "How about . . . could *I* try to bend your knee, Mr. Klenhard?"

"Sure," said Staley with a ghost of his former enthusiasm, "maybe you be better at it than me, huh?"

Crichton gingerly began to bend the knee. Staley yelped. This time Lulu started for Crichton, hands clawed, but the nurse again interposed herself between them.

"That's enough. My Karl has had enough."

Crichton frowned. "If we could just try his right leg—"

"No more," she said with that sudden determination that so far had kept anyone else from being assigned to the other bed in the room. "No more for my Karl."

"Mama," said Staley. This time he met that dark, ominous gaze with one of his own. "We gotta let the doctor find out what he can. One more leg, okay? Then we be all through here."

Another long pause from Lulu. Then finally, reluctantly, she nodded. "Okay. Once more. The right knee."

Staley steeled himself, then started to bend his right knee. One inch. Two. Six. He kept bending it. It was almost totally flexed before he suddenly winced and let it drop. He lay there panting, but he met the doctor's eyes triumphantly.

"Hey, I done good, huh, Doc?"

"You done wonderfully," agreed Crichton. "And that's it for today. In a few minutes they'll bring supper—"

Lulu said, "I think he's got too much pain to eat supper."

"Then you can eat it for him," grinned Crichton.

He made his notes on Staley's chart and departed with the nurse. Staley's eyes met Lulu's. He winked. She winked back.

"I'll make sure the nurse knows it was me ate your supper," she said. "Then during visiting hours tonight I'll sneak you in something from Jack in the Box—"

"Some of those fingerfoods I see on the TV," exclaimed Staley with enthusiasm. His voice was deep and full, not thin and quavery as it was when anyone else was around. "With some of those curly fries and a Coke . . ."

*   *   *

Marino was off working his secret hotel scam, but the three other literates in the *kumpania*—Yana, Immaculata Bimbai, and, surprisingly, fat Josef Adamo—were filling out registration applications in a variety of names, with return addresses all over the country. The DMVs of such friendly southern states as Georgia and North Carolina would mail valid auto registrations to anyone who paid the fee and sent in the forms, and already only fourteen of the cars were still in the Bay Area.

Immaculata Bimbai herself was still in town only because she wanted to hit a big Post Street jeweler before driving down to hit a similar establishment on Rodeo Drive in Beverly Hills.

As soon as fat Josef Adamo finished the Cadillac paperwork he would be heading for Seattle. His brother was already up there, organizing a much expanded version of the road-paving scam that was Josef's usual M.O.

Wasso Tomeshti was in the southland setting up the most ambitious con of his career, involving an East L.A. TV wholesaler and a contractor who was just finishing a fancy motel in the Valley. For this, the new Caddy was essential window dressing.

Heading for Florida was Kalia Uwanowich, planning on a big score in subdivision roofing just outside Fort Lauderdale.

Chicago for Nanoosh Tsatshimo, where a relative had rented a defunct metalworking plant under a phony name. Nanoosh's electroplating scam needed a physical place of business where the bogus plating work could be done, not just a mail-drop address.

Pearso Stokes was going to New York; she specialized in short-changing banks and she liked Manhattan because New Yorkers, even bank tellers, thought they were too streetwise to be taken. Which made them very easy to take indeed, especially with a hoary scam everyone had forgotten in this new electronic age of computer theft. Gypsies are nothing if not traditionalists.

No fewer than seven Lovellis, each with a new Caddy, were gathered in Reno to prepare for their annual round of the Midwest county fair circuits as palmists, curse-removers, mentalists, astrolo-

91

gists, telekineticists, tarot-card and tea-leaf readers, crystal-ball gazers, and similar divinators. All for twenty-five bucks a reading, quick in and out, wham, bam, thank you, ma'am.

All felt good about their work, because Christ Himself had given permission to the Gypsies to steal. As He hung dying on the shameful cross, a Gypsy stole the Roman soldiers' fourth spike—the one intended for His heart. A grateful Christ gave His absolution forever to all Gypsies who stole from the *gadje*.

Of course in this world of unenlightened souls, the *gadje*, just because they could not find the story in their Bibles, didn't believe in this dispensation; but the *kumpania* didn't worry about them. The *kumpania* could always outwit non-Gypsies.

Or had up until then.

CHAPTER TWELVE

O'B spent his Friday on the phone rooms. He started out in the morning by dropping around to the Public Utility Commission offices looking for a field investigator named Sturrock with whom he once had worked at a collection agency.

"Hey, Reverend, how's tricks?"

"O'Bannon, you old devil, what are you doing around here?"

O'B leaned close enough for Sturrock to smell the bourbon he'd swished around his mouth in the men's room.

"Well, I'm, ah, lookin' for work . . ."

Sturrock, that subservient ferret of a man, immediately darted down his burrow to safety. "Damn, O'B, you know with the recession and all, we don't have even entry-level jobs . . ."

Then, of course, guilty about dropping his old buddy like a used condom over that drinking problem, he had to take O'B around to meet the other field men before easing him out the door. Lots of heavy male guffaws, bluff manly hellos, *mano a mano* slaps on the shoulder, macho hearty handshakes all around—and O'B came away with *four* of the investigators' business cards he was after.

Each was worth its weight in gold because of the miniature—but official—Public Utility Commission seal in the corner.

At the phone company's gaudy blue building flanking Islais Creek, O'B pulled a soft wool cap down over his red hair before facing the uniformed guard on the door. This was a big red-faced galoot with mean little eyes who loved his pinch of power.

"Yeah, you wanna see who and why?"

Even as he spoke, the guard was examining the backside of a passing secretary with casual lust. Out came O'B's first card, William Ready, P.U.C., Field Investigator. Inspired by the guard's gaze, out came O'B's repoman voice and face. Out came O'B's hand to finger the cloth of the guard's jacket.

"Nice uniform. You rent-a-cops got a nice soft touch here, watch the door, watch the girls go in and out." Leaned close, let the guard smell his two-margarita lunch. "Watching 'em a little too close, pal? We been gettin' complaints . . ."

A guilty whine, "Listen, I don't know what you—"

"You're gone in a New York minute you screw with me, pal."

O'B sauntered on without signing in, flashing the second card— P. Dana Anderssen—from office to office until he got to Ms. Pegeen Gibson and knew he was home free. The lass had milk-white Irish skin and a fine peasant bosom and round cheeks and looked like she'd cop to a middle-aged redheaded man with a tired drinker's face and a rich line of Irish blarney. Besides, the phone company *loved* to cooperate with the P.U.C.—when it didn't cost them anything.

"Hey, Red, how did a carrot-top like you end up with a name like Anderssen?"

"I think it was the Vikings, raiding our coastlines and having their way with our Irish lasses, Pegeen o' Me Heart," grinned O'B. He was sprawled in the chair beside her desk. "Besides, Pegeen *Gibson?* 'Beautiful Pearl' in Gaelic—and a last name like a martini with an onion in it?"

"Maybe it's a pearl onion." She dimpled nicely looking at him. "Does anyone still drink martinis, Red?"

"Not with me. Bushmills with a water back."

"I wish all the investigators were like you. Harry was telling me on coffee break that this really nasty P.U.C. man—"

"I bet it was Will Ready," said O'B quickly. He was very glad his red hair had been under the soft plaid cap now folded in his topcoat pocket. "Trouble at home, makes him hostile."

Then, amenities observed, O'B got down to the storefront phone rooms. He mentioned nothing about Cadillacs, Gypsies, DKA, or Cal-Cit Bank.

"What I don't see is the P.U.C. involvement," said Pegeen.

O'B didn't see it either, now she mentioned it. Bright lass, this. He wished he'd worked on his cover a little better. Who expected a sharp mind in a bureaucrat?

"Um, a massive scam is being played on old people with Medicare payments due them, which makes it P.U.C. because the cons have been set up from these phone rooms."

She bought it, and brought up on her screen the eight phone numbers that Stan Groner had gotten for O'B from the bank's files. This being Head Office for Pac Bell, Pegeen's computer had them all.

She looked up at O'B. "What is it you need to know?"

"Who the phones were listed to. How they got them on such short notice with no waiting period. The addresses where they were installed, plus landlords' names. If they listed references of any sort, who they were, and *their* phones and addresses."

Her fingers flew over the keyboard, Pegeen frowning at the information being scrolled up. O'B stood up to look over her shoulder. He had never mastered a word processor and knew he never would, but he could read the screen and was already writing things down on his clipboard.

"This is very strange," she said. "For quick installation, you have to prove a medical emergency of some sort . . ." She scrolled again. " 'Sick child' . . . 'aged parent' . . . 'retarded son' . . . 'mother dying of cancer.' Those are all valid. And they produced the required 'To Whom It May Concern' letter from an M.D. But they all listed themselves as businesses—Tom's Paving, Sally's Dress Shoppe, Harry's Air-conditioning, Mary's Catering—and gave each other as references. *And* . . ."

Now O'B was glad she was a quick-minded woman. She was doing his work for him. "And?"

"Eight different phones, four different locations, four different counties, three different area codes—but the same San Francisco doctor. Rob Swigart, M.D."

"Four Fifty Sutter," observed O'B. "Doc Swigart must be one tired pup, running around the entire Bay Area on his rounds."

95

*   *   *

Doc Swigart had his shingle out at 450 Sutter, a medical-dental building with a prescription pharmacy on the ground floor. At that rent, he was no fly-by-night, so maybe he had been gotten at *because* he had a reputation to uphold.

Not yet four o'clock, the worthy doctor might still be probing and poking and billing outrageously up there on the fifth floor. He was. The nurse-receptionist was a big woman in a crisp white smock, with laughing eyes and an open face. Dr. Swigart was in but much too busy to see Mr. . . . Morrell, was it? Without an appointment? Out of the question. There were other patients waiting . . . O'B laid his third P.U.C. card on her desk.

"David Morrell of the Public Utilities Commission," he said primly. "Investigative branch. Telephone fraud."

She was frowning, but in puzzlement rather than hostility. She stood up behind her desk. She was nearly six feet tall.

"Well, I'll go tell him, but I don't see what—"

"Give him this list, too." O'B was writing the addresses of the phone rooms on her memo pad. "It might save a little time."

The addresses obviously meant nothing to her. She disappeared through the door behind her desk. To return two minutes later with the smile gone from her eyes and voice. The addresses obviously *had* meant something to Doc Swigart.

"The doctor can fit you in now," she said coldly.

Rob Swigart, M.D., was late 40s, lean, laid-back, sandy-haired, with quizzical eyes and a warm worried style of speech nonetheless conveying that here was a busy man. He came into the examining room holding the P.U.C. card in one hand and O'B's handwritten list in the other, as if they were urine specimens.

"See here," he checked the card, "Morrell. I don't—"

"Whadda the Gyppos got on you, Doc?"

"I'm sure I don't know what you're talking about."

"We're the P.U.C., not the A.M.A. We're bare-knuckle boys and I don't *like* docs, Doc. No old-boys' network for us, covering up your little peccadillos 'cause you're one of the club." He leaned forward and tapped the list of addresses with his finger. " 'Sick child' . . . 'aged parent' . . . 'retarded son' . . . 'mother dying of cancer' . . . This's phone fraud, Doc, and we can prove it. We can jerk your ticket for that."

Swigart had turned white. He sat down abruptly in the chair usually reserved for patients.

"Fraud?" he said weakly. "Look, if I explain, can—"

O'B had his hands up, palm-out. "No promises."

Swigart stood up and began to pace the confined area. O'B hiked himself up on the examining table to get out of the way and let Swigart's guilts do the talking.

"I . . . just feel so stupid, that's all." He looked at O'B. "Most doctors play golf Wednesday afternoons. I fly planes. Down the Peninsula, Palo Alto Airport."

This wasn't going in any direction O'B had expected, so he asked, to keep it going, "Own your own plane?"

"Yes. A Mooney 201. Got a great deal on it, fifty-five thousand used. But I've been wanting to get an old biplane. Prewar—from the thirties."

"I imagine you can afford it."

In knee-jerk defensiveness, Swigart exclaimed, "Everybody always thinks doctors make a lot of money, but the taxes and malpractice insurance and overhead . . ."

He'd flown his plane up to a small private airfield in Sonoma County to practice crosswind takeoffs and landings and there had seen an old Belgian Stampe, lovingly restored. He'd admired it aloud to the man and woman up on the reinforced wing panel just about to open the cockpit. They'd climbed back down, delighted at his praise.

"We restored it ourselves," the man said in Spanish-accented English. He explained that they were from the Argentine, in cattle. "Over a thousand hours to refabric and paint it . . ."

But now the health of Señor Gonzales's father was failing and they were going back to take over the *estancia;* alas, they were going to have to sell the plane. They'd rolled it out of the hangar, in fact, to show a possible buyer they expected in . . .

Swigart didn't want to profit from their misfortune, but if there was another possible buyer already interested, ah, what were they asking? They looked at each other, gave simultaneous Latin shrugs, simultaneous rueful Latin laughs. Since he had admired it so, and since they were so pressed for time, $20,000.

"How does that stack up with the going price for that kind of plane in that condition?" asked O'B.

"A steal. A *steal*. Should have been thirty, at least."

Old P. T. Barnum hadn't had it *quite* right with his "sucker born every minute" remark. Should have said every *second*.

"So you wrote them a down-payment check right there—"

"Of course. Five thousand dollars."

They'd given him a receipt, but the next week when he went back up to Sonoma to pay the balance, a stranger had the plane rolled out of the hangar and was about to fly it away. Swigart had been outraged, only to learn that *this man owned it!* Even worse, the cockpit had been broken into and irreplaceable original equipment had been wrenched right out of the control panel.

O'B couldn't help laughing. "The Brooklyn Bridge."

"I beg your pardon?"

"The Gyppos sold you the Brooklyn Bridge." He got down off the examining table, still chuckling. "Why in hell didn't you just report 'em to the cops? Bunco would love to . . ."

Swigart sat down all-at-once in the patients' chair again. He grimaced, squeezed his eyes shut as if he could barely face what he had to say. He finally opened them and looked at O'B.

"I . . . didn't want my wife to know that I'd been such a fool. Not her . . . nor my associates . . . nor the fellows at the club . . . Besides, those people had just . . . vanished. I didn't even know they were Gypsies until . . ."

"Until they showed up again?" supplied O'B. "Because you didn't go to the police?"

That had shown them he was vulnerable. So they wanted a "To Whom It May Concern" statement . . . if he wouldn't do it, they'd have to tell his wife and friends what a fool he'd been . . . But then they'd wanted another statement, and another, and another . . . And now here was the P.U.C. after him anyway, and . . .

"Did you stop payment on the check?"

"I tried, but it was much too late, of course."

"Where was it cashed?"

The doctor shrugged his shoulders, stuck his hands out in a search-me gesture. "I can't remember, if I ever knew. I could find out, of course, but I don't see what good that—"

"Find out."

"And the rest of it . . ."

"All I want is information," said O'B. "Anything you can tell me. Anything you can remember . . ."

A thin gruel, but suggestive. The airport up in Sonoma . . . the guy who actually owned the plane . . . where they had cashed Swigart's check . . . Detailed descriptions, of course . . . All of it, bits of tile in the mosaic . . .

CHAPTER THIRTEEN

But it was Dan Kearny, as you might expect, who actually drew first blood. He'd been let back into their nuptial bed from the spare-room couch, but with Jeannie still prickly as a hedgehog he'd fully expected to stay home all day on Saturday. Spend a little quality time with the wife, mow the lawn, maybe get a start at repairing the front fence whacked by Wednesday's windstorm. He'd even resolutely refused to bring any of the Gypsy files home with him for work over the weekend.

But by early afternoon, as he dumped the last bale of grass clippings onto the backyard mulch heap, he found himself still bugged by the name the Gyppo had used at all the branches of the bank. Angelo Grimaldi. Usually they went for the short, Anglo-Saxon pseudonyms, so why such an atypical name to open those accounts? All at the same bank? Maybe he'd just drive in to the office through the sparse Saturday traffic to check those files again. They needed to get some kind of handhold on the smooth surface of the con.

So he went into the house and called Giselle at her apartment in Oakland. Got her. And spoke almost accusingly.

"I thought you might be at the office."

"Nope. Washing dishes, and clothes, and my hair—I like to do that when I can't tell anymore if I'm a blonde or not."

"I thought you were going to talk with the bunco cop at SFPD who specializes in Gypsies."

"He's off until Monday."

"I'm going to run into the office and go over that folder on Grimaldi—"

"*I'm* off until Monday."

"I'll pick you up in half an hour."

He hung up before she could object. He knew she needed time for herself, to live some kind of normal life, meet the right guy, get married, have kids. At 32, her—what did they say—her clock was running? But not right now. Right now they had these Gypsies to contend with.

Until last year, when she'd learned how to drive and had gotten her license, Giselle had ridden in to work with him five mornings a week. He didn't realize it, but those forty-five daily minutes in the car had played a big part in DKA's success. Cut off from phones and interruptions, they'd reviewed operations, planned client strategies, discussed field men's productivity. They'd argued about computerized report-writing, insurance, health and pension and profit-sharing plans, automated legal and skip letters. They'd fought about hiring ex-cons as field men and about dying investigations and about dead skips.

During those drives, over the years, DKA had become DKA.

Now they tried to do it at his desk in the morning before things got too hectic, but it wasn't the same.

Giselle was dressed in jeans that looked like someone had spilled acid on them, and a mauve sweatshirt with figures leaping like lightning that spelled out *Alvin Ailey.* Without makeup and with her blond hair pulled back into a ponytail under a billed Giants cap, she looked about 12 years old. A tall, shapely 12.

But as she got into the car the angry gleam in her eye was anything but juvenile. On the other hand, she was carrying a fistful of folders. So she hadn't been as dedicated to free time on the weekend as she had let on.

"Dammit, Dan, I deserve a little personal time to—"

"You too, huh?" he interrupted without sympathy.

They were coming up to the metering lights on the Bay Bridge approach, inactive now for the weekend. She fastened her seat belt and squirmed around to get comfortable. She fought a grin. Finally nodded ruefully.

"Yeah. Me too. On Monday I'll check with the Gypsy guy in Bunco—an Inspector Harrigan—and the Better Business Bureau and the state Consumer Fraud Division."

"Why now, Giselle? This is a major, major con, one that's going right into the Gyppos' book of tall tales. Somebody really bright— obviously this guy calling himself Grimaldi—had to think and plan a long time to set this one up. Why'd he spring the trap right now?"

Out beyond her window and the whizzing railings of the bridge, the bay was whitecapped with hundreds of sailboats heeled over by a stiff breeze through the Gate.

"He was ready to move. He had everything in place, so—"

"I don't buy it." Kearny was frowning behind the wheel. "I think we ought to check with our law enforcement and P.I. informants around the country who work with Gypsies, find out if anything big is happening in their world."

"I thought we didn't want anyone to know about this case."

"We don't *tell* 'em anything—we *ask*." He paused. "Yeah, and when you see that bunco cop, check with him for any other odd incidents involving Gyppos and new Caddies during our time frame—hell, make that *any* Caddies during the past couple weeks. I think it's like you said—this guy Grimaldi was using that name to set up some nontypical Gypsy scam. Something really big, well-planned . . . It had to be something even bigger to make him endanger that by activating this Cadillac grift in such a hurry."

They were still kicking it around as they came down off the skyway at Eighth, intending to run out Harrison to Eleventh and the office. This was the heart of San Francisco's light industrial area, shabby and blue-collar with dirty intersections weekend-deserted, the lights clicking red and amber and green and red again in a senseless roundelay for nonexistent traffic.

Which made the car ahead of them in mid-block stand out. A white/blue Eldorado with the optional cabriolet roof. Without plates but with a paper sticker in the corner of the windshield.

"That's one of ours," said Kearny in a taut voice.

"You can't be sure, Mr. K—"

"Lookit the guy driving! Gyppo all the way. I'm sure." And he was, she knew. A savage intuition that made him the best in the business. "Get ready to slide over."

"Dan'l—"

But Kearny had drifted into the far left lane behind the Eldorado so he was close behind it. Too close behind it. When it braked for the red light at Tenth, he ran into the rear end.

"*Daniel*, are you *crazy?* What—"

But Kearny already had the car in neutral, motor running, and was jumping out. He left the door open. Ahead of them, the driver of the other car was doing the same, leaving his door open also, outrage flooding his dark, saturnine features. Giselle understood suddenly, even as she was sliding into the driver's seat. She wanted to pound the steering wheel with delight.

Outside, Kearny and the Gypsy—surely, he was a Gypsy—were meeting where Kearny's front bumper was just touching the Eldorado's rear one. The Gypsy was holding his neck.

"What the hell you do? Where the hell you learn to drive? I got whiplash—"

"It was your fault," Kearny exclaimed. "Running fast up to the light that way, then slamming on your brakes."

"Slam on my brakes? You were right on my bumper."

Giselle eased the door shut almost silently, just enough so the latch clicked to hold it in place, then backed up slightly. Kearny squatted to look at the bumper of the Cadillac her move had exposed.

The Gypsy started to squat, too, holding his neck and grimacing theatrically as if from pain. But then he shrieked and struggled erect again, now holding the small of his back also.

"Not a scratch on it," Kearny was saying.

"Besides my whiplash, I think I got a slipped disk." He was groaning, still holding his neck with one hand, the small of his back with the other. "And whadda ya mean about the car? Looka that crease! That indentation! That chipped paint!"

"Chipped paint?" yelled Kearny. "You're crazy!" He was erect again, pointing accusingly at the car, drawing the Gypsy's eye to the back of the Eldorado. "There's no—"

"There! There! And lookit there! And what about my neck? Very severe whiplash. And my back. Very dangerous slipped disk." He was growing paler by the moment, experimentally moving his legs

103

around beneath him, the knees now slightly bent as if he couldn't straighten them. "And torn ligaments in both knees, too, from hittin' them on the dashboard. That means I gotta see three doctors, go to hospital, get X rays, lose time on job . . ."

He was still holding his neck and holding his back and keeping his knees bent when the traffic light changed to green. Kearny simply walked away from him and slid into the driver's seat of the Cadillac. Belatedly, the Gypsy leaped erect beside the two cars, eyes bugging out, whiplash and slipped disk and torn tendons all suddenly and miraculously cured.

"Hey, what the hell you think—"

Kearny goosed the Eldorado across the intersection with the green light and the door still hanging open. The Gypsy ran after him for a dozen paces, shouting and waving his arms; then, as Giselle started to accelerate behind him, whirled to stand in her path, holding his arms out like he was herding sheep.

"Hey, you, stop—"

She whipped the wheel over, hard, floored it, bounced across the corner of the intersecting curbs with a loud *crash!* and screamed around the corner into Tenth Street. He slammed an angry hand against her rear fender, but she was already by him.

And gone.

As Kearny was gone in the Eldorado.

Ah. First blood.

CHAPTER FOURTEEN

Second blood to, of all people, Trinidad Morales. Who wasn't working the Gyppo files, wasn't even supposed to *know* about the Gyppo files, Kearny's paranoia about them being what it was. But on Friday afternoon he had snooped the supposedly empty file cabinet upstairs that seemed to hold so much fascination for Kearny, Giselle, O'B, Heslip, and Ballard. And had leafed through enough of the Gypsy material to know that almost any new Caddy with paper plates and a swarthy driver would be fair game.

Then he heard someone on the stairs, so he snatched one of Giselle's lists—the cars' colors and descriptions and model and I.D. numbers—eased the file drawer shut, and was halfway down the hall by the time Kearny appeared.

"Lose something, Morales?"

"Just findin' my office, Mr. K, just findin' my office. Lot different here from over to Seven Sixty."

Not that Morales intended to go out looking for Gypsy cars off that list. He had been hired to work the cases *abandoned* by those assigned to the Gyppos, and besides, there weren't any direct leads to work yet. For now he just wanted to know what was going on. Knowledge was power, and all that. And he would keep checking.

There might be a way to snatch some meat from the jaws of the other guys for a quick buck or two.

But that was Friday. Now, on Saturday afternoon, Morales was not thinking of Gypsies. He was, instead, over in the East Bay trying to find a welfare cheat Ballard had been chasing for his Mazda. Typical Ballard shit, he thought, booting the file all over the lot with that phony concussion of his.

He still hated Ballard's guts from the Maria Navarro thing.

Golden Gate Fields is shoehorned between I-80 and the fringes of the bay at Albany, just south of Richmond. This Saturday was a race day, and since a remarkably large percent of welfare checks in California, state or federal, are cashed at racetracks, and since the Mazda man had a history with the ponies, cruising the parking lots at the track offered good odds.

He waited until the third race, so most patrons already would be there, then for thirty minutes methodically checked for the blue 1990 Mazda 323/Protege hatchback with, noted from an earlier Ballard repo, a grey leaded-in left front fender.

Pretty easy to spot if it was around. It wasn't. And that's when he got his bright idea.

Racetracks were also dandy places to look for Gyppos.

Most of them were damned good with horses from the days when they rode around in wagons instead of Cadillacs; Gypsy horseplayers were legion, and a lot of others were seasonal trainers or grooms or even practice riders. For all he knew, there were even Gyppo jockeys. He'd never met a legit Gypsy yet, not one, not ever, but he guessed there had to be some.

There was a separate lot at the rear, on the other side of the access road, where owners and trainers parked dozens of R/Vs and horse trailers and big muddy luxury cars. Within five minutes he had spotted three new Cadillacs and felt the old adrenaline surge. Gyppos were the hardest game there was to track; to a manhunter, getting one was like wing-shooting a crow, that wiliest of birds.

And technically, he hadn't really gone looking for Gypsies, had he? Of course not. But if one of their cars should happen to fall into his lap, he couldn't be blamed for that, could he?

He parked across and down from the Caddies, studied the list of models and colors and engine I.D. numbers. Cad One was out. It had current California plates and it was just too soon for any of the Gyppo Cads to have plates—unless they were stolen or off a wrecking yard junker. Not likely, not yet. The Gyppos still would be thinking they were too smart for anyone to guess who they were, let alone find them. So, scratch Cad One.

Cads Two and Three were real possibilities.

But even as he thought this, a very tall, very lanky, very blond, very Anglo woman whose pale skin had the translucency of alabaster, wearing a beautifully tailored red hacking jacket and pearl-grey jodhpurs, appeared between the horse trailers. With her was a grizzled old man wearing a cloth cap and knee-high rubber boots spattered with dried horse manure. They shook hands and the blonde got into Cad Two. Before driving off she used her handkerchief to wipe the hand that the old geezer had shaken.

If she was a Gypsy, Morales was Madonna.

That left the silver Coupe de Ville loaded with one of the many Cadillac option packages. He itched to get out of his dumpy little company car and wander over there and try to get a squint at the I.D. number. But if it was one of the Gyppo cars, and he got spotted checking it out, they'd be gone in a flash.

When in doubt, do nothing. For the next twenty-seven minutes he kicked around what he might do if he *did* snag the car. He was on DKA time here, a field agent hired by the company, but the bank wouldn't know that. So could he turn it in on the sly, operating under his own still-active P.I. license? He'd probably get a hell of a lot more from the bank direct than the wages and expenses and— maybe—percentage of the repo fee he'd get from DKA. Assuming Kearny had cut DKA the kind of sweet little per-car recovery deal that Morales supposed he had.

No, ashcan that. He didn't like Kearny, but he was smart enough to fear him. He'd only get the one Gypsy car, then Kearny would find out about it and would have his butt. And if the state did lift his license, he would be out in the cold.

So, since there was no other option, be a good guy. Win one for the Gipper . . .

A short swarthy man and a beautiful girl of about 15—the age Morales found himself liking more and more these days—were coming his way. They both had brown skin and shiny black hair:

107

Gyppos, sure as hell. Man and wife? Gypsy marriages were arranged for bride price . . . Naw, by the way they related to each other, father and daughter. Now, if they stopped at the Caddy . . .

They did. Okay, then if he got a chance to grab it he would, even though he wasn't rock-certain it was one of the bank's cars. Without a key, he'd need a few minutes to break in unseen, check the I.D. against Giselle's list, pop out the ignition lock and substitute one of his own . . .

The girl got in behind the wheel of the De Ville but didn't start the motor. The man talked to her through the open window and Morales slipped out of his car unobserved, a plan half-forming in his mind. When the Gypsy started away between the trailers, Morales, who could pass for *rom* himself with his heavy features and cruel, thick-lipped mouth, angled quickly toward him. Gyps often posed as Chicanos when working welfare and street scams; Morales now planned to return the favor.

"Hey!" he called.

The Gypsy turned. "Yeah, what you want?" His voice was thick and guttural.

"*Za Devalesa.*" It was the sole Romany phrase Morales knew, a traditional greeting of some sort he had picked up in the Mission District as a kid. Something like Go with God, maybe.

He said it loudly so the girl in the car, too far away for anything said in normal tones, could hear it.

"*Za Devalesa,*" the Gypsy returned, obviously surprised into thinking for the moment that Morales was also *rom.*

Morales put an arm around his shoulders, walking him quickly down between two trailers and out of the girl's sight. To her, after hearing those exchanged greetings, it must seem that Morales was another Gyppo, a friend of her old man. At least he hoped that was the way it would seem to her.

"I got a good horse for you in the last race," he said to the Gypsy. "Saratoga Longshot."

"There ain't no horse in that race got that name."

"No shit?" Morales turned away, shaking his head as if in amazement. "Guess I forgot to get up yesterday."

He walked off leaving the Gypsy frenziedly checking his pockets in case Morales had been a dip. The Coupe de Ville was still there, the girl behind the wheel, the window still open. Morales put what he thought was a charming smile on his heavy face. His gold tooth glinted in the wan afternoon sunshine. She'd like that, he thought, Gyppos were like fucking magpies, they liked bright things. Anything gold, even teeth.

"Za Devalesa," he said to her. It had worked the first time, what the hell? He added quickly, "Your daddy said you should help me get my car started. Just over in the corner of the lot. He said you'd be back before he was."

He went around the Caddy and slid his ample bulk in beside her. After a moment, she started the engine.

Morales pointed. "Over that way."

And kept thinking, Go, move it. Even with her driving and him not laying a glove on her, she was a juvie and technically this had become a kidnapping as soon as they had started moving.

"Got a dead battery, been sittin' here since the start of the meet, my sister was supposed to pick it up but she got busted in Fresno behind a bum Murphy game beef . . ."

Seeing him with her old man on an apparently friendly basis seemed to have activated the Gypsy thing of strictly obeying the elders. She seemed to be buying it. Just two more minutes . . .

"There it is right over there, just needs a little shove to get it goin' . . ."

As he directed her across this almost deserted quadrant of the parking lot farthest from the track, he picked out an old Chev Corsica with a lot of room around it. He had her pull the Coupe de Ville up a few feet short of the rear bumper.

"You drive the Chevy, I'll push it. The keys are under the front seat. It's got a stick, it'll start real easy." The girl didn't even hesitate in opening her door and getting out. Morales slid over behind the wheel. Because odds were that the Chevy would be locked, he added, "First, check the bumpers when I come up behind it. I wanna make sure they match . . ."

Estúpida! She obediently went to look at the bumpers. Even began waving Morales forward, her eyes on the space between the two cars.

Morales merely put the Caddy into reverse, backed up, then drove away from there in a wide arc that left the Gypsy girl yapping in his dust like an angry Pekingese. Back toward the freeway through the parking lots, avoiding the trailers where her old man probably by now had discovered the Caddy was missing. He would come back, drop the company car on a towbar later, when he could be sure the Gyp and his disgraced daughter had departed.

Well away from her, he stopped to check through the windshield for the Caddy's I.D. number, which was fastened to the dashboard on a little plate. He looked for a match with the list he had stolen from the DKA file drawer that he now had on his clipboard.

Yeah!

Second blood.

CHAPTER
FIFTEEN

Larry Ballard didn't get to work many North Bay assignments because O'B couldn't resist all that sunshine when the City was freezing its butt off under a layer of coastal fog. So driving up to Santa Rosa that Sunday afternoon, Ballard was struck by how the land developers had bought effective control of Marin County's Planning Department when he wasn't looking. Almost every hilltop sprouted its dense crop of duplexes and triplexes; north of San Rafael, where he remembered a little French restaurant with a duck pond, a hulking PG&E plant generated power for all those hillsides acned with high-density housing.

Marin needed a spotted owl of its own, and fast.

Speeding north into still-rural Sonoma County on the six-lane 101 freeway, Ballard found himself wondering if Beverly would ever let him back into her life. They'd fallen into an easy routine of double-dating with Bart and Corinne, a movie and a drink afterward, then he and Bev over to her place for . . .

Trouble was, he'd liked her a *lot*, sometimes thought they were in love with each other. But one or the other had always pulled back from a lasting emotional commitment. Now, all gone.

He came off the freeway in Santa Rosa looking for the '30s-style stucco house at 15431 Redwood Highway. He'd stopped thinking of Beverly and had started thinking about work again. Well, maybe not totally about work. Speculating, instead, about the woman he had driven north to try and find.

Ballard hadn't had to look up the address in the old case file; it had leaped into his mind when he had decided to seek out the beautiful Gypsy fortune-teller named Yana. Some three years before, Yana had given him a lead that had helped DKA save its license from the state.

That wasn't all she'd given him. Against all known logic concerning Gypsies and *gadje,* Yana had gone to bed with him in the big motel down the road from the mitt-camp.

Just the one time; she didn't dare do it again. She'd been sold in marriage at 13 to some mean Gyppo bastard for $3,000, and ever since had been living with him and his mother, Madame Aquarra. Madame Aquarra hated her guts, had been single-mindedly devoted to getting something on her so Yana could be kicked out of the house with her husband retaining the bride price.

But Yana was the only Gypsy contact Ballard could think of, so he had to talk with her. Or, if she wasn't there any longer, with Madame Aquarra to find her. It had been night the other time, he'd spoken to the old woman for just a few moments, no way she would remember him now, three years later. Was there?

His speculations were academic: there was no 15431 Redwood Highway anymore. Just another stupid shopping mall. No one to ask where the mitt-camp might have moved to, and, it being Sunday, he couldn't even run a gag on the local post office for a possible forwarding. Anyway, few Gyps were literate so they didn't get much mail except government checks, anyway. Yana, he remembered, could only read phone numbers and street names, though she could fake newspapers and menus real well.

Since Madame Aquarra had an unlisted phone number, it took two hours to get a possible new address on her. Out in the burgeoning suburban sprawl west of Santa Rosa proper, where the old Calistoga Road meandered up off Cal 12 into the hills.

Spiritual Advisor, said the sign above the door, but it was a mitt-camp pure and simple. On the front porch of the stucco and red tile fake *hacienda* were primary-color ceramic pots, bright trashy

112

tourist souvenir figurines and ashtrays, and an exquisite Della Robbia ceramic medallion sunk in the stucco beside the door. A nearly life-size fuzzy stuffed gorilla sat in a wicker rocking chair with a dead cigar in his fist.

Ballard crunched across the gravel lot and up the three steps to the porch. He rang the bell. Bingo! Madame Aquarra, the mother-in-law. Smoking a long black stogie like the gorilla's which she whipped out of sight behind her back when she saw a possibly paying customer at the door.

"Madame Aquarra knows all," she intoned.

The same words she'd used three years ago. Obviously, she didn't recognize the supposed cop, half-seen in the darkness, who'd whisked her daughter-in-law away for a night in the pokey. Considering what he and Yana had so joyfully done together until dawn, it had been more like a night of pokey-pokey-pokey.

Now he was acting confused.

"I'm looking for the *other* Madame Aquarra."

She glared at him. Those same ice eyes, that same downy mustache adorning her upper lip, that same lustrous black hair, just slightly grey-shot, coiled about her head, that same extra fifty pounds stretching tight a bright silk skirt across her yard-wide *derrière*.

"There is no other Madame Aquarra. Down through the eons, in all lands during all centuries, there has always only been one Madame Aquarra at any one time to look into the future, to—"

"Damn!" exclaimed Ballard. "That's too bad."

"Too bad."

Not quite a question, not quite a statement. Willing to be informed. Almost, if not quite, smelling money in it somewhere.

"Yep. In her twenties—*rom* like yourself—"

"What you know of the *rom?*" she demanded quickly.

"I know they are the only true seers. I know only they are truly blessed with the second sight and the third eye."

He didn't know what he had just said, but Madame Aquarra seemed to like it. She nodded sagely.

"How do you know this?"

"The young *rom* woman I thought was Madame Aquarra. She told my fortune and eventually it made me quite a lot of money. I want her to have some of it."

"She told you this fortune here? In my *ofica?*"

Ballard thought fast. Yana obviously wasn't here, and he knew the old gal hated her; so he shook a chiding finger at her.

"You're testing me, aren't you, Madame Aquarra? Of course not here in your *ofica*. In . . ." He waved his hand in a dismissive manner. "But she's gone from there . . ."

He fell silent. Silence was useful: it might work even with this crusty old Gypsy woman driven by anger and greed.

"Madame Aquarra knows of whom you speak," she admitted in a suddenly mellifluous voice. "And of course Madame Aquarra knows the way in which she released your power so that you found financial success. So . . ."

Ballard just stood there beaming at her, his hands in his pockets. He had her. Goddammit, he had her! Or her greed did.

"So give me your gift for her and I will get it to her."

Ballard slowly moved his head from side to side, still without speaking, still with that silly grin on his face. The sudden anger he had hoped for suffused her features: *yes!* She hated her daughter-in-law hard enough to sell her out to a *gadjo*.

"How much for her?" Madame Aquarra demanded bluntly.

He brought his hand out of his pocket clutching two $50 bills. Madame Aquarra stared at them, then met his bland eyes with her angry ones. A shiver ran through him. She was a powerful presence despite her venality.

"Madame Miseria. San Francisco."

He gave her a single fifty. Silently. She spoke again, as if he were physically dragging the words out of her.

"North Beach."

Madame Miseria. Now he remembered her sign in . . . Romolo Place, that was it. He got around the City a lot, he knew most of the streets well. So Madame Miseria was Yana. Hot damn!

He gave Madame Aquarra the other fifty. Who immediately exclaimed: "Go! Find her! Destroy her! Rip her eyes out!"

Then Madame Aquarra slammed the door in his face.

Ballard went down to his car both elated and uneasy. He had found her—unless the old lady had conned him. No. She had stopped believing his story of a reward, she thought the *gadjo* wanted to bust Yana for something. Her hatred had fused with her greed and she had dropped dime on her daughter-in-law.

114

So it looked as if Yana had gotten away from her—and one way or another must have taken her bride price with her.

Ballard's unease came from the fact that he'd parked where Madame Aquarra could get his license number if she were so inclined. He didn't believe in Gypsy curses, but he did believe in the efficiency of their information network.

He drove off thinking, Maybe I ought to get word back to her that something really terrible has come down on Yana. That would make her happy and perhaps forget all about Larry Ballard.

Which would make Larry Ballard sleep better that night.

*   *   *

Sleep that entire weekend had been in short supply for Ken Warren. Somehow he had gotten it fixed in his head that those three days were some sort of test for him. Show Dan Kearny that he was a real carhawk, and the DKA job would be his.

There is a surprising number of things a guy with his sort of handicap can do to keep the bills paid, and Warren had done most of them, from civilian contract worker in Vietnam twenty years before (nobody with his kind of speech impediment could get into the military, he'd tried hard enough), to migrant laborer, to stevedoring on the docks, to pushing a big-rig, to, of all things, bartending.

But repoman was what he liked best, he was really good at it if they didn't try to make him talk to people. He got to use his smarts when he was a repoman. He got to figure out what the other guy had done and was going to do next. There was excitement and challenge and now and then intense danger. The perfect job.

Not that he'd faced any danger this weekend.

The woman with the can of coffee had taken off.

The guy with the big boyfriend hadn't come back.

But lots of other people had been home. Pedestrians now, every one of them. The guy in Fairfax in Marin County, up on the hill with the dirt road, who'd wanted to argue about his truck until Warren had picked him up under the arms like a baby and set him on a shelf in his garage as if he were a can of paint.

"Gnaw gnhew nthtay nere nhtil Ahm ghawn."

The guy didn't look like he understood the words, but he stayed there on the shelf as Warren drove away in his pickup.

The man and his wife down in Burlingame on the Peninsula with the twin his-and-hers Buick Reattas and the vicious watchdog. Warren had stolen the first Buick at 3:00 A.M., the second at 3:30, the first from the driveway, the second from the carport, without even waking up their Rottweiler in the backyard. In fact, he'd tied a big red bow he'd found in the back of one of the repos to the gate of the dog's pen as a little joke.

There had been one hairy moment in San Francisco's Castro District when a crowd of hostile gays had been watching him break into a Ford Aerostar van. But some guy had helped chill them out, and then, when Ken was about to drive away, had handed him the keys! The registered owner. He'd just stood there watching Ken take it, ashamed to admit being behind in his payments.

Then that other guy down South of Market, who had jumped on the hood of his own Plymouth Laser and spread his topcoat wide in front of the windshield in an attempt to keep Warren from driving it away. The Laser hit a phone pole, but still ran, so it came off better than the guy on the hood: he'd ended up in SF General with breaks and contusions and a bad case of gutter mouth from French-kissing a sewer grate.

No, the problems Ken Warren had faced hadn't been the subjects whose cars he was taking. The first was that along about 5:00 A.M. Monday he had run out of gas—him, not his car—and had fallen asleep on stakeout at 25th Ave and El Camino del Mar in Seacliff. The lady with the Beemer 535i never showed, and he woke bleary-eyed and fog-frosted at 6:30. He washed and shaved in the men's room at the Seacliff Motel up behind Sutro Heights, even had toast and coffee in their dining room before driving unwillingly back toward the DKA office.

Unwillingly, because that's where his other problem was waiting. He hadn't had a key to the DKA garage, so he'd street-parked the cars he'd repossessed around the block the office was on. Worse than that, when he'd run out of parking places he'd left the final repo right-angled across the sidewalk with its front bumper nudging DKA's heavy garage door.

He bet Dan Kearny was going to be really steamed about that.

CHAPTER SIXTEEN

When Dan Kearny got to the office at 7:33 Monday morning, he was really steamed. Some idiot had nosed a car across the sidewalk to block the DKA storage garage door. And wouldn't you know, there wasn't a single parking place in either direction where he could leave *his* car until he could move this one.

After double-parking in the street with the blinkers on, he went through the office deactivating the alarms, then out the back to unlock the heavy wooden sliding door and flick the switch on the little motor that rumbled it aside. Grumbling to himself, he got the car started and was backing it out into the street when Giselle double-parked behind it, boxing him in.

"What's that doing here?" she demanded.

"My very thought. I'm going to leave it in the street for the cops to tag and tow—"

"You can't. Until we turned in our files last week, I was carrying the paper on that one."

"I'll be damned!" said Kearny. "It must have been in that fistful of cases I gave Ken Warren on Friday. He must have grabbed it

117

over the weekend and parked it here because he didn't have a garage key. Not too shabby for a new man."

"There's another one of mine across the street."

"Got two? Hey, terrif!" He paused, suddenly uneasy. "Ah, listen, Giselle, I fired the cleaning service on Friday."

"You *what?* Why didn't you wait until I found somebody else who we can count on to—"

That's when O'B drove up and half got out of his car.

*   *   *

O'B had spent most of Saturday at the airfield up in Sonoma, trying to get a line on the Gyppos who had "sold" the ancient biplane to Doc Swigart—no luck—most of yesterday in the Old Clam House under the freeway near the Army Street off-ramp, and most of last night in an all-night steamroom on Market Street soaking clam juice out of his system.

One foot on the blacktop, he craned cautiously over the roof of his car as if he were still hung over despite his fresh-scrubbed, russet look from the steam. He shamelessly gargled his *r*'s for his best Blarney-stone brogue—a gone-slightly-to-seed Irish potato with bloodshot eyes.

"Faith an' bejesus, an' 'tis the wee leprechauns who've been busy this blessed weekend."

"Meaning what, exactly?" demanded Kearny, though he was starting to get an idea that he already knew.

"Makin' all the shoemaker's shoon in the night an' slippin' away at first light."

"How many of 'em are yours?"

O'B came around his car to slap a lean freckled hand on the hood of a green Cutlass Supreme right in front of the office.

"This." He turned and pointed down the block. "That one. And that pickup over there from Marin. Two more around the corner . . ." He grinned at Kearny. "Maybe now you appreciate just how much work I turn out in the course of a day's—"

Kearny had just begun pointing out that someone else had repossessed all those cars assigned to O'B, not the Irishman himself, when Larry Ballard drove up.

*   *   *

Ballard already had been around the block and through little one-block Norfolk Alley behind, and there was not one damned parking place to be found. Usually, early on a Monday morning, there'd be a dozen free.

And now this, people standing around in the middle of the street waving their arms. What was going on? A convention?

Or maybe it was trouble. Yeah, there were Kearny, Giselle, O'B . . . some guy's car blocking the garage . . . He squealed to a stop behind O'B's car and piled out, feeling behind the seat for his tire iron, only then belatedly realizing that nobody was there except the DKA crew. He went up to them.

"What happened?"

Kearny swept his arm around in an all-encompassing gesture. "How many of 'em were assigned to you, Larry?"

For the first time Ballard began checking license plates.

"I'll . . . be . . . damned . . ." He shook his head. "I see those his-and-hers Buicks from down the Peninsula, I bet I hit that address a dozen times without getting a *sniff* of those cars, just a big damn dog who tried to bite off my—"

"Don't say it!" exclaimed Giselle in alarm.

"—foot," finished Ballard, then said in equal alarm to O'B, "Nobody grabbed our Mercedes from Pietro, did they? I—"

"I didn't see it." O'B turned to Kearny, "How many guys *did* you have out in the field over the weekend, Reverend?"

Before Kearny could respond, Bart Heslip drove up.

*　　*　　*

He bounced out of his car like answering the opening bell.

"Who got run over?"

"Last week's cases," said Ballard.

"I don't get it."

"Somebody did. Repeatedly." Then it was Ballard's turn to wave his arm around like Balboa on a peak in Darién. "How many do you recognize, Bart?"

Surprise widened Heslip's eyes.

"That Laser with the front end bashed in was one of mine."

"I hope we didn't do the bashing," said Kearny quickly.

"I couldn't say. I never laid eyes on the car while I was carrying the assignment. I'd started to think the guy was made out of

119

smoke . . ." He interrupted himself in sudden panic. "Nobody got Sarah, did they? If I spent my weekend chasing Gyppos without a sniff and somebody knocked off that Charger—"

"I didn't see it on the street," said Ballard. "Unless it's inside—"

"The guys I had out over the weekend didn't have keys to the garage," said Kearny.

Heslip's eyes had lit on another of the parked cars. "Hey, there's that Aerostar van, the one that—"

"Out in the Castro," nodded Giselle, who had assigned the case to him in the first place.

"I only had it for a week," said Heslip defensively. "With all the other cases I was working—"

"The guy who got it only had it for a week*end*," Kearny interrupted in his most offensive manner.

Heslip was indeed offended. "What guy?"

"I only had two men out, and one of them is a green pea who just started Friday. So probably Morales—"

Just then Morales drove up *in one of the Gyppo Caddies!*

*   *   *

Instead of being grateful, Kearny, that *chingada,* was on him like a junkyard dog.

"What are you doing with that Cadillac?"

"Driving it," smirked Morales as he got out. He'd driven it the whole weekend, Jesus, what a boat! Power everything. "Bringing it in to make out my report and—"

Ballard had been looking through the windshield to check the I.D. number against their Gypsy Cadillac master list.

"Yeah, it's one of ours," he said in a crestfallen voice. "But what's this bastard doing working for us again, anyway?"

"*Chinga tu madre, maricón!* You wanna go 'round right—"

Heslip got between them but Ballard was ready to go—last time Morales had knocked him down, this time that wouldn't be so easy for him. Ballard was older, wiser, fitter, with a few years of karate under his belt.

Not that karate, come to think of it, had made much difference to Fearsome Freddi of the leather underwear.

Ignoring the ruckus, Kearny said, "We needed a couple of extra men to pick up the slack on the files you turned in so you guys could work the Gypsy stuff."

"Only a *couple* of extra men?" Giselle was looking around with a dazed expression. Apparently *all* the parking places were filled with repos. "Two guys? All this?"

But Kearny had remembered all over again that Morales wasn't supposed to even *know* about the Gypsy cases, let alone be working any of them.

"You snooped those Gypsy files!" he stormed. "That's what you were doing when I saw you in the front upstairs office on Friday afternoon! Dammit, Morales, I want—"

"Hey, I got one, didn't I?" Morales jerked a thumb at Ballard. "That's more than hotshot here did over the weekend." He stepped closer to Kearny, an insinuating look on his face. "Listen, I bet you're offerin' everybody a bonus on each Gyppo car they turn, right? Now it seems to me that if I was workin' Gyppo cases along with the rest of the guys . . ."

"No bonuses, and I can't trust you anyway," said Kearny flatly. "Not on something like this. You were hired to pick up the slack—"

"I'd still like to know who repo'd all these cars, since it obviously wasn't any of us," said O'Bannon.

That's when Ken Warren drove up.

*   *   *

He knew it, he just knew it. The car he'd left in front of the garage door now was backed halfway into the street, and Kearny was waving his arms at some Mexican dude in the middle of a bunch of people like maybe there'd been an accident.

He didn't remember a Spanish surname on any of the cases he'd worked, but he'd been knockin' 'em off pretty fast, he couldda forgotten a name. He'd never gotten a crack at so many easy repos in his life. These DKA guys must really *talk* to the man, like Kearny had said, instead of just grabbing cars.

Ken Warren really liked just grabbing cars.

He double-parked his company car like everyone else had, and sort of tiptoed down toward the group. Hey, they were all operatives, he bet. In fact, he bet he could figure out who was who just from reading the reports on the cases he'd been handed.

121

He couldn't place the Mex guy, but the Mick with red hair and freckles and boozer's face, that had to be O'Bannon, the one signed himself O'B.

The black guy he'd seen fight, that was Bart Heslip. Not very marked up for an ex-pro middleweight.

Kearny had said the tall good-looking blond lady was Giselle Marc, office manager. She also worked the field—he couldn't blame her there, that's where the action was.

And the lean handsome muscular guy, must do a lot of surfing or SCUBA-diving to have his hair bleached almost white like that, he had to be Ballard.

Inevitably, Kearny saw him. Came over working his face and waving his arms just as he'd been doing at the Mexican guy a couple of minutes ago.

"Warren, what the hell were you *doing* over the weekend?"

Giselle breathed, just loud enough for Kearny, "What do you think he was doing? Proving he *is* the greatest carhawk the world has ever known."

The rest of them had turned to stare at Warren as if he were from another planet—and he hadn't even opened his mouth yet. He shifted uneasily from foot to foot, trying to figure out what Kearny wanted him to answer. Then inspiration struck.

"*Hey, Mr. Kearny, Ah gnthalk ta gha man!*"

Kearny astounded him by busting out laughing. And then clapping him on the shoulder and demanding, "You talk to *all* the men?" He seemed to be getting the hang of the way Ken spoke.

"Well, no, juth nthoz who—"

"How many cars did you grab since Friday afternoon?"

He didn't have to consult his case files to answer that one. He'd counted them up during breakfast. "Nthevnteen."

"Seventeen?"

"Yeah."

"Police reports?"

"Yeah."

"Condition reports?"

He'd completed those over breakfast and he'd rather show than tell, so he held out the sheaf of completed forms. Kearny looked at them, then nodded and turned to the rest of them still standing around staring as if they were at Fleishacker Zoo.

122

"Ken Warren," said Kearny with a flourish, then added with masterful understatement, "he'll be covering for you while you work the Gypsy accounts."

"For *all* of us?" asked Ballard.

"Him and Morales, yeah." Kearny gestured at the repo-crowded street. "You got a problem with that, Larry?"

"Hell no, no problem, I just wondered how one guy . . ."

Ballard ran down. The guy had repo'd *seventeen* cars in three days! That was a decent score for a decent field man in a decent month. For the first time in his professional life he felt something akin to awe for another man's work besides Kearny's; the Great White Father, of course, was always the best. He stepped forward and stuck out his hand to Warren.

"I'm Larry Ballard."

"GnYm kGen Gwarren."

Then they were all crowding around and shaking his hand and clapping him on the shoulder, like football players mobbing the guy who took the opening kickoff and ran it back for a touchdown. Warren suddenly understood why they had been staring at him. Not because they'd heard he talked funny. Hell no. Because they were *impressed*.

For the first time in his life, the very first time, Ken Warren felt he was part of a group that didn't give a damn how he talked. However he did it, he spoke their language.

Kearny said, "Okay, Warren's got reports to write and cars to get back to the dealers. Giselle and Trin each have a Gypsy Cadillac to do the same with. The rest of us, the Gyppos aren't going to waste any time spreading the word that someone dropped a rock on a couple of their boats over the weekend."

"Hell, Dave," said O'B, "they were both gotten on drivebys. Maybe the Gyppos'll figure the law of averages just caught up with them. Only so many new Caddies on the street—"

"You really believe that?" demanded Kearny in disbelief.

"Nah."

CHAPTER SEVENTEEN

W e knew *somebody* would be looking," Marino offered tentatively. They were in the kitchen of Yana's *ofica*, and although he would never admit it, she was pretty impressive on her own turf.

"Track is always good place to look for Gypsies," agreed Ristik eagerly. But he came out sounding defensive just as Marino had, even though Yana was his kid sister, so he added, "Just some repomen getting lucky."

"That's some kind of lucky." Yana shook her head. "No. Somebody very good and very clever is after us."

"Repomen are not clever," said Marino disdainfully.

"These are."

"Or maybe your husband is up to his old tricks of selling our cars to the *gadje*, and maybe you are helping him . . ."

His voice ran down: he had gone too far and knew it. For a moment, her face looked like scraped bone; he felt a stab of superstitious dread. Then she relaxed and shrugged.

"If Ephrem can make money betraying the *rom* to the *gadje*, he will—but he gets no information from me. I don't know where he is and I don't want to know. Whether somebody is on to us or not, we have to tell the *kumpanias* two cars are lost. And I want to know for sure about the repo agency."

"Not too hard to find that out," Marino said.

At the same time, Ristik said: "Why tell the *kumpanias* yet? Most of our people are already gone from here—"

"Then find out," she told Marino, then told Ristik, "because if a repo agency knows about us, they'll try to follow us all over the country from here. Also, I can't leave yet—"

"Theodore Winston White the Third," smirked Marino.

She shot him a venomous glance.

"If you spent more time on your St. Mark Hotel scam and less on having your clansmen follow us around, hoping to take that fifty-eight pink convertible away from us, maybe you—"

"What do you know about the St. Mark?" demanded Marino in a furious voice. She laughed aloud, and whirled toward him so her full skirt flared out around her beautiful legs.

"What do I know? What I know."

"If you interfere with that—"

"Stay away from Teddy White."

There was a long pause. Finally, Marino nodded and stood up from the kitchen table, where he and Ristik had been sitting.

"Agreed."

She softened slightly. "I only need a few more days . . ."

"Also."

They stared into each other's eyes for a long moment. Then both of them burst out laughing at the same time.

"Want to be lady-in-waiting to my King after Zlachi dies?"

"Want to be court jester to my Queen?"

*   *   *

But clattering down the stairs a few minutes later, with no need to keep up a front, Marino was unsmiling.

Was there a detective agency good enough to tag them as the ones who had hit the bank for the Caddies? Couldn't be. No agency was that good. Yet as Yana had said, two cars in one weekend out of the fourteen still in the Bay Area were too many.

And meanwhile, time was tight and his people were having no luck at all in finding the pink 1958 Eldorado convertible. If she turned out to be right about the repo outfit, he'd use it to smoke out the ragtop. Not that he thought she was right.

As he started down the Romolo steps, a tall blond man with a hawk nose and cold blue eyes passed him coming up. Their eyes locked for a moment, like those of adversary eagles; then the man was gone. On a sudden impulse, Marino turned to look back up the street after him. Yes. Turning in at Madame Miseria's *ofica* just as Marino somehow had expected.

Theodore Winston White III? No. The man who fell for candle readings, and money that bled after a special-dye-soaked bill had been substituted for his, and probably a poisoned egg, and maybe even a cemetery dig, had never viewed the world through such bleakly realistic blue eyes. More likely, a cop.

Maybe she was in trouble. Good! He hoped she was.

*   *   *

Yana was saying, "We have to find out who repo'd those Cadillacs, and we don't have the contacts in the cop shop that Rudolph does. If someone in our *kumpania* could pose as—"

Ristik stopped her with a characteristic Gypsy shrug, the sort that involves eyebrows, hands, wrists, forearms, shoulders, and a tilt of the head to one side.

"I still ask, why bother?"

"Rudolph will use them to panic us into moving the pink Cadillac. He thinks then he can take it away from us and present it to the King as his own."

Ristik's eyes flashed. He shook a rigid forefinger at the ceiling. "He will not take it! Not while there is life in—"

Yana giggled.

"Thank you, Cornel Wilde. Or maybe Victor Mature?"

Ristik looked sheepish. "Okay. But if he thinks—"

The street buzzer sounded.

*   *   *

Ristik opened the door to stare up at the blond man who said, "I want to see Madame Miseria."

Ristik was glad that through habit he had centered himself in the doorway when he opened it. This guy looked like a cop. Yana didn't need any cops sucking around with their hands out or their backs

126

up, not with Teddy White responding so great. So Ristik's usually bright snapping eyes went dull with stupidity, his gutturals became thick as engine grease.

"Madame Miseria is not here."

He tried to shut the door, but the blond man's shoe was in it. Ristik raised his voice for the benefit of Yana waiting behind the curtain at the head of the stairs.

"*You need a warrant to*—"

"I'm no cop."

No cop. That made it easy. He tried to shut the door again. The foot had not moved. He put on his best threatening look. The tall blond man put contempt in his voice.

"You Yana's husband?"

Ristik was surprised; few *gadje* knew his sister's *rom* name.

"I know of no one by the name of Yana."

"Then lemme see your license for this mitt-camp."

"You said you were not police."

"I lied."

"Let me see your badge."

That's when Yana called from the head of the stairs, "Ramon. It is all right. Let him come up."

*   *   *

Ballard hadn't been sure he'd played it right, but here he was trudging up the stairs after the Gyp who had answered the door. And there at the head of the stairs staring down at him was Yana, more beautiful than ever. Beautiful, even with her face closed and unreadable.

She said, as he came up level with her in the hallway, "Ramon is my brother and he watches out for me."

She started down the hall toward the *duikkerin* room with the velvet drapes and crystal ball, talking over her shoulder to Ballard as she went, a bewildered Ristik trailing along behind.

"How did you—"

"Your mother-in-law."

In the room she turned to face him, took both his hands in hers, and started laughing. "How much did you have to pay her?"

"Enough."

"Too much, perhaps?" Her voice was teasing.

127

He said softly, "Never too much to see you again."

Ristik was looking from one to the other as if watching the U.S. Open. Yana was treating this *gadjo* like an old friend! He opened his mouth to speak, then felt the chill of Yana's piercing eyes. He shut his mouth, then opened it again, meekly.

"I'll make some tea," he said.

She nodded like a queen as she and Ballard sat down facing each other across the *boojo* table. They spoke in unison.

"So why did you—"

"So how have you—"

Both stopped. Both laughed. She took his hands across the table, as she had done with Teddy White, as she did with all the *gadje* marks. But wasn't this different? Surely very different?

"So why did you seek me out in Santa Rosa?"

"Old times?" asked Ballard.

She merely shook her head. He nodded. Gestured around the room with its long concealing drapes.

"Could we maybe go out somewhere to—"

"No."

He nodded again, going slow, letting her set the tone. She was all he had, but more than that, she was even more dazzling now than three years ago. And he'd been booted out by Beverly . . .

"Maybe later? Another time?"

Yana felt herself weakening, felt herself short of breath the way she had been last time. But she had been a girl then, rebelling against the dread return of her husband. She was a woman now, she must not give in to her attraction to this tall blond *gadjo*.

"To have your fortune told?" she asked almost coquettishly.

Ballard was staring at her, trying to read her.

"Whatever it takes," he said.

So he felt it too. But even so, it could not be. She had taught herself to read and write, and when her husband had come back and had beaten her for it, she had left Madame Aquarra's home and *ofica* with her bride price and had never returned.

Now, to the San Francisco *kumpania*, she was a woman of substance with her place in their councils. And very shortly, if she could keep Rudolph from getting the pink Cadillac, she would be Queen of all the Gypsies.

The pink Cadillac. The thirty-second Cadillac. If only . . .

And then she knew—*knew* before he said it—why Ballard was there. She shivered, because she had never believed in her own hocus-pocus: few Gypsy fortune-tellers did, or at least few would admit it. But here was the answer to her problem.

Ballard said, "You remember when we met that I was a detective looking for—"

"Yes. For a woman who had worked for your own company."

"This time I'm a detective looking for a bunch of Gypsies."

Yes. She had *known what he was going to say.* And now . . . now she knew that she was going to do to Rudolph just what he planned to do to her. She put scorn into her voice.

"So you come to my *ofica* asking me to betray—"

"I don't want you to betray anyone," Ballard said hotly.

He did, of course. That's why he had come to her. But . . . not really. Really, it was the memory of that velvet night . . .

Yana disengaged her hands from his, sat back with a judging look across the table, not speaking. Ballard cleared his throat.

"All the Gypsies in the country can't be your friends."

The draperies behind him parted silently, and Ristik started through with a tray on which were cups and a teapot and several diamonds of baklava, dripping honey. Yana narrowed her eyes at him and he just as silently withdrew again.

"No," she agreed gravely, "not even most of them."

"So if someone you felt no obligation toward has . . ."

"Has what?" she asked quickly.

"Has, um . . . stolen some Cadillacs—"

"*Stolen?*"

"Absconded with. Embezzled."

After a dramatic pause, she said, "And if I were one of those Gypsies who has done this, then I suppose you would—"

"Are you?"

Don't hesitate. The pause betrayed the lie. "No."

Don't hesitate. The pause betrayed the lie. "Even if you were, I'd look the other way."

It wasn't *really* a lie. He *would* look the other way. The rest of DKA wouldn't, but he would. Yana leaned toward him.

"There is another *kumpania* that has recently moved into the Bay Area, led by a man named Rudolph—I don't know his last name or what he looks like—I have never met him. But he is a bad man, a bold man, he will do almost anything for money. It is such people who give the *rom* a bad name among the *gadje,* and such a man might well be involved in something like this . . . this theft of these Cadillacs . . ."

Ballard felt his excitement rising. If he could just get some leads from her . . . "There are over thirty cars," he said.

"Of course if I am to ask around, perhaps learn something about their activities, where you might find some of these Cadillacs . . . I would lose money . . . be in some danger . . ."

"Hundred bucks for every recovery we make," said Ballard promptly, with no disillusionment in his voice. She would surely want payment hand-to-hand, and when hands touched . . .

She was leaning forward again, eagerly, like a child, excitement and intrigue in her eyes, as if the prospect of money had rekindled her personal feeling for him. She laid her open hand palm-up on the table. She almost giggled again.

And actually said, "Cross my palm with silver."

Ballard hesitated but a moment, then dug out his money clip and counted five twenties into her palm. That left him with three bucks. She closed her hand around the money.

"I wish to prove my heart is true," she said, "so I will find you a car, today. After today, if I have information for you I will leave a message only we will understand, and you will come, and I will tell your fortune, and you will—"

"—pay you for the reading," finished Ballard.

"And only you and I will know of it, no one else! I will be your . . . what do the police say? Your snitch!" She smiled complacently and leaned back in her chair. The $100 had disappeared. She glanced casually beyond him and added with delight, "And here is Ramon with the tea!"

Ristik came through the draperies with his tray again, as if just coming from the kitchen rather than lurking and listening behind the curtains. Ballard ignored him, wondering hopefully what else Yana might come to be for him besides his snitch.

CHAPTER EIGHTEEN

The two cheap metal plaques were placed so they would be facing anyone who sat down across the desk from the broken-down swivel chair in the narrow cubicle. One read, INSPECTOR HARRY CALLAHAN, with, underneath it, *Dirty Harry*. The other read, FEEL SAFE TONIGHT—SLEEP WITH A COP.

"Pretty good, huh?" demanded a voice behind her.

Giselle turned. The man wore an off-the-rack suit and Polo aftershave obviously applied in the men's room after seeing that she was good-looking. The cheap suit said honest cop; the Polo, and the leer he was giving her despite his wedding band, said son of a bitch. Said, to Giselle, don't trust the cheap suit.

She stuck out her hand and said, on that insight's impulse, "Inspector . . . Callahan? Gerry Merman, free-lance journalist. I want to do an article about the Gypsies, and—"

"Harrigan, not Callahan. Bunco." Going around the desk, he ignored her hand but not what she had down the front of her blouse. "The other guys gave me that plaque 'cause my name is Harry an' I get all the dirty jobs." To her silence he added, "You know, Dirty Harry Callahan . . . in the movies . . ."

Giselle finally nodded. Harrigan was the SFPD Gypsy man, and despite his wandering eye she needed his help.

"Clint Eastwood," she supplied.

"Yeah. As for the other plaque . . ."

"Very clever," she agreed too quickly.

"Yeah." A little sourly.

He lit a cigarette and leaned back and clasped his hands behind his head. Early 40s, Irish, red hair faded to pink by the grey in it, face full of sexual predation. Would once have been good-looking and would have known it, still would never regard his mirror with less than full approval.

Just the reverse of O'Bannon's bright blarney Irish coin.

"So, Gerry, you wanna do an article about me an' the Gyppos. Well, lemme give you an example . . ."

Two retired brothers, both in their 80s, lived in one of the showplace homes across the Boulevard from the Marina Green. A his/her pair of Gyppos had come knocking on their door claiming to be from the French Hostel welfare department . . .

"Musta staked 'em out an' followed 'em home, 'cause these old guys belonged to the hostel, all right—but they'd never heard of any welfare department there . . ."

Giselle realized that Bunco was even more depressing than Homicide. At least death had a hard truth. In Bunco it was all lies, lies to vulnerable old people who thought they had been helping the police catch a bad guy by cleaning out their trust account, only to learn they had given their life savings to some slime who'd dreamed up a new wrinkle on the pigeon drop.

"Anyway, the woman talks to 'em, prob'ly hints around about *doin'* 'em, y'get my drift . . ." He was leering at her through his cigarette smoke. "Meanwhile, her partner is goin' through the house. Gyppos know how to *smell* money. One old guy had thirteen hundred cash in the inside pocket of one of his suits in the closet, his brother had five hundred. That's eighteen hundred bucks!"

"Incredible," said Giselle, to be saying something.

"But the Gyppos made one mistake. They stole a gold pocket watch off the dresser, an old antique job. So of course I nailed 'em when they tried to pawn it."

"Of course." But her irony was unrecognized.

"Yeah, well, that's the kinda thing I do every day. As for what I do at night . . ." With another leer, he gestured at the plaque. "Interested? *Feel safe tonight. Sleep with—*"

"I already feel safe at night."

She needed a cigarette, badly; but Dan Kearny was being such a pain about it that she'd quit again. Thank God for her impulse to give Harrigan a false name and profession. Any call from this man to any woman on earth for any reason whatsoever would be an obscene phone call.

"You wanna feel even safer, girlie, you give ol' Harry a call—he practices safe sex." He started to guffaw, said again, "Safe sex. Course if a broad answers, hang up."

More guffaws. A broad. His wife. To hell with it. She took one of his cigarettes. Of course Harry was right there with a lighter, hoping for another peek down her blouse. Wouldn't you just know, the lighter was an old-fashioned Zippo with the 82nd Airborne crest on the side? She stubbed out the cigarette after one puff. It tasted like she was smoking an old tire. Wouldn't you just know that, too? You sin and it isn't even any fun.

She asked, "You hear anything about a Gypsy calling himself Angelo Grimaldi working the Bay Area lately?"

"Grimaldi?" He shook his head. "No Gyp'd choose Grimaldi, they go for short Anglo-Saxon names—Adams, Marks, Wells . . ."

"Great-looking, mid-thirties, charms professional women . . ."

"A class act?" Harrigan lit up again. "Now I *know* he ain't a Gyp. Gyppos can't bring off a class act. And he ain't local, either, I can tell you that. I know all the local Gyps."

"He's around," Giselle insisted. "Our angle is that this is a really unusual Gypsy we can build a story on."

"Yeah, well, they're putting the squeeze on welfare scams in New York and Chicago, so a lotta Gyppo scum is coming into California lately from over there. Maybe—"

"The land of opportunity," said Giselle wryly.

But it was his first interesting remark. Maybe Grimaldi was a recent arrival. Not for welfare scams, surely, but . . .

"They bring any news with them?"

"They might be gonna have to pick a new King—there's some rumors the old one's dyin' back in the Midwest . . ."

Better yet. A dying King would answer Kearny's questions about

133

the timing of the Cadillac scam. The Gypsies would want new cars to go back in style to the huge encampment of Gypsy *vitsas* and *kumpanias* necessary for selecting a new King.

"This dying King—who? Where? When?"

"Who knows, who cares, why bother?" His eyes were now unbuttoning her blouse. "Back in the Corn Belt somewhere."

She had to be careful; cops were notorious moonlighters, many of them as free-lance repomen, she didn't want to give him any hint about thirty-one Bay Area Cadillacs up for grabs. But she also needed whatever info he might have. So, turn it around.

"Any stories making the rounds about Gypsies with a whole fleet of new Cadillacs, maybe heading this way?"

"A fleet of 'em? Headin' our way? Don't I wish. A man could make himself extra loot knocking off those babies." He stubbed his butt. "But nah. I'd of heard of 'em, for sure."

"For sure."

"What the hell, the President's comin' in a few days, I won't be payin' any attention to Gyppos for a while. Everybody on Bunco'll be workin' the downtown pickpocket detail."

"Trying to catch the politicians in the act?"

"Hell no, the dips'll be workin' the crowds an' . . ." He stopped, belatedly realizing it had been a joke. He started to bellow with laughter. "Haw! Haw! Haw! Tryin' to catch the politicians in the act! That's good."

Giselle knew she'd had about all she could take of Dirty Harry Harrigan, but she had one more question.

"Any other Cadillac stories making the rounds?"

"Now you mention it, a bunco guy down to Palm Springs sent out flyers on a restored classic nineteen fifty-eight pink Eldorado ragtop got conned out of some used-car salesman." More guffaws. "Car salesman's out the money 'cause the Caddy wasn't his to sell— just borrowed by his boss for a promo!"

"Conned by Gypsies?" Giselle was leaning forward intently.

"Ay-rabs. Gal had a bodyguard with a big ol' knife, they scairt the guy into takin' a check an' signin' over the pink an' they just drove that ragtop right outta there."

"I take it the check bounced."

"Higher'n the Transamerica tower."

"Was it drawn on a San Francisco bank?"

"Naw. Arabia. Bahrain, somethin' like that."

Giselle was frowning. "Then why'd he circulate it to you? A few hundred dollars on a con game—"

"Few hundred? Try *sixty thousand!* Goddam Ay-rabs."

These goddam Ay-rabs interested Giselle vitally. It was easy to print phony checks that said Arabia, and there just were not a whole bunch of Arab conwomen around.

"Could the woman have been a Gypsy posing as an Arab?"

"Couldda been, I s'pose, but why would she take the chance? You're talkin' felony theft here. Gyps don't want old cars—it's always this year's Caddy to tool around in."

True. And yet . . . and yet . . . there was something here.

Maybe something like this: a Gypsy King is dying and a Gypsy who is using an odd pseudonym—one Kearny thinks has been created for a major sting already in place—recklessly endangers or at least complicates the sting by setting up a band of fellow Gypsies to hit a bank for a fleet of new Cadillacs.

Why? Because it's to Grimaldi's advantage that they drive those Cadillacs back to the Gypsy King's funeral?

Next, a classic pink 1958 Eldorado ragtop worth $60K is conned out of a used-car salesman—surely not your typical easy mark— by someone who could have been a Gypsy posing as an Arab. A big-time felony for a car not usually of interest to Gypsies.

To give Grimaldi an edge in choosing the new King?

But how could a '58 ragtop do that? She had to be missing some vital element. All of a sudden, Giselle wanted to talk to that used-car salesman in Palm Springs.

And wanted to know about that special-order limo Angelo Grimaldi had scored from Jack Olwen Cadillac.

And wanted to check whether any of the better San Francisco hotels had an Angelo Grimaldi registered.

Because if the Gypsy calling himself Grimaldi had a major con going, it surely would be timed to the President's arrival. The cops, tied up in crowd control as Dirty Harry had said, would be much less likely to catch the scam before it was too late.

A lot of ifs and mights and maybes, but they all added up to one thing: Grimaldi could still be here in San Francisco, waiting for the President's arrival. And if he was, Giselle Marc was going to nail him to the wall and . . .

135

She was brought crashing back to earth by Dirty Harry's dirty voice in her ear, his dirty hand on her arm.

"Listen, girlie, I got this one-eyed snake in my pants . . ."

Too much. She didn't really mind whatever dirty little fantasies he might have about her, but it was intolerable he thought she might want to share them. This particular girlie was going to have to do something about Harry's dirt . . .

"Okay, okay, you win—I'll admit it, you've got me intrigued." She added wickedly, "Come over to my place tonight, seven-thirty . . . I'll leave the street door unlocked . . ."

Even as she had given him a phony name, so she gave him a phony address, that of the Sappho Self-defense Dojo. Ballard, brown belt that he was, had told her in slightly awed tones about this extremely militant feminist lesbian martial-arts support group on Clement Street.

When Dirty Harry Harrigan swaggered into the place that night without knocking, she was sure they would give him, if not the sort of evening he fantasized, almost certainly the sort of evening he deserved.

CHAPTER NINETEEN

As Giselle was dashing heatedly off in several directions at once to look for Angelo Grimaldi, Rudolph Marino, cool as geometry, was looking for her. Oh, not for her specifically, but, through his SFPD contact, for the repomen who had knocked off the two Gypsy Cadillacs over the weekend.

He used a St. Mark lobby payphone; by now he routinely phoned from his suite only for room service and wake-up because the switchboard would be monitoring his calls. He asked for his tame cop in the gruff voice snitches so often have.

"Marino," he said when the man answered, gave the payphone number, hung up. When it rang three minutes later, he asked it, "What do you have?" then listened, nodding. "Morales . . . Marc . . . DKA? Which stands for . . . I see . . . Daniel Kearny Associates . . ."

He kept on listening. So Yana had been right. The same agency had picked up both cars. Bad news and good news. Bad news because the private detectives must indeed have figured out that it was Gypsies who had hit the bank for the Cadillacs. Good news because he could keep this information from Yana while feeding DKA information about her *kumpania* until she panicked and brought that '58 ragtop into the open where he or his people could grab it . . .

"*Giselle* Marc?" he exclaimed to the phone, surprised.

One of the repomen was a *woman?* He grinned whitely to himself. There wasn't the woman born he couldn't get next to.

Well, maybe Yana.

"Gerry Merman . . . yes . . . I understand . . . a journalist doing a piece about Gypsies . . . I see . . . free-lance . . ."

He hung up, frowning. Then he smiled. Gerry Merman, writer. Giselle Marc, repowoman. He'd never heard of a repo*woman*, but he liked her moves, posing as a free-lance writer to get a line on Grimaldi without tipping DKA's investigation. Free-lance, so if the cop had a highly unlikely I.Q. power surge and became suspicious, he couldn't check out her cover story.

Just her bad luck that Harry Harrigan, SFPD's Bunco Squad Gypsy specialist, also happened to be the cop in Marino's pocket. But her good luck that now he, Rudolph Marino, soon to be King of the Gypsies, would be feeding her info about Yana's *kumpania*.

Nothing about Stupidville, of course. If she learned of it, Giselle Marc sounded plenty smart enough to show up and grab some Caddies from a *rom* encampment called to name their new King upon the death of their old.

* * *

Their old King was not all that near death, actually, but Dr. Crichton, making his rounds, was worried about him all the same. Poor old Karl didn't seem to have a lot of will to live, and now the department store's insurance company was involved and insisting, in this age of skyrocketing medical costs, on more tests being run before they would okay even current expenses.

Bad for his patient, bad all around.

What Crichton didn't know was that Barney Hawkins, Democrat National Assurance Company's adjuster, was at that moment in Staley's room shoving ballpoint pen and release form under his aged nose. Hawkins had bad teeth and was overweight, with just a fringe of hair around the back of his head as if he had been tonsured for the religious life. Shifty brown eyes that Staley met with a hurt and hurting old-man's candor and bewilderment.

"Whazzis?" he mumbled in his overmedicated way.

"Just a release," oozed Hawkins. "So your medical bills will be paid and you can stay here in this nice hospital until you're all better."

Staley had taken the pen, but now it slipped from his lax fingers and his head tilted down to one side as if he suddenly were dozing off from his medications. He gave a snore.

"Here, don't do that. Just sign the form . . ." Victory seemed near and Hawkins made the mistake of grabbing an ancient shoulder and shaking him. "Hey, old man, wake—"

Staley reared up screaming. Hawkins jumped back, startled, to carom off the solid bulk of Lulu, who had been waiting in the bathroom for Staley's shriek to bring her charging out.

"*What you do to my husband?*"

As she grappled with the dumbfounded adjuster, the door burst open and in rushed Crichton and the redheaded, freckled nurse who accompanied him on rounds.

"*What's going on in here?*"

The nurse had Lulu by the arms to hold her back from Hawkins, who was exclaiming, "This crazy old broad attacked—"

"I was in bathroom, came out, he was shaking my Karl—"

"*Shaking* him?" Crichton, livid, shoved the adjuster back across the room. "You're *shaking* him? This man has a spinal injury from a fall down an escalator and you're *shaking* him?"

Staley moaned loudly from the bed. All eyes turned. "Want me to sign some paper," said his wan old-man's voice.

Crichton knew Hawkins only all too well. "A release form?"

"My Karl is not gonna sign no release forms," Lulu said in loud abrupt tones. "The lawyer told me that he shouldn't—"

"*Lawyer?*" cried Hawkins in alarm. "What lawyer?"

"The lawyer who said I should sign a paper with *him.*"

"Don't do that," said Hawkins with a terrible intensity. He'd had a shitty litigation loss-ratio last year, he didn't need this. "Don't sign any contracts with any lawyer—"

"Why not?"

"Well, ah, he'll, ah, take half of what you get from us. He'll, ah, cheat you. Just let us make you an offer and—"

Staley groaned again from the bed. Lulu said immediately, "My Karl in too much pain to be thinking about anything like that right now."

139

"Out," snapped Crichton, "everybody out. The nurse is here to give the patient a sponge bath." He laid a gentle hand on Lulu's shoulder. "You too, Mrs. Klenhard. Go get a cup of coffee at the cafeteria. Come back in half an hour or so."

Outside in the corridor, Hawkins glowered after Lulu's retreating form. "Y'know her old man's faking it, Doc."

"Nonsense."

"I tell you he's faking it." He riffled the papers in his hand. "Not one X ray here that's worth a damn."

"Not unusual; patients with acute pain can't lie still for X ray. I've conducted manual physical exams that more than—"

"Manual exams don't cut it with me, Doc."

"The man is nearly eighty years old! He fell down an escalator in a store you insure—"

"I want a spinal tap."

After a long, angry pause, Crichton said icily, "*I* make the determination of which tests should be run on my patients."

"Oh yeah? We've been through this before, Doc. I always go to the hospital chief administrator, and he always says . . ."

"The bottom line," finished Crichton hollowly.

The bottom line. If the insurance company refused to pay Klenhard's running medical expenses, the hospital would transfer the old man to a county-run facility that Crichton regarded as little better than a snake pit. He sighed in resignation.

"He has to *agree* to the spinal tap."

"Okay. But right now. Before that wife of his gets back."

The two men stared at one another with cordial mutual loathing. Crichton sighed and turned away. Hawkins smiled at his back. The old woman was the steel in the combination. With her out of the way, the old man would be putty in his hands.

The nurse had finished both Staley's sponge bath and that amazing nurses' feat, changing his sheets with him still in them.

Crichton dismissed her, said gently, "We've been discussing your case, Mr. Klenhard. We want you to submit to a spinal tap."

"What's that?" Staley was looking apprehensively from face to face for those answers not found in words alone.

"I draw fluid from your spinal cord to test whether—"

"Draw? What's that, draw?"

"Siphon off," put in Hawkins impatiently.

"Like with a needle?"

"Yeah."

"A *big* needle?"

"Yes," said Crichton suddenly, "a *very* big needle."

"It's gonna hurt, ain't it? A lot?" Staley's chin had gotten determined and his eyes had gone mule-stubborn. "I ain't gonna do it, I can't stand no more pain."

"Mr. Klenhard—"

"No."

Staley looked straight ahead as if alone in the room. Crichton took Hawkins to the window. Outside, April showers had come their way to bring the flowers that bloom in May.

"You heard. He can't stand any more pain."

"He wouldn't have known about any more pain if you hadn't tipped him off," snarled Hawkins. "A little needle prick—"

"Have you ever had a spinal tap, Mr. Hawkins?"

"No, but—"

"I thought not. I sincerely hope I get a chance to give you one. Meanwhile, I can't chance it over his objections." He amended, "I *won't* chance it. With his sensitivity to any added pain, the tap could result in further permanent injury."

"Further? I'm telling you, Doc . . ." The adjuster paused for a moment. Then he said in a low voice, "Okay, I'll accept reflex tests if administered right now in my presence."

"The same objection applies," said Crichton in equally low tones. "Any added pain—"

"If he's as bad off as he's claiming, he won't feel a thing. If he *does* inadvertently show pain, Doc, either we got us a miracle right here in River City . . . or he's been faking it all along. Right?"

Crichton hesitated. There had seemed no way Klenhard could profit from faking serious injury, but now the store manager had brought in his insurance company with the possibility of a settlement. Might not a destitute septuagenarian looking at a penniless old age be motivated to attempt insurance fraud?

"Okay," Crichton said abruptly, "I'll go along with it."

They turned from the rain-streaked window back to the bed, where Staley seemed to have fallen asleep again.

"Mr. Klenhard." No reaction. Louder. *"Mr. Klenhard."*

Staley stirred and opened his eyes. "Mama?"

"No. It's Dr. Crichton. We won't have to do the spinal tap after all, Mr. Klenhard, but we are going to have to perform some alternative tests on you right here in your bed."

"Like the last time? Bendin' an' standin' an'—"

"No. This will be with . . . sharp instruments."

"*Needles?*"

"*Little* needles. Like straight pins. And scrapers."

"See if I feel 'em, huh?" said Staley surprisingly, then added, more surprisingly, "Okay, if it's gonna help . . ."

Crichton put down the covers and bared Staley's legs and feet. He scraped them, seeking reflex reaction. Then, at Hawkin's insistence, he jabbed needles into the soles of the feet. Through it all, Staley lay on his back, motionless and relaxed, staring at the ceiling. He finally spoke.

"You can start anytime you want, Doc. I'm ready for it."

"We're finished," said a triumphant Crichton. He added to Hawkins, "Faking it, huh?" as Lulu appeared.

"What you doing to my Karl?"

Hawkins addressed a rude word to both of them and walked out without responding to either. Three minutes later, after reassuring Lulu that they had not harmed her husband in any way, Crichton also departed. Lulu sat down in the chair beside the bed with her purse on her lap.

"Did I stay away long enough, *Liebchen?*"

"Perfect," said Staley.

"Any trouble with the needles?"

"There never is if you know they're coming." In his youth, accidental falls had been his specialty; he knew all about how to control his reaction to the needle jabs of reflex testing.

"The spinal tap?"

Staley groaned very loudly. They both laughed.

The spinal tap that might have exposed their scam, because the fluid would have been clear, was safely behind them. Lulu opened her purse and took out some Nestlé's chocolate bars with bits of almond and toffee in them, Staley's favorite.

As he munched one of them, Lulu said, "That insurance man is gonna make us a nice offer in a few days."

"And you'll make him make us a lot nicer offer a few days after that."

Staley said it complacently, with not a little pride in his voice at his wife's abilities. He finished the bar and licked his fingers and started on a second one.

"I think tomorrow, maybe, you start word to the *rom* that I'm sinking fast. Prob'ly ain't gonna last out next week . . ."

"I think that's best," agreed Lulu comfortably. She stole a side-long look at her lord and master, and added slyly, "Think it's maybe time for a Queen of the Gypsies again? I been hearing good things about that Yana out there in San Francisco . . ."

"I don't know, my dumpling," said Staley judiciously. "I've been following the career of young Rudolph Marino . . ."

*   *   *

Marino and the other three sat in a semicircular window booth with a curved red leather seat, their backs to the glass. The maître d' had RESERVED signs on the flanking booths and on the tables in front of them. A balding man's waterfall fingers cascaded Gershwin's *Rhapsody in Blue* from a piano against the mirrored sidewall that was framed in thirty-foot-high red plush drapes. He had outlived his youthful self on the placard outside by a quarter-century, although his hair had not. Marino, against the others' objections to meeting in the Garnet Room, had said the piano would jam any listening devices pointed their way.

Redheaded Shayne, Hotel Security, smeared out his half-smoked Marlboro and fired up another.

"Your meeting, your agenda, Grimaldi."

Marino paused for a moment. They hadn't panicked and gone to the authorities, or by this time relay teams of Secret Service interrogators would be sweating him under bright lights in some anonymous federal office building downtown. But they hadn't accepted Angelo Grimaldi's offer yet, either; and the President was due in a couple of days.

So, another turn of the screw. He made his face devoid of expression and spoke from the corner of his mouth, tight-lipped.

"Assassination plot."

That almost did it. Harley Gunnarson went white around the mouth. If something happened to the President in a hotel he was managing . . . He had to clear his throat to speak.

"They plan to . . . to kill the *President?* In *my* hote—"

143

"Yes. You could notify the Secret Service *now*, of course," said Marino. "But . . ."

Smathers, lips parted, bird-bright eyes gleaming like those of a whiskey jay spotting a shiny coin, couldn't resist.

"But what?"

"You already didn't tell them about the bomb threat—"

"There haven't been any more," pointed out Shayne.

"That doesn't negate the one there was."

Dull, unimaginative Shayne, focus among them of opposition to Marino's sting, stubbed out his just-lit second cigarette. His resistance seemed to have given Gunnarson back some of the bluster the word "assassination" had scared out of him.

"I'm not so sure," Gunnarson said. "What if that threat was just some kook who thought he'd get his kicks making it? We have only your word that the Saladin even exist . . ."

Shayne added, "With the Secret Service guys and my own security people on watch, nobody can get through to do anything to the President anyway." He pressed his point. "So yesterday we decided that we don't need you or your 'people' on this."

Gunnarson concurred by refusing to meet his eyes, so Marino turned to Smathers, who lathered his little hands with the invisible soap of distress and squeaked, "I'm not management! As corporate counsel I can only advise! This decision was reached over my most strenuous objections! I was overruled!"

Marino had been counting on the tiny desiccated attorney, but now saw he'd been wrong. Well, he hated to waste such a beautiful vehicle, but his limo had been gotten as the final convincer, and this *was* the biggest sting of his life. So, better go over to Richmond and get it wired up by Eli Nicholas, who had served in 'Nam.

He slid out of the booth and smiled down at them. None of the faces was really happy. The limo would do it for sure.

"Your funeral," he said in his slightly grating Joisey voice. "Or rather, the President's." He started away, then turned back. "You're gonna get bloody on this one, y'know."

It was a hell of a good exit line, even if he had stolen it from *Lethal Weapon*.

CHAPTER TWENTY

Giselle and Ballard planned to talk about Gypsies over a drink at Fifi's on Union Street, but Ballard was late and Giselle, because of that pesky concussion he'd suffered, was feeling almost . . . maternal about him. Which was silly, since they'd worked together for eight years and were great friends. *Friends.* There could never be anything . . . *personal* between them.

It was just that he seemed so vulnerable and . . .

He also seemed to be twenty minutes late, she thought, but even her irritation was mild. Just like that Larry.

Leaving her wine and newly purchased pack of cigarettes and disposable lighter on a table facing Union Street through plate glass, she wormed her way through noisy bar drinkers to the payphone. Jane Goldson's noncommittal "Hello?" was the response prescribed for all unlisted DKA skip-tracer numbers.

"Jane? Giselle. Did Larry call in to say that he's still planning to meet me at Fifi's?"

"There's a message for you, luv, but not from Larry. From dear old Mr. Anonymous." Her cheery cockney voice changed to a reading singsong: " '*In Tiburon. Theodore Winston White the Third.*' "

Whatever that meant. She said, "I'm impressed—the Third, yet. But nothing from Larry . . ."

"No—well, a message *for* him, actually. A woman." Jane giggled. "Sexy-sounding wench, she was." The singsong again. " *'Rainbird Lounge. Tonight.' "*

Larry's call was none of her business, and Giselle's own anonymous call couldn't be about Gyppos. The only informant she had spoken with was Dirty Harry, who didn't have her real name or number. Besides, Theodore Winston White III was no Gypsy name.

Just to be sure, she tapped out 411. No listing for White in the Tiburon/Belvedere area. No listing for him anywhere in Marin County. And no way until tomorrow to run him down through the Civic Center records in San Rafael.

*   *   *

Sonia Lovari was 32 and looked 19, and helped nature along with simple artifice: since she had a short chunky body and swarthy skin and a round face with an inappropriate beak of a nose, she plaited her long hair into a single lustrous black braid that reached to the small of her back, wore jeans, run-over cowboy boots, and a fringed jacket of phony buckskin. Thus attired, she neatly fit the *gadjo* stereotype of squaw woman.

Sonia shook the one-pound coffee can with the slot in the top and MIWOK INDIAN SUPPORT GROUP—GIVE WHAT YOU CAN pasted around it. She kept it almost empty at all times; a few lonely coins rattling around inside attracted sympathy.

"The Miwoks are starving, sir. The Great Spirit will bless you if—"

"Everybody's starving," snapped the man she'd stopped.

He obviously wasn't. Florid face, fat stomach, three-piece suit, three-martini breath. Sonia welcomed the challenge. An argument always made other people stop and listen.

"Not like my people, sir. We—"

"You can't kid me—the last of the Miwoks died off last year!" he said with inaccurate belligerence. "Ishi, that was his name! There was a movie on Showtime about him—"

Sonia, who had never heard of Ishi, interrupted with glib and equal inaccuracy. "Ishi was a Tamalpais Miwok. We are Coast

146

Miwok." In her eyes were Native American patience and pain. "There are only thirty-three of us left—the same number as our dear Savior's years when He was crucified."

A crowd of curious commuters was gathering. The man looked around and saw only sympathy for Sonia on the attentive faces. He muttered under his breath while digging in his pants pocket for a crumpled bill to stuff into her tin can.

"Here, for Chrissake."

"The Great Spirit blesses you, sir."

But it was a Bay Area Rapid Transit guard, not the Great Spirit, who materialized behind her to lay an ungentle hand on her shoulder. "No panhandling in the BART station, sister."

Undismayed, Sonia displayed the bogus Chamber of Commerce "registered charity" badge that she'd paid a Gypsy documenter in San Jose $50 for. She didn't know what it said, not knowing how to read, but it always worked like a charm.

"I'm not panhandling, sir."

The guard's hostility had lessened. He gestured at the broad yellow line at the edge of the platform where the silver bullet-shaped BART projectiles would come roaring past.

"You still can't solicit in the BART station—it's just too dangerous for the customers." He gestured. "But you can do it upstairs, at the street entrance."

"I'm sorry. This is my first day. I'm only nineteen."

He hesitated. "Miwok, huh? I heard you say—"

"Only thirty-three of us are left, sir."

"Aw, what the hell?"

The guard shoved a dollar in the slot. Sonia thanked him and managed to rattle two more donations into her coffee can on her way up to the Market/Powell entrance. The streetlights were on and the stream of BART commuters had thinned to a trickle; until Memorial Day brought summer's tourist wave, she had to depend on the locals. Five more minutes, she'd quit for the day.

Rattle-rattle.

Clink.

"Great Spirit bless you, ma'am."

The Miwok scam was a new one for her; for years, up and down the coast, she'd done Navajos. But last month she'd been forced to spend an afternoon hiding out from a Marin County bunco cop at the Miwok Museum in Novato; since she couldn't read the captions under the displays, she'd followed around a schoolteacher explaining the exhibits to her second-graders. Sonia had immediately switched scams. In the Bay Area, she reasoned, local Miwok was bound to arouse more sympathy than far-off Navajo.

Still rattling her collection can, she started up the hill toward the Sutter-Stockton garage where she'd left her $50,000 Allante with its 4.5-litre V-8 engine and front-drive traction control system. Tonight, as usual, she'd swing over to the Rainbird Lounge for a little Miller time. Their happy hour always gave her useful bits of redskin lore and turns of phrase, and no one would come looking for her car there.

When she got the Georgia plates she'd applied for, the repossessors Rudolph Marino had warned her about would no longer threaten her Allante. And meanwhile, Rudolph would soon be King.

Leaving bitch Yana out in the cold where she belonged.

* * *

Larry Ballard was sitting opposite Giselle's glass of wine and pack of cigarettes when she got back from the phone. The red lump on his forehead was just about gone; all that remained was a slight reddish discoloration as if he'd gotten too much sun. Back to his old handsome self. Time to quit thinking Florence Nightingale thoughts about him, she didn't know why she was having them in the first place. Just silliness.

She shook her head ruefully. "I'd better change brands so I won't be so predictable."

"Or quit using disposable lighters."

"They give me the illusion the smoking is also disposable."

"I thought it was. Last I'd heard, you'd quit again." When she answered only with a shrug, he gestured at the huge plate-glass picture window. "Fifi's. I always feel like a French poodle at a dog show in this joint."

"You're sounding more like Dan every day."

"Yeah, sure. You get anything on Grimaldi from Harrigan?"

"Nothing. He said that if any Gypsy was operating with that name in San Francisco, he'd know about it."

"Except one is and he doesn't." Ballard paused. "You've been told the story about him, haven't you? They started calling him Dirty Harry in Vice, 'cause he was dirty—extorting money and tail from hookers in the Tenderloin. When he got transferred to Bunco his gross probably dropped fifty percent."

"He's still plenty gross enough for me."

"Dirty Harry put a move on you?"

They fell silent when the waitress brought Ballard's mug of draft beer, an automatic professional caution rather than any real worry about being overheard. But still they waited until she departed. Giselle lit a new cigarette, fumbling the lighter as she remembered the man's eyes crawling over her like spiders. Ballard grinned at her.

"Don't feel bad—he'd screw mud." To the look on her face, he added with quick diplomacy, "Not that I mean you're—"

"I think you think you just paid me a compliment."

She stubbed her just-lit cigarette in irritation. She didn't like their patter; she felt as if she were flirting with Larry. Good old solid Larry Ballard, for God sake! What was the matter with her? To cover her discomfort, she told him about the blind date she'd set up for Harrigan. Ballard broke up.

"So Dirty Harry'll show up at the Sappho Self-defense Dojo with his pocket full of condoms and his hand on his—"

"He did make a couple of interesting remarks," Giselle said quickly. "Three, actually. First, there's a rumor that the Gypsy King is dying back in the Midwest somewhere . . ."

"Which would explain Grimaldi interrupting his other operation for the Cadillac grab! Yeah! Go back in style to choose the new King . . ." He drank beer, added thoughtfully, "We need to know who, when, where. Maybe I can get a line on—"

"Harrigan wasn't really interested, so I couldn't be too interested myself, seeing as I'd just passed myself off as a free-lance journalist trying to dig up a story on—"

"Dirty Harry happen to mention a Gyppo named Rudolph?"

"No." She couldn't stop herself. "Why?"

Ballard grinned in an extremely sappy manner. "Oh, someone else mentioned him, that's all."

A sexy-sounding wench, Jane had said. Three years ago, a beautiful Gyppo fortune-teller'd had Ballard walking around with his tongue dragging the ground for a couple of weeks after DKA had put mob attorney Wayne Hawkley out of business for good.

"Your little Gyppo crystal-gazer from Santa Rosa?" she couldn't help demanding snidely.

Ballard frowned at her from behind his beer mug. What was this? Old Giselle gets out in the field and all of a sudden starts getting competitive about sources like any other repoman?

"Why do you ask?"

Giselle just shook her head and drank her Chablis, appalled at herself. She changed the subject yet again.

"Dirty Harry also said that some heavy-duty bad-guy Gyppos have been moving in from New York and Chicago . . ."

Ballard's momentary irritation seemed forgotten. "That fits, too. My informant said Rudolph had just hit town. She's never seen him, doesn't even know his last name, but—"

Again, Giselle couldn't stop herself. "*She* says."

"Why would she lie?" He licked foam from his upper lip and started trying to connect up the dots, one of the main hazards of the detective game—the irresistible urge to make all the data you had somehow fit together. "Think this Rudolph character could be Angelo Grimaldi?"

"Why not? Anyway, I'll check registrations for the Grimaldi name at the top hotels in town. If he *is* setting up some elaborate scam, it'll be timed to the President's visit . . ."

"Yeah. The cops'll be too busy on security and crowd control to check out every con game in town."

Giselle had finished her wine. She leaned toward him.

"I've already talked with Danny McBain at Jack Olwen Cadillac about Grimaldi's specially built limo. He said—"

"Specially built how?"

"Jack didn't know, the work was done by an outfit down in L.A. I've got a call in to them now."

"What was his description of Grimaldi?"

"Same as the bank's. Tall, lean, soulful eyes . . ."

"Man of my dreams." He added, a bit distractedly, "What's the third thing Harry told you about?"

Giselle started to tell him, then pulled herself up short. Uh-uh.

She'd always thought the competition between field men for the best monthly recovery record was childish macho nonsense, but now she understood the rivalry. When you were on the street, you wanted to be the *best* on the street. And who knew what Larry might pass on to his little Gypsy bimbo . . .

No, the Eldorado, though only a tenuous lead, was *her* lead, she wasn't going to . . .

Who was she kidding? She wasn't going to tell him about the 1958 pink convertible the Gyps might have snatched in Palm Springs for only *one* reason: because Ballard wasn't going to cop to his Gyppo crystal-gazer. It was simple as that.

She said, "Jane Goldson gave me a message for you. A woman. Wouldn't leave her name."

Ballard made impatient gimme-gimme gestures. When she stayed silent, he burst out, "Jesus Christ, Giselle, what the hell is it with you tonight? Every time I—"

" 'Rainbird Lounge. Tonight.' That was it."

It seemed hardly enough, but Ballard started grinning from ear to ear, that same foolish Tom-Sawyer-about-Becky-Thatcher kind of grin he'd used a minute ago.

"I'll be damned," he said softly, "she came through." To Giselle's cynically raised eyebrows, he added abruptly, "Yeah, her. Yana. Madame Miseria. My crystal-ball gazer from three years ago. My Gypsy informant. The one I paid a hundred bucks to this afternoon. There. You happy now?"

"You paid her one hundred dollars on the come?" The office manager in Giselle was genuinely offended at the idea of $100 being given to *anyone*—let alone some Gyppo princess—for information not only not tested for accuracy but not yet even received. "I suppose you think one of the Caddies will be parked outside the Rainbird with the key in the ignition and the engine still warm."

"Something like that, yeah."

"That's an Indian bar, you know. American Indian. Indians and Gyppos don't exactly love each other."

"O ye of little faith," he intoned in a pious inflection borrowed from O'B. He seemed to be having the time of his life, which made him very irritating.

She snapped abruptly, "I'm coming with you on this one."

"Like hell."

"I want to see the look on your face when there's no Gyppo Cadillac."

Ballard was silent for a moment. Then he smiled a slow superior smile. "Tell you what. You pay for the drinks here, and buy me dinner afterward, and you're on."

"The hundred dollars broke you, huh?"

"I've got three bucks."

"That's my Larry. Always a sucker for a woman with more in her bra than in her brain."

And *there* was a wonderful thing for Giselle Marc with an M.A. in history to say, she thought as they stood up. Quite enough out of you for one night, young lady, thank you very much.

As she scattered paper money across the table to cover their drinks and the tip, Ballard said abruptly, "I'm gonna really enjoy this. Eight lousy months in the field against my eight years, and you think you know all about it. Well, tonight, Giselle, the old maestro's gonna show you how it's done."

CHAPTER
TWENTY-ONE

The Rainbird Lounge, a neighborhood bar in the flats below Potrero Hill, had been rebuilt along with San Francisco after the Big One of '06. Then known as a "bucket of blood" to the South of Market Irish who frequented it, it became a speak for the Italians during Prohibition. In World War II it was a joint—the kind you drink in, not the kind you smoke—serving cheap booze to G.I.s being shipped out to the Pacific Theater.

After construction of the James Lick Freeway in the 1950s stubbed off its street into a dead end, it should have folded. But, inspired by the name "Rainbird Lounge," an alcoholic *muralista* hoping for free drinks forever—as Benny Bufano was getting free food for his fresco in a Powell Street cafeteria—painted a lurid *Custer's Last Stand* across the front of it. Lots of scalped horse soldiers littering the Dakota landscape.

His cirrhotic dreams died with a sale to new owners; but the name and the mural somehow became a draw for Native Americans adrift in the big city. Tribal artifacts traded for bar tabs accumulated to lure more Indians: beadwork, clay pots, kachina dolls, doeskin moccasins, woven blankets, even an antique turquoise and beaten-silver brooch hung from a light fixture.

The Rainbird was a comfy sort of place for those who were regulars, while turning a cold shoulder to outsiders who were not Native Americans. There was sawdust on the floor and a half dozen beat-up tables with mismatched chairs. Over the bar along the right wall was a twelve-inch TV tuned to the sports channel—with the sound off so country music could blare from the old-fashioned jukebox. At the Rainbird, a shot and a beer were a mixed drink, a bag of blue corn chips *haute cuisine*. Patrons drank heavily and fought often, making abrupt visits from the blues of the Southeast Station at Third and 20th inevitable.

*   *   *

The early-season A's game on the tube was silenced and the juke was between tunes, so Ballard could hear his entrance cut the babble of voices like ammonia squeaking on a windowpane. Every brown face in the joint turned toward his white one through the silence and pall of smoke and reek of stale beer.

There were only brown faces in the joint.

Ballard leaned across the stick and cleared his throat. "Uh . . . you sell cigarettes here?" He didn't want to ask for a drink for fear of getting scalped instead.

The bartender, whose face was right off the old Indian-head nickel, wore a cowboy hat with a burst of feathers on the crown. He jerked a brown thumb toward the rest rooms.

"Machine. Back there."

Ballard waded through utter silence to the swinging door beyond which were rest rooms, payphone, cigarette machine. As the door shut behind him, the babble started up again.

Three minutes later, sliding in under the wheel of the company car he'd left parked in the yellow zone outside, he dropped a red and white crush-proof box into Giselle's lap.

"I hope you like Marlboros."

She said sweetly, "Didn't want a drink after all?" He seemed too busy making a U-turn back out toward Vermont to answer, so she put the needle in again. "No Gypsies in swirling silks and high heels doing flamencos on top of the bar?"

"Rain dance," said Ballard shortly and sourly.

"I told you it was an Indian place. Admit it, Larry! Your precious Yana stiffed you for your hundred bucks!"

"DKA's hundred bucks. We'll go eat and come back."

"Can't admit he's wrong," sighed Giselle as if in sorrow.

She actually was delighted, of course, that there had been no Cadillac out in front, no Gyppo in swirling silks and hoop earrings beating a tambourine in one of the booths.

*   *   *

Sonia Lovari parked her shiny new Allante in the Rainbird's yellow zone a scant sixty seconds after they had departed. She had no feeling of impending danger: the car was safe there, as was she. She even had told the Indians in great detail about buying it from the insurance settlement of a fictional auto accident, so there was no overt envy over her fancy wheels.

When she had first started coming here, Sonia—known at the Rainbird as Maria Little Bird—had been unnerved by the broken pates, bloodied noses, and blackened eyes on the day the government checks arrived. But now, as a regular, she felt safe and welcome even though sometimes she had to duck thrown glasses and bottles, or grab her own glass and bottle up from the table as a large body crashed across it.

She was always apologized to; being small and an obvious non-combatant, she was never nabbed in the police raids; and at the Rainbird she was careful to never work the scams, cons, and grifts that made her so unwelcome in other South of Market bars.

"You see in the papers 'bout they wanna change the name of the Redskins football team?" asked Perching Raven, the heavy old Paiute woman on the next stool. She was very wide and brown and had the serene seamed face of a desert mountainside.

"K.C. Chiefs, too," said Comes By Night from the other side of Sonia. He was a sturdy Oglala Sioux who had been looking for work for two years and looking to live up to his name with Little Bird for almost as long. Work eluded him, and Sonia in her secret soul was a traditional Gypsy: no sex with *gadje*, which she guessed Comes By Night had to be since he wasn't *rom*.

"Atlanta Braves," nodded Hank Feathers, old Perching Raven's aged husband, not to be outdone.

"Red pride," said Perching Raven sagely.

"That's what I think, too," said Sonia. Being unable to read and disinterested in anything *sportif* except the odds, she hadn't the

155

slightest idea what they were talking about; but this was a safe remark. She gestured for another pitcher to share with her friends. "Us redskins gotta stick together, right?"

"Right," echoed the others as they filled their glasses.

*   *   *

"Hot damn!" exclaimed Ballard. He drifted the company Ford to the curb and stopped. "Didn't I tell you?"

Giselle looked at the spanking-new Cadillac Allante parked in the Rainbird's yellow zone. If the motor was warm and the keys were in it, she was going to scream. Ballard already had his Gypsy case folder open on his knees under the dash light, flicking awkwardly through the repo assignments for Allantes.

She ventured, "We don't *know* it's one of our Gyppo cars."

"Three Allantes, one of them a red hardtop convertible." He pointed through the windshield in a maddening manner. "Like that one. Right there. Red hardtop convertible."

"Shut up," agreed Giselle.

Ballard ripped away the key for the Allante he had stapled to the repossession order after cutting it himself per the code furnished by the dealer. He had his door open and one foot on the pavement. "You stay here and—"

"No, damn you! I'm not going to sit in the car while you're out there being Mr. Macho Man."

Ballard sighed and pulled his leg back in. Didn't she realize that even as they hassled here, the Gyppo who had arrived while they were eating might come out and drive away?

"One of us should stay with this car, Giselle. If—"

"So you stay."

"It's right in front of the bar. Bar repos can get nasty."

"Nasty? After your Gypsy sweetie set it all up for you? Heaven forfend!"

Ballard looked about to explode, but only gritted his teeth and said mildly, "Okay. We both go. But if any trouble starts, you get the hell out of there, car or no. All right?"

After a long moment, Giselle nodded. "All right."

The Allante's hood *was* still warm. No key in the ignition, but both doors unlocked with the windows down. Would a Gyppo leave his car that way? Maybe check the I.D. number . . .

156

The goddamn key didn't fit.

"I can't believe this shit," he muttered to Giselle.

As Ballard got back out of the car, she slid in to start working the key, raking it in and out of the lock, always with a slight sideways pressure to make it pop over if the tumblers decided to click. He bent to speak through the open window.

"I'll get my ignition switch to replace this one."

Giselle nodded, kept working the key.

Dammit, he thought, moving away, he really *should* check that I.D. since his key didn't work; but by this time he was determined to get the car if it was one of theirs or not. They could always dump it somewhere later if they were wrong.

From the company car he got the plastic letter file box that held his repo kit, and started back toward the Allante.

That's when the old man and the old woman, craggy of face, dusky of skin, came from the Rainbird. Injuns! He froze, hoping they wouldn't see Giselle ducked down in the Cadillac; but the bar lights shone right down into the front seat.

"Hey, whatta hell you doin' in Little Bird's car?"

Hank Feathers and Perching Raven started forward. Ballard gave a bellow and ran toward them, swinging the heavy plastic letter file in one hand like a weapon. They retreated hurriedly into the bar—but he knew they'd be back.

"Get outta here!" he yelled at Giselle. "Now!"

But the door of the Rainbird burst open to disgorge a dozen Indians on the warpath, led by a short squat girl who looked about 19 and seemed the stereotyped squaw woman.

"She's stealing my car!"

"*She's not an Indian! She's a Gypsy!*" yelled Ballard, not fooled by Sonia's bogus squaw woman looks.

At that instant the key turned under Giselle's fingers and the Allante roared into life. She knew the rules—get the car first, worry about your partner later—so she tromped on it and was gone as Larry stood his ground, whirling the plastic box around in front of him to hold them at bay for her getaway.

Huge craggy Comes By Night swung a two-by-four at Ballard's head. He ducked under it, rammed a karate blow known as a back fist up into the big man's crotch. Comes By Night said, "OOOF!" and went to one knee, holding himself.

Ballard ululated *"Yi yi yi yi yi!"* as best he could at his momentarily disconcerted foes. He had counted coup.

Giselle slid the Allante to a stop at the dead end of the cul-de-sac, slammed it into reverse, head and one arm out the window, and goosed it. Okay, she'd secured the car like she was supposed to; now she'd run down the goddam redskins if that was what it would take to save Ballard.

Who had just been caught on the shoulder by a thrown brick that knocked him off balance. He spun, the swinging box cracking the side of a face, his foot lashing out in a side kick that sunk into a beer-soggy gut. Stale beer sprayed his face.

A great red monster chased by a twinned fan of brilliant light roared backward out of the darkness upon them, horn braying, engine wailing. Giselle slammed on the brakes for a half-skid that scattered Indians in every direction.

"The window!" she yelled at Ballard.

Still spinning on one foot, he tossed the box in the open window on the rider's side and leaped in after it. But as the Allante roared away backward toward Vermont Street, someone grabbed Ballard's legs. He heard a ripping sound and felt cold air, heard a grunt of effort behind him—and a splintery two-by-four slammed against his bare butt with stunning force.

"OWWWW!"

Comes By Night had counted coup back at him by scalping his behind. Cars were roaring into life all around them. At Vermont, Giselle, still running backward, mashed the brakes and spun the wheel and simultaneously goosed it.

"Jesus!" Ballard took the Savior's name in vain as the torque almost tore him out of the window again.

*   *   *

It was Little Bird who stared sadly after the disappearing vehicles from in front of the emptied Rainbird—even the bartender had joined in the chase. But it was Sonia Lovari who sighed and started away on foot: she really had begun to think of herself as Indian, but eventually these genuine Indians would realize she was a Gypsy and would reject her.

And she knew who to blame. Only Yana would have told the *gadje* where to find her.

*   *   *

Giselle bit her lip hard enough to draw blood when one of the pursuing cars rammed the rear bumper.

"Hang on!" she yelled at Ballard, flooring it.

"What the hell do you think I—"

A brick whizzed by his head to scar the Caddy's paintwork. Cars were coming up on either side of them, the one on the right running with one set of wheels on the sidewalk, the other in the gutter. It hit a power pole and was out of the running, but another swerved around it to keep coming.

Giselle slewed into 16th Street as if she knew where she was going. Ballard hoped to hell she did; he didn't have a clue. He tried to pull himself inside, but the pursuer swerved in to crush him between the cars. He jerked up tight against the side of the Caddy as metal ground metal just below him.

Giselle screamed the Allante into broad Third Street, ran the red at the next intersection, horn blaring. They were outrunning their pursuers: the Caddy's big V-8 generated a lot of power. But a car shot across Third directly in front of her, she hit the brakes, slid almost sideways down the street, so numb by this time that she felt only a mild detached curiosity about whether she would miss it or not.

She did, but the skid had let the Indians catch up. They were cutting in, forcing her to the curb, roaring war chants.

But she was there! Horn blaring, she jumped the curb. Ballard, still half out of the car, hung on for dear life as the Allante leaped up three concrete stairs at a steep 45-degree angle to splinter the double doors at their head with its front bumper. A tire went BANG! The old-fashioned globe light above the cophouse door POPPED! to drift sharded glass down on them.

Uniformed cops, wearing astounded, half-scared faces, poured out of the Southeast precinct house past the Allante with guns in their hands. This flushed the covey of pursuing Indian cars, which burst out in every direction with squealing tires.

Ballard had managed to get his feet on one of the steps by this time, too dazed to know his ripped pants were puddled around his ankles so he was buck-ass naked from the waist down. He was waving his arms around in front of him, panting as if he'd just run a footrace.

159

"Peaceful repossession, peaceful repossession!" he yelped at the dozen guns' big unwinking eyes staring at him.

"The hell you say," drawled the Irish desk sergeant.

"From . . . the Rainbird . . . Lounge . . ."

"Ah," said the sergeant in soft understanding, and holstered his weapon. All the cops knew the Rainbird. After a moment, the rest followed suit, putting their guns away also.

Giselle staggered around the car from the driver's side, blood running down her chin from her bitten lip.

"I checked . . . I.D. number . . . we got . . . right car . . ." Then she saw Ballard and laughed weakly. "So this . . . is how it's done . . . maestro?"

"It got done," said Ballard with great dignity.

Looking at Giselle looking at Ballard, the sergeant said, with Irish rectitude, "Hey, Sam Spade, better get your pants on."

Ballard, suddenly realizing his condition, jerked his pants up with a savage gesture.

And shrieked in pain as the rough fabric scraped across innumerable splinters to drive them deeper into his bruised and lacerated rear end.

CHAPTER
TWENTY-TWO

Because Giselle was out in the field chasing Gypsies, Dan Kearny was stuck in the office with all the routine paperwork they usually shared. And it was making him feel old.

Time was, his field agents needed him to clean up their messes; now, he'd trained 'em to be the best in the business.

Time was, at Walter's Auto Detectives—before he founded DKA with Giselle and O'B and Kathy Onoda, God rest her soul—*he* was the best field agent in the business.

Now . . . Old. Mighty old.

His phone rang. Jane Goldson's voice was in his ear. "A man calling himself Ephrem Poteet is on line—"

Kearny, suddenly twenty years younger, punched into the blinking red light. "Whadda ya have for me?"

A recognized chuckle and heavy tones came at him over the wire. "Always right to business with you, ain't it, Kearny?"

"*Gadje* manners."

"Okay. Los Angeles. Silverlake District. Wasso Tomeshti. TV sets. And I'll take my hundred bucks now, up front."

"Not for that you won't. I need more. What's the scam?"

"Factory-direct to consumer. That's all you get."

Kearny recognized finality, but more than that, had a flash of inspiration.

"Your hundred's in the mail."

He hung up, sat there behind his desk. Fired up a Marlboro, forgot to shake out the match until the flame touched his fingertips. In all the years he'd dealt through various P.O. boxes with Poteet, they had never laid eyes on each other. He took a puff of his cigarette.

"No," he said aloud. "Not enough. Not nearly enough."

Not this time. This time he needed leverage, or Poteet would string out his info for weeks in an attempt to raise the $100-per ante—while the subject Gypsies scattered like quail.

Right now Poteet was calling the shots, and Dan Kearny didn't like anyone calling the shots on him.

He didn't like feeling old, either.

He shook his heavy silvered head, chuckled, jerked open a drawer to grab out one of the made-up Gypsy folders with everything they knew on each Cadillac. He didn't have a set of keys cut for the cars, but what the hell? Stay hungry.

As he went past Jane's desk, she piped up cheerily, "Where to, Mr. K? Your meeting with Stan at the bank isn't until—"

"Cancel it."

"But—"

"And hold my calls."

"But—"

"Hold tomorrow's calls, too."

"But . . ."

"And maybe the day's after that."

From her wastebasket he grabbed a discarded FINAL NOTICE window envelope with a canceled stamp on it—a shocking-red envelope designed to catch a delinquent's eye—and took a sheet of letterhead from her desk. Then he was gone.

*　　*　　*

Few would recognize Wasso Tomeshti in sleek Mr. Adam Wells.

Wasso Tomeshti was a greasy-curled *rom* who wore a heavy curled mustache with a day's beard, bright shirts, a brick-red bandana around his thick throat, and black jeans tucked into the tops of black leather hack boots. Mr. Adam Wells, his finest creation, wore a painfully close shave, too much cheap cologne, a gangrenous three-piece electric-green suit, a purple and gold plaid shirt, a paisley tie mostly orange, and black loafers.

"Want a little air?" Mr. Adam Wells asked expansively.

"No, I'm fine," said Sam Hood.

If Sam Hood thought Adam Wells sleazy—a compliment in Sam's book—he also knew Adam Wells was making enough of those big fat greasy bucks everyone yearned for to tool along Ventura Boulevard in a white Seville STS four-door notchback that went for $40,000 stripped. And this baby was *loaded.* Ultra-soft leather seats, hand-fitted to the car with French upholstery seams; air, Delco AM/FM stereo deck and C/D player, custom phaeton roof, power everything . . . still had paper plates and the new-car smell.

Like riding on a cloud.

"Trade every year," Wells was bragging. "One a these, then a Lincoln Town Car, then a Chrysler Imperial." A chuckle. "Gotta keep the Big Three going, y'know." Sam Hood knew. He also knew he wanted some of Wells's big fat greasy bucks. Wells added, "Yeah, strictly American, that's me."

"Except for TV sets?" Sam put a sly question mark on it.

"The TV sets are *business.*" Wells slapped the steering wheel with beringed fingers. "This here is personal. This here is love of country." He gestured with the stogie. "There she is, just ahead."

"She" was a nearly completed motel on the south side of the Boulevard near Tujunga that damn near popped Sam's eyes out of his head. Behind it rose green-foliaged hills studded with million-dollar homes. There was an obscene amount of construction going on along Ventura, but none of it was more opulent than this block-square U-shaped motel complex.

Wells pulled the Seville over to the curb to gesture.

"In the middle there's gonna be a fountain. Palm trees, lots of shrubbery. We got a Spago's coming in, shops, boutiques, indoor an' outdoor pool, sauna, a World Gym . . ."

Having a little trouble with his voice, Sam asked, "How many color TV sets did you say you're gonna need from me?"

"I didn't, but maybe three hundred to start. Sure, that's chicken feed, but we'll double-deck next year and'll need another five hundred. Not much even then, I know, but—"

"No, no—no job too small," said Sam quickly.

You bet your butt, thought Wasso. Three hundred would clear out this *gadjo's* stock on hand—he'd checked. That's why Wasso had picked him even though he might be connected. A dangerous man, perhaps, but hungry enough to be stupid.

When Wells had wanted "a few" color consoles for "his" motel at a discount off the already low wholesale delivery price that was Sam's stock-in-trade, Hood had pictured a couple dozen run-down units huddled around a postage-stamp pool with dead bugs floating around in it. But *this* . . .

This was money in the bank. His entire stock in one transaction! Since all his TVs fell off the back of the truck, anyway—with the driver's reimbursed cooperation—he was going to make a dizzying amount of money off this turkey.

Of course if Sam Hood, even tough as he was and with his underworld connections, had known this turkey was a Gyppo, he would have jumped from the Caddy and sewn his pockets shut. But he didn't.

"I'd love to show you around the place," Wells was saying regretfully, "but I'm doing lunch at LAX with a couple of Japanese investors between planes. So we'd better—"

"There's Jap money in this?" asked Hood, awed for sure.

"Nah, they don't fool with penny-ante crap like this. We got a seven-golf-course deal cooking that . . ." He broke off to laugh. "No you don't. Enough said about that." He opened his door. "I see the foreman there, can you wait for just a minute?"

Tomeshti was already out of the car and walking over to a man checking things off on a clipboard. He pointed at the roof.

"How high is that?"

The workman frowned at him. "Who the hell are you?"

"Who the hell am I?" Tomeshti took a step closer and pounded a fist into his other hand. "A taxpayer, that's who." He started away toward the Seville, then turned back to point at the nonplussed workman and yell, *"And don't you forget it, pal!"*

He got back in, pushing blood into his face to flush it.

"Trouble?" Hood couldn't help asking as they pulled away from the curb in a harsh shriek of rubber.

"Nah—it's just that you say three hundred TV sets are coming tomorrow, the rooms gotta be ready, does he say they'll be ready? Hell no. He says . . ." He shook his head, then brightened. "To

hell with all that. Let's go over to your office and sign that contract
for those TVs. I'll take delivery tomorrow no matter what the damn
foreman says. And pay you for all three hundred sets right then."
He looked over at Sam Hood as the big Caddy lanced through the
Ventura Boulevard traffic. "A check on the corporation account is
all right, isn't it?"

"Yeah," said a dazzled Sam Hood. "Money in the bank."

*   *   *

Dan Kearny's rental Cutlass took the Silver Lake off-ramp from
the Hollywood Freeway to a wide messy street of narrow messy
retail businesses with wide messy signs over them. Furniture
stores. Karate studios. Doughnut shops. Hairdressers. Clothing
stores spilling racks out across the sidewalk full of the sort of flowered sport shirts that make you want to roll a pack of cigarettes up
in one sleeve. Mostly brown faces crowding the sidewalks, a lot of
Habla Español signs.

After an hour of cruising he spotted the billboard:

FACTORY-DIRECT TO THE CONSUMER

Beneath that was:

MITSUBISHI—SONY—HITACHI—TV
ONE-TIME UNHEARD-OF PRICES

Kearny thought he got a glimpse of the con, and started to
chuckle. He found an open meter, parked and locked, walked back.
Bright sunlight, tempered with acrid smog felt in nose and throat,
was hot on the shoulders of his San Francisco-weight wool suit. He
looked into the empty storefront through recently washed windows. Floor fresh-swept, racks waiting to receive their sale TVs.
Sales counter in the back, glassed-in office partition behind that.
Realtor's sign still in the window. Phone number and an address
in the next block.

No Cadillac in the narrow dirt parking lot out in back, not that
Kearny had expected any when he saw the empty showroom. He
wove his way through the polylingual crowd to the realty office; he
had to know who Tomeshti was and when he would show.

Dusty pictures of commercial bargains nobody wanted crowded the front windows. Inside it was a narrow storefront with four battered hardwood desks down one wall and a manager's office in the rear. Latinas at two of the desks, the others empty.

A blonde with metallic hair that could break a fingernail came up from the office. She reeked of musk and greed. Too many teeth, a face-lift that hadn't helped blunt her icepick eyes.

"E. Dana Straub. 'Nye do for ya?"

"The empty storefront in the next block—"

"Din't you see the billboard?"

"Televisions factory-direct?" He shrugged. "Place is empty right now, today, and right now, today, it's just what I need for my retail electronics store."

E. Dana Straub got a look compounded equally of greed and regret. "Mr. Wells has already signed the contract."

"*Danny* Wells?" demanded Kearny in delight. "I can—"

"Adam Wells."

"Oh. But don't matter—I'll sublease from him instead."

"The terms of his lease stipulate no sublets."

Kearny brought out his flash roll—a hundred wrapped around a couple of dozen ones—and leaned suggestively across the counter with a dirty look in his eyes.

"Lease contracts can get lost . . ."

She sighed regretfully. "We remodeled to meet his needs, and Mr. Wells is moving his stock in tomorrow. At the end of the week he's giving me a check for the entire year's lease . . ."

Calling himself Wells . . . be here tomorrow . . .

Kearny put his roll away and shook her hand heartily, a good loser. E. Dana Straub had a warm sweaty palm. Out in the smog-browned sunlight, he thought that the Gyppo had to be very good indeed to con that stainless-steel lady into nothing down, pay at the end of the week—when both he and his hustled TV sets would be gone and she'd be stuck with her remodel.

*　　*　　*

It had been a lousy day for Ephrem Poteet on the Universal Tour shuttle buses. Every woman he sized up had her purse zipped, every man had his wallet in his front pants pocket instead of on his hip, and none of the kids was bratty enough to give the natural diversions he needed while he made his dip.

A lousy day. Less than a hundred bucks in seven hours.

The trouble'd begun when he'd donned the maintenance uniform and lifted all those wallets that one afternoon. So much extra security as a result of it that he was reduced to working only two days a week; even then he'd had a couple of close calls and been saved only by his disguises. He'd given his big score to the ponies, and now was barely making the rent. Kearny's $100 a car was suddenly looking damned good.

*   *   *

As he thought that, Dan Kearny went into the Universal City Post Office across Lankershim from the studio to check through the semi-opaque window of Poteet's P.O. box. Not even junk mail. Already picked up today? Still, worth a shot now he was here; it was the only place he could make physical contact with his man.

Behind the counter was a strikingly handsome black man in postal uniform, likely an actor waiting to be discovered. Kearny gave him the used red window envelope with its canceled stamp. Inside was his blank sheet of letterhead, now with five $20 bills folded into it and Poteet's handwritten box address showing through the window.

"This was lying under the bank of boxes. Guy must have dropped it when he picked up his mail."

"Sure. Thanks. I'll put it right back."

Kearny went back outside and, sheltered from the hot sun by an overhanging tree, sat in the Cutlass to keep observation on the P.O. boxes through the big plate-glass window. If Poteet did come in to check his, being a Gypsy he would be sure to spot anyone hanging around in the post office lobby itself.

*   *   *

Leaving the special-effects demo without scoring yet again, Poteet felt sudden rage roil up inside. Tomeshti driving around in a new Caddy, him riding the stinking bus. Well, he had a line on three other cars besides the Seville, and over the next weeks he would feed them to DKA, hundred bucks a pop, getting even with goddam Yana for making all this necessary . . .

He left Universal through the Main Gate, just in case someone was lying in wait for him at the Studio Tour gate. Maybe he would get drunk tonight, get in a fight. Get the bastard on the ground, knee-drop him—you could crush a guy's ribs that way, even kill him. Yeah! Grrr! Everybody said the Gypsies were conmen, nonviolent—but he'd done a hard deuce at Walla Walla during which he'd learned a thing or two. He'd show 'em.

Goddam bus was just pulling away when he got out to the street. It figured. Another half-hour wait.

May as well check the P.O. box again even though he'd checked it this morning—Kearny might have sent his $100 same-day delivery or something.

*   *   *

To pass the time, Kearny was playing the guessing game about those entering the post office. Three beautiful women in their 20s—easy, actresses from Universal. An older woman with white hair and the bearing of a queen—director, perhaps? A white-haired southern colonel limping along with his gold-headed ebony cane—aging character actor in a TV mellerdrama. A couple of suits—had to be execs from the Black Tower.

But no Ephrem Poteet, Gypsy. Not coming tonight. Kearny'd hang on for another hour just to . . .

Flash of red! The envelope, please. Never would have taken the old Kentucky colonel for Poteet, must be running a scam. Looking quickly around the lobby—Kearny was glad he was outside in his car—then ripping open the red envelope. Taking out the sheet of letterhead, staring at the $100 folded inside . . . Pocketing it, quickly caning his way out of the building.

Kearny already had slid down in his seat so he was not visible over the dashboard. This guy was jumpy as a cat. Watched the angled rearview until the Gyppo's retreating back came into it. Shifted around, staying low in the seat until the bus came and Poteet boarded it.

Tailing a bus is not as easy as it might seem, not during rush hour. You can get blocked off by other cars, lose your man when he debarks. But Kearny was an old hand at it, so he was driving by

168

when Poteet walked into a run-down residence hotel on North Main not far from the old Union Station, was parked in a meter space across the street when Poteet emerged minus his disguise thirty minutes later.

He was sipping a draft three stools down when Poteet got into an argument over liar's dice and got 86'd from the first of several bars he visited that evening. After the third, Kearny dropped out to buy a cheap camera and film and find a motel for the night. He settled on the Sherman Oaks Inn on Ventura. He still didn't know what Poteet's scam was, didn't have any leverage on him yet. Which meant a busy day tomorrow.

He didn't bother to call the office. Nothing to report.

Yet.

CHAPTER
TWENTY-THREE

With Kearny gone off somewhere, Giselle had been stuck behind her desk all day. Now, 7:00 P.M., the after-school girls had abandoned the automatic typewriters, the skeleton night staff had arrived—and Giselle was *still* here. And cranky.

The limo outfit in L.A. hadn't called back. Dan Kearny hadn't called in, no idea where the big bum was. Ballard was probably playing footsie with his red-hot Gypsy mama and getting all sorts of hot leads, while Giselle hadn't even time to ask any hotels if they had an Angelo Grimaldi registered, or to check out who Theodore Winston White III in Marin might happen to be.

And on top of everything else, she still hadn't found a new cleaning service whose work she'd trust, and the scrap paper was piling up and . . . oh, to heck with it for tonight. She reached for her purse. Field men were in and out all night, but when she worked the office she liked to be gone before seven. As she stood up, her personal phone that didn't go through the switchboard rang. Kearny. Finally. She picked up.

"Dammit, Dan, where are—"

"Yeah, where the hell is he?" Stan Groner. Pissed.

"Stan!" She put delight and surprise in her voice. "You're working late. You want to talk with Dan? He just—"

"Don't try to con me, Giselle. He missed a ten o'clock this morning, and Jane said he's out of town. Now, where is—"

"Hot lead on the Gyppos," she ventured promptly.

"Hot?" he asked in a slightly mollified voice, then turned hard again. As hard as Stan could get. "It better be hot. I'm getting a lot of heat myself, from the president of the bank."

"Hey, we got three of them already, Stan. What do—"

"Three out of thirty-one." He became his old querulous self. "What'd you guys do to that one Ballard got, Giselle?"

Since the Sonia Lovari lead had been dug up by Ballard, he had been credited with the Allante.

"We . . . he got it in front of an Indian bar, Stan," she said over the clatter of auto typewriters in the big echoing room.

"*Indian* bar? The Gyppo sold it to an Indian?"

"No, no—her street scam is posing as an Indian. Collects for nonexistent Native American charities and keeps the money."

"Jesus!" Giselle could almost see him shaking his head. "If they'd put that much energy into working they'd be—"

"Yeah. Rich. But would they have so much fun?"

"Whose side are you on, anyway?"

"The side with the big bucks."

"Right answer," he chuckled. "Listen, I want to see Kearny here tomorrow morning, ten o'clock. I mean it, woman."

Giselle grimaced. She had put down her purse and gotten a cigarette lit while they had been talking.

"I'm not sure he'll make it, Stan. To tell the truth, we're not in communication with him right now. Will I do?"

"I wasn't a married man, I'd take that as a proposition."

"Sure you would," she said, and laughed.

Giselle liked Stan, a lot, and knew he would back them as far as he could with the other bank officials. In the midst of her warm thoughts about him, he ruined her evening.

"Remember that old black gal, Maybelle Pernod?"

"Sure, I repo'd her car and she redeemed and—"

"Pick it up again."

"What?" Giselle was shocked. She had sympathized with Maybelle on some deep level not available to her conscious mind. "As I remember it, Stan, the next payment isn't due until—"

"The bank's declaring the contract null and void. They want it picked up for charges. Repo on sight." He added almost defensively, "Dan told me she's living out of the darned thing, Giselle, hooking at night, for God's sake!"

"I know, I know, but I really like that old woman."

"You know? Why didn't I know? Repo on sight."

Giselle heaved a sad sigh as she dug out Maybelle's file and typed up a new REPO ON SIGHT for her. Legally, if a conditional auto sales contract had late or repo charges pending, it could be declared null and void and the car picked up. She stapled copies of all previous field and skip-tracing reports face-out to the back of the assignment sheet, then handwrote and stuck a yellow Post-it note on the sheet that Maybelle had been last seen walking the dog around Divisadero and Turk.

Giselle sighed, "Oh . . . *dammit*, anyway!" as she put the assignment into the deadly Ken Warren's In box.

* * *

Fat black Maybelle Pernod parked in the shadows near her usual fireplug on Turk Street, and, as usual, had herself a good despairing cry. Then she dried her tears and heaved her hefty body, sausaged into its red sequined dress, out of the car.

If she could turn just three tricks tonight on the front seat of the Lincoln, what with the piecework at the dry-cleaning plant and all, she'd have enough for the April 30 car note and wouldn't have to do no more whoring again until mid-May.

She hated it, but what choice did she have? Times was hard, she didn't have no skills, she was 61 years old, she couldn't lose her car, no place to sleep if she did, and no money to buy another one . . .

She took up her stroll in front of Red Hot Ribs. The gal on nights, Edwina, didn't never drop no dime on her to get her busted for soliciting. Back and forth through the puddle of muddy-yellow light, tempting smell of scorching meat and barbecue sauce from inside, light, voices, laughter, people in and out. Black people, her people, she didn't get much trade from them—look at her, look away. White boys, mostly. Lookin fo Mama.

*   *   *

Several hours after the office had closed for the night, Ken Warren arrived to rifle his In box for new assignments, closeouts, memos, and skip-trace reports on current cases. He went through them quickly, stopping at the new REPO ON SIGHT assignment on MAYBELLE PERNOD, res add unknown.

"Oh, hndammit, nhanywhay!" he exclaimed aloud when he saw her name on the case sheet.

*   *   *

Lord, Lord, nuthin ever seem to work out the way you want it to. Maybelle sang in a soft rich contralto:

> *"Nobody knows the trouble I've seen,*
> *Nobody knows but Jesus . . ."*

No action, none at all on the street tonight. The ribs joint had closed hours ago, she was all souls alone out here, her varicose veins hurt, and not a single trick to show for all the hours, not one, not even gas money. And no chance of any now. Not much traffic on the street, let alone pedestrians.

Time to drive down and park in her usual spot under the freeway off Alameda where a lot of other homeless gave safety in numbers. Get her shower in the morning at the cleaning plant . . .

A long-bed pickup pulled over to the curb and stopped. It had a camper on back and three white guys in the cab. The window was open.

"Hey, lookit the nigger cow," exclaimed a cracker voice right out of south Georgia.

She didn't turn her head, just quickened her pace for the corner of Turk. These men wasn't no tricks, she wouldn't get no money from them, just trouble. Just a few more steps . . . But the truck backed up to keep pace with her, rolling slowly, motor mumbling, exhaust rising in white puffs on the chilly night air.

"Hey, Mama, how about you do us right here on the street?"

She turned the corner. They were behind her now. But the pickup backed around the corner into Turk and kept on coming. For the first time since she had started hooking, she wished a cop

173

would cruise by. Wanted to run but she was too old, too fat, too scared. Besides, it was when the deer ran that the feral dogs chased it and dragged it down, any country gal knew that.

Squeerg of brakes. Creak of doors. Hurried heavy feet on the sidewalk. She speeded up. Get to her Connie, jump in sudden, they wouldn't expect that, slam the door, hit the automatic door lock . . . Safe then. Just a few more steps . . .

The three men were upon her, surrounding her. Tall men, two bulky, the third lean and athletic. Maybe she could still make it turn out right. Maybe they'd be satisfied with some head, specially she didn't charge. She found a pathetic simper.

"Ah . . . you gemp'men lookin' for a little fun?"

"Lookin' at you, Mama, I'd say a *lotta* fun!"

He wore a soiled white cowboy hat and a soiled expression on a heavy red face with burst capillaries in nose and cheeks. Probably weighed 250. He hefted one of her massive mammy breasts with one hand. His fingers had black hairs on the backs of them.

"Dug of the month!" he exclaimed.

He ripped her dress down off her shoulder, half baring one breast.

"Flavor of the month—chocolate!" exclaimed the Athlete, making slurping noises with his mouth. He had styled blond hair and a striking profile and a high skinny laugh. White shirt under a blue and white sweater, the collar points outside the sweater in Joe College style.

"In the truck," said Cowboy Hat.

"In the back—in the *camper*," amended the third.

He was very wide, weight-lifter shoulders and chest, day's growth of beard, grimy green gimme cap with a darker green shamrock on it, a black warm-up sweatshirt with the hood back. Fleshy nose, heavy lips, slitted mean angry eyes.

Maybelle felt herself shrinking, heard her own voice, little, as she'd been when, pigtails sticking straight out from the sides of her head, she'd been chased into the barn by some white boys . . .

The little voice said, "Please, don't . . . hurt me . . ."

But by now they were already guffawing and pinching and feeling and poking. Cowboy Hat grabbed her hand, tried to shove it down the front of his pants. Athlete came up behind her, put his hand up under her tight red split skirt.

"Into the fuckin' camper," he ordered.

Maybelle wanted to scream then, because she knew that if she got into that camper they would hurt her real bad 'fore they let her out again. As if in confirmation, Green Cap suddenly had a big bowie knife in his hand.

"Into the camper, bitch, or I'll . . ."

Just as suddenly he was gone. Flying, had to be almost a dreamy sensation. Except a lamppost was coming at him, coming at him hard, CRUNCH! face-first into the curved metal cylinder, fell in a heap on the sidewalk amid his sharded teeth.

Athlete whirled, nimble and quick, reaching into the cab for his baseball bat—but the big mean-looking mother with short-chopped brown hair slammed the door on his wrist. He started screaming, high and thin like a grammar-school girl finding a snake in her bed.

The attacker picked up the bowie knife. Cowboy Hat ran, so fast his ten-gallon Stetson flew off and landed in the gutter. He was bald under it, somehow vulnerable without it.

The big mean-looking dude stood on the hat, ripped it in half with the knife, but let the man go. Maybelle was glad. She couldn't take no more people gettin' hurt, not even bad people.

Totally ignoring the fallen warriors, the man smashed in the windows of the pickup with the baseball bat, slashed all four tires with the bowie knife—in this part of town, no windows would go up, no police patrols would come.

Finally, he reached in and twitched out the keys to drop them and the knife down the nearest sewer grating. Then he came back to Maybelle and looked her up and down, thoroughly and unhurriedly, taking in her tight red sequins and too much lipstick and breast half-exposed by the torn dress.

Only then did he yell at her.

"Gnew awtta nbe hathamed!"

Ken Warren took off his tan corduroy jacket and draped it around her shoulders. Maybelle couldn't quit crying. She *was* ashamed, and terrified, and knew God had let him see her like this as punishment for what she was doing to keep her big fancy prideful Continental.

*   *   *

Warren drove the company car in on Post toward the Tenderloin with Maybelle sobbing beside him on the front seat as if her heart would break. He looked glumly over at her.

175

"Nthtop nhat!" he finally ordered.

Maybelle seemed to have no difficulty in understanding him. She reduced the crying to sniveling, then stopped altogether.

"Where you be takin' me?" she asked in a small voice.

His apartment, that's where, he told her. He'd just moved in last week, had this new good job so he was out all hours, anyway, looking for people, cars, how'd she think he'd found her? She could sleep there until she got something better.

"Lord, Lord, child, how'm I gonna get somethin' better?" she asked him, the tears coming again. "Ah cain't . . ."

She fell silent. She'd raised her son Jedediah without a man to home, raised him, as he'd always said with laughing eyes, with the Bible in one hand and the hairbrush in the other. Then God had forsaken her, and killed him. Killed her son. Her Jeddie gone, and her still here. Lord, Lord, it wasn't fair.

"Takin people's cars," she said finally. "Whut sorta job is that to—"

"Mbesth tI've never ntad," said Warren.

At his apartment over a liquor store he made her some soup, made up the couch for himself while she drank it, then got her into his bed when she started falling asleep spoon in hand.

Maybelle's last thought before going down, down into sleep between those clean, cool sheets, was that she knew, deep inside her secret heart, that Kenny'd been sent by God because Jesus was giving her one more chance to repent.

Then she was snoring, out cold, not even any REM going on behind her eyelids. Ken Warren shut the bedroom door quietly, tiptoed out of the apartment, and drove back out to the Fillmore to repossess her Lincoln Continental for the bank.

No more of that streetwalking shit for Jedediah's mother, even though his buddy was eighteen, no, nineteen long years dead in the jungles of Vietnam.

CHAPTER
TWENTY-FOUR

The aging rock musician bore the stylized stigmata of his tribe: a Gibson slung down his back on a worn leather strap; a bright felt-covered baseball-style cap loaded with glittery beads bill-backward on his shoulder-length hair; leather vest with more beads, big brass belt buckle of crossed miniature wheel lock pistols, faded jeans with the knees out, black scuffed combat boots. Obligatory shades.

"You see that there big ape?" he demanded of a little girl at the King Kong exhibit. "My daddy caught him for me."

The little girl's eyes got very big. She had blond hair and a gap in front where two teeth should have been. She lisped in wonder, "For *you?*"

He pulled the guitar around and strummed a simple chord progression and sang in a flat Bob Dylan sort of voice:

> "*Big ole ape, apin' on a vine,*
> *My daddy caught him, made 'im mine.*
> *Swingin' away in his jungle gym,*
> *What you gonna feed 'im—*
> ANYTHING HE WANTS!*"

The mother, who thought he was part of the entertainment, laughed at his shouted last line as he lost his balance and steadied himself against her and lifted her wallet. The long drought was over. The Rock Musician, one of Poteet's most potent personae, was scoring like the Golden State Warriors.

But when he was about to put the wallet back into her purse, some old grey-haired geek with a big jaw wanted to take their picture in front of the ape.

"Hey, sure, that's great, man," he mumbled, thinking, Get outta my face, geek, or I'll knee-drop you for sure.

But, ever alert, he used the photo opportunity to slip the wallet back into the woman's handbag—minus a couple of twenties, of course. The grey-haired guy ended up sitting next to him on the bus, real talkative and a real bug with that camera, *click, click, click,* all the damned time.

"My grandchildren are coming out from back east next week." The old geek's smile lit up a rather hard and heavy face. "So many things to do while they're here, my wife sent me out on a little recon mission so we don't miss anything."

"Recon . . . that like a scoutin' trip, Dad?"

"Very like," agreed the grey-haired man solemnly.

He took so many pictures of everything and everybody that pretty soon Poteet sort of forgot he was there.

Click, click, click!

*   *   *

Up in the Bay Area, Eli Nicholas hauled the backseat out of the brand-new Fleetwood limo. Unlike Poteet, Nicholas absolutely would have known what a recon was, and actually did play the guitar professionally: on the weekends he strummed wild Gypsy tunes for a group of *gadje* amateur flamenco dancers in a neighborhood bar on El Cerrito's San Pablo Avenue. He was a slight swarthy man with a lined joyful face and strong fingers callused by three decades on the strings.

During Vietnam those hands had learned another trade, one that led him to now have both back doors of the Fleetwood limo open and the backseat out on the concrete. Midday of a midweek workday, most of the parking slots under his Richmond apartment building were empty. The deserted area, backed by a high wooden

178

fence, was well-hidden from the street. The afternoon was balmy, so both men, in work pants and shirt sleeves, were sweating lightly from pulling out the seat.

"Why under the backseat?" asked Rudolph Marino.

"It's under where *he* would sit," said Nicholas patiently.

Fact was, Marino was shook-up, nervous, a state of mind so foreign to him it was like a fever in his brain making it not work right. His biggest score, sure—but he only wanted to con some people, he didn't want to blow them up.

From a cardboard box with a construction company's logo on it, Nicholas was taking a foot-square sheet of whitish putty-like substance a quarter inch thick and backed with adhesive strips.

Marino asked almost shrilly, "What's that?"

"Sheet C-4." Nicholas said it casually as he was peeling away the protective layer from the adhesive.

"C-4? *Plastique?*"

"Yeah. *Plastique.* Ninety percent RDX, the most powerful chemical-composition explosive known, ten percent inert binders so it can be pressed into sheets like this here."

He got into the back of the limo with the square of stolen explosive and, with the flat of one hand, began pounding the square casually down into place on the contoured metal floor where the seat would fit back in.

"*Careful!*" yelped Marino.

Nicholas ignored him to finish, then got back out of the car to squint at him through habitual cigarette smoke.

"Before we put the seat back in, I'll push an electrical blasting cap down into the C-4. We'll use a radio transmitter to detonate. When you want it to go off, you just attach a radio receiver preset to a certain band to the cap's wires. You'll have a pocket radio transmitter with you, so you just—"

"What if somebody else has a transmitter set to that band?"

"They won't, but anyway, you connect the receiver to the blasting cap at the last second—in the garage. Then get behind a pillar and turn on your transmitter and . . ." He suddenly threw his arms wide with a joyful laugh, "POOF!"

*   *   *

PLOP!

The broken egg had slid down the curved side of the mixing bowl just a split second before something small and dark and gleaming and hunched dropped in after it.

"No," said Ramon Ristick, "too slow. Way too slow."

Yana fished the little dark gleaming pellet-like object out and palmed it. When she destroyed the next egg, the black object fell so smoothly that it landed in the bowl to glisten evilly up through the yolk as if it had preceded it.

"Perfect," pronounced Ramon.

Yana broke another egg. "It has to be perfect *every* time."

Ristik, watching her practice in glum silence, suddenly said, "I didn't like what happened to Sonia's Allante."

"That was Rudolph's fault. I had to give Sonia to the *gadjo* after Rudolph threatened us . . ."

PLOP! Perfect yet again.

"He'll know it was you told the *gadjo* where to look."

"Maybe he'll blame Ephrem again," she said indifferently.

After two more, they scrambled and ate the eggs she had been practicing with, discussing when and with what trappings of the occult—and speculating for how much—they would work the poisoned-egg effect on Theodore Winston White. The Third.

* * *

Even from the outside, Theodore Winston White III's house looked to Giselle like something out of Hammett's "The Gutting of Couffignal." Part stone, part wood, probably twenty-five to thirty rooms, three stories on grounds that were a wilderness of native California trees and shrubs able to thrive despite the now-broken drought.

Giselle had driven up a winding drive to the top of a Tiburon hill and climbed the broad stone stairway to the hardwood door. She banged the iron gargoyle-face knocker and turned away to look at the City, rising from the far side of the sparkling bay like a misplaced Camelot: distance lent it a bogus charm absent in close-up.

When the door was opened by a slender blond chap in his 30s, a big tiger-stripe tomcat scooted out between his legs and bounded off down the steps.

"It's okay," he said quickly, "he does it all the time."

There was a moment of silence. Once the office-work crunch had eased, Giselle had been in a great hurry to follow up on her anonymous phone caller's lead. So she had gotten White's address from the tax assessor's office at the Marin Civic Center, and had driven directly here without even phoning ahead. She had not even formulated a plan of attack or worked out her cover story.

So she cleared her throat and said, "Ah . . . I'm looking for Theodore Winston White the Third."

"That's me. Teddy White."

"This might sound a little strange, but do you perchance know any Gypsies?"

His slightly too close-set eyes lit up. "Madame Miseria's incredible, you know. She's changing my life."

It all fell into place. Madame Miseria. Ballard's Yana, the Gypsy fortune-teller. Giselle's anonymous caller obviously was some Gyppo opposed to Yana. Giselle smiled. Brilliantly. The kind of smile men felt all the way down to their toes.

"Mr. White, I'd love to drive you down into town and buy you an espresso," she said.

*   *   *

Drinking muddy Turkish coffee in the office, Wasso Tomeshti could see his sister and mother and two cousins feeding the shopping frenzy surrounding his purloined color TVs. He'd priced the sets for quick cash sales, so was also collecting and pocketing the 7.25% sales tax to help offset the bargain prices.

Wasso figured he had today and tomorrow before some officious bureaucrat came around asking to see his sales permits; so tomorrow he'd give E. Dana Straub her check and pack up his remaining sets and move on—to be gone by the time it bounced. No sweat about Sam Hood's check bouncing—Hood didn't know where to find him anyway. Life was good.

"Mr. Adam Wells?"

Tomeshti looked up from his paperwork—bogus optional service guarantees on the sets, also paid to him in cash—into cold grey eyes above a granite jaw. Cop face. But they couldn't have got on to his scam yet, so . . .

So he said, "That's me, King of the Cash Sale—"

181

The guy shook his head. "No. A Gyppo named Wasso Tomeshti." He showed some I.D. "Private detective." He held out his hand. "The keys to the Seville, Gyppo."

The coin dropped. Yana's call warning him that some P.I. might have a line to their Caddies. He was unworried. He was a big man, heavy-waisted and four inches taller than the square, grey-haired man's five-nine. Never actually violent, but this *gadjo* couldn't know that. He came around the counter.

"You better get to hell out of here, pal, before I . . ."

Hard-face merely picked up the phone and tapped out a number with such confidence that Tomeshti waited just too long.

"Yeah, gimme Sergeant Block in Bunco." He listened to the canned voice saying, *At the tone*, *Pacific Daylight Saving time will be*, then said, "Larry? Dan Kearny here. I'm at . . ."

Tomeshti's thick fingers depressed the hooks on the phone. Kearny laid those cold grey eyes on him once more.

"And my next call, Tomeshti, is to the guy you conned out of those three hundred TV sets."

Kearny didn't know if Tomeshti had conned the sets out of anybody or not, but it was a safe bet—and conmen were easily conned. Tomeshti slid the Seville keys across the counter.

Saying, "Goddam you," in a heartfelt voice.

He followed Kearny silently out through the bedlam of the store, careful to arouse no hot-blooded *rom* hostility against him: what if the guy *wasn't* bluffing? Sam Hood was the kind of man would live up to his name if he knew he'd been ripped off.

Wasso had left the Seville parked out in front as a sort of advertisement. Kearny opened the trunk and curbside doors.

"Please remove your personal possessions from the car."

"Hey, listen, can't we—"

"No." Flat voice. No give. No leeway. "Just do it."

Kearny watched as Tomeshti put his personal gear in a rather messy pile on the curb. Prospective customers were starting to gather around and watch also, highly diverted. In that neighborhood, repos were no novelty.

Wasso's beautiful Seville pulled away, the radio blaring golden oldies. He turned sadly back to the store—and stopped dead. Facing him was brass-haired E. Dana Straub.

She bared all those teeth in a supposed smile. "I need the year's lease payment in cash right now, Mr. Wells, instead of a check tomorrow," she said with transparent ferocity.

Aw, *hell*.

* * *

Giselle Marc, back from Marin only twenty minutes ago, dropped the receiver onto the hooks and leaned back in her creaking swivel chair to slam a fist against her thigh in delight.

"*Yes!*" she exclaimed.

Still no callback from the limo people in L.A., but *whammo!* the St. Mark, the very first hotel she'd called (she'd had to start somewhere), had turned up an Angelo Grimaldi registered in one of their penthouse suites.

A day or two, scout his scam, take him down. But before that, using the wealth of information Teddy White, that sweet, simple, confused little rich boy, had just given her without knowing it, she'd take down his incredible Madame Miseria.

Yeah, she'd show Yana she couldn't take Larry away from . . .

No, wait a minute, that was nonsense. This was strictly business. This was about purloined Cadillacs, not men.

Dammit, it *was*.

* * *

When the dice passed to Ephrem Poteet, he could feel a jolt like electricity run up his arm. He'd picked it up in the joint, had come to like it. And he just knew he was hot tonight.

"I shoot twenty," he said. "Look out there, gimme room."

Seven. He scooped up crumpled bills.

"Read 'em and weep, boys."

The "boys" were another Gypsy and six *gadje*—three blacks, a Mexican, an Anglo, a Chinese—all of them in a closed poolhall on run-down Temple near Beaudry Ave. Poteet again rolled the dice out across one of the green felt tables.

"Gimme the news. Don't hold nothing back!"

The dice bounced off Robert Byrnes's classic, *Standard Book of Pool and Billiards*, resting on edge inside the far end of the table as a backstop, and tumbled to the felt showing two twos.

"Twenty says I can do it!"

He was covered. Rolled a nine.

183

"The point is four," he chanted. He rolled again. "C'mon, little Black Joe. Hah! See that? I shoot the roll."

The side bets were getting fierce. He rolled. Five.

"Feevy's the point—fever in the south. I'm coming out."

He came out. And sevened out.

Next point, eighter from Decatur.

Snake eyes. Crapped out.

And crapped out again . . . and again . . . and . . .

*   *   *

"Goddammit!" Ephrem Poteet muttered to himself.

He was trying to sober up (black coffee and chili dogs slathered with relish) in a little white tile, chrome and glass all-night hot-dog joint on Hollywood Boulevard. At the next table was a burly bearded man with a knitted cap pulled down over his ears and wearing heavy skiing mittens, reading that day's *L.A. Times* through sunglasses. Behind the counter was a soft-eyed Iranian who looked about 12 years old except for a fierce black mustache and a scar running down one side of his face from below his eye to the collar of his shirt. The place smelled of fried onions and dead hot dogs and stale coffee and sour milk.

The chili dogs and coffee weren't working. Or were working too well. Poteet was coming down and didn't want to. In the crap game he'd lost his case money, the day's take from Universal, and the $100 in the mail from DKA the night before.

Goddammit.

A stack of photographs was slapped down to splay out across the shiny red Formica tabletop. Photos shot at Universal that very morning. He was in every one of them, every time with his hand in somebody else's pocket or pocketbook. The voice jerked his eyes up to the man just settling down across from him.

"I turn these over to the cops, Poteet, and it won't be back to T.I. for another vacation. It'll be serious time upstate at Q for you, pal."

The grey-haired old camera freak from Universal! Poteet half started from his chair. He'd knock the bastard down, knee-drop him to smash in his goddam ribs, snatch the photos . . .

"I wouldn't," said the man in a disinterested voice.

Poteet already knew he wouldn't. He never did. Women, yeah.

Them he could hit. Them he could beat up. But other men . . .
He always *thought* he would, but when it was down-and-dirty in
some alley . . . or in some Hollywood hot-dog joint . . .

He sat down again, heavily. He never had any luck. "Aw, Jesus
Christ!" he moaned in disgust, almost to himself.

"No. Dan Kearny."

Dan Kearny! During the years he'd been selling information to
Dan Kearny over the phone, and hearing stories about him, the
man had assumed almost legendary status in his mind. Kearny had
once found a relative of Poteet's hiding in Palm Springs under her
brother's wife's maiden name.

The capped and gloved man at the next table suddenly heaved
himself to his feet, glaring at them, and stalked away to a farther
table muttering, "Goddam zoo at feeding time!" Kearny was picking
up the photos and stuffing them into his inside jacket pocket. He
tapped the pocket.

"These were just to get your attention—*if* you give me everything you have or can get on those Gyppo Cadillacs. Right now.
Without stringing it out or getting tricky with me."

"And you want it all for free," said Poteet bitterly.

"No, our original terms stand. What I want it, is NOW."

Hey, maybe there were angles to be worked here. He drank
coffee, tried to figure percentages . . . and tried to meet those
bleak eyes. No. Too much danger in them. As if to confirm it,
Kearny again tapped the picture pocket suggestively.

Poteet sighed. "How'd you make out with Tomeshti?"

"In the barn."

Of course. He wouldn't have expected anything less from Dan
Kearny. He leaned forward across the table, his decision made.
Play it straight all the way. Dump the bag for Kearny and get more
for him later. And *from* him. Hell, at $100 a car, Ephrem Poteet
would make out all right.

"Okay. Seattle. Chicago. And tomorrow right here in Beverly
Hills."

CHAPTER
TWENTY-FIVE

It was midmorning of the next day. O'B drove his company car sedately along Bayshore Boulevard. At the foot of Geneva was the railroad siding from whence, if the circus was in town, elephants would parade trunk-and-tail, trunk-and-tail, all the way up to the Cow Palace from the Barnum & Bailey train.

O'B loved the circus. But he wasn't after elephants today.

Gyppo Cadillacs. In fact, one particular hypothetical Gyppo Cadillac O'B had deduced was out there in the same way that an astronomer who sees there isn't anything in a particular patch of space deduces it is holding a black hole.

The trail had been tortuous, but then O'B had a tortuous sort of mind. His last two days had been spent chasing a set of assumptions that went something like this: (1) since the Gyppos who had conned the $5,000 check out of Doc Swigart had then (2) turned around and blackmailed him into giving them (3) the medical documentation needed for storefront phone rooms from which (4) the Cadillac scam had been worked, then (5) it stood to reason that these same Gyppos already would have ended up with (6) one of the purloined Cadillacs as a reward. Right? Right.

That was the Cadillac O'B wanted.

First, he'd gone back up to Sonoma yet again to talk with the soils engineer named Oleson who owned that old Stampe biplane the Gyppos had so blithely sold to Rob Swigart. Oleson, alas, had never laid eyes on them so he couldn't confirm Swigart's description. But the kid who pumped gas for the airplanes maybe had and maybe could. At least he remembered a swarthy man and woman hanging around for a couple of days and driving an old car.

Aha! An old car! Please, let the kid be a car freak.

He was. Rusty old '74 Plymouth Road Runner, green, with a wide flash running back from the headlights along the side under and then up behind the window to the roof. O'B remembered those Road Runners—he'd picked up enough of them for Fellaro Dodge/ Plymouth/Chrysler on Geary Boulevard during their heyday.

He dared barely whisper it: license number, maybe?

And would you believe, the kid had a partial plate because it wore the same digits as the license on his Harley: 444.

Of course just the digits, without the letters, were useless, because there had to be about a zillion different three-letter combinations on California license plates ending in 444.

Dead end in Sonoma. But what about San Francisco? The reluctant Doc Swigart should have gotten back his canceled $5,000 check by this time.

Swigart, now that O'B wasn't *really* a P.U.C. investigator, didn't want to cooperate. O'B picked up the phone to call the worthy doctor's wife and tell her all about how stupid her husband had been. Then, like magic, Swigart managed to dig out the canceled check.

Used to open an account (closed again as soon as the check had cleared) at an American West Bank on Geneva Ave near the Cow Palace. The check endorsed on the back with, and the account briefly opened in the name of . . . *Tucon Yonkovich!*

A *Gypsy name.* Could Tucon be guilty of one of those gaffes even the best occasionally make when dealing with doctors—whose credulity is legend among conmen because they believe they can never be wrong? Could Tucon have chanced his *real* name because he needed the check to clear before it could be stopped?

O'B stayed on the line while SRS in Sacramento computer-checked DMV records for possible driver's license and auto registration data linking Yonkovich, Tucon, with a 1974 Plymouth Road

Runner whose plate ended in 444. Yeah! Tucon had been thusly stupid. Such a car was registered to him in the 300 block of Oriente, Daly City—which O'B knew lay just south of the San Mateo County line near the Cow Palace. As the bank where Tucon Yonkovich had cashed Swigart's check was near the Cow Palace.

By now the Road Runner doubtless had been sold to somebody in a bar; but eventually the Caddy should turn up at that address.

* * *

A wrecking crew was tearing down an old white frame house in the 300 block of Oriente. For one dismal moment O'B feared it was *his* house: the subject address. No. Four doors away. And squatting right on the subject address was a new Eldorado two-door notchback with paper plates. What could be sweeter?

O'B, pulses quickening though he'd done this thousands of times, parked his company car around the corner and got out with his ring of keys coded to all of the Gyppo Cadillacs.

The Eldorado was unlocked with the driver's-side window down. O'B began running his keys, not even bothering to shut the door—the window was frozen open until he found the right key, anyway. Besides, Gyppos were talkers, not fighters, and O'B figured he could hold his own with any talker who ever lived.

Missed the right key on his first hurried run-through. He patiently started back at the front of the ring.

"HEY, WHADDA FUCK YOU DOIN' IN MY CAR?"

O'B looked up through the windshield at the man bearing down on him, and his airy quips in response—having a picnic, flying to St. Louis, like that—died on his lips.

Because this wasn't just a Gyppo, this was, for God's sake, Paul Bunyan! Seven feet tall and three wide, black curling beard, black curling hair, snapping black eyes, wearing a red plaid lumberjack shirt with the sleeves rolled up almost to the shoulders and even carrying an axe in one hand.

Well, a sledgehammer, really, but at a time like this who the hell cared?

O'B frantically worked his keys, at the same time calling, *"From the bank, from the bank, about your auto loa—"*

The sledgehammer came whistling in an arc through the open window at his head, wielded by a Schwarzenegger arm lumped and knotted with muscle. O'B ducked; as the sledge took out the windshield from the inside, he threw himself across the soft leather seat, jerked the door handle, and slid headfirst out the far side of the car as the huge man grunted with the effort of his next swing. This one knocked the door off the glove box an inch behind O'B's departing right heel.

O'B ran around to the front of the car, held up a placating palm. His other hand rested on the hood of the car.

"You don't understand! I'm from the bank. I'm not a car thief, I'm the legal repre—"

The sledge smashed in the hood where his hand had been a moment before. He ran back around to the driver's side as his pursuer yelled, "You sonna beech, I gonna *kill* you!"

Jesus, that huge guy was fast. O'B fled down the side of the car with Paul Bunyan tight behind. Swinging.

CRUNCH! Driver's door.

SMASH! Rear door.

THUD! Trunk lid.

O'B was able to dive back in through the rider's side to get in a couple of twists with the next key because the sledge stuck for a moment in the hole it made in the trunk. The next blow just missed his ankle and demolished the Eldorado's C/D player and tape deck as O'B dove out again.

Going around the front of the car as the big guy came out the driver's side, yelling, *"Gypsies are supposed to be nonviolent!"*

Paul Bunyan paused to rip out the front seat and throw it across the street.

"I'll GYPSY YOU, BASTARD SONNA BEECH . . ."

As O'B ran yet again, the sledge smashed in the headlights and grille. Back through the car, twist another key, *the motor started*, leave the key there, out again, run around it again, there went a hubcap wobbling away across the street, a blow at his legs took out the muffler. Back inside, slapped it into gear, crouched in the bare space behind the wheel, *goosed* it.

Gimpy-gimpy jerk-jerk but fast, must have bent an axle somehow, goddamnedest Gypsy he'd ever . . .

"*KILLYOUKILLYOUKILLYOUKILL YOU* KILL . . . YOU . . . KILL . . . YOU . . . KILL . . . . YOU . . . . *kill* . . . . . *you* . . . . . kill . . . . . ."

THUDS, CRASHES, CRUNCHES as Paul Bunyan ran alongside belaboring the Eldorado with his hammer. O'B finally began pulling away. Just as he reached the corner, Paul Bunyan threw the sledge after him, SMASH, there went the rear window . . .

Safely away.

*   *   *

Jackson B. Gideon, president of California Citizens Bank, had a poor big devil of a stomach that, like Cyrano's nose, marched on before him by a quarter of an hour. He also had John L. Lewis eyebrows crawling like hairy caterpillars around the top of his face, a beaked fleshy nose, pouting lips Sly Stallone would have killed for, and two chins with a third working on its growth portfolio. He splayed out of his dove-grey wool double-breasted suit the way a sausage splays out when you cut its skin.

"It just won't do," he said. "It just won't do at all."

They were in the bank's cul-de-sac storage lot behind an old factory backed up against the base of Telegraph Hill. Ballard, whose butt still hurt and who thought he was there to be praised for his good work, not reamed out by a bank president, started to speak—but Stan Groner cut in smoothly.

"Well, J.B., they *did* recover the car under very difficult conditions, and—"

"And the city wants to bring suit against the bank."

Ballard was astounded. "What the hell for?"

"New door for the precinct house," explained Stan. "New light fixture. New front steps. New balustrade. New—"

"They were trying to kill me, for God sake!"

"Would have been cheaper if they had," sniffed J.B.

Not that the bank had any intention of paying the city one red cent—J.B. had elucidated the policy at that day's board meeting—but field men had to be kept firmly in their place.

He added in disdain, "Since it occurred in the course of a recovery action by Daniel Kearny Associates, I feel that the costs should come out of your company's recompense."

"Now just a damned . . ."

Stan Groner caught Ballard's eye and shook his head slightly. Ballard stopped talking, face rich with unspent anger. Gideon, that smug bastard, had never been out in the field in his life, what did he know?

Stan had once been the same way. But they'd gotten him liquored up at one of Kearny's infamous spaghetti feeds, and had taken him out on a salty repo in the Hunter's Point housing projects, where a favorite sport at the time had been shooting windows out of Muni buses. Sitting behind the wheel, Bart Heslip had read the repo's operating manual aloud to Groner by dashlight, hoping to find out how to release the handbrake, while the registered owner had been running upstairs for his shotgun.

They had made it away with nothing worse than a trunk lid full of buckshot, but Stan had been on their side ever since. Even now he was trying to pour oil on the troubled waters.

"I'm sure this sort of thing won't happen again, J.B. Gypsies are nonviolent creatures who . . ."

His voice was drowned out by a terrible racket echo-chambered and amplified by the sounding-board walls of the deserted factory. RATTLE! of loose tinwork, COUGH! of ruptured muffler, SCRAPE! of rubber on pounded-in fenders, BANG! of misfiring engine, THUNK-THUNK of flattening tire.

All eyes turned toward the cacophony of noises coming their way; all breaths were bated. Somehow, all three of them knew.

Yes. Oh yes indeed. O'B. In a brand-new Eldorado.

Brand-new? But how could this be? Fenders smashed in, a tire flat. The top was crushed down to the window tops, the windshield was gone, the door panels were pounded in, the trunk was flattened, the hood was history, the grille was gone, various fluids dripped as smoke rose from both ends of the car.

O'B stepped gently on the brakes as he came up level with them. The engine died with a *pop, pop, grunt, grunt, poof* . . . silence. He had found a plastic bucket somewhere to upend where once the sleekly upholstered seat had been, and was hunkered down on it, under the flattened roof, as he drove the car. He shoved a shoulder against the door to open it. The door fell off with an agonized CLANK! of overstressed metal.

Totaled.

O'B stepped out and said jauntily to Stan, "The lighter still works, Reverend."

"But . . . but . . . but . . . this . . . this can't be . . . be . . . one of *ours* . . . ," Groner managed to stammer out.

"It can. It is. He beat it to death trying to get me."

"Gypsies are nonviolent," snapped J.B. in his nastiest give-the-teller-hell voice.

Stan the Man wilted into Stan the Boy. Ballard turned red trying to keep from laughing. O'B, who had made out a condition report when he had stopped to get the plastic bucket seat, held the completed form out to J.B. Gideon with a straight face.

"If you'll just sign for it, Reverend, I'll be on my way."

Gideon stared at him with real hatred, then turned to Stan the Boy. "I will expect you in my office in sixty minutes, Mr. Groner," he said thickly. "We have a great deal to discuss."

He stalked unevenly away across the rubble-strewn storage lot. Stan ran after him for a few paces, but Gideon was already in his Lexus LS400 and slamming the door with eloquent rage. The car sped off. Stan turned blindly back to O'B, who was laughing, and Ballard, who was too solemnly checking the car's serial number against his list of the Gypsy cars' I.D. numbers.

"I'm ruined," groaned Groner.

O'B guffawed and shoved the condition report under his nose. Stan started to automatically scrawl his signature across the bottom of it, but Ballard held up a detaining hand.

They both turned to look at him.

"What?" demanded O'B a bit shrilly. The expression on Ballard's face had made the laughter die on his lips.

Ballard waved an airy hand at the Cadillac. "This isn't one of our Gyppo cars. Its I.D. number isn't on our list."

O'B turned bone white. His freckles looked like measles against that suddenly ashen skin. "But . . . it has to be . . ."

"Okay, you've had your fun," said Groner. "Now go *give the man back his car*—and get me the right one. Right away. Reverend." Then Stan the Man started an ugly chortling sound.

He was laughing.

CHAPTER TWENTY-SIX

Dona Dulcinea Inez Mattheu Duchez Escobar, incredibly beautiful and incredibly wealthy Brazilian coffee heiress—recently widowed—passed through the gilt-edged motor-driven plate-glass door of *bascom's (rome, london, paris, amsterdam, beverly hills)*. Even in parlous economic times, these first few blocks of Rodeo Drive north of Wilshire in Beverly Hills are . . . well, Rodeo Drive. Occasionally Worth Avenue in Palm Beach *pretends* to the crown, but . . . after all, Florida . . .

The diminutive button-eyed youth behind Dona Dulcinea wore the Beverly Wilshire's distinctive livery and was festooned with boxes: square boxes, oblong boxes, oval boxes, boxes large and boxes small, boxes flat and boxes deep, boxes broad and boxes skinny. All bearing labels from the most exclusive shoppes and boutiques up and down Rodeo Drive.

"My hotel has call," announced Dona Dulcinea imperiously.

Her hotel hadn't, but nonetheless Monsieur Bascom himself surged forward with her entrance, practiced eye agleam at the compulsive-shopper possibilities suggested by all those boxes.

"Ah, yes, of course, Madam . . ."

"*Dona* Dulcinea Inez Mattheu Duchez Escobar of São Paulo.

193

Brazil." Her accent made "Bretheel" of the final word. Monsieur
Bascom inclined his beautifully greyed *coiffeur* as she added,
"Someone should help the . . ." She gestured helplessly at the
bellhop. "Mmmm, how you say, young servant man . . ."

M. Bascom was already snapping his fingers without looking
around. He had a patrician face with a thin nose pinched at the
sides, and thin lips that could by a sycophantic pucker become a
rosebud or by simple compression a white line of fury.

"Could the word be 'bellhop,' madam?"

"*Sim!* Bellhop! The hotel has give . . ." She broke off, looking
extremely sexy as she almost giggled. "No, has *lend* me the bellhop
to help with my . . ." She rolled around the word on her tongue.
". . . mmm, buying. You sell diamonds, *não?*"

"Yes, of course. We sell . . . *diamonds.*"

Bascom gave the final word the reverence usually reserved for all
the names of God. His snapped fingers had brought a magnificent
salesman to help the bellboy jettison all those boxes as M. Bascom
led the fair Dulcinea to the gleaming glass cases where *bascom's*
most stunning creations dwelt in luxury.

"If one could inquire as to madam's diamond needs . . ."

Again that charming almost half-giggle. "I no really know . . .
but I weel when I see!" Her eyes got very wide and round and her
mouth formed a lovely little "O." "But whatever you show me
must be most . . . tasteful. Nothing, mmm . . . vulgar, *não?* The
absolute . . . how does one say . . ."

"*Crème de la crème?*" suggested Bascom.

"*Sim. Exactissimo.*"

Bascom had little Spanish and less Portuguese, so he found himself utterly charmed by Dona Dulcinea's accent as she went through
thirty minutes of brooches, earrings, and necklaces "not quite
right" for her needs. Of course, since he had an addiction to scoring
sexually with wealthy women no matter what their age or looks, he
was already in thrall to the Dona's bounteous feminine charms.
Finally, he suggested that if she could perhaps tell him the occasion
she sought to enhance with diamonds . . .

Sim, but could she have a glass of Pellegrino, perhaps . . . ver'
hot in here . . .

Refreshed and restored, she explained that it was a little—pronounced "leetle"—somet'ings for her first dinner party at the *haci-*

enda since the death . . . close to tears here . . . of her beloved "hoosban'" eighteen months before . . .

Dwelling on this untimely death made her feel "a leetle faint" again, but she recovered quickly when he showed her loose teardrop diamonds set in gold which could be worn as singlets, clustered as a pendant, worn around the neck on a gold chain . . .

Yes! Dona Dulcinea's interest quickened at the sight of them.

For some time the bored bellhop had been following them around the store, staring at the wonders being displayed, but unfortunately was just too far away to help catch Dona Dulcinea when she swooned and fell heavily against M. Bascom.

As her unexpected dead weight bore Bascom to the floor, her hand struck the edge of the velvet display tray upon which the diamonds nestled. Teardrops flew in every direction. Before the salespeople could converge, the bellhop was crouched beside her, mouth working as in distress, cradling her head with his hands.

He gulped back tears. Immediately, her beautiful dark eyes fluttered open and she gazed deep into M. Bascom's blue ones.

"I am so ver' sorree," she said in a little voice. The eyelids fluttered again. "The loss . . . of my hoosban' . . . sometime it has seem . . . I cannot . . . go on . . ."

More Pellegrino, a few minutes in a brocaded chair by the office, and Dona Dulcinea was much restored. But too upset to, mmm, how you say, do more shop today. For now, she would return to the Beevairly Weelsheer to rest . . .

Without qualms, M. Bascom led her solicitously to the door. One teardrop was missing, a stone valued at $7,000, but she could not have taken it. She was, after all, very wealthy in her own right; and she had been in her swoon at the very moment the diamonds had become vulnerable. Staff was still looking, probably it had rolled under some distant display case . . .

Dona Dulcinea gave M. Bascom her hand to kiss and flashed her big round eyes at him. "If it is not found by tomorrow when I return, I mus' pay for the diamon' who is missing!"

"No need, madam," said Bascom gallantly. "It will turn up."

"But I insist—and I have just decide. Tomorrow, I weel buy *ten* of the teardrops!"

At the curb was her beautiful cream and grey Fleetwood Sixty Special four-door sedan. A grey-haired heavy-jawed man, obviously her hired driver, was doing something under the dash. But as Bascom reached out to open the door for the *dona,* the man started the Caddy and accelerated away into traffic without a backward turn of his head.

Leaving Bascom on the curb with his hand outstretched and his mouth, for once, hanging open in utter astonishment. He turned to Dona Dulcinea for enlightenment, and was even more astounded to see the Brazilian heiress running out into Rodeo Drive, skirts flying, face contorted, vapors forgotten.

"You son of a bitch!" the *dona* screamed after the departing Fleetwood. "I know who you are, faggot repo bastard! I curse your eyes and the eyes of your children! I spit into . . ."

Dona Dulcinea caught herself, realizing the figure she was cutting, and turned back to the curb with an embarrassed little *moue.* But her accent had derived from no farther south than, say, South Jersey, and, since diamonds were involved, this stripped off a good bit of Bascom's veneer. His shit-kicker granddaddy had come west from Ada, Oklahoma, during the dustbowl '30s, after all, to get land-rich during the postwar California '50s, and Mama Bascom hadn't raised no fools.

So Immaculata Bimbai spent two most uncomfortable hours in *Bascom's* office with Bascom himself and a brace of Beverly Hills cops, during which time it was discovered that the Beevairly Weelsheer had never heard of her *or* the bellhop, and that the boxes he had been carting around all day were empty.

But finally they had to let Immaculata go, along with her young servant man. Lying to a jeweler, even a Beverly Hills jeweler, is no crime, and she was getting vocal in the way only a *rom* woman can while extricating herself from trouble. Most importantly of all, however, a separate strip search of her and her son—the cops never uncovered their real names or relationship—could not turn up the missing *bijou.*

So Immaculata came away scot-free; it was her son Lazlo who had a few bad hours in their West Hollywood motel. He ate many a slice of Wonder thin sandwich bread to coat the swallowed diamond on its way through his intestines, and brought forth just about the time Peter Jennings did the same with the evening news.

They cleaned up the teardrop and admired it, a wonderful $7,000 score; but their elation was tempered by the loss of their lovely loaded $50,000 Fleetwood Sixty Special. Not even all of Immaculata's Gypsy curses could bring *that* back again.

*   *   *

Just about the time Lazlo swallowed the diamond, O'B poured beer for Ballard at Ginsberg's Dublin Pub on Bay Street up in San Francisco. Under cover of CCR's "Bad Moon Rising" on the juke, O'B was pleading, actually pleading, for assistance, which gave Ballard a wonderful chance to be sanctimonious.

"Absolutely not," he said, not for the first time, "I am not going out to Oriente Street with you, and that's final."

"But Larry . . ." O'B again plied Ballard with beer. "Think of all the times I've helped you out—"

"All the times you've got me in trouble, you mean. No! I keep telling you, O'B, since we got no plate numbers you gotta check those Gyppo serial numbers *before* you grab the cars!"

Conveniently forgetting he had done the very same thing on the Sonia Lovari Allante. But *that* had been the right Caddy.

"There just wasn't time, Larry. It was squatting right on the address. You know I usually always make sure before I—"

"Usually always," said Ballard, then added, "Fairfield."

In Fairfield late one St. Paddy's Day, a tipsy O'B had grabbed a hearse while Ballard was inside the mortuary learning the undertaker had just caught up the payments. Even worse, O'B hadn't checked the rear of the vehicle . . .

"The guy paid with a rubber check," said O'B virtuously. "And we dumped that personal property at Eternal—"

"I don't want to hear about it. The answer is still no."

Actually, there was a certain logic to Ballard's refusal. Returning the car could get messy, and a cryptic message from Yana at the DKA office meant that tonight he was getting his fortune told. And maybe getting some other treasure besides?

"Paul Bunyan really tried to kill me, Larry. I go back out there alone, and . . ." O'B drew a slicing hand across his throat.

Two beers later, Ballard relented, drove O'B back to the storage lot, and helped get the Eldorado started. He even found another bucket to sit on—gingerly, his lacerated butt was still sore—so they could plan strategy while riding out to the Portola District together. He considered it simple.

197

"If he isn't around, we just drop it at the curb and run."

"If he *is* around, we hit him on the head with a tire iron until we get his attention."

"He can't be *that* big and tough, O'B."

"Bigger," said O'B. "Tougher."

*   *   *

They couldn't ease the Eldorado back to the curb exactly where O'B had gotten it, because another car was parked there. You guessed it. Another brand-new Eldorado. With paper plates.

"That's Yonkovich's car!" bellowed O'B as they came rattling, clunking, banging, and thunking up the street. *"I'm sure of it!"*

"Maybe," Ballard yelled back cautiously over the din.

O'B shouted, *"In your heart you know that it's the—"*

"It's nice to sneak up on him this way!" shrieked Ballard.

O'B eased the totaled Eldorado to the curb in front of the house being torn down a few doors away from Yonkovich's place. He killed the engine. Ballard rubbed his tortured ears.

"I'll check the I.D., you run the keys," he said firmly.

O'B responded weakly, "Oh Jesus Christ!"

Ballard turned to follow his stricken gaze. Thundering down the front steps of the half-demolished house was the biggest biped he'd ever seen outside 49ers game days at Candlestick Park. Before they could move he was upon them, engulfing O'B's right hand in his own, roughly the size of a Virginia ham, and pumping it up and down with great energy.

"Geez, am I glad to see you! I really gotta apologize." He turned to include Ballard in his remarks. "I got this terrible temper, see—"

"I wouldn't have known that," said O'B mildly, trying to massage feeling back into his fingers. "Anyway, no harm done. At least, not to me . . ."

By this time, Paul Bunyan was examining his car with professional interest, hands on hips, shaking his head fondly.

"Geez, see what I mean? My dam' temper. I roont it." He turned back to O'B. "Called the friggin' bank soon's you was gone an' I calmed down. Tol' 'em I was sorry they hadda send somebody— got so much demolition work goin' on around town I just dead forgot to make the payments. Tol' 'em I was payin' it off—penance, y'see what I mean? Authorized a transfer right on the phone. They said they'd check an' get you right back out here with the car, an' here you are."

O'B cleared his throat. "You, ah, was this, ah . . . I mean, which bank did you . . ."

"B of A, of course. Dumbbutt I talked to didn't even know they'd sent you out after it, but that's okay. Here you are an' here it is." Paul Bunyan laughed a great laugh. "Yeah, here it is! Jeez, here it is!"

Ballard opened his mouth to say something, then shut it again. What was there to say? Luck of the Irish?

"Couple days, I call the insurance company an' say it was stole. Cops get it on the hotsheet, find it parked somewhere, like this . . ." His massive head suddenly swung toward them, his brows drawing down frightfully. " 'Less you got some moral qualms 'bout sticking it to the insurance company . . ."

They protested qualmlessness with upraised palms. Paul Bunyan laughed and nodded and again hoped O'B had no hard feelings and again shook hands with both of them. Then he turned and nodded at the other Eldorado. And laughed again.

"Same freakin' car, 'cept for the color."

O'B said smoothly, "And would you believe, sir, that we also have a repossession order on that very car? That's why I brought my colleague with me when I came back . . ."

"No kiddin'!" He almost collapsed into helpless laughter as they walked over to the Gyppo Caddy. "How the hell you gonna tell it's the right one, without a license plate on it yet?"

"I.D. number," said Ballard, this time very firmly.

And began checking it. As O'B began working his keys on the locked door.

"Right car," said Ballard.

But he used a desperate *sotto voce* because the door of the house had burst open and seven obviously Gypsy males were running down the walk at them. And still the keys stubbornly refused to work here in the right car, when they had perversely worked fine in Paul Bunyan's *wrong* car.

Ballard went into a defensive stance, but Paul Bunyan stepped in front of him to pluck the Gypsies' obvious ringleader from the ground with one hand, and shake him. The man's eyes bounced

199

around in his head, his hands flapped at the ends of his arms like clothespins on a line. The other Gypsies faded back.

"You owe the bank on that car?" roared Paul Bunyan.

"Yee . . ee . . ee . . ees . . . sss . . . sssirrrrr . . ."

"Then you give that man the keys, y'hear what I'm sayin'?"

He slammed Yonkovich back down on his feet like slamming a beer mug back on a table. Tucon dug through his pockets with shaking fingers to find the keys and give them to O'B.

Using them, O'B asked, "Any personal possessions in here?"

Yonkovich shook his head mutely. Perhaps all of his voice had been shaken out of him with "Yessir." O'B gave Ballard the keys to his company car, knowing Ballard would figure it was parked around the corner out of sight.

He paused to shake hands with the hulking demolition man. "Thanks for savings our butts, Mr. . . . er . . ."

"My pleasure!" roared Paul Bunyan. "I hate the kinda deadbeat s.o.b.s get their cars repossessed!"

Luck of the Irish, thought Ballard fatalistically as he trudged away to get O'B's car and drive it back downtown.

CHAPTER TWENTY-SEVEN

That same evening, back in Iowa, the first tentative bands of Gypsies were gathering around the edges of Stupidville like rime ice at the edges of a pond at the first freeze of winter. No ice crackled in the corridors of the Stupidville General Hospital, not yet, but it was coming. Oh, it was coming.

Inside the hospital, Barney Hawkins, Democrat National Assurance Company's adjuster, was red in the face as he strode up and down Staley Zlachi's room with short, jerky steps. Veins swelled dangerously along the sides of his neck. His suit coat was thrown across the empty other bed. Sweat mooned his armpits.

"Lissen, *Klenhard*"—his voice made the word an epithet—"you know an' I know you're faking it, but—"

"Not by the reflex tests," said Lulu calmly from her chair by the window. "You watch 'em yourself, mister—by them, my Karl, he got no feeling in his legs."

As for Staley, he said nothing. In his Klenhard persona he lay on his back under the blankets with his eyes closed.

"Goddammit, man! Are you even listening—"

"You'll bring on another attack," warned Lulu.

Hawkins stopped in the middle of the floor and bent over almost

201

double, like a man in pain. He finally straightened up and sighed deeply. "Look, I know you've got some shyster lawyer you won't even tell me his name, but I've made a good offer—"

"Fifteen thousand," said Lulu in disdain. "For my Karl living the rest of his days precarious-like, in pain and possible danger of being paralyzed forever?"

"Twenty."

Lulu didn't even deign to reply. Hawkins's face became scarlet again. With visible effort he got control.

"You're nothing, you know. Shit on a stick. But I wanta get you off the books because I have some really important cases piling up. So I'll tell you what I'll do. I'll go to the absolute limit." He lowered his voice. Staley opened an eye to squint at him. "I'll go to twenty-five thousand." Hawkins pasted a smile on his face. "And I'm a man of my word. Twenty-five thousand, I got the papers in my briefcase, you can—"

"Seventy-five," said Staley. And closed the eye again.

"And not a penny less," chimed in Lulu instantly.

Hawkins snatched up his jacket and stormed out. In the hall he yelled, *"I'll see you both in hell before I go one cent over twenty-five!"* As he charged off and the door slowly shut on its pneumatic closer, his voice got smaller and smaller like a Louis L'Amour hero riding off into the sunset. *"Crazy bastards think . . . wouldn't give my* mother *a seventy-five-K settlement . . ."*

Staley threw back the bedclothes and slid his bare feet to the floor. He began striding up and down the narrow room, his crumpled white hospital gown fluttering open behind him.

"Are the *rom* gathering?"

Lulu nodded, then frowned. "Yes. I'm keeping them away from the hospital—you're too sick to see them. But . . ."

"But you're right, Lulu darling. We can't stall them much longer. Guess it's time to settle with Hawkins."

Just then the doorknob turned. With remarkable agility, Staley leaped into bed and jerked the covers up as Lulu, out of her chair with equal alacrity, grabbed up his glass of water and dashed it in his face. Crichton entered to find Staley flat on his back, tossing his sweat-beaded head from side to side on the soaked pillow.

"I heard Hawkins all the way down in the doctor's lounge," Crichton began apologetically. "Did he . . ."

"Terrible abusive, he was," snuffled Lulu. She was dabbing the moisture off Staley's contorted features. "He swore an' called my Karl names . . ."

Crichton sighed. "I'll see he doesn't get in here to bother you again."

They grinned at each other as the door closed behind him.

"Three-four days oughtta do it," said Staley.

"Yes, my beloved," said Lulu warmly.

*   *   *

In San Francisco, it was a night for lovemaking. And con games. And maybe jealous rages.

Bart Heslip and his forever lady, Corinne Jones, were buying a house together above Parnassus in that maze of little streets twisting up the side of Twin Peaks. It was a Victorian with dark hardwood walls and floors, big front windows, an upstairs, an old-fashioned swing on a front porch with chunky balustrades, and a modern kitchen with a microwave and an electric stove that Corinne had installed herself and loved.

Walking uphill from the bus at six o'clock, she found Bart in the kitchen with lamb chops in the broiler, mashed potatoes warm on the stove, brussels sprouts in the microwave, and a green salad on the countertop he'd laid tile by tile.

"My God!" she exclaimed, folding herself into his thick black arms. "It's a miracle!"

"C'mon, I do *lots* of cookin' around here . . ."

"Microwave popcorn," she said, opening things and peeking into things and sniffing things. "Hot dogs. But lamb chops . . . and even a crucifer . . ." She laughed over her shoulder at his sour face. "What you want? You must want somethin' . . ."

Bart suddenly grinned. "How about you?" he said.

"That can be arranged."

It was.

An hour later they sat down to dinner by candlelight, Bart waving his arms around as he told her just how much he wasn't accomplishing on the Great Gyppo Hunt.

"Everybody's grabbing cars but me! Even Trin Morales got one of 'em, for God sake! Morales!"

By soft candleglow, Corinne's black eyes gleamed in her heart-shaped brown face. She was a beautiful woman, with high cheek-bones off an Egyptian wall painting and a wide warm kissable mouth. Bart was stirred again just looking at that face.

"You always said he was a very good detective."

Heslip laid down his knife and fork to gesture some more.

"Also a son of a bitch, unlike the other Latinos I know. Point is, he doesn't know anything more about Gyppos than I do—but *he's* scored. Larry's got his fortune-teller feedin' him leads, Giselle's got some secret informant, O'B just busted one out by the Cow Palace, the Great White Father is down in L.A. knocking 'em off . . ."

"And poor little Bart Heslip is a pseudo house-husband stuck at home baking cookies for his wage-earning cutie."

"Well, damn near."

They both laughed, and tinked their wineglasses gaily; and the phone rang. Corinne wiped her mouth as she stood up.

"It'll be the office."

The year before, she had taken over as manager of the downtown travel bureau where she had worked for several years; she and Bart were even talking about buying in when the owner retired. The promotion had meant more money, but in the recession crunch the agency had taken to staying open until seven o'clock weekday evenings, and problems were usually bounced back to Corinne even if she had gone home for the night.

But it was Giselle Marc's familiar voice on the phone. After hello-hello, Corinne said, "I hear you have a mysterious Gypsy informant all of your own."

"Mysterious is right," said Giselle. "One cryptic phone call that led me to a mark who led me to Larry's fortune-teller."

"Jealously among the Gyppos?" asked Corinne.

"Something like that, maybe I'll know more tonight." She added quickly, "Don't tell Bart that, he'll tell Larry and—"

Corinne chuckled. "Gotcha." Giselle had told her all about Yana and the claws she had in Larry.

"Speaking of Bart the Incredible Hulk, is he around?"

"And grouchy as a bear."

"Then I think I have some good news for him."

Heslip was standing beside her when she turned to look for him; he always knew when she was talking with Giselle. The two women had gone through a couple of things together that had made them the same kind of real friends he and Larry were.

He took the receiver from Corinne's hand, making a kissing mouth at her as she went back to her dinner before it got cold.

"Ed McMahon called, I'm worth millions?"

"Next best thing," said Giselle. "Dan has a chokehold on Poteet and the man is paying off like a drilled slot machine."

Cutting lamb, Corinne watched Bart write things down. She knew him so well. They had met just before he had quit the ring, and for years she had hated his being a detective as much as she'd hated his being a boxer, had even convinced herself she hated Dan Kearny for making him a DKA associate. But finally she had realized that Bart defined himself by the game, and his game was Me against You, whether in the ring or in the field.

Me against You, and no color, no social status, no educational differences to worry about. Delinquent debtor, deadbeat, embezzler, skip, defrauder, personal injury cheat, they were all the same. For Bart, just Me against You, physical if you wanted it that way, but usually outguessing, outthinking, or outfacing you to bring you down. In a way she'd even come to approve of it—she couldn't deny that sort of excitement and challenge to her man . . .

Who was writing and mumbling, "Yeah, yeah, I got it, mmhmm, Seattle . . . Yeah. And that's . . . Okay, J-O-S-E-F—that's with an 'F'—A-D-A-M-O. And his scam . . . Road paving. We got an address or . . . Just check on new subdivisions, huh? Okay, Got it. And Chicago . . . hold it a sec . . ."

He started another REPO ON SIGHT order.

"In Chicago it's . . . Mmmhmm, N-A-N-O-O-S-H . . . what was the second . . . T-S-A-T-S-H-I-M-O—Tsatshimo, that right? . . . Yeah . . . Metal plating? What the hell is . . . Okay, got you . . . Yeah . . . Either likely to be using his real name? . . . Okay, sure, I'll call you, give you my motel soon's I get . . . Yeah, I'll fly tonight. Soon's I can get to the airport . . ."

He talked a few moments more, hung up, turned to Corinne wearing a face alight with excitement.

"Honey, old Dan Kearny turned this L.A. Gyppo upside down and shook him, and out popped—"

"Seattle and Chicago and a couple of Gyps with names like rare diseases."

He chuckled. "Think you're so smart! Anyway, I gotta—"

"Soon as you can get to the airport?"

Her tantalizing Mona Lisa smile made Heslip realize he was going to be several long days—and nights—away from her sweet face and sweet body and that sweet loving he'd just had some of not long before . . .

"Well, baby, all that 'soon' talk is relative, isn't it? Gotta find out when there's a Seattle flight, no use hanging around the airport for hours . . . What's 'soon,' after all . . ."

Somehow, they never did finish that fine dinner house-husband Heslip had slaved over.

CHAPTER TWENTY-EIGHT

Ramon Ristik met Teddy at the door. "Do you have the egg?"

Teddy held up the old battered yellow gym bag as if it carried the Hope diamond. "Still in my Reebok. Just the way Madame Miseria told me. And the money, all I could raise."

Ristik nodded and stepped aside to let him by. It was all part of the mumbo jumbo, but also Yana had not been quite ready for the night's charade. They had been arguing, truth be told. About the tall blond *gadjo* with whom Yana had a relationship Ristik really didn't understand. And didn't trust at all.

But Ristik had dropped it: after all, who knew what powers Yana might *really* possess? Ramon always had secretly believed that his sister had been born with "a veil over her forehead" as the gift of second sight often is described by the *rom*.

She appeared at the head of the stairs when Teddy had limped halfway up—the snake down his flank was severe. Yana was back in her bright filmy Gypsy clothes, but tonight it was without anything under them so her beautiful figure was outlined mistily by the light behind her.

Ristik approved of the tantalizing display, it kept Teddy off balance. But he couldn't approve of the blond *gadjo*. How did Yana know him so well? From when? From where? She almost acted as if they once had been . . . *lovers*. But *rom, gadjo* . . .

"You have come," said Yana in that eerily deep voice she could assume at will.

"Ye-e-es," quavered Teddy.

"To learn whether evil had hatched out or not."

Yana was as beautiful as ever, but Teddy noted there were shadows under her eyes—skillfully applied, which he didn't notice—and her skin was pale, almost translucent. He didn't realize, either, that she had dusted pale powder on beforehand and that her parrot-bright silks were to heighten the effect.

She said, "All day I have been feeling . . . a *presence* . . ."

Teddy was led to the *boojo* room. Flickering candles made shadow demons dance in the corners. They sat down across from one another at the table. No crystal ball tonight; instead, a single small bone-white ceramic bowl like that in which his money had bled. Ristik had disappeared. Yana gripped both of Teddy's hands hard in hers.

"Let us pray now to Jesus Christ the Savior," she said.

Teddy panicked—he hadn't prayed in years, so he could think of nothing except "Now I lay me down to sleep . . ." Yana started a Hail Mary, but suddenly stopped and released his hands.

"It is no good!" she exclaimed harshly. "The emanations are too strong . . ." She transfixed him with her sudden fierce gaze. "You brought all the cash you could raise?"

"Yes," said a terrified Teddy. He didn't say he had cheated, that it was all he could raise without starting to cash in the investments his stepfather had left for him. "Over five thousand dollars. But . . ."

"*But!* Do you wish to die?"

"No, but—"

"Die horribly?"

Teddy slumped in his chair. "No." His limbs twitched. Sweat poured down his face. Yana softened.

"Perhaps it will not come down to the money."

As if on cue, Ristik appeared, pale. "The omens are bad! You must not do this!" But she waved him away.

"I must. Leave us. Be ready if I cry out."

He seemed to struggle against her, but finally disappeared silently through the curtains again.

Yana turned back to Teddy. "Put the egg on the table."

He opened his old yellow gym bag and took out the Reebok. If he had felt silly putting the egg in the shoe, he didn't now. Now he felt disoriented, terrified, feverish. Out of the shoe he carefully took the sweatsock in which he had rolled the egg. He put the egg carefully beside the bowl.

"If the demon has not hatched, the egg will be pure. If it has . . ." Her voice trailed off, fraught with horrors.

"How . . . will we . . . know?"

"We will know."

"And if it . . . if it *is* in the egg, what happens?"

She only whispered it. "It will pass from the egg to me."

She took up the egg and rolled it gently between the palms of her flattened hands. When she did, she began to tremble. Suddenly, with one convulsive jerk of her wrist, she cracked the egg against the rim of the bowl. She bent forward.

As did Teddy. He looked into the bowl. He screamed.

Staring up at him was a tiny bilious green devil's head with black exclamation-point eyebrows, a black goatee, and gleaming minuscule horns. Tiny evil eyes burned redly up into his through the mucous mess at the bottom of the bowl.

Even as he glimpsed it, Madame Miseria sprang to her feet, whirled around three times, and fell to the carpet where she rolled to and fro, shrieking, gnashing her teeth. Ristik leaped into the room and grabbed her shoulders, trying to hold her down.

"Help me!" he cried. "The demon has passed from the egg into her! Goddam you, help me!"

The terrified Teddy threw himself on her, but she was tremendously strong. Her shiny teeth snapped at his face like a dog's, narrowly missing his nose. Ristik was chanting in *rom*. The squirmings and spasms of her body beneath Teddy's were like obscene lovemaking. He felt disgust for himself: even as she fought for *his* life, he wanted to possess her sexually!

Her convulsions began to lessen. Finally, the thrashing ceased. Ristik, panting, stood up to lean against the table, looking down at them. He crossed himself.

209

"It . . . it has . . . gone."

Yana sat up, a dazed look on her face. She was wringing wet. She whispered hoarsely, her vocal cords strained by her battle with the forces of evil, "The . . . demon is very strong."

She struggled to her feet. Teddy did the same, couldn't help looking into the bowl again. The devil's head was gone!

"Yes," Yana nodded. "From the egg to me. It nearly took me, but now it has passed from me back whence it came."

Teddy knew where that was. He knew what had to be done.

"So my money is—"

"Cursed. Indeed, it is cursed."

The demon's whirlwind passage had knocked the gym bag off the table; the paper bag's money was spewed out across the floor.

As Teddy stared at it, mesmerized, Madame Miseria whispered, "It is the only way. Only then will the curse depart."

Ristik had brought forward a thirty-gallon metal trash barrel and a poker and a box of decorative wooden fireplace matches about a foot long. Yana picked up the money, folded the top of the paper bag down over the thick sheaf of bills. She slipped the package into her bosom, crossed her arms over it.

"You have the strength to do what must be done?"

Teddy squared his shoulders. "Yes."

She hesitated, then took the tightly folded package from her bodice and handed it to him. Ristik jerked involuntarily, made a strangled sound. Yana ignored him to light a long match and hand it to Teddy. Her eyes glowed, her voice deepened.

"Theodore Winston White the Third . . . *burn the curséd money!*"

Trembling as if with the ague, Teddy put the flame to a corner of the package. It began to wisp smoke.

"Drop it in the pail."

He did. With a WHOOSH! the crumpled newspaper in the barrel, soaked in lighter fluid, shot flames two feet above the rim, driving them both back. Ristik stepped in with the poker and stirred the contents vigorously as Yana chanted in her strong, almost guttural voice, *"Te avis yertime mandartay te yertil o Dei, te avis yertime mandartay te yertil o Dei . . ."*

The flames died. The money was gone. She embraced Teddy.

"You have been very strong," she said. "Very brave."

"And the curse . . . what of that?"

She shrugged in the Gypsy manner. "We shall see if this money was enough. Go home. Feel if the snake in your body withers away—perhaps you will have no more need of me."

"I will always need you!" cried Teddy despairingly. He could not face the uncertainty of life without her help.

But she had melted away through the curtains and was gone. Teddy found himself being firmly herded by Ristik from the *ofica* and down the stairs to slanting Romolo Place.

*   *   *

Ristik returned to be waltzed around the room by his manic sister at the success of the "burn-up"—so called because no evidence of the con is left, supposedly it has all been burned up. By the dimming light of the candles their shadows capered like those of cavorting goblins.

"I was the best I've ever been . . ."

"When you handed him the phony package to burn—"

"Did you see the switch? The smoothest . . ."

"If he had looked inside—"

"I had stage money in the prepared package . . ."

Yana took Teddy's $5,000 package from the pocket inside the bosom of her blouse, and put it on the *boojo* table. Next to it Ristik laid the tiny hand-carved devil's head he had scooped from the bowl just before Teddy had stood up. Just as he had flipped the gym bag to the floor so the money would spill out.

Yana gestured at it. "Half is yours."

Ristik protested, rather weakly, "You did all the work . . ."

"Equal partners, brother of mine." She embraced him again, and laughed at him. "Go! To your poker or dice game . . ."

He laughed almost sheepishly as he took $500. "Keep the rest for me, Yana. Otherwise I will just gamble it away."

"We will get much more than that with the cemetery dig."

"You truly believe that he will go along with that? What if his sciatica clears up?"

"He will still *think* it is there." She extended a foot like a ballet dancer on *pointe*. "He would lick this shoe if I asked him." Her laugh was not pretty. "He is mine. I own him."

After she had gotten rid of Ramon, she smiled a secret smile and

211

went to put on perfume. She had another fortune to tell tonight. She knew Ramon's ingrained *rom* disapproval, but Ballard was necessary to save the pink Cadillac so she would be Queen of the Gypsies. She merely had to get him to . . .

The trouble was, conning Teddy had her in a state of sexual arousal. Seeing Larry would heighten and focus that arousal.

* * *

From her vantage point in the recessed doorway of a small grocery store at the head of Romolo Place, Giselle had seen Teddy White enter the *ofica.* She hadn't tried to dissuade him previously in Tiburon over *caffe latte:* there was one born every minute, and what Yana did to him interested her not at all.

Unfortunately, what Yana did with Larry interested her a great deal—to her eternal shame. Oh God, acting like a jealous teenager! Over *Larry,* always only a friend. If he knew how she felt, he'd laugh at her. Yet here she was, consumed.

She watched the dazed Teddy eventually go back down Romolo toward Broadway with the limping, shambling gait of a drunk. Minus, she was sure, that silly damned egg wrapped in a sweatsock and stuck in the toe of his running shoe. Minus, also, whatever money he'd crammed into the gym bag with it. Poor fool.

She sighed. A wasted stakeout, what had she accomplished? What had she learned? Who was the bigger fool?

But still she stayed.

The door emitted a swaggering Ramon Ristik. The brother, off to celebrate a successful con in a bar or poker game.

And *still* she stayed. Waiting for what now? What other shoe was there to drop?

Larry Ballard climbed the steep side of Telegraph Hill to Madame Miseria's door, was admitted.

Of course. *That* was why she had waited. For the final humiliation at the hands of Yana. Oh, the bitch!

* * *

"You have come."

"To get my fortune told?" Ballard made it a question.

Yana drew him up the stairs, her hand hot in his. Wearing the same sort of flowing silks as that first time in Santa Rosa. He found it so erotic he got a strong erection just walking hand in hand with her down the dim narrow curtained hallway.

He finally broke the silence. "Did you have . . . a séance here tonight?"

"A reading. Theodore Winston White the Third."

There was an electricity in the air, a tension so palpable it was almost unpleasant. Also a tremendous excitement in her—as if she had just made love. He told himself it had been just another con, nothing physical, but he felt a stab of jealousy.

He tried to keep his voice neutral. "Successful, I hope."

"Very."

"For him or for you?"

The *ofica* was dim, he could smell snuffed candles; now the only illumination was the glowing crystal ball back on the table, beautiful and cool and disturbing. She stopped and turned so abruptly that he collided with her. The length of her body pressed against his. Her eyes gathered light like a cat's.

"For me," she said in a low intense voice. She was speaking almost into his mouth. "It was a poisoned egg. It is a cruel deception, but he is only a *gadjo*."

Ballard's arms had come up around her. She was naked under the thin silk, her body almost feverish to the touch. She made a small despairing sound in her throat. She must not. She was *rom*, Ballard was *gadjo*. But she felt the same wild excitement as the first time with him. She belonged to no man, no concept: only to herself. Therefore she could give herself to any man she desired, *rom* or *gadjo*, couldn't she? Yes!

Their mouths met, their tongues sought. Their bodies began to move together in that most ancient rhythm of life even as they were sinking to the floor, even as his hands went up under the silk garments to open her waiting flesh, even as her hands almost magically freed his stiffened member so it could enter her.

Above them, the crystal ball faded slowly to darkness.

*   *   *

When the dim light was gone from the front room, Giselle left her stakeout, feeling humiliation almost as vindication. No wonder Dan Kearny kept DKA out of domestic investigations: they were degrading. No more of this for Giselle Marc, not ever.

CHAPTER
TWENTY-NINE

Ken Warren sat upon the edge of the couch and looked at his wristwatch. Not quite six in the morning. He yawned and started to stand up and fell back in a sitting position with a grunt of surprise. He had to put his hands on his knees and push to get himself upright, his knees popping like dry kindling. Goddam couch. Old and not very good quality in the first place.

In the shower, hot enough to turn him lobster red, then cold enough to chatter his teeth, he knew that he would have to get his bed back. Which meant getting Maybelle an apartment.

Yesterday he'd returned her Connie to the dealership, only to be faced by an edgy Giselle when he'd got to the office.

"Ah . . . fast work on that Continental, Ken." He'd shrugged, but she wouldn't go away. "You . . . ah . . . have any trouble?"

He faked amazement. "Nthixty-one an' phat an' hmblak?"

She put her hands on her hips and tried to stare him down.

"All of those," she said, "and a hooker besides. But also a human being who deserves some decency and a few breaks."

Ken had patted her shoulder and walked around her and gone up to type reports. When he had looked up an hour later, Giselle was leaning in the doorway with her arms folded, waiting.

"You know she was sleeping in that car?" Warren nodded, kept hitting the keys. "Now where's she going to sleep?"

Unwillingly, still typing, he said, "Nthees ngoht frenz."

Softly, "Thanks, Ken." When he looked up, she'd been gone.

None of that helped with this morning's aching back. He'd give Maybelle this apartment and move into a furnished room in a minute—but she'd never stand for it. No, she had to have legit work that paid enough better than piecework at a dry-cleaning plant to let her get a place of her own.

As he turned off the icy stinging water and rubbed down vigorously with the napless towel, he started to laugh. She was big, strong, eager, and the job was there. He'd *make* it happen.

Meanwhile, he'd repo'd all the easy ones the DKA gang had left for him. Today he wanted the tough ones.

*   *   *

Today Giselle wanted Angelo Grimaldi.

She would uncover his scam, then take his big black limo away from him. To hell with Larry Ballard and his Gyppo broad. Today she was Boadicea, war queen of the Britons, slashing Roman legionnaires to bloody ribbons with flashing blades fixed to the wheels of her chariot.

Since she was going to the St. Mark, she wore pale yellow silk under her lightweight full-length back leather coat, and wrapped a very expensive almost Gypsy-bright silk scarf about her throat. Her attaché case of repo tools looked full of dynamite legal papers. She would never be spotted as a hard-nosed repoman.

Ah, repowoman. Repoperson?

Boadicea, armored. Angelo Grimaldi, dogmeat.

Except she couldn't even get from DKA to the top of Nob Hill. Her radio told her why: the presidential motorcade was arriving from the airport. Finally, she parked in a supermarket lot on Larkin and rode the California cable in.

At the St. Mark she went through the fancy revolving doors into the venerable thick-carpeted lobby and almost asked the tall blonde at the check-in counter, who looked *simpática*, if Angelo Grimaldi was in his room; but showing interest would tip her hand too soon. Instead, attaché case in hand, she went to the elevators. Check the garage first, she might just get lucky.

*   *   *

Rudolph Marino, wearing yet another $1,200 suit, strolled from the coffee shop just in time to miss the descending car the tall beautiful sexy blonde was getting on. A knockout! But no time for blondes now, not even blondes that stunning. So he tipped sometime lover Marla at the check-in desk a wink—she might still be useful—and waited for the next down-car.

Just before his continental breakfast, he had attached the receiver to the detonator embedded in the C-4 *plastique* under the rear seat of his limo, thus arming it. The transmitter was in his pocket. Today an unsuccessful terrorist attack on the President would make Rudolph Marino $75,000 richer.

*   *   *

My God, there was the long black Gyppo limo conned out of the bank by Angelo Grimaldi! Giselle had intended to scope out Grimaldi's scam before seeking the limo, but this was better. With the car in the barn, maybe she could turn him. He'd make a dynamite informant, even better than Dan's Ephrem Poteet, light-years better than Larry's Ms. Gyppo Slut.

The garage was full of men in business suits coming and going, standing around in little groups talking. Giselle got out the key she had cut for it, and, looking every inch the ambitious young attorney, strode boldly over to the Gyppo limo and started to insert the key into the door lock.

That's when half a dozen suits seized her from behind, twisting the key out of her hand and slamming her face-down against the car's fender, her arms up behind her back.

*   *   *

Rudolph Marino stepped from behind his pillar to check that nobody was near his limo before he detonated the C-4 under the rear seat, and saw the Secret Service agents roughing up his beautiful sexy elevator blonde. *Devalesa!* She had to be Giselle Marc, the repo queen! He changed his plan instantly.

*   *   *

216

"You have the right to remain silent . . ."

Giselle felt cold steel bite into her wrists. "No! Wait! You don't understand—"

"You have the right to an attorney . . ."

"It's all a mistake—"

"If you cannot afford an attorney . . ."

"All I was trying to do—"

"Stop this disgrace!"

The voice was such a whipcrack of authority that the chunky man in the Brooks Brothers suit stopped reading Giselle her rights from the soiled card in his hand. Even Giselle, despite her awkward position against the car, twisted to see who it was.

The most beautiful man in the world.

Dusky skin . . . raven ringlets . . . long curved eyelashes . . . a strong nose, beautifully shaped lips, strong, cruel chin . . . meltingly handsome, romantic, dashing . . . Obviously . . . *Angelo Grimaldi!* Whoever the hell Angelo Grimaldi really was.

"Who the hell are you, buddy?" A short weasel of an agent had his chin thrust out.

"The lady's husband." Somehow, Marino was at Giselle's side, his arms around her. "Are you all right, my darling? Have they hurt you?"

She almost managed tears. "They frightened me, sweetheart, and they put these cold . . . *things* on my wrists and—"

He whirled on them, eyes blazing.

"Remove those handcuffs immediately! My wife makes a simple mistake, and . . ."

Weasel had planted himself in front of Marino, hand out. He said, "I.D." Marino didn't move. Weasel smiled. Not a nice smile. "No? I like that." He gestured. "Take him, too."

"Better not," said Grimaldi.

Giselle, half-forgotten, had managed to straighten up and twist around. She was close to openmouthed at the unbelievable *chutzpa* of this Gypsy calling himself Grimaldi.

Who was saying, "I am Ali Akbar Zuhrain, underambassador from Kuwait, here in San Francisco to confer with your President." A pause. "At *his* invitation."

The man who had been reading Giselle her rights furtively but feverishly began thumbing through an appointment schedule.

217

"Ah . . . Ali Akbar Zuhrain, uh, yes, he . . . is the, uh, underambassador. And he had a meeting scheduled for, ah, three P.M. in the presidential suite . . ."

Grimaldi snatched Giselle's repo key out of the hands of the man who had taken it. He jabbed it at the door of the presidential limo. It wouldn't even enter the lock.

"See? Comprehend? It does not fit." He turned to gesture across the garage. "But if you will look over there . . ." All heads swiveled. "You will see an identical vehicle." He handed the key back to the man. "I insist you try this key in the door of *that* limo."

Looking dazed, the man walked away. Giselle hoped to God she had cut the key right to fit Grimaldi's Fleetwood.

"That limo was delivered to me yesterday, it is almost an exact replica of this one. My wife is not yet familiar with it, so she went to the wrong vehicle—and you *bêtes* assaulted her."

Weasel was beginning, "I still want to see some I.D.," when the key turned in the lock and Grimaldi's limo door opened. There was a release of pent-up breaths, and sheepish voices rose in apology. Giselle felt the steel fall away from her wrists.

*   *   *

Pietro Uvaldi was on his way out, wearing Gianni Versace's latest overdraped sports fashions. He opened the door to stare at the chest of a very big, scary-rough sort of man with short-chopped brown hair and a quizzical face and a hard, taut, animal body. The man was just pointing a finger at Pietro's doorbell.

Oh my *God*, ring my bell indeed! Somehow Pietro managed to find his normal speaking voice.

"May . . . I help you?"

The delicious hulking brute said, "Gha Merthades."

"My Mercedes?"

"Ah hthnorry, buddy, it'th goin'!"

"*Freddi!*" he cried, realizing what the man was.

At the same time he almost danced to the coat closet. Didn't they ever learn? He came around with the shotgun, only to be slapped, very hard, across the face. At the same time the gun was wrenched away as if his fingers were made of Play-Doh.

"F . . . *Freddi!*" he shrieked.

"Gha gnkees," snarled the beast, hand extended.

Keys. Surely that's what he meant. Keys. God God God! Don't enrage the animal further. In a moment Freddi would arrive from the back of the apartment to pulverize him . . .

The beast took the keys from his shaking fingers, turned to go— and Freddi made his charge, roaring, arms out and head back to deliver a head-slam such as had disabled poor Larry Ballard.

Timing is everything. At the exquisitely perfect moment of impact, the big man raised the shotgun beside his cheek just as he moved his head slightly to one side. Freddi slammed headfirst into the wooden gunbutt with a *crack!* like bighorn sheep slamming bosses of horn in ritual battle. Freddi's feet went up and he lay down four feet off the floor. From whence he crashed down on his back like a dropped side of beef.

"You *killed* him!" Pietro shrieked. The big man, turning away, shook his head. Pietro momentarily abandoned his lover to run after him, hugging him from behind, trying to kiss his hand, crying, "Don't go! I love masterful men!"

The masterful man said, "Fnuk ohnff!" and was gone.

Only then did Pietro drop on his knees to minister to the unconscious Freddi. But even as he did, his thoughts were all with that delicious scary brute who had simply *dismantled* Freddi.

Even as he was whispering to his fallen defender, "My poor, poor darling . . ."

CHAPTER THIRTY

M y poor, poor darling!" exclaimed the man who called himself Grimaldi, then started to chuckle. "Giselle, you are very quick, to see what I was doing and play along—"

"What choice did I have? And how did you know about what's-his-face? The underambassador? Ali Akbar Zuhrain?"

"I read the President's schedule in the *Chronicle.*"

"And how come you know *my* name?" Almost an accusation.

"Who do you think left the phone message leading you to Theodore Winston White the Third?"

"Your real name wouldn't happen to be Rudolph, would it?"

He shot her a surprised look. Marino was tooling the long sleek black limo out California Street through the tranquil wide-street richness of Pacific Heights.

"You're really good, you should be a Gypsy yourself."

"Rudolph what?"

"Look in your crystal ball." Then he shrugged. "Marino."

Giselle opened her window to let the air blow her blond hair around. She put her silk scarf on the seat, began doing airplanes with her right hand in the slipstream outside, as she used to do on car trips with her folks when she was little. This Marino was just the kind of guy to get her into a lot of trouble. Well—defiantly—maybe a lot of trouble was what she needed.

Painfully casual, she said, "You ever hear of a mitt-reader calls herself Madame Miseria?"

"Aha! Little Yana has been whispering in your ear."

"Not my ear," said Giselle bitterly.

Out of sudden memory and insight, he said, "A tall blond man perhaps? Hawk nose, hawk eyes?"

Dismayed, she yelped, "How did you—"

"Gypsies know things." He nodded thoughtfully. "Dear, sweet little Yana. I bet she said she didn't know me . . ."

"Never even met you."

Marino felt a dangerous urge to tell this *gadjo* woman real truths about himself. He contented himself with facts instead.

"We grew up together. We were betrothed when she was seven and I was fifteen."

"So she's a liar besides!" Triumphantly.

"Can you blame her?" His mildness would have surprised Yana. "I want to be King of all the Gypsies, Yana wants to be Queen of all the Gypsies. One of us must fail."

Giselle said, "Outstanding," softly. She was recovering from her dismay. Help him, hurt her. How? There'd be a way.

He turned downhill on Lyon Street, parked at the long-since-locked Broadway gate of the Presidio. They got out, the pungent cat-box odor of the eucalyptus groves beyond the chain-link fence rolling over them. He leaned in the open rear door as Giselle came around the back. She watched him detach a small radio receiver from some inconspicuous wires going under the backseat.

"Standard issue for limos this year?"

"Disarming a bomb."

He waited for her to be shocked, but she merely raised her eyebrows for him to continue. A woman worthy of a *rom!*

"Inept terrorists were going to try to blow up the President, but fortunately were going to get the wrong limo . . ."

"Only I stepped in and tried to repo the President's limo instead, and screwed up all your plans!"

"Screwed them up?" Mischief glinted in his eyes as he looked over at her. "Made them better. To the Secret Service I said you were the underambassador's wife, but to the hotel management I will say you were a blond terrorist . . ."

Giselle clapped her hands in the delight of discovery.

"Blackmail! The hotel management! I was working to your command—"

He said, a little stiffly, "I am a *rom*, not a blackmailer."

Then, struck by the incongruity of it, they both laughed.

*   *   *

Ken Warren had once spent a couple of weeks as a substitute meter reader for PG&E, and still had a contact or two there. One of them, just this morning, had let him know that a new San Francisco utilities connection had been made by a Sarah Walinski.

His Sarah Walinski, formerly Heslip's Sarah Walinski?

After dropping Uvaldi's Mercedes 500SL back at the dealer, he cruised the tall narrow streets that overlooked James Lick Freeway from Bernal Heights. Modest row houses built after World War II for returning vets but with price tags no longer modest. Working-class, racially mixed, just the right kind of anonymous rabbit warren in which his Sarah would rent a burrow.

Heslip said she was big and quick and powerful and without inhibition concerning violence to others, which made Ken wary. You couldn't hit a woman, not even to defend yourself, but he didn't want to get axed or coffee-canned, either. Nor did he want her alerted to skip again, so he'd have to start looking for her and her car all over somewhere else. So, cruise the area, talk to a couple of bartenders, the local ma-and-pa . . .

But as he started uphill from Jarboe, a Dodge Charger pulled over and stopped on the other side of the street, facing down. Right address. Right year. Right color. Right license.

Right car!

In his rearview he saw a woman get out and start up the front steps with a twelve-pack. Right woman, too, from Bart's description. A fireplug with weight-lifter arms and beautiful taffy hair glinting in the spring sunshine.

At the top of the hill he parked to consider his givens:

—She bought the car in Jersey City and skipped.

—She ran another repoman off with an axe and skipped.

222

—She belted Heslip with a can of coffee and skipped.

—She put her boyfriend in the hospital and skipped.

Conclusion: he'd only get one shot at Sarah and her car.

He gave her twenty minutes to pop a tab and tap the tube, then got out, locking his car and making sure no papers on the seat or over the visor betrayed it as a repoman's. Unhappy subjects liked to get even by icepicking your tires or sugaring your gas tank before you could get back to pick up your own car.

Sarah must have stopped for a couple on the way home: car window open, door unlocked, wheels uncurbed so the steering wheel wasn't even locked. The slightest of turns would lock it, but if he could put the Charger in neutral and let it roll downhill out of sight of the house before he fired it up . . .

He eased off the handbrake, let it roll. So far, so good, but since he couldn't turn the wheel, he couldn't steer it. By the time it hit the flat intersection it was in the wrong lane. And then it lost momentum. And stopped.

"Grrrrr!" observed Ken.

He cast a look up the hill—nothing—and bent down under the steering wheel to get at the ignition lock.

"You got troubles, pal?"

Ken came up from under the dash, his fingers still up behind it trying to find the ignition lock ring washer. When he straightened, his shoulder was tight against the steering wheel.

Click.

Now it was locked.

A head was in the window. Guy from a road crew around the corner Ken had noted on the way up, young, beefy, brash, semi-belligerent, looking for something to liven up a cigarette break.

"Hgnoh!" Ken exclaimed crossly.

"What was that, pal? You tryna wise off?" *Why* couldn't he talk like everyone else? Just this once? He kept silent. The intruder didn't. "Ignition's busted, huh, pal?"

Still silent. Fingers, do your work.

"Hey, how'd you get it down here in the middle of the intersection without no key to it?"

Had it! His fingers turning the ring washer as his eyes found the rearview mirror he'd tilted so he could see up the hill. Holy Christ, here she came boiling out of the house!

223

"Can't leave it here in the intersection, y'know, pal."

Ignition lock out. He could unfasten the wires, but even if he got it started, with this guy hanging in the window . . .

"GODDAM THIEF!"

The beefy kid turned his head—but kept his elbows firmly in the open window. Ken jerked the wires out of the old lock, started fumbling them around the posts on his own lock.

"GODDAM THIEF! GODDAM THIEF WITH MY GODDAM CAR!"

She was running now, downhill, full out, something long and glittering in her right hand. As Ken started to put his key into his now-live substitute ignition lock, the beefy guy grabbed his arm and sent the key flying.

"Hey, you! Who's the broad yelling thief?"

Fumbling around on the floor for the key, *got it!* stick it into his lock now dangling at the end of the ignition wires.

"I'm talkin' to you, pal!"

Sarah was coming off the curb a dozen yards away, the huge butcher knife in her right hand raised for stabbing. With desperate calm, Ken tried harder than he'd ever done in his life to articulate well.

"Hmy whife!" he managed to yell.

And twisted the key. The engine started.

But Sarah's shoulder sent the beefy guy bouncing out of the way like a helium balloon, too late to roll up the window—the knife flashed down at Ken's unprotected neck. But the car was easing forward so the blade gouged uselessly down the rear window and the knife was knocked from Sarah's hand by the frame.

The amazed construction worker, flat on his butt in the street, yelled, *"Your wife? Pal, you* do *got troubles!"*

Sarah was knifeless but still running alongside, clawing at Ken's hair and face, grabbing the door frame, being dragged several feet before he could stop the car to save her injury.

Dead stop. Leaving him a sitting duck, helpless against her attack. She pulled back her fist for the knockout blow, her red rage-contorted face filling the open window.

Ken kissed her on the cheek.

Her mouth fell open in astonishment, as did her fist. Ken tapped the accelerator, the Charger moved away. In the rearview Sarah, dumbfounded in the middle of the street, was staring after him. Then her right arm came up, again fisted. But the fist dissolved. Thick fingers, as of their own accord . . . *waggled.*

The dragon, transformed to fair maiden by a kiss, was waving Ken Warren and her Charger a bittersweet goodbye.

*   *   *

"If not a terrorist and not a blackmailer, then what?"

They were back in the limo, driving back in toward Nob Hill. Marino used the lighter on both their cigarettes.

"A knight in shining armor to *stop* the terrorists."

"Who do not exist. You made them up."

He patted the pocket with the transmitter in it. "Who is to say they are made up? With proof such as this . . . And a blond terrorist trying to break into the President's limo . . . But you can see my dilemma. Even a white knight must have his great black stallion on which to ride to the rescue."

"Only I have a repo order on your stallion."

"The steed of a man who saved you from arrest, disgrace, torture? Perhaps even from . . ." He twirled an imaginary mustache, Giselle laughed, she seemed to laugh a lot with this man. "Something *worse?* But *me* . . . I can make you an offer—"

"I can't refuse?"

"Exactly! I will give to you Cadillacs being driven by Yana's clan—"

"But you got those cars for them in the first place!"

"*Devalesa* gives, *Devalesa* takes away. Yana is betraying *my* clan to your friend with the hawk eyes, yes? So let me finish my business with the hotel while giving your DKA many cars . . ."

Giselle stubbed out her cigarette. What could she lose? He wasn't going to give her the limo, anyway, and she couldn't take it away from him. Not now. And if he fed her other Gyppo cars . . . and helped destroy Yana in the meantime . . .

"Tell me just one thing, Rudolph. Who is Angelo Grimaldi?"

"Who else could he be but Mouthpiece for the Mob, offering to rub out the terrorists for a fat fee?"

Giselle broke up. It almost would serve the hotel people right if they bit on that one. He was going on.

"We will work out a telephone code, you will be a business

woman joining me at my hotel for conferences; I will give you the time and place to steal many cars."

"Recover," she said automatically.

"Whatever." He paused. "Deal?"

"Deal."

He reached over and solemnly shook her hand. Ballard had *his* Gyspy informant, she thought defiantly, she'd have hers. A disturbingly attractive Gypsy informant . . .

Very disturbingly attractive . . .

CHAPTER THIRTY-ONE

After dropping Giselle at her car, Marino found a payphone and called Gunnarson's office at the St. Mark. He repitched his voice to the bogus Arab gutturals of his previous terrorist call and became more and more excited, speaking faster and faster in a higher and higher register.

"We failed this morning, but we will strike again. You have opposed us and taken one of ours, so now the St. Mark Hotel is our target! Even if your President escapes our vengeance!"

And hung up. Back at the hotel, he holed up in the Garnet Room while sending word to Gunnarson they had to meet right away. He made it even money whether the Three Stooges or the feds would show up this time, but hoped Gunnarson and his cohort were in too deep to cry wolf now.

He had a drink, then a second, rare for him; not, oddly enough, because he was nervous about a possible federal bust, but because he had been shaken by Giselle Marc.

He *wanted* her. Physically. Usually, with *gadje* women, he just serviced them as part of some con he was running. But Giselle was not only stunning, she was *rom*-smart, smart as Yana. Despite their mutual attraction, she would be using him while he was using her, and he found that intensely exciting.

Curly, Larry, and Moe paused in the doorway of the lounge to tell the maître d' to keep other patrons away from around their table. Marino felt himself relax. No feds.

So, as Grimaldi, he opened with, "Now do you believe me?"

"Believe you about what?" demanded a harried Gunnarson.

Marino realized his fears had been groundless. Call in the feds? These stupid bastards hadn't even made the necessary connections to do so—connections transparent as glass to him.

Grimaldi snarled, in his Bronx accent, "Whadda ya think? The terrorists. The blonde in the garage this morning, trying to get into the President's car so she could set a C-4 *plastique* bomb—and then do a remote detonation by radio signal."

"What sort of fools do you take us for?" demanded hulking red-headed Shayne. "The underambassador of Kuwait's wife tries to open the wrong limo, and you try to make her a terrorist?"

"The underambassador from Kuwait, a devout Moslem, has a blond American for a wife?" countered Marino witheringly.

Shayne blustered, "The Secret Service agents—"

"Are stupid." Not that he really thought so; it was just that he had been running cons since he was three years old, and fortunately these particular agents, hustled, had bitten. "That was not Ali Akbar Zuhrain who took the blonde away from them."

Little desiccated Smathers bubbled, "But . . . but . . . the key fit the underambassador's limo, they drove away together . . ."

Grimaldi casually laid on the table a perfectly harmless penlight that looked like an engorged ballpoint pen, and then proceeded to ignore it. Which assured the others couldn't keep their eyes off it.

"Yeah," he said sarcastically, "sure. You got it. The underambassador and the terrorist drove away together."

"You're trying to tell us," sneered Gunnarson, "that *another* terrorist walked in there and rescued her and drove her off in his limo? Just like that?"

"No. I'm telling you that *I* walked in there and drove her off in *my* limo—just like that."

Shayne chuckled, "And took her where?"

"Out," said Grimaldi bleakly.

Smathers suddenly had to take off his eyeglasses and start to polish them with his display handkerchief. The quaver was back in his voice, which was almost a whisper. "There . . . *was* another phone call . . . saying . . . we had taken one of theirs . . ."

Shayne couldn't let go of it. His voice was low, intense, furious. "You're claiming you knocked off this blond bimbo?"

Grimaldi ignored him, spoke instead to Smathers.

"I've learned their usual M.O. is to threaten the involved institution directly when they lose one of their people . . ."

"Well-l-l . . . yes, the call did . . . threaten us, but . . ."

Grimaldi drummed his fingers on the table, frowned, sent bleak eyes around to each of them in turn.

"You don't have a lot of time, gents."

Gunnarson demanded abruptly, "Do you have any proof the blonde was a terrorist? Any proof the phone call was real? Any proof that you . . ." he stumbled over the word, "*removed* her?"

"What is proof? I imagine the real Ali Akbar Zuhrain has had his meeting with the President by now, am I correct?"

"Yes, but—"

"And has left the hotel, since he is not staying here?"

"I believe so, yes, but . . ."

"Zuhrain didn't have a limo, you can check that out. I do. It's parked down in the garage with the blond bitch's scarf lying on the front seat, if you want to go look. Here are my keys." Grimaldi dumped them on the table in front of Shayne. Shayne made no move to pick them up. His ruddy countenance had paled slightly. Grimaldi pointed at the harmless penlight. "I took this off her body . . ."—he dropped his transmitter beside the penlight—"and this from her attaché case."

"What . . . are they?" quavered Smathers, his calendar age at last. Grimaldi flicked the penlight with a contemptuous finger.

"Pen-bomb. Inside are a miniature receiver, detonator—"

They started back, blanching. "A *bomb?* Are you—"

"I removed the C-4 from it. It's harmless." Grimaldi tapped the transmitter. "Transmitter, present to the same frequency as the receiver in the pen-bomb. Once the President was in the car, all she had to do was—"

"My God!" Gunnarson looked as if he were about to faint. "And now they are threatening the hotel itself . . ."

A subdued Shayne began, "What if the Secret Service or the FBI or the police find out . . . find the blonde . . ."

"She went swimming about thirty miles out," said Grimaldi. "Got tangled up in some scrap iron and dove out of a small plane that happened to be wave-hopping under the Coast Guard radar."

"Did you—"

"Personally. One of my people dumped the body, of course." He said it offhandedly and stood up, pocketing harmless penlight and transmitter. "She's a freebie, but it's seventy-five K in forty-eight hours for the rest of them. After the forty-eight there's nothing I can do for you. My principals are tired of your delays, and I need an answer for them."

Gunnarson was wiping sweat from his forehead with one of the cloth napkins. "You're talking about . . . *killing* people! You can't expect us to just—"

"They plan to kill you," said Grimaldi reasonably.

The forty-eight-hour deadline was genuine—that was as far as he could stretch the Grimaldi persona, then the real Grimaldi was due back to New York from his Maine fishing trip. When he found his apartment rifled and his credit cards gone, he would hit the street yelling and his cards would hit the stolen-card hotline a few hours after that.

Forty-eight hours for $75,000. Or zero.

Same with Giselle Marc. Tomorrow she would come to the hotel and he would feed her some leads to a few of the Cadillacs being driven by Yana's people. And afterward . . . perhaps . . .

*   *   *

It was nearly midnight when Dan Kearny let himself into the office. He had driven directly there after his flight from LAX, rather than home, because he'd had his fun in the field and suddenly, dog-tired as he was, had to touch DKA again. Truth to tell, what was worrying him most was what he and Giselle could do about the mountains of wastepaper and layers of dust accumulating since he'd foolishly dumped the janitorial service . . .

He stopped dead just inside the front door, keys forgotten in his hand. All the lights were on in the middle of the night, and the whole place was spotless. Almost in time to the gospel music from the back room, he swiped a hand across a desktop—no dust. Giselle must have found a dynamite new service that . . .

Gospel music? From the back room was coming gospel music!

He went hurriedly back between the deserted desks and through the open doorway. At Giselle's desk was a fat black woman of about 60 whom he'd never seen before. She wore black stretch pants and a scarlet sweater and her head was wrapped in a bright-hued bandana to keep the dust away. In one hand was a poorboy, in the other a Styrofoam cup of coffee. Her eyes were shut, she was rocking her head from side to side in time with the music, crooning along with it in a rich dark contralto.

This was the new cleaning service?

"Ma'am, pardon me . . . ma'am . . . *ma'am*—"

She shrieked and jumped up, arms and legs going every which way, eyes popping wide in a caricature of black surprise.

"It's okay," said Kearny soothingly, making little palm-down shushing movements with his hands. "I just wondered if—"

But she was in motion, hitting the stop button on the boombox and dropping her sandwich into a paper bag and draining her coffee and dropping the cup into a big trash bucket that stood upright on a two-wheeled cart beside the desk, with brooms and mops sticking out of it. Meanwhile, she kept up a running barrage of chatter as she sped about.

"Scairt me half to death, you must be Mr. Kearny, yessir, all finished up in here, jus on my way out, yessir, finishin up my snack an Ah be outta here, yessir, everything done jus apple-pie nice, didn't mean to set at no desk, neither, nossir . . ."

And, pushing the big metal trash bucket on its two-wheeled frame, she was through the back door and gone. Kearny blinked after her as if he'd just seen a UFO, then shook his head and went back out to the front office and down to his desk.

He stood there idly leafing through the teetery mountains of billing, subconsciously hearing voices coming down from the second floor through the narrow stairwell behind his desk. Somebody working late. Dozens of files. Looked like the place ran better without him . . . than . . . with . . . him . . .

The top file on the stack was PERNOD, MAYBELLE.

Maybelle Pernod, fat, black, and 61, streetwalking to keep her impossibly expensive Continental. Giselle had fallen for her hard-luck story like a ton of bricks . . .

New cleaning lady, fat, black, probably 61 . . .

And it was Giselle's voice he was hearing from upstairs, along with a male rumble out of which he could pick no words. No she didn't! Giselle didn't get away with *this* crap!

Kearny took the stairs two at a time, went along the hall to a cubicle where Ken Warren was typing, a thick stack of finished reports beside the machine. Giselle was sitting on the edge of the desk, swinging her feet and talking.

". . . and he's been running this elaborate scam on—"

She broke off abruptly when Kearny appeared.

"No," he snarled.

"No to what?" She stood slightly taller than he, and so slid off the desk to look down at him as she always did when they were about to go at it.

"Maybelle Pernod. No way she's going to—"

"Hnyeth thnee ith! Hnit wasth hmy indea!"

Kearny was frozen in openmouthed astonishment. Warren, having had his say, began doggedly hitting the keys again.

"Ken repossessed her Continental as ordered," said Giselle, talking fast. "She's living at a friend's apartment until she gets enough for first and last and security deposit on her own."

"Yeah, well, she ain't gonna get it from us."

Warren ripped the report from the typewriter and stood up. He jerked his windbreaker off the back of the chair and started to shove his arm into the sleeve all in the same motion.

"Hnen Agh nquitt!" he exclaimed.

CLOSE AND BILL on WALINSKI, SARAH.

CLOSE AND BILL on UVALDI, PIETRO.

The guy was an absolute killer. Kearny got in Warren's way as the big man tried to storm out of the room.

"You can't quit," said Kearny reasonably. "I need you to go down to L.A. with Trin Morales and ferry up a couple of Gyppo Cadillacs. Besides, your registration hasn't come back from Sacramento—and your raise hasn't come through yet."

Storm clouds still churned in Warren's eyes. "Hngmaybelle?"

"A steal at forty a night, Dan," said Giselle quickly.

"Hear that?" said Kearny. "A steal at forty a night."

Warren looked suddenly flustered; he ducked his head and mumbled something and gathered up his folders and patted Giselle on the shoulder and was gone.

"What'd he say?" asked Kearny.

"He has to drive Maybelle home."

"*He's* the friend whose apartment she—"

"Yep. He knew her son in Vietnam. I didn't know that when I assigned the reopen REPO ON SIGHT to him. He went out on it and rescued her from some rednecks and *then* repo'd her car."

"How the hell do you find out all this stuff? The guy doesn't say two words to me, and when he does I can't . . ."

"Maybe 'cause I listen?" she said. Kearny shrugged, half shook out two cigarettes, extended the pack to her. She took one, adding, "And how'd you know I'd started smoking again?"

He gestured at the ashtray of butts. "Warren doesn't."

They lit up. Giselle said casually, "Maybelle does a hell of a job, doesn't she? A steal at forty a—"

"Yeah, yeah, I heard you the first time."

*   *   *

Ballard and Yana both came at the same time, crying out together wordlessly in their mutual release. After a long minute of dying spasms and thrusts, they fell apart and lay on their backs, sweating, panting, staring up through the semi-darkness at the plush hangings over Yana's bed. Incongruously holding hands.

Almost unwillingly, Yana rolled toward him and put her head on his shoulder and gave him a few leads on some Marino clan Cadillacs. And then asked him for that favor she had in part brought him back here a second time to get.

At such a moment, what man in his right mind would say no?

CHAPTER THIRTY-TWO

If it isn't raining in Seattle, it's overcast. In fact, a publisher who wanted an aerial panorama for a book jacket once had to wait eight months just to get a clear day for the picture.

Take today: overcast, moist, but not raining; none was forecast until after the weekend. Which suited Big John Charleston right down to the waterlogged ground. Scraped out of the piney woods by his bulldozers here southeast of Seattle on Maple Hill Road, Big John had a subdivision he'd figured for a sure thing. Urban refugees fleeing California for the good life in God's country, what did they care about a few trees got axed to give them space? How could he miss?

But despite a hell of a lot of money paid under the table to various officials, the permits and zoning and environmental impact studies had taken so long that the goddam recession had its claws in when he'd been ready to roll. So Big John had fifty lots all platted out, sewer and utilities in, roads dozed and graded for blacktopping—but no buyers. Not even Californians.

He needed loan extensions from the banks, but to show the project was viable he had to pre-sell lots, which meant paved streets. And now the goddam envirofreaks were double-dipping for a second share, and there was an injunction against him getting any more work done until some other goddam study had been made. Well, screw that. He'd do it anyway—except that all the local contractors, knowing he was broke, wouldn't work on the cuff.

"We got assets." Little Johnny was Big John's son by his first wife, and, sadly, a mere sliver, not a chip, off the old block. "We got this model house done and three others framed, and the lake and the park and the golf course staked out—"

"We got dirt fucking streets is what we got." Big John was the size of the late John Wayne, whom he would have resembled if Wayne had worn Jay Leno's outsized jaw. "It starts raining and the streets turn to mud and *we* turn to mud."

"Joe Adams Road Paving, Inc., is really big down in Los Angeles, Pa. *Really* big. He's got prospectuses and photographs of jobs he's done, ten times the size of ours. His specialty is getting in and getting the job done before the environmentalists can get a restraining order. He says even after they got one, like with us, it's awful tough to tear up paved streets once they've been laid. He's just moving into the Northwest, that's why he's willing to give us such a good deal."

"But he wants the whole sixty thousand cash money up front," said Big John, "and we got thirty thousand eight hundred sixty-one dollars and twenty-two cents in the corporate account."

"Maybe offer him half down, Pa, give him the rest after we get the bank loans renegotiated. Meanwhile, all the streets in the subdivision will be blacktopped and ready for buyers—"

"Shut up. Lemme think."

Big John heaved himself to his feet with a grunt, went to stand in the open doorway of the sales office in the model house. Overhead was the huge illuminated billboard Little Johnny had insisted would catch the eye of motorists passing on Highway 169:

BIG JOHN'S BIG BUNGALOWS
BUY! RENT! LEASE!
FIVE MODELS TO CHOOSE FROM
FISHING—HIKING—BIKING—GOLF
CAREFREE MINUTES FROM THE CITY

He rubbed Jay Leno's massive jaw. Southern California road contractor. Designer jeans and dark glasses, prolly driving some shitty little foreign bug a real man couldn't hardly get his butt into. But here Big John was, with an unfinished subdivision would belong to the bank if he didn't get those streets paved. So his kid's $30,000 down wasn't such a bad idea.

"We'll see," he said at last. He had no other options.

A filthy mud-spattered pale blue Cadillac Seville STS, the new one winning all those auto mag best-car-of-the-year awards, swung in from the highway. California plates, on the door the silhouette of a big black bird with the tips of its spread wings going off into ribbons of blacktop road. Below that:

JOE ADAMS, INC., CONTRACTORS
ROAD PAVING OUR SPECIALTY
GLENDORA, CALIFORNIA

A very fat man got out of the Seville. He wore a stained blue workshirt with the arms cut off above the biceps and khaki work pants riding low under a balloon belly. The bottom two buttons on the shirt had strained open, showing a tepee of hairy skin with a navel deep enough to hide a golf ball. His neck was thick and his arms enormous and sweat stood on a face too shrewd for one so fat. He stuck out his hand.

"Joe Adams."

Big John took the hand. "Big John Charleston," he said.

Truth be told, Big John liked everything he saw. Even drove American, not Japanese. No flash—hell, construction game, a man needed a heavy car to drive around in—not afraid to get dirty, not afraid to put a sign on the door of his car. But Big John crossed belligerent arms over his own wide torso.

"That's a substantial amount of money you want. Ain't any way I'm gonna pay the whole contract off up front in cash."

Adams had a heavy, almost guttural voice that went with his massive physique. "There's reasons I'm askin' for that."

"I'd like to hear 'em."

Adams gestured at Little Johnny, hovering behind his pa like a family dog waiting to be told whether he's going to be allowed to ride in the car or not.

"I thought I made 'em clear to your boy there."

"Make 'em clear to me, too."

"Primo, you're in trouble with your bank." Big John swung around to glare dangerously at his son; Adams put up a detaining hand. "Not him. I got connections, even up here in Shitburg."

"You mean God's country," chanted Little Johnny in the Northwest's knee-jerk mantra about their heavenly land.

"Yeah? All God does up here is piss on a flat rock."

"No rain's slated 'til Monday," said Big John literally.

"Good. I can finish the job by then, and our work is guaranteed. In writing. Second, you got the Greenies breathin' down your neck. But Joe Adams, Inc., Contractors, we just do it—and once it's *in*, it's hard to tear out. That's why we can undercut anyone else's bid by fifty percent. And that's why we get our money up front."

Unfortunately, Big John still had only half the needed cash. But then Little Johnny surprised him with, "It isn't good business to pay you up front for a job you haven't even started."

"Tell you what," said Joe Adams. "Thirty thousand Monday morning, the other half in sixty days. Fair enough?"

Yes indeed! Big John was proud of his son for the first time in the kid's miserable weak-kneed life. All he had to do was figure out a way to hold this guy off on the second $30,000 until he could scratch up the dough. He stuck out his hand.

"Couldn't be fairer," he rumbled.

*   *   *

As Joe Adams drove away from BIG JOHN'S BIG BUNGA-LOWS up in Seattle, down in L.A. Ken Warren was turning his company car into the Sherman Oaks Inn on Ventura and Coldwater. Ignoring the office, he went down the sloping drive and turned left, as Kearny had instructed, to check the under-the-building parking stalls.

"There they are," said Trin Morales.

Next to the end wall was Dona Dulcinea's Fleetwood Sixty Special four-door sedan. In the stall this side of it was Adam Wells's Seville. They'd flip a coin to see who had to tow the company car back up north. But Morales spoke abruptly.

"I'm staying over." He dug an elbow into Warren's ribs. "Just came down 'cause I got a little *chiquita* lined up, 'course I couldn't

tell Kearny that. You drive one Caddy back up, tow the other—
I'll keep the company car. Got it, dummy?"

Without answering, Ken Warren got his towbar from the trunk
and tried the key Kearny had given him for the Seville. It worked.
Kearny's other key worked in the Fleetwood. Only then did he
turn back to Morales.

"Hndon' cat'th AIDTH," he said.

*   *   *

The others had already left when the nigger showed up. Wasn't
nothin' wrong with niggers playin' wide-out for the Seahawks, say,
goin' long for them bombs and them Hail Marys. But not around
Big John's subdivision. Hell no. Niggers was lazy and couldn't keep
their eyes and hands off your women.

This one was a little feller, couldn't go over 160 pounds, but had
the widest shoulders Big John'd ever seen on a man his size. Stood
looking around the staked-out subdivision under the lowering skies,
clipboard in hand.

"Looks like you're going to have some road-paving work done,"
he said pleasantly. "All graded and ready to go."

Big John fisted his hand around the roll of nickels he'd gotten
from the desk drawer before coming down the steps.

"Ain't any work, that's what you're after."

"Not looking."

"They're all sold, closed escrow on the last one yestiday."

"Before the streets are in," marveled the nigger. "Before the
houses are even framed up. In a recession economy. You're a hell
of a salesman, Mr. Charleston."

"You gettin' wise-ass with me, boy?"

The nigger just shook his black poll and said, "Wouldn't know
where I could find your paving contractor, would you?"

"Joe Adams? Try his office."

"Which is . . ." Ballpoint poised.

"In Seattle." Big John chortled at his own wit, then demanded
abruptly, "What ya wanna see him about, boy?"

"I'm with the State Contractors Licensing Commission . . ." Big
John put a hasty hand in his pocket to deposit the roll of nickels
there. "Question of whether he has the necessary permits and has

paid the necessary fees." He was looking into Big John's eyes for the first time, and there was unexpected steel in his gaze. "We don't want him to do any road paving here on your subdivision until it's cleared up. Do you understand?"

The nigger obviously didn't know about the Greenies' injunction against *any* work being done on the subdivision.

"I most surely do," said Big John evenly.

He'd keep away from the job over the weekend, in case this guy *did* come around and catch Adams paving without a permit. And just to be sure he'd . . . But he stopped his hand on its way to his money clip. The nigger somehow looked like a bribe offer might not set too well with him. And hell, wasn't no need. No gov'ment pussy'd ever worked the weekend in the entire history of bureaucracy, and the paving would be done by Monday.

Which gave Big John his really brilliant idea.

Make *sure* this pansy coon came around with his pansy little clipboard on Monday, after the job was finished, so he'd arrest Adams, at least shut him down for operating without a permit. Maybe Big John'd get himself a $60K job for *zero* K bucks.

"Mr. Adams plans to start work on the project first thing Monday morning," he said. "You can catch him here then."

*   *   *

Bart Heslip drove away satisfied. Josef Adamo indeed was in Seattle, calling himself Joe Adams. And would be out here at this subdivision Monday morning bright and early in his Seville.

But as he headed north on Empire Way, Bart got thoughtful. Big John Charleston had been too cooperative. What if the work was going to be done over the weekend, not next week?

Considering that rain was forecast for Monday, and considering what he'd learned that day going around to recyclers and paint wholesalers in the greater Seattle area, he'd hold off until Monday. He laughed aloud as he jinked over to the I-5 skyway that would take him all the way up to Seattle Center.

Monday was going to be a whole lot of fun.

Bart didn't like bigots any more than bigots liked him.

*   *   *

"Sir, you can't leave those cars there fastened together like that . . . *sir!*" Ken Warren, already out of the Fleetwood, just waited. "You'll have to uncouple them to park them here."

Fair enough. Ken bent to the task of getting the Seville off the towbar. He had taken U.S. One up through Big Sur to see firsthand the post-quake repairs they had made on the highway. Had seen HIGHLANDS INN, below that, *Pacific's Edge Restaurant,* on a sudden urge had snaked the linked Cadillacs up the one-way black-top drive to the restaurant looking out over the vast sweep of Pacific. He'd always wanted to eat in one of these fancy places, and Kearny had given him a raise and promised all his expenses on this trip would be paid besides . . . So why not?

The trouble was his towbar. New, it had cost him $396.83 including sales tax, and he just knew every son of a bitch in the world would like to steal it. So he wrapped the towbar in an old horse blanket he found in the trunk of the Seville, left the keys with the blond-headed car-parker, and sauntered across a tiled patio filled with fragrant flowers and green sprays of foliage and small carefully tended trees in great terra-cotta pots.

Inside Pacific's Edge were thick carpets and a two-tiered dining room with low redwood-beamed ceilings and slanted skylights of tinted glass. He paused at the reservation table. A beautiful brunette with Betty Boop curls dancing beside her cheeks stared up at him in undisguised astonishment.

Seeing heavy boots, blue-check shirt, thick moleskin trousers resistant to the battery acids often encountered when hotwiring under the hood. Smears of grease on his face and hands. Cradling something metal and lumpy wrapped in a horse blanket as if it were a baby rescued from a Dumpster.

To her, Ken Warren looked big, dumb, and dangerous.

And sexy. She asked faintly, "May I . . . help you, sir?"

"Hndinna," he got out.

She shivered slightly. She could just *feel* this inarticulate tree falling on her in the night, but Ken didn't notice. He was staring out over the tops of the down-slope trees outside, awed by the incredible sunset dying on the Pacific rim.

"Dinner for one? Very good, sir. Ah . . . would you like to check your . . ." She wasn't quite sure what sort of metal monster he was clutching to his chest, but it looked vaguely automotive. Ken shook his head, so she added brightly, "I'm sure your, um, will be safe at your table, sir."

Heads turned, heads were shaken, as Ken followed her down to the very front corner of the lower level in front of the wide picture windows. She didn't care. She was feeling a tingle in the loins very like that felt by Pietro Uvaldi after Ken had slapped him in the face and wrenched the shotgun away from him.

A waiter in crisp black and white showed up to hold Ken's chair for him. Before sitting down, Ken put his towbar very carefully in the chair facing him across the pastel tablecloth.

"Would you like something from the bar to start, sir?"

Ken shook his head conscientiously. He was driving. The waiter nodded and handed him a menu. "Enjoy your meal," he said.

Ken did. The kind of meal he hadn't known existed. His appetizer was a seafood carpaccio served with Chinese black beans, his entree a brochette of scallops and shrimp on a spicy cilantro parsley *beurre blanc*. The salad had *flowers* in it—actual flowers! His raspberries were the best he'd ever tasted.

When he finally left the restaurant, he gave his last $20 bill to the hostess. He didn't get home until four in the morning, making it only by siphoning gas from the Seville into the Fleetwood's tank—the dinner had taken his cash, all of it.

Maybelle woke up when he dragged into the apartment; they sat up until dawn as she extracted from him every last bit of his adventure. Then a crazy thing happened. She threw her big fat mammy arms around him and hugged him close and wept down his shirt. Good tears. The kind they cry in romance novels.

Craziest of all, Ken found himself crying right along with her.

CHAPTER
THIRTY-THREE

Talk about the luck of the *Irish*.

Trinidad Morales spent Friday night slipping the old banana to his *chiquita*, then very early Saturday morning had to go out a window when *chiquita*'s husband came home unexpectedly. So with the early sun creating long black low-angle shadows across the pavement despite the morning chill, he found himself strutting along Olvera Street puffing his cheap cigar, overnight bag in hand as if he had just hit town, unwittingly projecting earnest, honest, and stupid—none of which he was.

"Pardon me, sir . . ." A diffident Spanish voice at his elbow. Morales turned.

A tall thin stooped man in a brown suit, apparently a Chicano like himself. Worried brown eyes and a *bandido* mustache that bracketed his mouth like an inverted horseshoe.

"Yes?" Also in Spanish.

The man looked around nervously, edged a little closer.

"I am . . . Sir, I need . . ." Another look around. "Do you know an attorney, sir? One of our own people whom I can trust?"

Morales stood stock-still for a moment, the soft birdsong of Spanish voices around him, the smoke from his cigar rising straight up into the morning air. Then he shook his head sadly.

"Sir, I am sorry," he said, raising his overnight case slightly, "but I have only just arrived from . . ."

He stopped, suddenly as secretive as the tall stooped sad man beside him. The man found a faint smile. "From elsewhere," he supplied.

"You misjudge me," said Morales a little stiffly. "I was born in this country, I have money in the bank, transferred here from Florida so I can open a business with my brother-in-law who is a very fine taco cook. I am most sorry I cannot help you . . ." A delicate pause. "The Yellow Pages, perhaps?"

A violent headshake. "No! I cannot trust anyone unknown with this. I have something . . . I need advice that . . ." They were walking through the crowds, the tall man stooped and almost whispered in his ear, "I am an illegal, sir."

"For this you need no attorney unless you are caught."

The lips came closer yet, the voice lower still. "But sir, I have won the lottery!"

Morales stopped dead, gaping in surprise. Then he grabbed the thin man's arm and hustled him across the narrow street to a playground flanked by an elementary school with vivid murals painted on its walls. They sat down on a concrete bench facing the street, where no one could approach them unseen.

"The *California* lottery?"

"Yes. Last Wednesday's."

"Jesus, man, that's worth . . ."

The man put his long narrow hand on Morales's thick blunt one to make him lower his voice. Morales nodded, pulled a folded *L.A. Times* from the side pocket of his rumpled suit coat, found last Wednesday's winning number, proceeded in quieter tones.

"You hold *that* ticket? That one right there?"

"I do, sir."

Greed shook his voice. "Let me see it."

The man got out an ancient cheap imitation-leather wallet. From it he removed a battered lottery ticket. It was bent and folded and soiled from being taken in and out of the worn billfold many, many times, but it bore Wednesday's date and unmistakably matched the winning number from Wednesday's drawing.

"Blood of Christ!" said Morales in an awed voice that prevented it from being a curse. "That jackpot is seven million dollars! Even if others also hold the winning number . . ."

The man returned ticket to wallet, wallet to pocket. "You see now my problem. If I present myself with the ticket, being an illegal, perhaps instead of getting my money I will be seized and held by the immigration and sent back to my country."

"Why not get someone else to cash in the ticket for you?"

"I know no one in this city, sir, except you." A delicate pause. "And even you, I do not know your name, sir."

"Morales. Trinidad Morales."

"Jesús Zaragoza."

They shook hands, then sat on their bench in companionable silence, contemplating the problem in the unhurried, Spanish way. A distinguished middle-aged gentleman who also looked Latin, wearing a three-piece suit and a dark tie and highly polished black shoes, sat down on the adjacent bench. He took off his old-fashioned Borsalino and with his display handkerchief mopped the brow thus exposed.

Immediately, a couple of pigeons fluttered to the bricks at his feet and strutted about, cooing and cocking sharp eyes at him as if anticipating his 79-cent Big Bite of Granny Goose popcorn. While scattering fluffy white kernels he caught the eye of Morales and Zaragoza. He gave them a small courtly bow.

"Truly," he said, "it is too hot to wear a suit and tie."

Other pigeons converged, slipstreaming in to walk and talk and peck. The newcomer beamed at them, dispensed more popcorn.

"When I complete a saddening deposition such as the one just taken, I come here and feed popcorn to the pigeons. It makes me feel less disheartened by the follies of mankind."

Morales caught Zaragoza's eye. "Deposition?" he asked after a delicate pause. "Such as a lawyer might take?"

The distinguished middle-aged man brought out a business card and leaned across to hand it to them.

Manuel Cerruli
Attorney at Law

Below that was a Los Angeles address and phone number.

"Immigration law, perhaps?" asked Morales hopefully.

Cerruli shook his head. He shrugged. "Nothing so grand. Small things . . . wills, divorces, contracts . . . but it is a living and I feel I serve a useful purpose to my community."

"We . . . have a problem . . ." began Zaragoza hesitantly.

Of course the whole story came out. When he and Morales were finished, so was the popcorn and Cerruli was sitting back on his bench, wiping his face again with his handkerchief.

"Unfortunately, sir, I am not a man with the necessary knowledge of INS rulings and immigration law to be of any help to you . . ." He sat up suddenly, a light coming into his eyes. He checked his watch. "But I have a friend, of our race, who works in the INS office here in Los Angeles."

Zaragoza shook his head quickly, fear in his eyes.

"Immigration? No! He will just . . ."

"*She* is, I assure you, a friend. From my neighborhood." Señor Cerruli stood up with decision. "She works Saturday mornings, I will call her and present her with a hypothetical case." He eyed Zaragoza shrewdly. "Perhaps you can offer her a fee . . . some small percentage of your winnings . . ."

The three of them ended up crowded around a payphone, each with his ear close enough to the receiver to hear.

"Immigration and Naturalization," said a crisp male voice.

"Ms. Trejo, please," said Cerruli in excellent English.

Concepción Trejo spoke English with a Latin slur, and became first excited and then cautious at the hypothetical case presented to her. *Sí, la Migra* would hear of this illegal's attempt to cash in his winning ticket, and would find a way to deport him—with the ticket disappearing into some corrupt agent's pocket. The only way to do it was through a third party, a native-born American impervious to INS pressures. Morales eagerly snatched the telephone receiver from Cerruli's hands.

"I am such a one! I can cash in the ticket in my name!"

And who was he? They explained. But . . . delicately . . . how could they trust him? He became indignant. She was firm. As a favor to her old friend Señor Cerruli, she would meet them, they could talk this thing through, but . . .

They ended up driving up and down and around and through

245

the curving streets of Echo Park in Señorita Trejo's splendid new Cadillac Brougham as they thrashed out the details of a transaction that had rapidly become anything but hypothetical.

Señor Zaragoza, as the actual holder of the winning ticket, would receive one-half of the lottery winnings—$3.5 million.

Señor Morales, as the man who would present the winning ticket and have to face all of the attendant public scrutiny, would receive one-fourth of the winnings—$1.75 million.

Señorita Trejo and Abogado Cerruli, for picking a way through the INS and legal minefields, respectively, would each receive one-eighth of the winnings—$875,000 each.

If there were other holders of the winning number, all of these winnings would be scaled down proportionally. So all of the problems were solved except the greatest one—that of trust. Morales, after all, would have to be given the winning lottery ticket—*the winning ticket!* There had to be some deterrent that would keep him from making off with it and leaving the others without recourse . . .

"I am an honorable man," Morales protested. "You need only ask anyone in Miami whether I can be—"

"Unfortunately, this is Los Angeles," said Señorita Trejo. She was a handsome full-figured woman with snapping black eyes.

"His brother-in-law?" suggested Zaragoza diffidently.

"He would be very difficult to find on a Saturday like this," said Morales quickly, almost overplaying his hand because, of course, there was no brother-in-law. "And besides, if he heard of this he would want a percentage for his testimonial."

"There is a way," began Cerruli carefully. "It is not perfect, perhaps, but it would assure some safety to all . . ."

What? How?

"How much money have you had transferred from Miami to your bank here for the purpose of starting this taco place with your brother-in-law?" asked Señorita Trejo.

"Fifty-three thousand dollars," said Morales, but quickly added, "but I cannot . . . do anything with that money. It is from all the members of my family."

"You must," said Cerruli gently. "They all will benefit."

Señorita Trejo took it up. "It is the only way. You withdraw the money, give it to Señor Cerruli to hold, to show us that you are acting in good faith. Señor Zaragoza gives you the lottery ticket to show that he is acting in good faith. It is he who is at risk. As soon as you divide the first payment between us, he will return your money to you."

Morales argued and cajoled, but in the end he acquiesced, it only made sense: after all, $53,000 against $1.75 million . . .

The other three would wait in a taco joint across the street from his bank with the ticket. Morales would get his money before the 1:00 P.M. Saturday bank-close. He was sufficiently excited as he slid out of the booth that he knocked the señorita's purse to the floor. He gathered up the various items that fell out of it, returned it to her, and crossed busy Glendale Boulevard with his overnight bag for the money.

A few minutes later he recrossed the boulevard from the bank in which, of course, he had no account. Nor did he cross to the coffee shop. Instead, he went directly to the Brougham.

Morales opened the door of the Cadillac with the keys palmed when he had knocked Señorita Trejo's purse to the floor. He tossed in his overnight bag, and followed it into the plush interior. The engine caught instantly.

As the three furious Gypsies boiled out of the taco joint to hurl useless threats and imprecations after him, Morales flipped them a bird and drove quickly away. An hour later, the police informed of the repossession and the company car on a towbar behind the Brougham, he was on his way to San Francisco.

He had known the lottery ticket was real, of course, and it really had borne Wednesday's winning number. But Morales also had known that it was for *tonight's* drawing, purchased on Thursday after Wednesday's winning number had been announced.

For a skilled Gypsy documenter, child's play to change May 6 to May 9. For a private detective of Morales's experience, equal child's play to spot the alterations. He would not have been the first mark they had hit on with their scheme; but he would have been the first who must have seemed just right: an out-of-towner with money in the bank and a larcenous itch.

So . . . luck of the Chicano?

Or perhaps just what Bart Heslip already had remarked, a hell of a detective—even if a son of a bitch personally.

CHAPTER THIRTY-FOUR

Midafternoon on Saturday, Giselle went out the DKA back door and couldn't believe her eyes: a 1958 pink Eldorado convertible was parked in the storage lot with Ballard beside it, hands on hips, gazing at it in a proprietary way. Florida plates, but it *had* to be the one Dirty Harry had told her about. The one ripped off from the Palm Springs used-car salesman . . .

Beautiful Arab woman, posing as an American blonde.

Or beautiful Gypsy woman named Yana, posing as an Arab?

Elaborately casual, she asked, "Who'd you repo it from?"

"No repo. Just storing it for a friend for a few days."

"A Gyppo friend?" she asked flatly.

Ballard seemed to exude sexual smugness. "You know how it is, Giselle, I massage her back and she massages mine. Yana came through for me the other night with a lot of info . . ."

Yana came *through* the other night? Just say Yana *came* the other night. While Giselle, to her eternal shame, was down on the corner hanging around under a streetlamp like Lili Marlene. Never again, not for Ballard, not for any man.

"Don't be disgusting," she said to him.

Why didn't he . . . Of course! She'd never told him about the

248

Caddy lifted in Palm Springs! She'd wanted to track that lead down herself. He didn't know its significance. She walked around the car, peering inside, opening doors, kicking tires, secretly memorizing the I.D. number inside the driver's door.

"What do you figure it's worth?"

"Hell, I don't know," he said. "Classic ragtops in this condition can bring a lot of bucks, I know that." He looked over at her. "How'd you make out with the great Grimaldi hunt?"

"He's, um . . . no sign of him yet." She was *glad* to lie to him; he was sleeping with Ms. Gyppo Slut and bragging about it.

"Too bad. The President's gone, that means he's probably worked his scam and taken off." He patted her arm. "I know how much you wanted to nail that limo. But hey—we ought to be knocking off a bunch of Gyppo cars in the next few days. I'll leave some assignments on your desk—"

"Don't bother! I'll find my own cars!" She whirled away to storm quickly into the office.

Now what the hell was bugging Giselle? Ballard turned to the '58 Eldorado as if for an answer, but it told him nothing. Not yet.

*   *   *

After just forty minutes on the phone to Palm Springs, Giselle had Jeeter Pickett's calculated Fonzie-voice in her ear, asking about her measurements as if he had one hand in his pocket and she were Dial-a-Porn. All that ended when she asked about the '58 pink ragtop Eldorado.

"Them goddam Ay-rabs!" he erupted. "I'm not ever gonna get beyond what they did to me!"

Working off his debt over that damned car, he was still peddling used iron at Wonderly's Wonderful Wheels, instead of raking in big bucks over to the Mercedes agency in Palm Desert where he belonged . . . Giselle brought him back to the main points: first, the Eldorado's I.D. number; second, could the Arabs have been Gypsies *posing* as Arabs?

—How'm I gonna remember a car I.D. number, doll?

Well, could the bodyguard's mustache have been fastened on with spirit gum?

—Wasn't looking at his mustache, doll, was looking at that flick-blade of his.

How about the woman's blond hair? Maybe a wig?

—Wasn't looking at her hair . . . a greasy chuckle, Leastwise not *that* hair, you get my meaning, doll . . .

Giselle kept patiently at it, emerged with the following:

The number, gotten from the original loan agreement for Wonderly's HAPPY DAYS promo, matched the one on the Eldorado in the storage lot.

The woman, minus blond wig, *was* Yana.

The man, minus mustache and flickblade, *was* Ramon . . .

So out in the DKA lot was the car grabbed by Yana for some arcane Gypsy purpose, and then hidden at DKA by Ballard. She was hiding it from *someone*—almost certainly Rudolph. Could Giselle ask Larry to find out all the whys? No. By this time he was too far gone to lift a finger against his little Gyppo.

But now Giselle had her own Gypsy intimate, and the one thing Yana seemed to have that he didn't was this pink Eldorado. So wouldn't he tell her all about it if she showed up *driving* it?

Yes! She didn't stop to think about the situation any more than that, she just checked that Larry was elsewhere, got her pop keys and hotwire, and headed for the lot.

*   *   *

Why had Giselle's reaction to the pink Eldorado been so casual? Why had her rejection of Yana's easy repos been so angry? Ballard was at a second-floor window, taking a break from laboriously typing REPO ON SIGHTs on the Gyps Yana had given him, when the ragtop, top down, shot out into Eleventh Street with Giselle's unmistakable blond head behind the wheel.

Ballard took the stairs three at a time, was into his company Ford by the time she was jinking over to Ninth Street a few blocks up, lost her at Market, briefly spotted her going up the Larkin Hill, caught a flash of pink turning into California.

So. Heading for the luxury hotels atop Nob Hill. He slowed going by the Cathedral Apartments where Brigid O'Shaughnessy once gave Sam Spade the runaround; when Giselle turned in at the St. Mark, he immediately dropped his own car into the Masonic Auditorium garage across from Grace Cathedral.

A few minutes later he sauntered into the St. Mark, making himself bland. She was not in the lobby, nor in the coffee shop.

250

He drifted into the Garnet Room past its purple velvet rope. One of Scott Joplin's tinkling piano rags tinged the air with sadness when he caught sight of Giselle's gleaming blond hair and exquisite profile bent forward intently toward the handsome guy across the table from her.

In the lobby Ballard found a discreet chair, tried to think it through. The handsome guy was swarthy and black-haired and looked like an Italian mobster. Sure as hell, the Gyppo calling himself Angelo Grimaldi whose complicated long con—give that one to Kearny—apparently wasn't finished yet.

Real name, obviously Rudolph something.

What the hell was she doing with him? Working him to find out where he'd stashed the limo? Or working him for the other Gyppos' Cadillacs and *not* trying to find where he'd stashed the limo? Or . . . Ballard, conveniently ignoring his own identical arrangement with Yana, shied away from that particular *or*.

He felt a little grimy staking her out—Giselle, for God's sake!—but he was driven by an emotion he didn't even know he was feeling, let alone that the emotion was jealousy.

*   *   *

"Won't they recognize me as the underambassador's wife who was too dumb to know her own car?"

"The Secret Service left when their President left."

"What about hotel management? If one of them should—"

"They never saw you. To them that woman was a terrorist, remember?" Rudolph Marino chuckled. God, he was a handsome brute! For his part, he was charmed to be telling a *gadjo* woman things he would never tell a *rom* woman, not even Yana. "Besides, I haven't explained to you yet what happened to you . . ."

Giselle was getting high on Cordon Rouge, not their first bottle. "Whatever happened to *her,* if they see *me* here—"

"What happened is that I offed her."

"You *what?*"

Giselle's delighted squeal made him cover her pale long-fingered hand with a brown muscular one. He sighed theatrically.

"Alas, she is now somewhere in the Pacific with scrap iron tied to her ankles. Now, if they see me with a beautiful blonde, merely . . ." He kissed his fingertips. *"Cherchez la femme."*

Giselle finished her champagne and frowned sternly. She had something to ask him. And tell him, too. This was, after all, a business conference. Not like Ballard with his bimbo.

"First, Rudolph, why did you run all of those Caddies through one bank? If you'd used different banks, with different central computer systems, you would have had more time to . . ."

She stopped because Marino was chuckling in embarrassment.

"When I laid the idea out to the other *rom* . . ." He paused again and shook his head. "I wanted to use four banks, it would have been easier, but they said one bank . . . four branches . . ."

"But it doesn't make sense—"

"The stars said it did." A shrug. "The *rom* . . ."

Giselle shrugged in turn. He acted as if he didn't believe in superstition, but he'd gone along with it. "Okay. Now I want to know all about a nineteen fifty-eight pink Eldorado Biarritz convertible."

For perhaps the first time in his life, Rudolph Marino was speechless. He opened his mouth, shut it again, blinked, yawned like a confused cat, and then just stared at her.

"What has that car got to do with whether the Gypsies get a new King or a new Queen?"

Devalesa! This woman! But . . . with a typical Gypsy shrug he told her of the dying King's wish to be buried in a restored 1958 Eldorado convertible because he had ridden in one to his coronation in 1958. She was laughing before he was through.

"No no no no no! You have to have a casket and an embalmer and burial certificate and—"

"*You* do. Not us, we are the *rom*."

She leaned suddenly across the table toward him, so their faces almost touched. "Would you give me all the other Gypsies' Cadillacs for that pink Eldorado?"

Her voice slurred "Cadillacs" so it ended with a slight but distinct "sh" sound. Yet, even here, even now, even tipsy, she was working him. He loved it. He shrugged again.

"Of course. But even if you could and I did, you must understand that the *rom* are never long in one place . . ." Except Stupidville next week, but she was not to know of *that* encampment, ever. "We Gypsies are like the wind—"

"I have it," she said. For the second time that evening, he was momentarily struck stupid. She almost giggled as she pointed at the floor as if in confirmation. "I drove it here."

Not like other *gadje* women, no, not just useful to him . . .

But still useful. On Monday he had to be heading for Stupidville because the real Grimaldi would make his departure imperative . . . somehow, he *had* to be driving that pink Cadillac.

"Let's go down to the garage and take a look at it." He could barely disguise the greed in his voice.

Giselle shook her head with a lazy smile. "I didn't say it was in the garage. If Lar—" She stopped with a surprised look on her face. Champagne. She covered by saying, "Kiss me."

He did, using lips and tongue, working on her in turn . . . *Devalesa*, maybe this woman had hidden *rom* blood in her, after all. Just her kiss made him stiff.

But meanwhile, *Lar*. Larry something. Of course! The tall blond man with the hawk eyes. Yana must have asked him to hide the Eldorado for her at their repossession agency, where Rudolph would never think of looking. How admirable of her! But he merely shrugged at Giselle.

"It is of no moment. We can go out to dinner in the limo." He gave it the lightest possible touch while feeling his heart actually pound as it had when he had lost his virginity at the age of 11. Champagne, of course. It could be nothing else. "Or . . . we could get room service . . ."

This was it, wasn't it? Giselle had felt her body go soft and creamy when they had kissed. This was what she had come here to find out, admit it. About herself. About him. All questions answered, even apart from getting leads to Gyppo Cadillacs . . .

Ballard was probably with Ms. Slut right now.

"With more Cordon Rouge?" she asked almost defiantly.

"For us both," he said. "And with oysters for me."

*   *   *

Ballard was watching the blonde behind the reception desk, name-tagged MARLA, because she was a pale shadow of Giselle and because she was so obviously angry. Eyes glued to the entrance of the Garnet Room, mouth a downturned arc so compressed her lips had disappeared. Then her face tightened in barely repressed fury—and Giselle and the Gypsy came across the lobby to the elevator banks, arms around each other.

Arms around each other! Giselle and the Gyppo bastard! And Ballard was stuck. He couldn't get in the elevator with them, obviously; and if he caught the next up-car he wouldn't know their floor or room . . .

Giselle with that slimy Gypsy bastard who'd screw anything hot and hollow . . . He realized he was sitting with his teeth gritted and his hands white-knuckled on the chair arms. Jesus, Larry, get a grip. Giselle'd never cared what he did with who, just as he'd never cared what she did with who, either. Except as a friend. Sure, that was it. Friendship. He hated to see his friend sleeping with . . .

Bullshit. Jealously. White-hot, searing jealousy. Unexpected, totally out of left field. But it *hurt. Burned.* Like drinking goddam Drāno straight out of the can.

But still Larry Ballard sat there.

Why? To find out how tough he was? Or to some purpose . . .

Then the blond woman named Marla was relieved at the desk, and Ballard knew what that purpose was. In the coffee shop she looked up, startled, when he sat down across from her. He flashed a laminated yellow State of California registration card with his color photo in the lower right-hand corner.

"I'm a private detective working on a case involving that blonde who got on the elevator with Mr. Grimaldi," he said in gruff professional tones. "I'm hoping you can help me . . ."

Could she. An hour and four cups of coffee later, he knew all about Angelo Grimaldi from New York, and terrorist calls, and— although Marla didn't—a whole lot about a Gyppo named Rudolph. He even had figured out the way the Gyppo, as Grimaldi, had used her in running—again, unknown to Marla—a damned clever scam on the hotel management.

Later for that. For now . . .

He went down to the garage. In all this the '58 ragtop was significant, perhaps vital, but Giselle would be bringing it back; and besides, it wasn't on his REPO ON SIGHT list. Rudolph's long black limousine was. And Larry Ballard, no matter how much Drāno he might have drunk, was a professional.

*   *   *

Third time lucky: Marino and Giselle made it absolutely in synch, then fell apart gasping. The champagne was still cold, so they lay companionably on the king-size bed, sipping bubbly and smoking cigarettes while their hearts slowed.

Their loving had been fierce, not tender; during her final involuntary rhythmic contractions, Giselle had felt Rudolph's ultimate frenzied thrusts not only in her vagina but in her heart, perhaps even in her soul. For the first time in her life, she had wanted to be a succubus, to contract her whole body down around a man and greedily suck up all the juice he had in him, everything, everything . . .

She looked over at him in the warm glow of city lights far below their aerie, and felt a great joy and sadness together, as if something in her wept at a loss of ecstasy not yet known, and she was roused to give this man something, something fabulous . . .

Well, what about a Kingdom?

"The pink Cadillac," she said to Rudolph. "It is yours."

But with that highly feminine perception that made him so irresistible to women, he understood her gift and returned it.

"*Cara mia*," Rudolph said, "if you do that, Larry will know you have taken it and have given it to me. I can't let you—"

"I want him to know," said Giselle grimly.

CHAPTER
THIRTY-FIVE

Larry knew bright and early Monday morning.

He had gone to DKA to drive the limo to the bank's storage lot, but instead found himself staring at the empty space where the pink Cadillac had been—just as Giselle came striding in. Through the open garage door Ballard could see the cab that had brought her. She was wearing the same clothes as Saturday.

She stopped dead at sight of the shiny black limo, a flush mantling her cheeks; Larry must have followed her to the St. Mark on Saturday, so he must know she had just left Rudolph snoring on his king-size bed in oyster-depleted sleep.

"*Bastard!*" she hissed in her embarrassment.

As he thought, She spent the *whole weekend* banging that Gyppo fuck, and *then* she gave him Yana's pink Cadillac besides!

"*Slut!*" he snapped in his hurt and confusion.

It was war.

*　　*　　*

Not for O'Bannon. He had arrived in Hawaii midday Saturday following the trail of a Rudolph clan member named Ral Wanko who had shipped a long sleek white De Ville to Honolulu, his home

256

base, the day after the big Cadillac grab. That was all O'B had, so Kearny had lined up a P.I. contact for him on Oahu.

"Little Jap guy named Shinji Ueda. I met him on Maui during the P.I. convention at the Kaanapali Beach Resort last year," he explained. "Size of your thumb, but smart—he'll probably have Wanko picking you up at the airport in the De Ville."

Not quite. But Mr. Ueda was there himself, holding up a big neatly lettered O'BANNON sign on a wooden stick. Ueda was short indeed, about five-two, and a crow among peacocks. Instead of the usual *aloha* shirt and shorts and *zori*, he wore a three-piece dark suit, a dark tie, and highly polished black oxfords.

He bowed. "O'Bannon-san. Shinji Ueda."

O'B returned it. "Make that O'B-san, Ueda-san."

Ueda had a round head and crinkly cheeks and narrow bright inquisitive eyes. Driving the Ala Moana Highway from the airport to Waikiki, he cast O'B a long worried sideways look.

"I have made certain inquiries."

O'B had his window down so warm moist air delightfully heavy with flowers could ruffle his russet hair. "And?"

"Is very dangerous. Ral Wanko is a very bad man indeed, with very bad friends. They steal very nice cars to order. Repaint, or take apart to use parts for other cars—"

"Chop shop," said O'B.

A short bow behind the wheel. "Even so." A pause. "They move auto-altering establishment many times a year. Hard to find." Ueda drove with his hands at ten and two in the proper manner. He bowed again, slightly. "But I go find for you."

O'B took him at his word. He dug his toes into dazzling white sand in front of his high-rise hotel, swam in the ocean, drank at the beachside bar, saw the Banyan Tree, and at sunset wandered along the Ala Wai Promenade watching the sailboats ghost by. After dark he went downtown, barely avoided a fight in a poolhall, rejected the advances of a truly stunning *hapa-haole* hooker, and went to bed alone feeling sober and virtuous and that he hadn't had so much fun since his Army days.

That was Saturday.

*   *   *

On Sunday, Mr. Ueda took him up to the incredible verdant freefall of the Pali, where many brave warriors had gone to their death, then out to the rich exclusive streets off Kahala Avenue. Not a word of business. Mr. Ueda had his golf clubs in the backseat and was one of the peacocks today, wearing a short-sleeved flowered shirt that showed a chest and arms suggesting he spent a lot of hours in the *dojo* breaking bricks with his bare hands.

They came around a sweep of drive to a stunning view out to the Pacific past the shoulder of decayed volcano known as Diamond Head. Blue-edged fluffy clouds dreamed on the distant horizon. Ueda gestured at a long sleek red Jaguar XJ6 parked at the curb.

"That one," he said. "Tonight."

O'B craned around at it. "That one what tonight?"

"They steal. You follow to chop shop. De Ville be there."

They had rounded the Diamond Head crater, were entering Kapiolani Park. In the moist heavy air, the lush vegetation rang with the squawks and shrieks of the zoo's exotic harsh-voiced tropical birds.

"How do you know all this stuff about 'em?" asked O'B.

Ueda laughed, hee-hee-hee. "Call in lotta favors. Sam Spade, huh?" He slapped O'B's knee in almost shocking intimacy. "I give you car to drive, you stake out Jaguar, you catch 'em, be big hero with Five-O." Another hee-hee-hee, a punch on the arm. "Book 'em, Dano!"

The car stopped under the frangipani bushes flanking the hotel parking lot. Heat bounced off the sun-softened blacktop. The hotel balconies were a white ladder climbing a blue heaven. They could have been in Dallas. O'B cleared his throat.

"Ah, Shinji, maybe you'd like to, ah, come along tonight, share in the glory with Five-O." He gestured. "I bet you know judo, karate, kung fu, aikido, all that martial-arts stuff . . ."

Alarm passed across Mr. Ueda's face. "Oh no no no no. No know martial arts. Know golf." His seamed face split into a huge grin. "Low eighties."

That was Sunday.

*   *   *

After midnight, thus technically Monday, O'B was parked under the shadows of some anonymous estate's tall hibiscus border when he heard the almost silent rush of a bicycle-built-for-two manned by two massive figures in *aloha* shirts. Far down the wide curving expensive street, the one riding behind slid off to dart over to the Jag XJ6. His partner kept pedaling.

Pretty slick. No wonder no one ever heard the thieves.

Motor. Lights. Red wink of taillights, one marred by the "X" of black electrician's tape O'B had put over it earlier. This helped him track the Jag through still-heavy Sunday night freeway traffic to the Pali Highway Interchange, over to Ward Avenue, and into the industrial district.

There O'B had to drop back so far that he lost it, but going by an abandoned-looking warehouse he saw double doors sending out a widening wedge of light. When the Jaguar entered and the doors closed again, O'B's vague silhouette slid through the final sliver of light behind it. Inside, he crouched beside a BMW, panting with excitement and perhaps even terror.

The two huge men both looked Hawaiian. But as one got out of the Jag, the other said, "Any trouble, Ral?"

So the hulking driver was the Gypsy, Ral Wanko. Who shook his head and said, "Like silk," then stopped to stare at the tape on the taillight. "Hey, bruddah, whadda hell's this?"

"Who cares? We got da kine work to do."

Their upper halves disappeared beneath the Jag's hood. Beyond the midnight mechanics was the De Ville O'B was after, and beyond that, through another set of wide-open double doors, an enclosed parking area and an alley. By merely going around the block, O'B could have snuck up on the De Ville and grabbed it.

But now he was trapped. Closed automatic doors behind him, the two midnight mechanics between him and the De Ville and the safety of the open doors beyond it. *Huge* midnight mechanics. He couldn't go back, through, or around.

But could he go *over*?

The peaked tin roof was held up by two-by-six beams bolted together in rectangular patterns, supported by angled crisscross two-by-fours bolted to other beams above. If he could get up there, could he hump his way along one of those horizontal beams to the far wall where a rough ladder of two-by-fours waited?

O'B crept back to the similar ladder fastened to the wall behind him. Ten agonizing minutes, one rung at a time, a fly on the wall in plain sight, freezing each time one of the car choppers emerged from beneath the hood.

Just as he straddled a beam far above them, Ral Wanko laid down his wrench and wiped his hands on a greasy red rag.

"Gotta go take a dump."

One gone. Do it now. Grip the beam ahead with both hands. Lean forward, weight on arms, slide butt forward eight or ten inches. Again. Again again again. And yet again. He was almost directly over the Jaguar now . . .

"Hey, bruddah, you one dead man."

Whirling, O'B lost his balance, saved himself only by grabbing one of the angled two-by-four support struts. Wanko was directly behind him on the beam, grinning ferociously, a short-handled sledge for beating out fenders upraised in a hand that made it look like a doctor's reflex hammer.

O'B should have remembered Wanko was a Gypsy, one of the world's ultimate survivors, which meant one of the world's ultimate paranoiacs. That "X" of tape had sent him into ambush to see if some unwary quarry would break cover. Unwary O'B had.

"Listen," O'B said in a voice that wobbled with earnestness and *bonhomie*, "I'm not the cops and I'm not here to—"

Wanko swung the sledge. O'B ducked, it splintered his two-by-four support, he went off the beam sideways, arms windmilling wildly to no avail, struck the roof of the Jaguar feet-first. They went from under him, he shot off the slick curved surface to land on the floor just as the massive Hawaiian charged him.

O'B jinked, his attacker smashed headfirst into the side of the Jag. Wanko couldn't get off the beam quickly without rupture, so O'B walked across the goal line for the score. He gave them a digit salute while burning rubber out of the garage.

By noon Monday the De Ville was in bonded storage waiting shipment back to the mainland, Five-O had a copy of the report, and Mr. Ueda was driving a *lei*-laden O'B to Honolulu International for the long hop to Florida, where Yana's info had sort of pinpointed another Gyppo Cadillac.

O'B hadn't had this much fun even *in* the Army.

*   *   *

That same morning in Seattle, Bart Heslip, seeking some fun of his own, parked his rental car half a mile from BIG JOHN'S BIG BUNGALOWS. He left the keys on top of the left rear tire and the completed paperwork in the glove box; he would call Avis with directions where to pick it up if he was successful.

The paved streets of Big John's subdivision were black and smooth and gleaming in the muted light that managed to get through an angry cloud cover. Bart hunkered down behind the signboard and thought, Hot damn, it looks like rain any minute.

When the rain began, that was when the fun would begin.

* * *

A two-year-old Chrysler Imperial pulled up in front of the sales office. Big John and Little Johnny got out. Big John was carrying a satchel. Little Johnny looked at the gleaming streets of the subdivision and got inordinately excited.

"Pa, those streets look fantastic! People come out here, drive around, they'll just start laying their money down!"

"Yeah, but where's that nigger gonna take Adams down?"

Little Johnny looked a little scared. "Pa, you sure you wanta . . . uh . . . This Joe Adams looks pretty . . . tough . . ."

"Ain't us going to do anything, son," said Big John. "It's just the man from the State of Washington gonna do his duty."

Just then Josef Adamo's Seville turned in from the highway. The fat Gypsy grunted his way out from behind the wheel and came around the back of the car, leaving his keys in the ignition. With a look of great self-satisfaction he waved his arm at the ribbons of tar laid over the flattened landscape.

"What I tell you? You ever see a better job than that?"

"It's terrific!" enthused Little Johnny.

Big John had $30,000 in the satchel; it was a hell of a job at the price, but it would be a hell of a lot better job if the price was zero, nothing at all. Stall 'til the nigger got there.

"It looks okay, but that's what we're paying you for."

"Speaking of getting paid . . ."

"Yeah, well, you were promising written guarantees . . ."

"I got 'em right here in the car."

So Big John was able to stall him twenty minutes, reading things he didn't give a damn about anyway, all he needed was the roads laid—they were—and the nigger there—he wasn't—but then just a few little drops of rain started falling and Joe Adams got impatient and uptight and almost abusive.

"What the fuck you waiting for, Charleston? I laid your goddam streets, now gimme my money!"

Big John reluctantly handed over the satchel, buying more time because Joe Adams had to count his money. But then the rain started to come down in earnest—and *still* no nigger—and Adams was abruptly and surprisingly satisfied. He shook hands, tossed the satchel into the Seville, and started to get in himself only to be arrested by a sharp voice at his back.

"Are you Joseph Adams?"

Adamo backed out awkwardly and looked around. A compact very wide-shouldered black man had materialized out of the rain.

"Who the hell wants to know?"

"Would you step away from the car, please?"

Adamo got a confused look. "You a cop? This a roust?"

The black man totally ignored the rain that was really pelting down now, sparkling in his tightly curled black hair, running down his face in rivulets.

"He's from the state licensing bureau!" burst out Little Johnny in gleeful triumph. "He's going to get you!"

"Please. Step away from . . . thank you."

The black man moved forward as Adamo shuffled awkwardly aside.

Big John felt wonderful under his rain slicker and hood. It was going to work out; even his kid showed promise. "Sir," he said respectfully to the black man, "I had no idea he was going to illegally blacktop my roads without the proper permits . . ."

He stopped because the most extraordinary thing happened. The black man from the state stepped right by Joe Adams and into the Seville and slammed the door. The automatic door locks clicked shut. The car moved away around the traffic circle back toward the main highway. Everyone woke up at once.

Adamo started running after the still-slow-moving vehicle.

"MY CAR!" he bellowed. "MY CAR!"

Big John, yellow rain slicker flapping, suddenly ran too.

"MY MONEY!" he shouted. "MY MONEY!"

Little Johnny was staring at the beautiful blacktop roads.

"OUR STREETS!" he yelled. "PA! OUR STREETS!"

Big John checked at his son's cry. Looked.

His beautiful shiny streets were dissolving under the pounding rain into mud, their blacktopping running down the ditches beside them. Just as Bart Heslip had known they would, because Josef Adamo had bought up just about all the recycled crankcase oil and cheap paint thinner in Seattle. A mix of paint thinner and crankcase oil applied to a road surface looks exactly like high-class road paving—until it rains.

Then the glistening new surface just melts and vanishes.

Screaming his fury, Big John Charleston flung himself on fat Josef Adamo.

Bart Heslip's last view of BIG JOHN'S BIG BUNGALOWS was through sheets of torrential rain as two hefty tar babies rolled over and over in the mud, flailing ineffectually away at each other. Even as the downpour obliterated the sight, the third figure, jumping up and down and waving its arms, lost its footing and rolled down the muddy slope into the fray.

It wasn't until he hit the Idaho line on his way to Chicago that Bart stopped to check out the bag that Josef Adamo had tossed into the Seville.

Thirty thousand dollars—in a pig's valise! Bart Heslip cracked up. As Jane Goldson would say in her Limey accent, Dan Kearny *really* was going to do a bird over the personal property in this baby!

CHAPTER
THIRTY-SIX

Rudolph's actually scant data to Giselle was now going out, as Yana's also scant data to Ballard already had, so people were on the road for the second wave of repos before the first wave had even hit the beach. Kearny still was holding off on referrals to affiliates around the country, and even to DKA branch offices: he didn't want to make assignments until he had specific cars, names, and addresses to give them.

Both O'B and Bart Heslip had called in.

The Spanish Lottery Gyps' car was in the barn and Morales was on a plane to Cabo San Lucas, where an unnamed Gyp was maybe using his Cadillac in a lost-goldmine scam on some yachtsmen. In Baja, a Spanish-speaker was a must; hence Morales.

Ken Warren was driving Sarah Walinski's Dodge Charger into the sunrise feeling well-content even though still not involved in the Great Gypsy Hunt. Their client on the Charger was a Jersey City used-car dealer who thought DKA's three bids on the car were too low. Ignoring the fact that drunks' cars get beat-up very rapidly, he thought DKA was jerking his chain. He wanted the Dodge ferried back to Jersey for resale off his own lot.

Which ticked Dan Kearny off enough to tell Ken to get cash or certified check for all costs before handing over the Charger. Ken was glad to. Don't get him started on Jersey City . . .

The real point was that Dan Kearny had promised to give him any east coast Gypsy assignments that might develop while he was on the road.

*   *   *

Giselle Marc needed a shower and clean underwear. She couldn't call Rudolph, the hotel switchboard would be listening in, but she needed to tell him that Ballard—*damn* him—had grabbed the limo she'd promised Rudolph he could keep until his hotel scam was over. So she'd told Jane Goldson to put through any call from Mr. Grimaldi immediately—but no others. She was so upset she didn't realize Ballard overheard the instructions.

The phone rang. Giselle grabbed it up.

"*Cara mia*. I missed you when I awoke this morning."

"Me too." She paused. "Rudolph, I . . . have to tell you . . ."

*   *   *

Everything fair in love and war, right?

And this was war.

So when he saw Giselle's extension light up, Ballard punched in and shamelessly eased his receiver off the hooks.

To hear Giselle's voice, "Rudolph, I . . . have to tell you that . . . um . . . Larry, uh, repossessed your black limo over the weekend. Took it right out of the St. Mark garage."

Rudolph's hearty chuckle came over the wire, tightening Ballard's hand around the receiver as if around Rudolph's neck.

"*Cara mia* mine, that is all right—let your Larry have his dog's leavings, his Yana will dump him when she learns *I* have the pink Cadillac! He is meaningless to me."

"I can hardly wait until tonight," said Giselle in a dreamy little-girl voice that made Ballard want to fwow up.

"Nor I, my love," said Rudolph. "I will count the hours until I hold you in my arms again."

He made kissing noises into the phone, and hung up. So did Ballard—a tiny bit carelessly because he was fighting his gag reflex. Giselle caught the sound of the receiver going down.

Ballard! Listening in on her call!

She leaped to her feet, on her way upstairs to rip the sneaky bastard's ears off, when she saw *his* extension light up. When it stayed lit, she sat down again and punched into it and carefully and silently lifted the receiver. Love and war . . .

Larry was speaking when she eased the receiver to her ear.

". . . find out about that pink Caddy and about tonight."

"Of course tonight!" exclaimed a voice that could only be Yana's. "But the pink Cadillac—I need it before then, the danger has passed, it is perfect to . . . conclude my business with Teddy White tonight. Let us meet at that little café in North Beach . . ." Ballard was silent long enough for alarm to enter her voice and for Giselle to think, Maybe Ms. Slut's clairvoyant after all. "The Eldorado *is* safe, is it not? It is vital—"

"Ah, sure, sure, it's fine. But why's it so important?"

"This afternoon for that, my love. And then tonight . . ."

She gave a throaty laugh and hung up.

Giselle, gloating, slipped her receiver back on the hooks when she was certain she had a dead line. Ballard and his Gypsy princess were about at the end of the trail. When he couldn't deliver the pink Cadillac to her this afternoon . . .

But to make sure, tonight, before going to Rudolph's bed, she would stake out Teddy, and he would lead her to Yana, and somehow she would mess up Yana's scam and Yana along with it.

*   *   *

Ballard hadn't told Yana he'd lost the pink Cadillac because he didn't have to: he'd gotten something that morning over the phone from Marla at the St. Mark that he expected would let him teach Rudie-baby how to play hardball.

*   *   *

Angelo Grimaldi shot his cuffs so his antique gold links could be seen glittering at his wrists, then pushed open the door to Gunnarson's office. He finally was playing match-point in the ultimate game of hardball he had come to San Francisco to play.

Delia, Gunnarson's lanky but full-bosomed secretary, looked up at him with smouldering eyes, very different from the eyes with which she had regarded his first demand to see her boss. Obviously, Gunnarson had been pillow-talking to her about Angelo Grimaldi,

and her look said she might find sexual congress with a lean dangerous Mafia attorney much more exciting than with a dull overweight
hotel manager. Alas. Never to be.

"They're waiting for you inside, Mr. Grimaldi."

He nodded, caressed her with his eyes, and went through the
inner door she buzzed open. Gunnarson, Shayne, and desiccated
little Smathers were drawn up in a row across the room as if to
repel a cavalry charge.

Grimaldi grinned at them. This was the moment every conman
waited for, the moment of truth. Whichever way it went, the game
had been worth it. He threw Shayne's words back in his face.

"Your meeting, your agenda, gentlemen. But briefly. I have a
plane to catch."

Smathers must have gotten the short straw. He stepped forward
almost formally and cleared his throat.

"Mr. Grimaldi, we have carefully considered your . . . offer to,
um, er—"

"Blow the fuckers away," supplied tough Angie Grimaldi in his
Bronx voice, "before they blow up your fancy fucking hotel. But
your forty-eight hours have passed, so I'm on my way to—"

"Goddam you, we're paying!" burst out Shayne in a hoarse voice.
"All right? We're paying!" He stepped closer, his red face ugly.
"But we know who you are and where you are, and if you're fucking
us over and the Saladin attack our hotel—"

"When I leave this room, gentlemen," he said with a totally
straight face, although the blood was singing in his veins and his
stomach was quaking with suppressed laughter, "to all intents and
purposes the Saladin will have ceased to exist. You have my personal guarantee that they will never bother you again."

Gunnarson put a satchel on the desktop.

"Seventy-five thousand dollars. It's also gotta guarantee that
whatever happens, the hotel's name won't be connected—"

"Connected with what? With who? I will never have been here.
We will never have had this talk. There will never have been a
blonde. It's what the politicians call deniability."

Gunnarson opened the satchel, his associates pressed forward to
bid a last fond farewell to the banded bundles of greenbacks stacked
inside. Not Grimaldi. He merely leaned across the desk to push
the intercom button.

"Delia, please come in here. Leave your steno pad."

As he released the switch and snapped the satchel shut, Shayne began, surprised, "But don't you want to count . . ."

Delia entered, looking puzzled because it had been Grimaldi's voice on her intercom. He handed her the satchel.

"Tell Marla at the front desk to have this sent down to the garage and stowed in the trunk of my Cadillac with the rest of my luggage. And have the car brought around to the front entrance."

Delia looked at Gunnarson, who nodded slightly.

"Ye . . . yes, sir, Mr. Grimaldi."

Grimaldi extended a $20 bill also. "For the flunkie who takes down the luggage and brings up the car."

Hesitantly, she took satchel and bill and departed. Grimaldi spoke to the three hotel officials as if there had been no interruption.

"You know who and where I am—but I also know who and where *you* are. So I don't have to count the money, do I?" There was a chorus of assent to his negative. He nodded in a courtly way. "Then, the best goodbyes are the shortest, gentlemen."

And was gone, drawing the door shut behind him as if on a wake, fighting laughter out past Delia's unattended desk. But she was entering as he left, brushing up hard against him, and he grabbed her wrist, spun her around, pushed her against the door frame to grind her pelvis against his own as he kissed her with hard contempt on the mouth.

He finally released her. "A pity, *cara*," he said. Then he went out the door quickly and down the hall to the front desk.

He had been rough with her because she was not Giselle—and because he would never see Giselle again. Inescapable, but . . . for just this once, if he could have *not* been a Gypsy . . .

But he was. Not just a Gypsy, but soon to be *King* of the Gypsies! Going out the heavy ornate doors to the traffic circle in front of the hotel, he blew a kiss to Marla. She gave no acknowledgment, which he found interesting and at the same time unsettling. But what matter now? It was finished. He had won!

At the curb, he gestured to the doorman.

"The pink Cadillac, my good man."

It was his first sight of it, now all his own. Gleaming and exciting in the bright San Francisco sunshine, the top down so its thorough-bred lines showed to best advantage. Worth, literally, a King's Ransom, and looking it.

The tall well-built car-parker, his face shadowed by his uniform hat, brought the Caddy almost ceremoniously up to the entrance. Rudolph came around it to the driver's side.

But the car-parker didn't get out. Instead he tipped his hat to the back of his head to look up at Rudolph. Blond hair. Hawk features. Hawk eyes that drilled into Rudolph's. Whose mouth fell open in sudden recognition and surprise as Ballard waved the $20 bill languidly under his outraged nose.

"Thanks for the tip, Rudie-baby. See you around."

And tromped on it. The Caddy shot away from the hotel and zipped across Powell Street under the nose of a startled cable car, to disappear down the California hill. Marino ran a few paces after it, fists clenched, face congested, eyes ablaze. Stung! Totally! By a *gadjo*, yet. With the help of another *gadjo*, the casually dismissed check-in clerk, Marla.

Then Rudolph stopped. Took a couple of deep breaths. Chuck-led. Ballard was besotten, wasn't he? So he'd deliver the car to Yana, wouldn't he? Yana would drive it to Stupidville.

Where Rudolph Marino would take it away from her.

His $75,000, so superbly scammed out of the St. Mark Hotel executives? Gone also. But if Rudolph knew his Yana, eventually most of that money would find its way into her hot little Gypsy hands. And Rudolph was a master at taking things away from Yana.

Meanwhile, no other *rom* need know he'd lost it, right? So his scam would stand among the best in the great legends of the Gypsy oral tradition—and help him get his Kingship.

With a rueful grin, Rudolph turned back to the uniformed door-man to whistle him up a cab for the airport.

*   *   *

Larry Ballard figured Rudolph's $20 tip was the easiest money he'd ever made. Of course he'd had to give one of the St. Mark's car-parkers $50 for a blind eye and the use of his uniform—but that was DKA's money, not his.

After he removed and itemized the personal property in the car, he would return it to Yana. Who need never know he had temporarily lost sight of it, right?

So she would come to him willingly in the night.

This night.

CHAPTER THIRTY-SEVEN

Yana's thoughts of the coming night, *au contraire*, were hard-edged. In a couple of hours, she would meet Larry to get back the pink Cadillac; she had given it to him for safekeeping after getting word that Rudolph had pinpointed its hiding place. Now its safety didn't matter: tonight, after her ultimate coupling with Teddy's bank account, it would be on the road.

Because she had him hooked so hard, Teddy himself had come clamoring for his own destruction the day before yesterday. His phone call caught her still in bed not long after six o'clock on Saturday morning: the bed Ballard had left not an hour earlier, sneaking down the stairs shoes-in-hand so Ramon would not know of their frenzied lovemaking.

"Madame . . . Madame Miseria? This is—"

"Theodore Winston White the Third."

"You knew it was me?"

"I always know it is you." Her voice hummed like a stroked harp. She knew her man as she knew the contours of her beloved crystal ball. In the warm afterglow of sexual satiation, she was perfectly pitched to exploit him. "I receive certain emanations from you when I pick up the receiver."

Actually, Teddy's voice was unmistakable, thin and reedy and hesitant and unsure of itself, much like Teddy. She took a chance— not much of a one at 6:00 A.M., not with Teddy.

"You are calling me from your bedroom, you are barely able to get up, the snake has crawled deeper into your body."

"Yes!" The eagerness of the hypochondriac expatiating his illness quickened his voice. "It . . . it's like a red-hot cable down the back of my leg. I want . . . I need . . ."

"It is as I feared," she said. "When the demon entered my body from the egg, my terrible battle to expel him told me that the evil is very strong indeed."

She was sitting up in bed now, smelling rich strong black coffee, Gypsy coffee boiled in a big old enameled pot with the grounds and an eggshell. Perhaps Ramon himself was a mind reader; or perhaps he had heard her on the phone, taking care of business on a 6:00 A.M. Saturday. It might even be his way of making amends for his intransigence about her love life.

Even so, she was glad he hadn't seen Larry sneaking down the stairs. Meanwhile, Teddy was still whining on the phone.

"You know what you must do," she said in ringing, apocalyptic tones. "And quickly. Midnight Monday."

"Midnight? Monday?" Alarm squirmed in his voice.

"It is your stepfather you have offended," she reminded him inexorably. "It is the only way."

"Oh God!" moaned Teddy softly.

This was it, the culmination, the final sting: after that, he would never see her again. She said, "Tam Junction. Midnight Monday. The fruit stand where Tennessee Valley Road leaves the Shoreline Highway. Alone."

His voice shivered. "How . . . how much do I have to—"

"Seventy-five," she had said abruptly, and had hung up.

Monday was the earliest he could assemble the cash money she was asking for, so for the rest of the weekend, to avoid possible backsliding, she had not answered her phone.

*   *   *

Now it was Monday and tonight Teddy would bring her $75,000—if he came at all. Naming a particular sum was a calculated risk, because if that sum stripped his estate, lawyers and bankers would start asking questions. Seventy-five thousand would be by far and away the biggest score Yana had ever made.

And afterward, that's where she would be—far and away. Out of the state, out of the jurisdiction. Her kind of fraud was not federal, so if California ever came after her for it they'd have to identify her first, find her second, and extradite her third. Which, given that she was a beautiful Gypsy *boojo* woman in a time of criminal rights, would be very difficult indeed.

She would drive the pink Cadillac Larry would bring her this afternoon, and Ramon would drive their sturdy three-year-old Jeep Cherokee that served the same function the Gypsy caravan wagon served their *rom* forebears a century earlier. They would rendezvous in Sacramento at dawn, to travel together over the Sierra and east across the Great Plains to Stupidville.

They systematically stripped the *ofica* of all its Gypsy paraphernalia, packing it carefully to be set up at some new location elsewhere after the funeral of the dying King. Although it looked exotic and richly furnished by the dim *boojo* lighting, it was all an illusion created by the heavy drapes, a couple of antique chairs, the specially constructed crystal-ball table, the highly portable ornaments and props. Holy pictures, tinkly lamps, books of divination and necromancy, charts, figurines . . .

As a matter of honor they were leaving with three months' unpaid rent: it was the Gypsy way.

"Be careful of the crystal," Yana said as Ramon added the priceless globe to one of the huge sacks of his *gonya*, a heavy leather strap with a bag at each end.

"Do you think I am a fool like your *gadjo* lover?"

"He is no concern of yours," she snapped.

When the bags were filled to about equal weight, he put the strap across his shoulders and came erect. His body was tensed and lumped with the strain of supporting the weight of the loaded *gonya*. He met her eyes steadily.

"I know he slept with you Friday night."

She drew herself up to her full height, eyes flashing.

"And if he did?"

"Yana . . . he is *gadjo*, and you . . . you—"

"Will be Queen of the Gypsies because of him, don't forget that," she snapped. "Besides, it is ended now."

No auto traffic was allowed on Romolo Place; but as the street had to be available to fire trucks, three posts sunk in concrete at the foot of the street could be removed in an emergency. Somehow they had been set aside for yellow warning flashers; the Cherokee was parked right in front of the *ofica*.

As Ramon grunted his way down the stairs under his laden *gonya*, Yana thought, Yes, Larry is a *gadjo*, but he is also the only man who has ever clutched my heart in his two hands.

No more. Their meeting this afternoon, then she would never see him again. She knuckled her eyes in a little-girl gesture, then snapped at Ramon when he appeared, panting, at the head of the stairs.

"We must hurry, there are still the arrangements to be made over in Marin."

* * *

Over in Marin, Teddy White was busy about *his* arrangements, all of which were financial, all of which were cash transactions. Closing out this brokerage account, cashing in these stocks and bonds, pillaging that bank balance, realizing the value on those government bonds, everywhere facing the same sort of financial advisor questions and comments.

"In this financial climate is this is a prudent move?"

"In another month, the capital gains allowances, even though reduced, would give you a tax advantage that . . ."

"On Friday I wanted you to roll these over. Now . . ."

"I must strongly advise against taking all this cash . . ."

"If I knew what this is for, I could better . . ."

To each he gave the response Yana suggested: a once-in-a-lifetime investment opportunity. She had also told him to take less than $10,000 in twenties, fifties, and a few hundreds from each of eight different accounts. Teddy was secretly appalled at the amount she named, secretly pleased it was not more, secretly guilty at being pleased it was only some fifteen percent of his net worth.

How could he be so petty, so mercenary? Hadn't Yana already endangered her life just so he could survive to this moment? Couldn't she very well be endangering it again tonight?

* * *

274

Giselle, staked out on the street below his house with binoculars, picked Teddy up when he came home with the money. At least, when he took from the backseat a dark green plastic garbage bag bulging with its contents, she assumed it was money.

So *much* money?

She waited, first thinking of revenge on Yana, then drifting into thoughts of later silken hours in Rudolph's bed . . .

*　　*　　*

Over coffee Yana had been withdrawn, edgy, even a little sad, but she probably was preparing for the Teddy White scam that night. So Larry Ballard was also thinking of the night to come, when she would be finished with Theodore Winston White III and waiting in her bed for him . . .

Where would it end? What was going to happen? He didn't know. He didn't care. He didn't want to think beyond this coming night with her. He was well and truly hooked.

*　　*　　*

Meanwhile, on Florida's Gold Coast, O'B was looking for Kalia Uwanowich, supposedly running a large-scale roofing scam in one of the bulging suburban areas near Fort Lauderdale, Broward County's financial and commercial hub shoehorned in between Miami to the south and Palm Beach to the north.

But which suburban area? O'B was doing what O'B did best— driving around, looking, talking, stopping in bars and lounges, having a drink with the good old boys. Soaking up information— and booze—like a sponge.

*　　*　　*

In Baja, in Cabo, Trin Morales already had spent several hours nosing around the fancy tourist hotels perched high up on the rocks overlooking the Pacific, or strung out along the white sandy beaches on the Sea of Cortéz side. Then he'd parked the ancient rattling yellow VW Bug he'd rented at the airport on Cabo's main street, and had just walked and talked. Up and down narrow potholed dirt streets, chatting with people in shanties of beaten-flat tin nailed to scraps of wood.

The Giggling Marlin, he'd learned, was where most of the *gringo* yachtsmen hung out. He would go in there, nurse a drink, wait. Where the yachtsmen were, the Gyppos eventually would be.

With the Cadillac Morales was after.

* * *

In Nebraska, Bart Heslip was driving west across the prairie along a gunbarrel highway remarkably flat and straight. It just cut right through all the rolling plains and undulating hills like a chainsaw through pine logs.

He'd phoned Kearny about the $30,000 in the valise, and Corinne to tell her he missed and loved her. Next stop, Chicago, and Nanoosh Tsatshimo's bogus electroplating operation.

* * *

In Reno, the Lovellis were packing up to head east. Nearly a hundred Gypsy men, women, and children, twenty-two cars (seven of them Cadillacs ripped off from Cal-Cit Bank), and two pickups full of the paraphernalia they would need for a summer spent working the Midwest county fair circuit. East through Utah, Wyoming, a corner of Colorado, and then out across the rolling Nebraska plains toward the Mississippi and the Stupidville encampment.

* * *

In his Stupidville hospital room, Staley and Lulu were plotting the downfall of Barney Hawkins and the Democrat National Assurance Company—to the tune of $75,000. Staley was willing to come down to $50,000; Lulu didn't think they'd have to.

* * *

At DKA, Dan Kearny was starting out the back door when his private phone rang. He sighed and went back and picked up to hear Ephrem Poteet's voice.

"I got something for you, Kearny."

"A Cadillac?"

"Something better. A King."

CHAPTER THIRTY-EIGHT

Giselle Marc had to pee. It was all very well, in detective novels, for the writer to gloss over the gross stuff when someone was on stakeout for countless hours. Also, men had a natural spigot that interfaced just fine with an empty Styrofoam cup. A woman had some engineering problems with that. Worse, there were no adjacent bushes; if she drove off to find a gas station, Teddy would choose just that moment to depart.

So she'd just held it, waiting for dark; Yana, after all, was a creature of the night. Now it was nearly *midnight*. If he didn't move soon . . . Then her binoculars caught Teddy coming down the front steps, heavy plastic garbage bag over his shoulder.

She tried to figure out how to drive with her legs crossed as she tailed him down Tiburon Boulevard to the 101 freeway overpass to Mill Valley, the lights of Sausalito winking from her left across broad placid Richardson Bay.

They ended up on the Shoreline Highway in Tam Valley, where Teddy stopped his little red Alfa beside the closed old-fashioned fruit stand on the dirt verge of the Tennessee Valley Road intersection. Eleven forty-five. Obviously, a rendezvous set for midnight.

And an old cemetery was nestled on a tree-shaded hillside above Tennessee Valley Road. Odds-on, a cemetery dig.

She kept going, found some bushes where at long last she could ease her bladder, returned to the fruit stand for a tremendous shock. The pink 1958 Eldorado ragtop was just pulling up beside Teddy's Alfa! One of the most beautiful women she had ever seen got out. Black-haired and exotic . . . Yana! Had to be!

Oh, that bastard Larry! Somehow he had gotten the pink Cadillac away from Rudolph and had given it back to Yana.

Giselle wasn't going to let him get away with it. At a 7-Eleven she bought a box of heavy green plastic garbage bags and three newspapers, returned to Tennessee Valley Road seeking an easy way up the hill to her left. She stopped where the high cutbank dipped for a dry wash, half-choked with brush and ginestra, overhung with a live oak.

Giselle got out her flashlight and stuffed a garbage bag with ripped newspaper. At least she had running shoes in the car. She looked both ways; then, wishing for slacks instead of a dress, hiked her skirt up around her waist and started climbing, using her flashlight only to keep from running into a tree or getting stuck in the eye by a branch.

Ten minutes later, scratched and breathless, she hit a wide packed-earth path that slanted up the hillside to her left. Five more minutes on that, and she emerged at a hairpin turn of a narrow blacktop road. Beside the road was an abandoned wheelbarrow with a rake, a hoe, and a shovel in it.

*　　*　　*

The brown sign with the green tree painted on it read:

IRONWOOD CEMETERY
AND MORTUARY

Yana swung the huge car left into the steeply slanted blacktop drive. The top was down and Teddy felt chilled of body and mind. In the backseat was a shovel and $75,000 of his stepfather's—no, he meant his—money.

"I wish Ramon was here," he said in a shaky voice.

278

Yana stopped just short of huge black iron double gates, flanked by grey massive concrete cubes twenty feet square.

"He would not come." Her stunning eyes burned into his. "He does not approve of this. If you wish to withdraw now . . ."

"No, I . . . The curse . . ." His hands were like ice while his forehead was clammy with sweat. "But the cemetery's closed, the gate's locked . . ."

Yana made a strange quick graceful gesture at it with both hands and intoned loudly, "*Nashti jas vorta po drom o bango.*" Just the Gypsy proverb "You cannot walk straight when the road is crooked," but it was the prearranged signal and was why the Eldorado's top was down.

Before Teddy's astounded eyes, the long-hasped padlock struck through the joint of both gates clattered to the ground as the right-hand gate slowly swung wide. Yana put the Eldorado through the opening. The narrow blacktop road continued by a long grey massive concrete mortuary building set into the hill like a bunker; a few scraggly patches of ivy grew on it.

Yana sent the big car questing up by it into darkness.

* * *

Ramon trotted out to close the gate in case a security patrol came by. He previously had picked the lock and set it back, open, to fall off when Yana signaled him to pull the thin strong black wire he had attached to the right-hand gate.

When he heard Yana's car returning, he would reopen it.

* * *

It was just after midnight at the Giggling Marlin, and Morales had miscalculated. He'd drunk three of the Marlin's goldfish-bowl-size margaritas, and his lips were numb. His head was swirling. Now he was shoveling in *refrítos y arroz y pollo*—but it was much too late. He was blasted.

So was just about everyone else in the place. The Giggling Marlin was a huge box crowded with dozens of tables, all jammed with babbling patrons, mostly yachtspeople. Mexicans, *Norteamericanos*, other *gringos*—Australian, Scandinavian, German, English, Dutch, French, Italian, Spanish . . . A dozen languages, a hundred accents fenced in midair.

Against the left wall was a heavy pulley and tackle such as sports fishermen use to haul up by the tail and display the big game fish they have caught. On the wall beside it in bright cartoony colors was painted an eight-foot marlin up on his tail, with sunglasses and a deep-sea fishing rod. He was laughing.

Morales turned to look over the room yet again, and there they were. Four *gringos* and two swarthy men who looked Mexican but who had to be his Gyppos, because one of them was pocketing a set of Cadillac keys. All of them were drunk and boisterous.

Morales staggered to his feet and out the door—*Madre de Dios*, how he was drunk! A serious miscalculation. A group of Mexicans was laughing and exchanging remarks in highly accented English with the *gringos*. One wore a leather vest and no shirt; a three-foot-long iguana was perched on his shoulder, its long whippy lizard tail curled down against his naked chest. The iguana's eyes mirrored with lidless lizard contempt Morales's own vast contempt for mankind.

"He is your friend?" he asked the Mexican in Spanish.

"My dinner," said the Mexican, and they all laughed.

Morales said, "I wish to see the rich North American's Cadillac."

"The new Cadillac? With the word 'Brougham' on the trunk lid? With the wire wheels and the leather seats and the tinted glass and the cornering lights and—"

"The very one," said Morales gravely.

"I have not seen it."

They all laughed again. Morales found a crumpled $20 bill, said with great assurance, "But you can discover it."

The Brougham was found, but it had the d'Elegance option package, which included a theft-deterrent system. Morales had no key for it. *Caramba*, he wished he wasn't so drunk; he couldn't remember where he'd left his own car, with his repo kit in it.

Even with the kit, and sober, getting away with the Caddy wouldn't be easy. Cabo was at the very southernmost tip of Baja, where the Gulf of California met the open Pacific. There was only one paved road north to La Paz, capital of *baja del sud*.

He had to find a way to get a head start on them.

Morales returned to his half-eaten *frijoles* and latest margarita, caught the arm of a passing waiter to talk earnestly about the Gyppo *without* the car keys. Greenbacks changed hands. The waiter departed. Soon a threesome of waiters appeared. One carried a tray with a huge brimming margarita on it. The second carried a big black frying pan and a heavy metal ladle. The third carried a funnel.

Suddenly the lights dimmed, flickered. The waiter with the funnel grabbed the Gypsy under the chin and tipped his head back to shove the funnel into his mouth. The one with the frying pan beat it lustily with his ladle. The one with the margarita poured it into the funnel.

As the Gypsy gagged and choked and thrashed and blinked his watering astounded eyes, everyone in the room clapped, whistled, and cheered his macho performance. He got more drunk and out of it by the second, intoxicated not only by tequila but by the crowd's flattery of his all-important *machismo*.

One down. Morales finished his beans and paid up, then talked earnestly with the waiter again. Again, money changed hands. Morales moved over to lean against the wall near the tackle and pulley and the painted giggling marlin.

His waiter and several more suddenly charged the other Gypsy. Gripped by the arms and legs, he was dragged from his chair and rushed over to the pulley and tackle. Lights flickered. The waiter beat his frying pan with his ladle. The crowd shrieked, clapped, cheered. The Gyppo squawked and yelled and struggled to no avail.

They laid him on the floor and whipped a padded leather cuff around his crossed ankles, pulled it tight. Then they unceremoniously hauled him up into the air, upside down, like a gaffed marlin being avenged by the giggler painted on the wall. Flashbulbs popped.

The waiters usually let their victims remove everything from their pockets before being upended; this time they seemed to have forgotten. Change, wallet, keys, pocket knife, and money clip all rained down on the floor beneath. In a drunken flash, Morales sat down heavily amid them. Struggling to his feet, he returned them courteously to the drunk and disoriented Gyppo once the photo opportunity was finished.

All except the Cadillac keys. Morales had a use for those.

*　　*　　*

The Cadillac's headlights carved a tunnel through the forest of live oak, bay, ginestra, and acacia they were penetrating. The narrow blacktop road switchbacked up the steep hillside, eucalyptus trees now forming a row of tall grey ghostly sentinels beside them. Off to Teddy's right on the far slopes beyond Tennessee Valley Road were scattered lights.

"Just . . . just k-keep going . . . It's up near the top," he quavered. His teeth were chattering, not just from the lowered convertible top. "Right-hand . . . side. I'll . . . know it . . ."

A sharp switchback, their lights picked out a packed-earth path sloping away down the hillside, an abandoned wheelbarrow with a rake and a hoe in it. Oddly, no shovel, but Yana had no need of one; she had her own in the backseat.

Around the next curve were the gravestones, up- and downslope, some recent, some very old. The cemetery was well-kept.

Teddy chattered, "He-here. Stop here."

"You are cold?" she asked sharply as she braked the car.

"I'm frightened."

She cut lights and motor, they got out. From the backseat she got a foot-high statue and an old-fashioned kerosene lantern with a glass cylinder to shield the flame from the wind. She worked the little metal arm to raise the glass so she could insert a match and light the wick.

There was a low moan; Teddy realized it had come from him.

"You are sick?" asked Madame Miseria.

"Still frightened."

"Rightly so." Then she added, "Bring the shovel and the money," and started off up the gentle grassy slope, holding the statue against her breast in the crook of her left arm, lighting their way with the lantern held high in her right hand.

"You . . . you know where my . . . my stepparents are buried?" demanded Teddy in awe.

She turned to look down at him over her shoulder. "There are few things on this earth I do not know."

She didn't say that she and Ramon had been all over the small cemetery earlier to find the Whites' grave in this newest corner close to the edge of the hardwoods. As Teddy took off his jacket and with a frightened look around started digging, she placed the figure at the head of the grave and the lantern on the tombstone. The lantern vaguely illuminated a Christ figure and some of the letters incised into the stone:

282

Beloved parents of . . . In loving memory of . . .

Yana's statue was of the Blessed Mary holding the Christ Child in the crook of her left arm as Yana had held it. Mary was very dark of visage; her blue gown, His red one, were crusted with jewels and gold and wondrous embroidery. On their heads were jeweled golden crowns, with halos of what looked like beaten gold fastened behind.

"The Black Virgin," Yana explained when she saw Teddy gaping at it. "To protect us. Dig, my child—dig."

Teddy dug. *Down into his stepfather's grave!* He had a moment of terror, revulsion. Wasn't this sacrilege? But Madame Miseria was standing at the foot of the grave with her arms wide, her head back, her eyes closed, her features stern as the cold stone itself. Her pose aped the spread-armed Christ incised into the reddish marble slab. The lantern's pale light emphasized her striking resemblance to the Black Virgin.

"*Te avis yertime mander, ter yertil tut o del,*" she chanted. If you will forgive me all I have done to you, I will forgive all you have done to me. "*Ta avel angla tute, tai kodo khabe tai kado pimo tai mange pa sastimaste.*"

This Gypsy service for the dead would quiet the spirit and keep it in the grave. Better to be safe than sorry, no?

Teddy was sweating and smeared with soft loam. His hands were blistered, his right calf hurt from pushing his foot down on the rim of the shovel to help force it into the ground. The snake writhed fiercely up his left leg.

"It is deep enough," said Madame Miseria abruptly. "Put in the money and cover it over."

Shoveling the grave full was easier than digging it out.

"No one must ever disturb this site again," she told him. There was a terrible and utter finality in her voice. "If they do, you will surely die."

As the brown clods covered the green plastic bag, Teddy could picture the $75,000 in the dark earth, eventually rotting away and disintegrating just as his stepparents were doing. No, he would never disturb this grave. Not ever.

As they got back into the pink Cadillac, Teddy turned for a last look. He seemed to see a shadow moving at the edge of the trees behind them. He was glad to get away from there.

*   *   *

Ramon's Cherokee nosed cautiously up the road. He parked where the Caddy had been, got out, started up to the grave with his shovel and flashlight. Twenty minutes later he hefted the big green garbage bag onto his shoulder and almost ran back down to his car. He didn't like being alone in a cemetery at night.

*   *   *

Giselle rode the elevator up to Rudolph's penthouse suite. A triumphant Giselle, despite being filthy, disheveled, hair hanging down in her face, one knee skun, pantyhose run, and still wearing her running shoes. First, a hot shower in Rudolph's big tiled bathroom; then, fragrant with the hotel's expensive soaps and perfumes, mating with her wild Gypsy lover in the big bed . . .

He wasn't there. The night clerk was gravely attentive to her dilemma. "Mr. Grimaldi checked out, ma'am. Early this morning. No forwarding address. Of course if you want to contact Bookkeeping during business hours, perhaps . . ."

But Giselle was gone. She'd known all along it had to end, but . . . but . . . not *yet*. Not like *this* . . . A single word rose up unbidden in her mind.

Gyppo.

*   *   *

As Ballard, over in North Beach, started his hand toward the bell push beside Madame Miseria's door, he stopped. The seamed Gypsy palm and Madame Miseria's sign were gone. He jabbed an overcoated elbow through the glass.

Stripped of its Gypsy artifacts, the nondescript flat had reassumed its real character: two tiny bedrooms, a living room with a bay window, a kitchen, and a minuscule bath with water stains on the ceiling from some long-ago overflow in the apartment above. Bare pine floors, bare plasterboard walls in need of paint, still bristling with the nails from which had been strung the wires for the heavy drapes. Nothing of Yana remained.

He'd known it would have to end. But not *this* way. Not *now* . . . A single word came unbidden into his mind.

Gyppo.

*   *   *

As, in Sacramento, Yana and Ramon stared wide-eyed at one another across the open tailgate of the Cherokee. Between them was an upended green plastic garbage bag, its contents heaped around it.

Torn-up newspapers, courtesy of Giselle Marc. The same word rose unbidden to both of their lips.

Gadjo.

CHAPTER THIRTY-NINE

It was getting hot. Trinidad Morales licked his crusted lips and bunched up his round brown face against the exquisite thunder inside his skull, gathered his courage, and opened his eyes. And SCREAMED.

Facing him from a foot away was a monstrous dragon, tongue flicking, unwinking eyes staring into his own with cold intensity and contempt. He tried to thrust himself back from the terrible monster, but he was gripped by a giant's hand that . . .

Oh. The seat of the Brougham. Which was parked on a flinty narrow track in the desert, starting to cook in the morning sun. When he had screamed, the three-foot iguana had fled to the far corner of the dash on which he had been sunning himself. He crouched there now, hissing in terror and defiance, long whippy tail lashing his distress.

Morales groaned. He opened his door and staggered out into the sunlight. To one side were nearly vertical rock faces. He began sending a seemingly endless yellow stream down over the rusted narrow-gauge railroad tracks beneath his feet . . .

Railroad tracks?

Hand-laid on rough-hewn ties, they ran toward the rock face and disappeared into the black mouth of a tunnel with a broken-down miner's shack beside it. Glassless window, gaping door, sprawling shamelessly in the desert sun like an overused harlot.

He shook, encased, zipped. Shards and snippets were coming back. The Giggling Marlin. Margaritas. Drunken Gypsy. Upside-down Gypsy. Cadillac. Mexican ready to eat an iguana. Cow looking in through the windshield, *cow?*

He remembered getting the keys, going outside, *buying* the iguana, taking it with him in the car. Driving north through the warm black night toward La Paz, the twisting rising falling blacktop, the lights picking out cattle all over the open-range desert, the road itself . . . Almost off the road. Cow looking in the windshield, front bumper two inches from its legs. Mooo.

Morales scrunched his way across the mine tailings to the shack. Legless chair, three-legged table, what once could have been a bench to put a bedroll on. And a Mexican comic book. A romance, shamelessly saccharine. He left it for the next pilgrim, crunched back to the Brougham.

After the cow, mountains. Terror. Drunk. He'd seen this rocky track off to his left, taken it until he was out of sight of the road, had switched off and passed out. End of story.

The iguana was on the driver's seat. Staring at him.

Good to eat; in Mexico, as often as not they were the chicken in your *pollo.* Tasted like chicken. They said that about everything from rattlesnake to, he bet, monkey meat. Tasted like chicken.

Morales had bought the iguana because the Mexican was going to eat it and Morales didn't want him to. Between him and the lizard was a gut connection, one of the few Morales could remember making with any living thing. He opened the car door.

"Okay, kid," he said in English, "beat it." The iguana stared at him unwinkingly. He made shooing gestures with his hand. "*Vamoose, muchacho.*"

The iguana waited a moment longer, then flowed down over the edge of the seat past him, scuttled off a few yards across the rocky terrain of his natural habitat. Stopped, swung head and trunk around to regard Morales from those ageless eyes.

"*Vaya con Dios,*" said Morales.

With a sudden whip of his tail, the iguana was up on his toes and sprinting gracefully off across the rocks with a dry scrabbling sound, out of sight and gone forever.

Morales got into the Brougham and started the engine and backed out toward the blacktop. He would follow it north to La Paz, and, eventually, nearly a thousand miles north of that, to the U.S. border entry point at San Diego.

Meanwhile, Trinidad Morales had just done the first good deed of his entire adult life.

*   *   *

Giselle Marc stormed into Larry Ballard's second-floor cubicle with a heavy green plastic garbage bag over her shoulder. She thudded it to the floor by the corner of his desk, eyes flashing, fingers unconsciously hooked and ready for clawing.

"What did you do to him?" she demanded.

"To whom?" asked Ballard casually and grammatically, taking the precaution of getting to his feet for a few quick defensive moves if she started clawing. As in eyes out.

"You know who—Rudolph! You tricked him out of the pink Cadillac and—"

"It was Yana's in the first place."

"It actually belongs to a restorer in Palm Springs, so don't give me that Yana stuff. If you hadn't taken it, Rudolph never would have gone off without telling me and—"

"No?" Ballard leaned forward intently. "How do you think I knew I could snatch that pink Cadillac away from him?"

"H . . . how?" Giselle felt her face getting tight and hot.

"Marla, the check-in clerk, he was banging before—"

"That's a lie!"

Ballard caught her wrists before her nails could bite his face. "Yeah. Cheap shot. Sorry." She stopped raging and he released her. "Anyway, she told me he'd settled his bill the night before and was leaving by midmorning yesterday. I bribed a car-parker for a uniform and brought the car up for him." Smugness entered Ballard's voice. "Only I drove off in it myself. I rubbed his nose in it!"

Giselle upended her plastic garbage bag over his desk. Out cascaded great heaps of small-denomination greenbacks, some banded, some loose, spilling out and eddying down to the floor. Clods of dirt fell out also as she glared defiantly at him.

"The Teddy White score—I took it away from your precious Yana and rubbed *her* nose in it!"

Ballard's brows were terrible to behold. He looked like a berserker from Norse mythology. They were face-to-face, inches apart, quivering with anger and hurt, their voices crescendos.

"You drove her away from me!"

"She didn't need me to leave you!" she yelled. "She was on her way out of town with her brother—their truck was packed to the roof with all their cheap gimcracky Gyppo crap."

Ballard grabbed up Marino's satchel from behind the desk. Clicked open the top. *"Yeah? Well, look at this!"*

The satchel was stacked to the mouth with orderly banded packets of greenbacks. Giselle stared with stricken face.

"Rudolph spent three weeks—"

Dan Kearny's voice crashed down on them from the doorway like a huge breaker on hapless swimmers.

"QUIT ACTING LIKE GODDAM TEENAGERS THE PAIR OF YOU!"

"He—"

"She—"

"Cry on your own time." But advancing into the room, he stopped to stare openmouthed at the money on Ballard's desk. He faltered, "What in heaven's name . . . is going on in here?"

They talked over one another like siblings vying for a parent's attention, Kearny listening with darkened face.

"What pink Cadillac?" he asked finally in ominous calm.

"The pink Cadillac the dying King wants to be buried in."

Giselle added, "Rudolph wants to be King—"

"And Yana wants to be Queen," finished Ballard.

"Dying King, huh?" said Kearny, a sudden gleam in his eye too brief for either of them to catch. "Pink Cadillac. Yana. Rudolph." He looked from one to the other of them. "What the hell else don't I know?"

"Nothing," they chorused too quickly, not meeting his eyes, then told him they didn't even know where the King was dying.

"Steubenville, Iowa." This riveted their attention: where the

King was dying, there would be Rudolph and Yana. He suddenly thundered at them, *"Put that goddamned money in the safe until I figure out what to do with it!* Get hold of O'B in Florida and Bart in Chicago and tell them to meet us in Steubenville. Counting the one in Baja last night, we've only repo'd eleven, leaving us twenty to go—twenty-one if we add that pink Cadillac. Most of them ought to be at Steubenville."

They started moving, reaching for the satchel and stuffing loose greenbacks back into the green plastic garbage bag.

"You two ought to fit right in there." He smiled like a fat-smeared bear trap smiling in ambush under the dry leaves. "The locals call it Stupidville."

*   *   *

Under the bluffs a mile downriver from Stupidville, on the wide rolling field of a farmer who'd needed the money, the Gypsy encampment was swelling. Trailers and RVs and pickups with camper beds on the back, vans and trucks and dozens of new and beat and battered Cadillacs, fifty other cars of assorted makes and ages. Even a dozen horses and three or four old-fashioned Gypsy caravans. They had been brought out to honor the dying King born in the early days of the century when creaking canvas-covered horse-drawn wagons were the Gypsies' only transportation.

Hundreds of *rom,* more arriving by the hour, in every conceivable sort of dress. Underfoot and assaulting the ears, countless dogs and cats and children, even chickens. Overhead, a pall of sweet-scented applewood smoke from their cook fires.

In town, the encampment's presence already was being felt. Christ Himself, remember, had given the Gypsy a dispensation to steal from the *gadjo;* so Stupidville's original pleasure to have so many new spenders in town was being hourly reduced to dismay.

All the tools had disappeared from Klinger's Garage.

Ben Franklin Five and Dime was seeing its shelves cleared as if by goods-eating locusts.

The Deli Ice Cream Shoppe ("I'll Be Dipped!") had been forced to remove all their sugar cones from the front display case, and were considering locks on their freezers.

All the summer dresses—along with their mannequins—had disappeared overnight from Sylvia's Dresse Shoppe's front windows. Sylvia had checked her insurance, closed her doors, and gone visiting her sister in Dubuque.

Himmler Clothing ("Boys' Wear to Outwear the Boy") avoided similar problems only because Doug Himmler had played nose-tackle for the Ohio State Buckeyes and would break bones if anyone messed with him. Gypsies were partial to their bones.

Kay Wenzel's Jewelers ("It's Okay to Owe Kay") had a sophisticated alarm system and put all of their stock in the safe at night, so they were so far untroubled by missing jewelry. Of course Immaculata Bimbai had not yet hit town.

Also untroubled were Steubenville General Hospital, the adjacent Hansel and Gretel Park ("Has Public Water Access"), and the block-long marina ("The Boat Float") the hospital overlooked.

But there were reasons for that. To have Barney Hawkins realize Staley was a Gypsy—*King* of the Gypsies, no less!—would be fatal. Until Democrat National coughed up money for Karl Klenhard's terrible tumble down the escalator stairs, Lulu had to keep the *rom* away from the hospital.

*   *   *

The tableau was familiar: Staley lying on his back with his eyes shut; Margarete in her chair beside the bed, bird-bright eyes fixed on the pudgy Hawkins; Hawkins pacing up and down the tiny free area in the middle of the room.

"All right, I got a little . . . upset last time," he said. "But *goddammit* . . ." He got control of his voice. "But I have to get this thing settled." He turned to Lulu. "Mrs. Klenhard, you have to see my position—"

"Seventy-five thousand dollars," said Staley in sepulchral tones. Lulu kept silent.

"That just isn't reasonable, Mr. Klenhard. Now, the offer I made last time, twenty-five thou—"

"Seventy-five thousand dollars," said Staley.

"Okay, because I gotta close this one out, thirty—"

"Seventy-five thousand dollars," said Staley.

Hawkins's veins and eyes were beginning to bulge again. He had stopped, squarely facing Staley on the bed. Even though Staley's eyes were closed, it was *mano a mano*. Lulu was out of the loop and glad of it. Staley had never lost *mano a mano* in his long life.

"Thirty-five—"

"Seventy-five thousand dollars."

"*Forty*, and that's the last—"

"Seventy-five thousand dollars."

"Goddam you, fifty, and if you think—"

"Seventy-five thousand dollars."

"Fifty-five—"

"Seventy-five thousand dollars."

Hawkins was red as a turkey wattle. "Sixty—"

"Seventy-five thousand dollars."

"Son of a bitch bastard, sixty-five—"

"Seventy-five thousand dollars."

Hawkins threw up his hands in defeat. He'd like to choke the scrawny old bastard to death, but the wife would probably kill him and his company would have to pay for his burial.

"All right!" he yelped. "All right all right all right! You win! Seventy-five . . ."

Staley at last opened his eyes. Was that a twinkle deep in their opaque depths? "Acceptable," he said.

Barney Hawkins left the hospital within seven minutes of his humiliating capitulation. As he drove south out of town along the river, he sneered at all the bums and drunks and hoboes and homeless who were congregated in some hick farmer's field back under the bluff . . . Except, Christ, he might soon be one of them. He had made a $75,000 settlement when the home office was expecting $15,000! Beaten by some 77-year-old fart you had to move from place to place with a shovel!

Which old fart at that very moment was polkaing his lady in a breathtaking whirl around his hospital room to oompah music from the radio, both of them giggling like teenagers, until the sound of Dr. Crichton's footsteps in the hall sent them scurrying to hit their respective marks in their little domestic farce, his the bed, hers the chair.

Seventy-five thousand dollars.

Yes!

CHAPTER FORTY

The burly Jew in the skullcap took the tarnished metal object from the black man's fingers and said to his young bright-eyed assistant in Yiddish, *"Vi heyst dos?"*

"Vaz."

"Yo, yo, vaz," he said impatiently. He moved the vase slightly. *"Zilber?"* The assistant shrugged. He turned back to the black man. "You want to know if this is a silver vase?"

The black man grinned. *"Yo?* Good word." He gestured at the beat-up-looking vase. "How much to get it replated, or whatever you call it?"

The Jew turned the object over with his fingers, looking up with probing eyes. "Old family heirloom, I suppose?"

"Yeah, sure, somethin' like that. Look, bro, you don't wanna do it—"

"And you think it is silver."

"Ain't it?"

"No."

"Well, shit, then, whut you be wastin ma time for?"

The black man snatched back the battered vase to swing away through the street crowd on this part of Chicago's South Drexel

Boulevard near the university, where the Jews' secondhand stalls catered to South Side blacks. He heard something with *zilber* in it that ended with a laugh and *narish schvartz*. *Zilber* had to be silver and he knew *schvartz* was black man. *Narish* probably was something like dumb or stupid—which he wasn't.

So he swung back to say, "African-American, hymie," then pushed his way on down the street with the worthless vase he had bought at another street stall an hour before.

*　　*　　*

Was the skull-capped Jew really a Jew, wondered Bart Heslip as he blew on his coffee to cool it, or a Gypsy posing as a Jew? Chicago's blacks often had tensions with the Jews, but they had no time at all for Gyppos. A skullcap and a few scraps of Yiddish did not make a Jew; and laughing at the dumb black who didn't know his stolen vase wasn't silver was more Gyp than Jew.

Meanwhile, he'd been in Chicago for nearly twenty hours with no luck at all in finding the elusive Tsatshimo and his equally elusive four-door 4.5-liter V-8 fuel-injection Fleetwood sedan. Since metalworking and electroplating plants had yielded zero results, in desperation he'd started working the street stalls, looking for people selling gold and silver plates at prices that guaranteed they weren't gold or silver. So far, also zero.

Bart sighed and gulped his coffee. There still was something about the old Jew that hadn't rung quite right. Maybe tonight, come back for a second look . . .

*　　*　　*

O'B was feeling desperate himself down in the Sunshine State. He'd found out that (a) Florida developers could destroy wetlands with the best of them, and (b) local Florida governments would sell out to them even quicker than their counterparts in California. What he hadn't found was a Gypsy named Kalia Uwanowich and a new Cadillac Allante hardtop.

And now he'd gotten a call from Giselle telling him to drop everything and hightail it to Iowa for a Gyppo encampment. Hence the desperation, because O'B had his pride. He didn't want to show up without Kalia Uwanowich's Allante. What had some far-out Frog writer once said? That genius was not a gift, but the way one

294

invents in desperate situations? Out of his desperation was born his wonderful invention, a new way of looking at his problem.

He'd been acting as if Uwanowich really *was* a roofing contractor. Acting as if he really *would* be buying large quantities of roofing materials. Uwanowich was running a Gypsy scam. He wasn't going to roof anything. He wasn't going to buy anything. He was going to rip off a subdivision.

So O'B had started to look at *existing* subdivisions with homeowners' associations. These associations set up neighborhood Crime-Watch programs, told you what color you could paint your house, how often your lawn had to be mowed. Why wouldn't a homeowners' association—stick with him here—tell its members that all their houses had to get reroofed at the same time? Why wouldn't they contract to have it done, collective bargaining being a lot cheaper than individual deals?

It was worth a shot.

And west of Tamarac, on a tract between West Atlantic Boulevard and the Sawgrass Expressway, O'B saw thirty roofs without shingles, without even the tar paper that goes on under shingles. Even better, discarded shingles were lying all over lawns and sidewalks and even out into the streets.

In front of one house a tall fortyish man with reddish hair and a long pink homely face was picking up ripped-off shingles. O'B sauntered up as he dropped the armful on a stack beside his driveway. He straightened up with a hand to the small of his back, then wiped his forehead with his shirt sleeve.

"See you're getting your roof done," said O'B.

"Yep." He squinted up at the roof along with O'B, and waxed eloquent on his subject. "Ted's Roofers had a sixty-man crew out here today, rippin' off shingles from all the houses."

"I thought roofers usually carted away the old shingles."

The man chuckled. "At the price we're gettin', we gotta stack 'em, then they haul 'em." He had a Midwest accent. What did they call them here in Florida? Snowbirds? "It's all part of the contract."

"Offered you a real good price, huh?"

"The best. He comes in with a big crew, does it, and gets out again in a single day."

"But he didn't finish the job today," O'B pointed out.

"One day to strip 'em, the next day to roof 'em. Homeowners

association pays him after the old shingles are already stripped. Ted, he insisted on that, didn't want nobody to say they paid for something they didn't get."

"I bet he insisted," said O.B. A nice touch, that.

The man looked at him shrewdly. "You're in the market for a roofer, you can't beat Ted's prices."

"Where do I find him?"

"Secretary of the association, feller named Hank Sawtell, he lives right down the street, twenty-seven sixty-eight, he'll have all the dope. Has the association books right there in his house. Say, you want some iced tea? The missus . . ."

O'B begged off, hurried away. The trouble was, the roofs were already off and Ted's Roofers wouldn't be back to the subdivision in the morning to replace them. Not then, not ever. He was speeding down the wide curving suburban street, dodging kids' toys and picking up house numbers off mailboxes, because his only hope was that Ted—surely, Kalia Uwanowich—hadn't scored and soared yet. Soared a long way from here.

He needn't have worried; Ballard should have been there to bitch about the luck of the Irish. Parked in front of 2768 was a spanking-new red Allante hardtop with Florida plates.

O'B parked around the next corner out of sight, got out the dealer key and his repo order with the Allante's I.D. number on it. He confirmed the I.D., got in, fired it up. In the rearview, just before he passed out of sight around the curve of the suburban street, he saw a swarthy man sprinting down Sawtell's walk, waving his arms and yelling.

See you in Stupidville, baby.

O'B dropped the paperwork and keys for his rental car into a mailbox, notified the cops of the repossession, checked out of his motel, and headed north and west for Iowa.

*   *   *

Nanoosh Tsatshimo had started out in his 20s with an instant rechroming scam he'd learned from a great-uncle who'd had a wealthy and sympathetic *gadjo* take him into his home and pay for his education. Such men, called *rai* by the Gypsies, were considered part father, part fool.

Anyway, the great-uncle had been good at chemistry, and had taught Nanoosh how to dissolve mercury in a weak nitric acid solution and then apply it to something made of copper. The nitric acid ate a little of the copper, which formed an amalgam with the mercury. This gave the piece a shiny surface like chrome or silver plating.

But it was a short con, because the nitric acid goes right on eating away, so after a few hours it destroys the mercury amalgam and the item looks like copper again. As he got older himself, Nanoosh began to search for a long con without those short departures. He found it in gold and silver electroplating.

Soon he was selling "solid silver" flatware; soon after that, lead plates (same approximate weight as solid gold) electroplated with a micrometer-thin layer of real 24-carat yellow Saudi gold. It could be gotten cheaply in Arabia with the right connections, and the plates could be sold as solid gold.

Now he could set up and sell the whole season in one place, having calibrated almost to the day when the microscopic layer of gold or silver would wear through to show the base metal beneath.

Tonight he had an appointment in Lincoln Park with a man who wanted a service for twenty of solid-gold plates and flatware. The mark was a 26-year-old stock futures options player who had just gotten his seat on the Exchange and a condo overlooking Lake Michigan. The mark planned to screw blind the old Jew in the skullcap who ate kosher and kept the holy days—not knowing the old Jew was really Nanoosh, who planned to maybe leave him his pants.

Nanoosh used Lake Shore Drive north to go get him.

*　　*　　*

Bart Heslip had his window open and the Cubs game on the car radio as he drove south on Lake Shore Drive. The old skull-capped Jew who maybe wasn't Jewish at all deserved another look.

As always as he drove, his eyes were busy on cars passing in the other direction, some unconscious computer in his skull ticking them off, ready to register only if one of the big, dark, bulky cars he was passing was the Nanoosh Tsatshimo Fleetwood.

Lincoln Continental . . . Acura Legend sedan LS . . . Mercedes-

Benz 300 . . . Buick Riviera . . . Chrysler Imperial . . . Lexus LS400 . . . Infiniti Q45 . . . BMW 750iL . . . *Cadillac Fleetwood Sixty Special* . . .

His old skull-capped Jew behind the wheel! Bart was in the fast lane: even as his mind registered car and driver, he was spinning the wheel and slamming the brakes to put the Seville into a controlled skid. Bounce! thunder! crash! across the grassy center-divider, goose it, hit pavement, tires shrieking, *he had it*, back on the highway but in the northbound lane.

Eight cars behind the Fleetwood. One car back by the 31st Street intersection. Crowding its tail where Lake Shore splits at Cermak. Ran it off the road not far from the aquarium.

Nanoosh, his nephew, and two young Gypsy bucks in the backseat came boiling out of the Fleetwood even as Bart slammed the Seville to a stop behind it.

Nanoosh bellowed, "WHADDA HELL YOU T'INK—"

Bart roared, "I'M FROM THE BANK AND I'M TAKING THAT CAR!"

"The bank? The California bank?"

"Cal-Cit, you bet." Bart was flying on an adrenaline rush. *It was the right car!* "Take out your personal crap—"

That's when the nephew of Nanoosh made a bad mistake. He threw a punch at Bart. Bart slipped it, snapped his head back three quick times with three left jabs, breaking his nose on the second, then came up with a good right cross to put him away.

Nanoosh stayed out of it, leaned placidly against the fender to watch his young Gypsies take Bart apart. But they were bloody and reeling, Bart had only a skinned cheek and a fat lip when the cops arrived, a salt-and-pepper team of suits who came up with only nightsticks because it seemed that kind of beef.

Nanoosh quickly put his skullcap back on. "We are on our way to temple, the black man runs me off the road, tries to steal my car. My sons they defend me . . ."

That's when Nanoosh's nephew made another terrible mistake. Still half-blinded by tears from his broken nose, ashamed of the tears, he swung at the black cop because he thought the cop was Bart. Black is black, right?

Wrong. *Thwock!*

Nightstick on skull. He folded.

"Peaceful repossession," panted Bart. "They're Gyppos."

The black cop started to laugh as he put the cuffs on the recumbent nephew. "*Peaceful* repossession?" He laughed again. "That's a damned nice right cross you got there."

"Used to scuffle for a living," said Heslip.

"We'll take the lot of them in," said the white cop.

*   *   *

Bart talked the black cop into not charging the nephew with anything worse than disturbing the peace, then spent a half hour side by side with Nanoosh on a hard wooden bench at the cophouse.

"You're the one from this afternoon," said Nanoosh finally.

"Yep," said Bart.

"How'd you know to look for me in Chicago?"

Bart just shrugged and looked wise.

"It was them fucking Lovellis, wasn't it?"

Bart looked even wiser.

"I knew it! Son of a bitch bastards! Well, let me tell you something about *them* . . ."

Bart stayed silent, looking as wise as Solomon, which he proved to be—Nanoosh told him *all* about the Lovellis.

Finally, the cops admitted that Bart was Bart, that the Fleetwood was a Fleetwood, that Cal-Cit Bank was a bank, and that Bart was indeed their legal representative.

"I want to thank you guys a lot for your help," he said. "I'll just take my cars and—"

"What about the writ?" asked the white cop.

Not being a Chicago boy himself, Bart said, "What writ?"

"The writ, the writ, *the long green writ!*"

Maybe not Chicago born, but no hayseed. Fifty each to the salt-and-pepper team, then from his expense roll Bart started dealing twenties like a hand of cards, one to every cop in the station house. Ten cops, ten twenties. Pick a card, any card.

Back at his motel just across the river from the Loop on South Canal, he found Larry Ballard's message about Stupidville. He left Larry a more urgent message of his own, got the number of the Jersey motel where Ken Warren would be staying, and finally looked up truck rental outfits to call in the morning.

Bart Heslip had a PLAN.

CHAPTER
FORTY-ONE

Ken Warren had been born in Jersey City, within a mile of Journal Square; his father had worked for Colgate. So he had few illusions about the place. Before returning Sarah Walinski's Dodge Charger to Andy Anhut's A-One Autos on Kennedy Boulevard, he put something bulky in his topcoat pocket and called a taxi. He gave the cabby an address near Anhut's, and enough money to keep him waiting there. Ken himself waited across the street from the lot until the two burly salesmen—they looked more like made men—had gone to lunch. Only then did he drive in.

At the back of the lot he went up three wooden steps and into a little frame office strung with dismal glittery tinsel. Inside was a scarred wooden desk bearing a telephone, a heap of curly black hair the size of a Norway rat, and the shoes of a man reading a skin magazine. Looking at him, Ken remembered a Sunday school phrase about Jacob's brother Esau: *He was an hairy man*.

In almost every respect, Andy Anhut was an hairy man. It sprouted above his eyes, it tufted from his nostrils and ears, it matted the backs of his simian fingers and wrists, it curled exuberantly in the open V of his sport shirt and made a nest for the gold medallion on his chest.

Almost every respect. He was bald as a billiard ball. A squashed-down billiard ball with a cigar screwed into the middle of it. He sprang to his feet and clapped the Norway rat to his head when Ken's shadow fell across his magazine.

"Whadda fuck ya doin' sneakin' up?" he yelped.

Ken sent the DKA invoice spinning across the desk with a flick of his wrist, and leaned forward. He was taller, broader, meaner than Anhut; no man can look tough adjusting his toupee.

"Ngcahsh," expelled Ken.

"Cash? Wadda fuck ya mean?" That seemed to be Anhut's favorite phrase. He was out from behind the desk with the invoice, heading for the door. "Lemme see the fuckin' unit."

Ken waited. Outside, Anhut was snapping and nipping at the Charger's heels like a terrier driving a cow at sunset. He came back shaking his rat-nest head.

"Naw, naw, naw, fuckin' car's in terrible shape, I'll give ya fifty bucks for your trouble an'—"

Ken stepped away from the desk and put his hand in his topcoat pocket. The hand looked larger in there than a hand should look unless fisted around some bulky object. Anhut, caught up short, stared at him, measuring him. Then he shook his cue ball again.

"Nah," he muttered to himself. He bared his teeth in a death-rictus grin. "My boys come back from lunch, they'll—"

Ken jerked his hand from his pocket with something in it. Anhut went back an involuntary step. Ken's hand put on the edge of the scarred wooden desk . . . a red ripe tomato.

Anhut blanched as if someone had dipped him in boiling water and peeled him like . . . well, like a ripe tomato. To the mob, a Jersey tomato was dynamite—literally. A juicy red stick of overage, unstable dynamite. The tomato sitting on the edge of his desk was a statement that DKA, though a west coast firm, was connected on the east coast.

Statement or bluff? Well, Ken was heading for the door.

"*Wait!*"

Anhut cursed and brought out a huge roll of cash money, counted off enough hundreds, threw them on the desk. Ken didn't ask for a receipt. He rode the cab back to his motel to pack, but there was a message from DKA. According to Ephrem Poteet, a Gyppo

301

woman named Pearso Stokes was working the midtown Manhattan banks out of a silver Eldorado with M.D. plates on it.

Warren paid another night on his room, because Jersey prices beat New York prices, then rented a little red Toyota and headed for Manhattan. He'd just blown off a Jersey City used-car dealer with hardly a word being spoken and no overt physical threats made! It had to be a first. And now he was chasing Gyppos just like the rest of the gang!

*   *   *

Just about when Ken was paying the Holland Tunnel toll-taker on the west bank of the Hudson, Giselle was parking her company car on Teddy White's hilltop in Tiburon. She had his $75,000 in a plastic suitcase, but left it locked in the car until she could ease Teddy into her revelations about Madame Miseria.

She pushed the bell and Teddy opened the door and the same big tiger-stripe tomcat scooted out between her feet and bounded down the steps. Teddy even started again, "It's okay, he does it all . . ." before exclaiming, "Oh! Ms. Marc! Hello."

"I, ah, wanted to tell . . . that is, I have something to . . ."

Teddy looked five years younger, two inches taller, and his face eased of all the lines of pain. He came by her out onto the stoop, leaving the door open.

"Let's sit out on the steps to talk, this sun is so nice."

Giselle sat with her feet primly together, smoothing her skirt down over her knees almost nervously.

"I . . . have something to tell you about Madame Miseria. She knew your name, all about your stepparents and your dead real parents because . . ." She cleared her throat. "She got it all from her brother. He picked your pocket in that bar—"

"Not possible," said Teddy. "But please—go on . . ."

"The bleeding dollar bill—when you went to get the bowl of water, she just substituted one soaked with red dye for the one you'd put on the table."

"Of course she didn't," he said, untouched. "But even if she had, that's what convinced me my money actually was cursed."

The big tomcat came up and started to rub against Giselle's calf and purr. She scratched the back of his head and behind his ears absently. She was fuming.

"The poisoned egg—that was just sleight of hand. She had the devil's head in her hand when she broke your egg. She just dropped it into the bowl and—"

"Where is all this leading, Ms. Marc?"

"It was all a series of cons," she said stridently. "I bet she burned up a bunch of money that night too, didn't she?"

"Yes. Five thousand dollars."

"*Five* . . ." Giselle got control of her voice. She said very precisely, "She didn't burn up that money, she kept it. She and her brother just burned up a different envelope full of—"

"Paper bag."

"*What?*" Her voice was shrill.

"It was a *paper bag* full of money she burned up. But . . ." He gave her that goofy grin of perfect peace again. "But even if she kept the money, she would be entitled to it."

"I . . . don't understand. If she *conned* you and—"

"She cured me. Better than any doctor could have done."

Giselle sighed. Out between Angel Island and Alcatraz a big oil tanker down to its marks was waddling in with a bellyful of crude for the Standard Oil Refinery at Point Richmond.

"Okay," she said briskly. "She cured you. But also, two nights ago, she took you out to the graveyard in Tam Valley and there you and she buried a great deal of money in your stepfather's grave. Seventy-five thousand dollars, to be exact."

Teddy stood up abruptly. Suddenly there was panic in his eyes. "You didn't *dig it up* . . ."

Giselle started to say yes, then checked herself. She stood also. She put a gentle hand on his arm.

"Ramon Ristik did."

His reaction was totally unexpected. He started to laugh.

"No he didn't. You're mistaken."

"I *saw* him dig it up!"

"You couldn't have," he said with total conviction, "because I'm still here."

"You're still . . . I don't understand."

"That money was put there for the demons. If anyone digs it up, I die. But since I am still alive . . ." He flapped around awkwardly on the stair like a drunk in a dancing-chicken suit. "And *cured* . . ."

303

Giselle was finally getting it. "So if someone should return seventy-five thousand dollars to you—"

"I wouldn't take it. Because it wouldn't be mine. Mine is buried in my stepfather's grave." A sudden sly grin. "Besides, if Ramon took the money, how did you get hold of it?"

"I took it first, and substituted another garbage bag full of torn-up paper for it?" It was a question, not a statement.

"Ramon wouldn't be satisfied with torn-up paper," said Teddy delightedly. "So, if you have any money in your car, it isn't mine. The demon has mine." He chuckled. "And I'm cured."

Giselle found herself standing on the steps alone with the cat. It was a nice cat. She scratched it behind the ears. It was a nice day. Teddy was a nice man. Yana was not a nice woman. But then neither was Giselle Marc a particularly nice woman. She remembered a line from a favorite kid's book of her childhood. A book about a goldfish seeing the world.

"Sunny Sunfish wiggled his tail and wondered."

Giselle wondered if she was wiggling her tail on the way down the stairs to the car.

*   *   *

Dan Kearny wondered if he'd ended up in that place Peter Pan went back to—Never-Never Land, that was it—instead of the executive offices of the St. Mark Hotel. Lined up across the desk from him like the Three Stooges were the hotel's General Manager, Corporate Counsel, and Head of Security. All because he'd just thumped their satchel full of money down on the desk.

"There it is, gents, all of it. The seventy-five thousand dollars a man calling himself Angelo Grimaldi extorted—"

"That's a great deal of money," said the heavy-set one, Gunnarson, the manager.

The little wizzled-up one, Smathers, the corporate counsel, cleared his throat. "Yes. A great deal of money, Mr. . . ." He looked at the business card in his hand. "Mr. Kearny." He smiled a toothy smile. "But guests leave their valuables in the safe at the front desk—not here in the manager's office."

"But it's not my money," said Kearny with a great show of reason. "It's *your* money."

The big redheaded one, Shayne, with the gun under his arm,

suddenly said, "I don't know what sort of games you guys play back there in Washington, Kearny, but out here—"

"Washington?" Kearny jerked a thumb at his own chest. "Like the card says, Daniel Kearny, licensed private detective right here in San Francisco . . ."

Gunnarson waved him silent with almost a smirk.

"You're a licensed private investigator from California. We accept that." He opened his hands and beamed. "So why won't you accept that we never had a guest at this hotel named Angelo Grimaldi? No Angelo Grimaldi ever tried to extort money from us. And we certainly—"

"His real name is Rudolph—"

"*Please.* And we certainly never gave any Angelo Grimaldi any seventy-five thousand dollars." He turned to look at his two associates, and chuckled. "Why, we wouldn't keep our jobs very long if we went around dishing out free cash to just anyone who came through that door, would we, fellows?"

They also laughed. Dan Kearny looked from face to face. Never-Never Land? Alice down the rabbit hole, for Chrissake!

"Grimaldi told you that a blond terrorist was going to blow up the President and he said he killed her and dumped her body in the ocean . . ." They were all staring at him blandly. He added with a dash of desperation, "The blonde isn't dead—she's my office manager, for Chrissake! I can get her in here—"

"A terrorist for an office manager?" Smathers made little tutting noises with his birdlike mouth. "I don't know if this is a bet, or a prank, or what, Mr. Kearny, but we're busy men . . ."

Shayne picked up the satchel, clicked it shut, and slammed it against Kearny's chest so Kearny had to grab it or let it fall to the floor. And he suddenly understood.

They hadn't told the feds about Marino's threatening phone calls! So now they could never admit anything *to anyone!*

Back at the office, Giselle Marc was sitting on the top of his desk, idly swinging her legs and smoking a cigarette.

"He wouldn't take back the seventy-five thousand dollars," she said.

Kearny set his satchel down next to her plastic suitcase.

"Neither would they." He fired up one of her cigarettes, then shrugged. "But at least I can take a triangle flight up to Seattle

305

tonight on my way to Steubenville, and give *that* guy back the thirty thou Bart found and messengered to us."

* * *

"Nossir, I don't know nothing about no thirty thousand bucks I was supposed to of paid some road contractor."

Big John Charleston was glowering at him from across the desk in the office Big John could no longer pay for on Queen Anne Ave near the Seattle Center.

"He was a Gypsy," said Dan Kearny, trying to keep tension out of his voice. It was happening again! "He put crankcase oil mixed with paint thinner on the roads of your subdivision—"

"I ain't got no subdivision," snarled Big John.

"Because you guys at the state took it away from him!" chimed in Little John from his smaller desk in the corner.

"I'm not from the state! I'm a private investigator—"

Big John was on his feet.

"Then investigate how to get to hell outta my office 'fore I throw you through the window! You guys ruin me an' then come around tryin' to trap me into damaging admissions . . ."

Which meant Dan Kearny had to fly *back* to San Francisco to redeposit the $30,000 before catching a flight east to Iowa. He didn't know what else to do with it—for the moment. But all that money was giving him ideas . . .

The flight back to San Francisco, however, was going to put him into Stupidville well after the fireworks had started there.

And in Nebraska.

And in New York City.

CHAPTER

FORTY-TWO

Pearso Stokes was a beautiful Gypsy woman of 26 who managed to look like a misfit Iranian student of 19. Her lustrous coiling black hair was skun back into a bun with a rubber band around it, huge glasses magnified her truly astonishing eyes into terrifying bug eyes. She carried a chemistry and a physics textbook under one arm, though she could neither read nor write.

But boy, could she count! She entered her fourth midtown bank of the day to work the scam supposedly originated by the legendary Tene Bimbo some seventy-five years before. The con was so old nobody remembered it anymore, especially not the harried Manhattan tellers to whose windows she shuffled. Here she put down her books and fixed the teller with her fearsome bug eyes.

"My fadder has send me money from Tehran."

The teller leaned forward. *"What?"*

Her accent was truly atrocious, guttural and thick, her voice low. He could barely understand what she said. While honking at him again, she dug through her voluminous purse for a crumpled $500 bill she handed him like a fragment of the Koran.

"What?"

—"I said I want five one-hundred-dollar bills."

But as soon as she had them, Pearso changed her mind.

—"No, no, wait. I need three hundred in fifties and two hundred in twenties."

The teller started over again with fifties and twenties. The line of impatient customers behind Pearso was growing. She picked up her new money, hesitated, thrust it back again.

—"Make the fifties tens, and one of the twenties fives."

Somebody behind her exclaimed just loudly enough, "Aw, for Chrissake!"

Pearso was undeterred. The teller was flustered. He had just finished the count when she gave it all back again.

—"No. I need four fifties, ten twenties, nine tens, ten dollars in quarters, and fifty dimes."

He had to write that one down. The line behind her was grumbling like a thunderstorm. He lost his count twice.

After all that, she exchanged the silver for two $5 bills, got another ten and four twenties, and the rest in hundreds. The patrons behind her started clapping as she left. Pearso didn't mind: she could laugh all the way *from* the bank. Her silver Eldorado with its M.D. plates had the driver's-side visor turned down to show her printed sign, EMERGENCY—DOCTOR ON CALL, so the car was unticketed even though left in a No Parking zone.

She had palmed one of the original hundreds.

Then a fifty and a twenty.

After that, two tens and a five.

On the final exchange, a fifty, two twenties, and a ten.

She had given the teller $500, had gotten $500 back, and had palmed an additional $295 that the teller wouldn't discover was missing until he tried to balance at the end of the day.

Time for tea at her sister's mitt-camp in the Village. But a cruising Ken Warren spotted her at Seventh Ave and West 14th, and fell in behind her. Everything fit. Eldorado. Silver. M.D. plates. Woman driving who looked like a Gyppo.

Follow until it roosted, then drop a net over it.

*   *   *

Despite the fancy shingle out front, READER AND ADVISOR, it was a mitt-camp. Ken parked a short block away on the narrow busy street, started to get out—and there was a wiry little guy with a sharp nose who didn't look like any Gyppo Ken had ever seen just getting into the Caddy.

He unslotted the Toyota, followed him. When the guy stopped, Ken would grab the Caddy. Only he picked up two more guys and some luggage. One was tall and bony and middle-aged, not much heat if Ken had to dance with them. But the other one was an elephant in clothes. Not a fat elephant, either.

Not good. Not good at all. Ken couldn't have handled him one-on-one, let alone wearing the other two around his neck.

And then, to make matters worse, they headed north out of the city along the West Side Highway. He'd topped off, but the Caddy with its outsized tank would have the range on him if they went over a couple hundred miles.

*   *   *

They didn't. Two hours later the Cadillac made a turn onto Oak Street in a little town called Dudson Center and pulled up on the gravel driveway just shy of a chain-link fence behind the old-fashioned two-story white clapboard house at number 46. Good. No garage.

Ken steered the red Toyota past, made the next right, the next left, and parked. Maybe they were Gyppos after all; the big guy, who looked like two pro wrestlers at once, had sat in the backseat waving a tambourine around on the way up.

Didn't matter. Two minutes and the Caddy would be his. He retraced his route on foot, shambling along round-shouldered and thrust-jawed like an ill-tempered dangerous bear.

The Eldorado had been left unlocked. Ken slid in behind the wheel. Man, it was loaded—cruise control, a/c, cassette player, reading lights, extremely woodlike dashboard trim. As he keyed the ignition, a bread company van pulled in behind him, filling the rearview mirrors and blocking his exit.

"Hey," Ken said. He leaned out to look back at the van's driver. Hell of a time for a guy to make a delivery. "Moo fit!"

Instead, the driver switched off the van's engine, pulled on the emergency brake, and stepped out to the driveway, calling toward the house, "Andy! Mayday!"

And hell, here came another one, climbing over the driver's seat to get out on the same side as the driver. That made five of them. The new one said, "Who is he, Stan?"

"No idea."

"What's going to happen?"

"No idea."

Ken hit the button that locked all four doors, tried his keys, kept working them. Once the Caddy started, he'd push the van back out of his way and be off about his business.

People erupted from the house; first the two who'd been in the front seat of the Caddy on the way up, then a not-bad-looking woman making unconscious motions like a person lighting a cigarette off the stub of another one, then the big guy, finally a really mean-looking old dude. He and the woman stayed on the porch. The three he knew about came over to join the two from the bread truck. They were all looking in at him. He could hear them talking through the closed window.

"What's going on?" the guy Stan had called Andy asked.

"No idea," Stan said. He turned to the other bread truck guy. "Wally?"

"That man was in the car," Wally said, in great excitement, "when we got here."

"He's still in the car," Andy said, and rapped on the glass in the driver's door, calling to Ken, "Hey! What's the story?"

He found a key that popped over, and the engine purred. Ken looked over at the right-door mirror to back up and push the bread truck out of the way, when he saw a heavy-laden pickup pull into the driveway behind the van, filling the driveway and blocking the sidewalk as well. A handsome blond guy in cut-off jeans and a T-shirt that said *Work Is for People Who Don't Surf* got out and strolled curiously forward.

"What's the story here?" he asked.

"No idea, Doug," Stan said.

This was getting confusing. All these people to keep straight. Could he push both the van *and* the pickup? He had to try, get on out of here. He shifted into reverse—and watched a green and white taxi pull up to the curb, parking crosswise just behind the pickup. A feisty little woman in a man's cloth cap got out of the cab and joined the crowd beside the Cadillac.

"What's happening?"

"No idea, Mom," said Stan. "Dortmunder, do you . . ."

The other guy who had been in the Cadillac just shook his head. Ken considered the chain-link fence. No: the metal pipe supports were embedded in concrete. Get the elephant mad, he might pick up the Cadillac and shake it 'til Ken fell out.

The feisty little cab-driving woman went into the house. Andy leaned close to the glass separating him from Ken.

"We're gonna put a potato in the exhaust!" he yelled. "We're gonna monoxide you!"

Ken was feeling very put-upon, very confused. For the first time, he studied this mob around the Cadillac. They just didn't look right. Could he have made a mistake? But the car was right: make, model, and color. The M.D. plate was right. He'd picked it up in front of a mitt-camp, for God sake! There was even a tambourine on the backseat.

Still, *something* was wrong. Tambourine or no tambourine, these people just weren't Gypsies. As the woman cabdriver came out of the house carrying a big baking potato in her hand, Ken cracked the window beside him just far enough to talk. He announced through the crack, "Ngyou're gno Gnipthy!"

Andy reared back: *"What?"*

"Gnone of gnyou are Gnipthyth!"

"He's a foreigner," Stan decided. "He doesn't talk English."

Ken glared at him. "Ngyou makin funna me?"

"What is that he talks?" Stan's mom asked, holding the potato. "Polish?"

"Could be Lithuanian," the elephant rumbled doubtfully.

Dortmunder turned to stare at him. "Lithu*a*nian!"

"I had a Lithuanian cellmate once," the elephant explained. "He talked like—"

Ken had had enough. Pounding the steering wheel, "Ah'm thpeaking Englith!" he cried through the open slit of the window.

Which did no good. Dortmunder said to the elephant, "Tiny, tell him it's our car, then. Talk to him in Lithuanian."

Tiny. That figured. He said, "*I* don't speak Lith—"

"Ikth's *gnot* your car!" Ken yelled. "Ikth's gha *bankth's* car!"

"Wait a minute, wait a minute," Andy said. "I understood that."

Dortmunder turned his frown toward Andy: "You did?"

"He said, 'It's the bank's car.' "

311

"He did?"

"Fuckin' right!" Ken yelled.

Stan's mom pointed the potato at him. "*That* was English," she said accusingly.

"He's a repoman," Stan said.

"Ah'm a *hawk*!" Ken boasted.

"Yeah, a carhawk," Stan said.

Wally said, "Stan? What's going on?"

Stan explained, "He's a guy repossesses your car if you don't keep up the payments." Turning to Andy, he said, "You stole a stolen car. This guy wants it for the bank."

Ken nodded fiercely enough to whack his forehead against the window. "Yeah! Nghe bank!"

"Oh!" Andy spread his hands, grinning at the repoman. "Why didn't you say so?"

Ken peered mistrustfully at him.

"No, really, fella," Andy said, leaning close to the window, "no problem. Take it. We're done with it, anyway."

Handing Doug the potato, Stan's mom said, "I'll move my cab."

Handing Stan the potato, Doug said, "I'll move my pickup."

Handing Wally the potato, Stan said, "I'll move the van."

Wally pocketed the potato and smiled at Ken as if he'd never seen a repoman before.

Ken, with deep suspicion, watched all the other vehicles get moved out of his way. Everybody smiled and nodded at him. The other woman and the mean-looking old man came down off the porch. The woman smiled and did that thing like lighting a cigarette off an old one again.

The mean-looking guy said, "Kill him."

They all turned toward him at once. "Huh?"

The old guy waved his arms. "Drag him out through the crack in the window. Bury him in the backyard in a manila envelope. *He knows about us.*"

"He knows *what* about us?" asked Dortmunder reasonably.

Everybody nodded and turned back to Ken, still all smiles. The mean-looking old guy lapsed into moody silence.

Ken lowered his window another fraction of an inch and said, "Ngyou dough wanna arngue?"

Andy grinned amiably at him. "Argue with a fluent guy like you? I wouldn't dare. Have a happy. Drive it in good health." Then he leaned closer, more confidentially, to say, "Listen; the brake's a little soft."

The other vehicles were all out of the way now, but people kept milling around back there. The van driver returned from moving his van to lean down by Ken's window and say, "You heading back to the city? What you do, take the Palisades. Forget the Tappan Zee."

Ken couldn't stand it. Trying hopelessly to regain some sense of control over his own destiny, he stared around, grabbed the tambourine out of the backseat, and shoved it into the van driver's hand.

"Here," he said, "this ain't ghu bank's." For some reason, it was probably the clearest sentence of his life.

The blond guy stood down by the sidewalk and gestured for Ken to back it up, so he could guide him out to the street. Ken put the Cadillac in reverse again, and the woman from the porch came over to say, "You want a glass of water before you go?"

"Gno!" Ken screamed. "Gno! Jus lemme outta gnere!"

They did, too. Three or four of them gave him useful hand signals while he backed out to the street, and eight of the nine stood in the street to wave goodbye; a thing that has never happened to a carhawk before. Only the old guy glared after him with hate-filled eyes. Only the old guy knew how to act.

Ken had his Cadillac, but as he drove away, he just didn't feel very happy about it. Much of the fun had gone out of the transaction. There were right ways and wrong ways to do things. A repoman *took* a car, the people driving it *resisted*. That was the way it had always been, that was the way it would always be.

But not with these cheesecakes.

Halfway back to the city, however, the Toyota behind him on the towbar, Ken brightened. First Gyppo blood for him, right? He turned on the radio and started to drum his fingers on the steering wheel in time with the music. He'd finally figured out what was wrong with those screwy people who'd just *given* him the Caddy without any argument.

They were crooks; and you just couldn't trust crooks. Crooks

313

never did what was right and proper. Only the old guy who'd wanted to kill him had it right.

* * *

Back in Jersey, there was a message from Bart Heslip. Meet him and Larry Ballard in Grand Island, Nebraska, as quick as he could get there. Drive all day, all night if he had to.

Ken checked out and was on the road twenty minutes later in Pearso Stokes's new silver Eldorado. What a great road car for eating up the miles!

CHAPTER FORTY-THREE

Late that night, as Ken sped west through moonlit darkness toward Nebraska, O'B was getting himself arrested on a bluff overlooking the Mississippi just south of Stupidville.

It came about this way.

He arrived from Florida that afternoon to find that Giselle had reserved rooms for everyone at the Bide-A-Wee Motel.

But Dan Kearny had not checked in yet.

Bart Heslip had not checked in yet.

Ken Warren had not checked in yet.

Larry Ballard had checked in the day before, but then had left again, saying he would be back "in a day or two."

Giselle Marc had checked in but was nowhere around. No message. So O'B, at loose ends, did what he did best.

He played liar's dice in the Pirate's Landing ("Choice Steaks, Cocktails")—"I'll drink to that"—played horse in the Blue Moon Cafe ("DW—Dipped Walleye—Our Specialty")—"I'll drink to that"—shot pool at Kreuzer's Sportsman's Hall ("You Catch It— We Cook It")—"I'll drink to that"—played shuffleboard at the Gallery ("Where the Elite Meet to Eat")—"I'll drink to that"—and at nearly midnight had a hamburger at the Marina Mooring ("Deck Dining May to September")—"I'll even drink to that."

Alas, with all those drinks in him, it seemed to O'B like a good idea to scout out the huge conclave of Gypsies camped in Dieter Braun's field a mile south of town. Local kids liked to go up to the bluffs overlooking the field and park, he had learned, but the cops had been chasing them away because of reported "scandalous doings" in the encampment below.

O'B, knowing that the Gypsy society is among the most rigorously modest on earth, felt the tales of scantily clad dusky women parading around campfires was more adolescent wishful thinking than anything else. The Town Meeting scheduled for tomorrow night at the Elks Lodge would examine, he was sure, the Gypsies' endless thieving rather than any scandalous doings.

Anyway, O'B staggered back to the motel and got his car, by trial and error found the narrow dirt road winding through the hardwoods up to the big open-view area overlooking the moon-silvered Mississippi. There were no other cars.

Knee-high in sweet-smelling grass, he scoped the encampment below the edge of the bluff with a pair of binoculars he'd found in the glove box. There actually was enough light from campfires and the moon to let him pick out several new Cadillacs beside the tents and trailers. Easy pickings for DKA tomorrow . . .

Headlights transfixed him, a harsh voice snapped, "Hold it right there, mister!"

O'B turned, squinted into the lights, holding the hand with the binoculars up to shield his eyes. Two burly uniformed policemen moved in on him from either side of the headlights.

"Tryna get a look at them Gypsy women?" demanded one cop.

O'B started to reply with something zesty—like, What are those binoculars in *your* hands for, Officers?—then remembered how much he'd had to drink. Whoa! Easy, hoss!

"Think we oughtta roust the bastard, Lloyd?"

"Let's let him go this time, Frank . . ."

They waited as he walked back to his car—thank God for the uneven ground, it would account for any slight unsteadiness of gait—got in, and drove away. To find a track into a nearby cow pasture where he hid his car under the hardwoods, killed the lights and motor, and waited.

Roust him, indeed! Let the bastard go, indeed! They had started to believe the tales of the kids they'd sent home, that was it, and wanted him out of there so *they* could spy on the Gypsy women. But he was here on a *professional mission!* It all got his Irish up, begorra! He'd *carry out that mission!*

Of course a little basic caution was called for. Some camouflage, that was the ticket. And he knew just where to find it. Kalia Uwanowich, that Gypsy scamp, must have had a sideline for times when the bogus roofing trade was slow: O'B had found a trunkful of "novelty items" and "marital aids" while itemizing the personal property for his condition report on the Allante.

Ten minutes later the police cruiser went by, heading back to town. A little sober voice deep inside whispered that O'B should just return to the motel and go to bed—tomorrow was another day. But the booze was positively shouting in his ear, *Action! Action!*

Chuckling to himself, O'B opened the trunk on its spate of thoroughly ingenious—if often grotesque—devices from Japan to plug into auto cigarette lighters, insert into various body cavities, and the like. There were two cartons of explicit photo magazines from Australia ("XXX Nonviolent Erotica, All Models Over 18"). And, perfect for O'B's purposes, two boxed Anatomically Correct Life-size Inflatable Latex Sex Dolls ("You Need Never Do It Alone Again") made right here in the good old U.S. of A. One blonde, one brunette.

O'B chose the blonde.

By the time he managed to get her blown up, he was red-faced and panting, about ready to forget the whole thing. But from a dozen feet away, sitting on the front seat with the door open and the overhead light on, she looked extemely lifelike, from the tippy-tips of her red rubber toes to the Dynel champagne-blond crown of her inflated latex head.

But also extremely *nude*. Extremely *naked*.

Well, he was, after all, going to a lover's lane. But he would drape his sports coat decorously around her shoulders. And by parking broadside and very close to the edge of the bluff, he could lean across his anatomically correct companion, put his elbows on the edge of the open window, and glass the encampment below. All anyone would be able to see of her was her hair. To the casual glance, just a guy snuggling up to his gal.

But he found that the booze was dying in him, his head was

starting to ache, there was a distinctly chilly breeze blowing up from off the river, and nearly all of the Gypsy campfires were out. He couldn't see a bloody thing. To hell with it.

He started to draw back into the car, barked his knuckles on the window frame, and dropped the binoculars on the floor. In leaning down to grope for them, he unwittingly pulled his coat off the inflated nude figure.

Damn! The glasses had gone under the seat. He leaned down farther still, his face pressed firmly into the dummy's Dynel-ornamented anatomically correct lap, his other hand groping for the doorframe. By bitter mischance, it closed around one of the latex doll's extremely lifelike triple-D breasts.

That's when the policemen sneaking up on his car shone their flashlights in the windows.

"He's got her buckass nekkid and his goddam *face* in her *lap*, Lloyd!"

"An' grabbin' her *tit*, Frank!"

O'B tried to sit up, cracked his head painfully on the underside of the dash.

"That ain't no woman, Lloyd! It's one of them sex dolls!"

"We got us a damn *pervert*, Frank! Spyin' on the women down there to the campground, then up here with his face in—"

Guns were suddenly pointed at him.

"OKAY, YOU, OUTTA THE CAR! HANDS ON TOP OF YOUR HEAD!"

"YOU GOT THE RIGHT TO REMAIN SILENT . . ."

Busted.

* * *

Dawn in Nebraska. Grunts of effort, grate of trenching tools against stone as three kneeling figures dug a hole in the rocky soil big enough to bury a midget or a large dog.

"Good enough," panted one. "They'll be coming soon."

The three men in black jumpsuits donned black ski masks, picked up their weapons, and separated to their assigned posts.

* * *

The twenty-two-vehicle Lovelli caravan rolled east through the plains along a two-lane highway. The rising sun dazzled their eyes while showing that the early May buffalo grass, nevermore to be cropped by its namesakes, was still green and lush. In a month it would be sere and silver. A low hill rose from the prairie ahead; the road cut straight through it, flanked on both sides by rock faces of shale deposited by the shallow inland seas that had once covered the region. The Lovellis drove toward it.

*　　*　　*

The black-clad figure prone on the rounded apex of the hill took his binoculars down from his eyes. He said into his walkie-talkie, "Here they come, guys! ETA three minutes."

*　　*　　*

As it reached the far side of the narrow cut through the hill, some three city blocks in length, the lead car of the caravan squealed to a stop: crosswise on the highway in front of it was a car-trailer used to haul new cars to dealers. It completely blocked the road. As the caravan skidded to a stop, a second big car-trailer came bouncing out of a sandy-floored wash to block the highway just behind the last Gypsy vehicle.

Trapped.

Yojo Lovelli, the clan patriarch at 55, got stiffly out of the lead car—a new Cadillac Coupe de Ville from Cal-Cit Bank, as it chanced—tested his knees, and looked around. There was a moment of relative silence except for the grumbling of the engines and the soughing of the prairie wind.

Then there was the unmistakable harsh metallic sound of a shotgun shell being jacked into a chamber. A man in a black jumpsuit and wearing a black ski mask over his head came around the front of the car-trailer with a sawed-off 12-gauge shotgun.

Yojo, not yet intimidated, began, "Hey, whatta hell you—"

To be drowned out by a bullhorned voice from above them. "NOW HEAR THIS! NOW HEAR THIS! YOU ARE SUR-ROUNDED!"

Another shotgun shell was jacked into another chamber; a second man, dressed and armed like the first, appeared above them on the lip of the embankment with the bullhorn. Behind them, yet a third shotgun was worked to bring a shell into its chamber.

"REMAIN IN YOUR VEHICLES!" ordered the bullhorn. There

was a scrambling back of unarmed Gypsies who had started to get out of their cars and pickups. "EXCEPT FOR THE NEW CADILLACS . . ."

Yojo was poised on a knife-edge of resistance: he didn't want to lose his Coupe de Ville. He didn't want to lose face with his clan. But he didn't want to lose any of his people to these madmen, either. His moment passed.

"Goddammit!" he said as he stepped away from his Caddy.

Within twenty minutes, the seven Cal-Cit cars were lined up on the shoulder of the road, empty of people and possessions, engines whispering. The man on the hilltop stayed there, watching for any approaching highway patrol vehicle. None showed. Where they had real luck was that no other travelers appeared on the road from either direction; of course it was early and the Gypsies themselves had chosen this route for its relative lack of use.

The driver of the truck blocking their passage east climbed up into his cab and ran the truck forward so one lane of the highway was open. The man on the top of the hill just couldn't resist his bullhorn one last time.

"EASTWARD . . . *HO!*"

The caravan moved. Yojo's wife, Vera, cursed the car thieves through her open window in passing.

"May your testicles wither! May your members be soft! May your wives cuckold you! May your children be born dead!"

As the last car began to move, the other truck pulled around on the shoulder behind it. The driver jumped out to pull down the truck's clanking metal ramp and fix it in place.

Because occasional cars were passing in each direction now, the three men quickly stripped off their jumpsuits and ski masks to become Bart Heslip (front truck), Larry Ballard (hilltop), and Ken Warren (rear truck). They tossed their attack clothing and sawed-off shotguns into the sage along the shoulder of the road. Within fifteen minutes, all the cars were loaded, along with Bart's and Ken's two other Cadillacs they had kept hidden in the arroyo.

"Think the Gyps'll flag down the highway patrol?" asked Ballard a little nervously.

Ken Warren shook his head. "Gno."

"Guess not, at that. 'Hey, Officer—somebody stole our stolen cars!' "

"And the closest town is two hours away," said Bart Heslip. He was feeling mighty good about this coup he had engineered. A lot could have gone wrong, from the highway patrol showing up to a Gyppo buck trying to jump one of their shotguns. None had. He added, "Ken and I'll be on the interstate inside of *one* hour."

Larry shook hands with them before they started off, yelling after them, "GO GETTEM, BEARS!" That had been Kathy Onoda's invariable order as she sent them out into the field, and since her death it had become a DKA rallying cry.

When the rented truck-trailer rigs had disappeared to the west and no traffic was in sight, Ballard dumped the discarded jumpsuits, ski masks, and shotguns into the predawn hole they had dug. In the unlikely event the Gyppos did blow the whistle, no incriminating evidence would be found on them.

As he filled in the hole, artistically replanting over it an uprooted clump of rabbitbrush, the only observer was a ferruginous hawk *kweee-e-eing* down at him as it passed in its rocking, side-to-side flight half a hundred feet above his head.

Finally, he recovered his rental car from beneath a pile of brush in the dry gulch, and turned its nose east toward the Mississippi, and Stupidville—and, hopefully, Yana.

The recovery count in the Great Gypsy Hunt had just risen from fourteen to twenty-one.

CHAPTER
FORTY-FOUR

In those same predawn hours that the DKA boys dug the grave for the contraband black jumpsuits and artistically sawed-off shot-guns Bart had bought in Chicago, Lulu Zlachi was practicing some artistry of her own on Staley in his room at Stupidville General Hospital. The *rom* would be descending on the place at first light, and the King had to be ready to receive them.

"Hey, that stuff feels good," exclaimed Staley.

"It *is* good," she said complacently. "A mix of St. Ives Swiss Formula Firming Mask and Johnson's Baby Oil. Mineral clay— make you look good and beautiful."

"Make me look good and dead," grinned Staley.

Lulu smoothed more of the mixture onto his hands and face. "Good and *almost* dead," she amended.

"Close enough so they'll believe I'm gonna go any minute?"

"But not so close you can't have a miraculous recovery."

Yes, it was a thin artistic line indeed that Lulu walked. Or rather, smeared.

*   *   *

At 9:00 A.M. a terrifically hung-over O'B, with only hazy recollection of the previous night's events, was brought over from the four-cell town jail to the county courthouse and arraigned before Judge Konrad Spitz on charges of lewd and lascivious conduct and possession of pornographic materials.

Thank God, there was Dan Kearny himself, wearing a suit and a tie and a sour expression. What did he have to be so sore about? O'B was the one with the headache, wasn't he? And sundry itches that suggested the jail needed a good fumigating.

Judge Spitz was a white-haired man with muttonchop whiskers and wire-frame glasses. He peered over them first at O'B and then at the two complaining officers.

"All right, what do we have here?" he asked.

Lloyd and Frank testified as to what had happened the night before. The whole courtroom was laughing—mostly drunks up from the tank, and their lawyers—when they had finished.

Dan Kearny cleared his throat and said, "Your Honor, may I address the court?"

"And you are, sir?"

"Daniel Kearny from San Francisco, Your Honor. This man is in my employ. We are in town to try and recover a number of illegally obtained automobiles from the Gypsies in the encampment south of Steubenville. In his capacity as a private detective, Mr. O'Bannon recovered a car from a Gypsy in Florida . . ."

Kearny explained away the pornographic material found in O'B's trunk. O'B had been on the bluff, not to ogle Gypsy women, but to ogle Cadillac cars. It was unfortunate that . . .

Et cetera.

O'B then explained that he had inflated the doll so he would look like a harmless necker rather than a tough private eye, but he had dropped his flashlight and . . .

Judge Spitz began, "From the look of your eyes, sir—"

"You ought to see them from in here, Your Honor."

Kearny looked stormy, but Judge Spitz allowed himself a small grin. Then he turned to Frank and Lloyd.

"Gentlemen," he said in a deceptively soft voice, "I know of no law against parking with an inflatable latex doll. Especially since you arrested Mr. O'Bannon outside the city limits." He leaned forward and roared, *"Outside your jurisdiction!"* He SLAMMED down his gavel. *"Dismissed."*

Kearny and O'B crossed the street in silence to the Dew Drop In Coffee Shop ("Wake Up with Our Bottomless Cup"), where the waitress found them a booth in the corner so bright light couldn't pierce O'B's sunglasses. He tried a little levity.

"What I really need, Reverend, is a Bloody Mary."

"Buy it on your own goddam time!" snapped Kearny.

"Listen, Reverend, I saw a lot of Cadillacs out there last night. When the rest of the crew gets here—"

"You won't see them there this morning. It's all over town—redheaded Irishman claiming he was repoman from San Francisco getting busted on the cliffs overlooking the Gyppo encampment! All the Cal-Cit cars are gone."

"Gone where?" asked O'B stupidly. His head was even worse.

"Why the hell didn't you just keep your mouth shut last night? You knew I'd be here to bail you out."

"I . . . don't remember what I said," admitted O'B sheepishly.

"Well, you'll have a lot of time to figure it out on the plane back to San Francisco," said Kearny.

"What do you mean?"

"G'wan. Get out of here. Screw up somewhere else." He suddenly stood, throwing some money on the table to cover their coffees. "I mean it, O'B. I'm sick of your goddam boozing."

Alone in the booth, O'B sipped his coffee and tried a little toast. One bite was all he could stomach.

Hell, his drinking wasn't *that* bad. Just social. He could take or leave it alone . . . couldn't he?

As O'B wandered disconsolately back to the hotel to sleep it off—Kearny wouldn't *really* send him back to California, would he?—Kearny himself was trying to think of a way to salvage the situation. He knew what he wanted to do, he just didn't know how to arrange . . . But once again, necessity inspired genius. Kearny had an idea. Maybe even a brilliant one.

He went in search of Alvin Crichton, M.D.

*   *   *

Until Kearny saw him, Doc Crichton thought he was going crazy. The hospital grounds, park areas, rooms, hallways, and elevators were jammed with Gypsies. Gypsies in droves, paying no attention to visiting hours, eating and drinking everywhere, passing their food and drink around, spilling it on the floor, bothering staff and patients alike.

Swarthy-skinned, brightly dressed, clamorous *Gypsies*. The cacophony was deafening, defeating, head-splitting. In a *hospital!* *His* hospital! What were they *doing* here?

Well . . . stealing.

Everything movable, portable, or salable in the way of hospital furnishings and equipment. Several of them had been stopped trying to dismantle the X-ray machine and cart it away. Apprehended, they just grinned and shrugged and walked off—to be instantly lost in the throng of other Gypsies.

And a shifting population of some fifty *rom* seemed to be crowded into the room of his patient Karl Klenhard at any given moment. On the bed lay Staley, eyes mostly closed, looking ghastly, his fishbelly skin slightly tinged with almost luminous green, as if he already had started to decompose.

He lifted his eyelids with difficulty. His voice rasped in his throat. "It is . . . so good for you . . . all," he managed. "So good . . . so loyal . . ."

Lulu chimed in, "Please, your gifts—if you could take them to Three Forty-seven Riverview Avenue where we were staying when Staley . . . when Staley . . ."

She broke down and started to sob. A dozen Gypsies supported her to her chair beside her husband's bed. Voices were clamoring, making so much noise that no one heard the door open behind them or saw Dr. Crichton framed in the opening.

"Mr. Klenhard!" Crichton's voice burst out. "Mrs. Klenhard! What is this all about?"

Staley quickly shut his eyes and played—almost literally—dead. Lulu quickly took over. "The meanin' of what, Doctor? These are friends, relatives, come to pay their respects—"

"They're *Gypsies! You're* Gypsies!"

"Even Gypsies gotta have relatives and friends, Doctor," she said reasonably. "They heard that my husband was sick, they come to pay their respects—"

"They're destroying my hospital and I won't have it," said Crichton. "You have to get them out of here."

Staley opened his eyes. He said in a weak voice, "Well, gee, Doc, if that's the way you feel about it . . ." His voice quavered, his fingers plucked wanly at the coverlet. "I thought you was my friend . . ."

But Crichton was not to be swayed.

"I'm sorry, but you've gotten your settlement from the insurance company, a very fine settlement, and you now can afford private care facilities if you have not recovered . . ."

From the corridor outside came a nurse's voice.

"Make way here, please! We have a patient here. Make way, please. Coming through . . ."

There was stirring in the Gypsies crowding the doorway and spilling out into the corridor. A gurney was thrust through them into the room. On it was a sheet-covered middle-aged man with grey hair and a heavy face and a strong profile. He was very pale, and looked almost as sick as Staley was pretending to be.

"This man is post-op and needs quiet to recover from surgery," said Crichton. "I have to ask your friends—"

He was drowned out by angry denunciations from the Gypsies, who were, however, in their turn drowned out by Lulu's voice.

"Romale—men of Romany."

The formal salutation grabbed their attention; silence fell. The nurse, ignoring them all, was transferring her patient from the gurney to the bed. Lulu was going on in quieter tones.

"This man, he's sick, he's got a right. If you stay, you gotta be quiet . . ."

Staley opened his eyes again. In his weak voice, he said, "To-night, at the encampment, I'm gonna choose my successor . . ."

His eyes drooped shut and he fell silent. The nurse completed her work with the patient in the next bed, and she and Crichton departed.

* * *

Out at the encampment a feature writer from the Sunday *Minneapolis Tribune*, calling herself Gerry Merman, was interviewing Gypsies for an in-depth look at the ritual of choosing a new King. She was a tall blonde and she was getting a lot of good stuff from the *rom* women. Gypsies are never averse to sympathetic publicity, and this one was a sucker for their stories and opinions.

"Honey, we Gypsies gotta live together because we can't make it apart."

"What about love affairs with *gadje?*" asked the reporter in an oddly nervous voice.

"Sure, some of us have 'em—but they never last," said a young girl who looked like a heavily made-up disco queen. "I had a *gadjo* lover once, but I was too lonely."

"Join the group," said Merman.

Everybody laughed.

A girl recently married, alone with her, said, "I gotta get pregnant quick as I can. Right now I live with my husband's parents, and it's killing me. I'm just a servant to them."

It was the old women, however, who were most vocal—and most opinionated. One who called herself Aunt Bessie invited Merman into her trailer for tea. She waved a vile cigar while explaining why the Gypsies stayed apart from the mainstream.

"We send our kids to your schools, what happens? They get beat up! Or they get raped by black men! I'd be crucified like Jesus before I'd let my granddaughter go to school."

Scribbling madly in her reporter's narrow fat notebook in short-hand learned as a part-time after-school girl working at DKA, Giselle found herself wishing she really were a journalist. Some of the stuff she was getting was really good.

Well, she wasn't a journalist. She was a detective.

And a woman, too. A woman not getting what she so desperately desired, a glimpse of Rudolph Marino.

Or even a glimpse of the pink Cadillac; because wherever that car was, Rudolph would not be far away.

CHAPTER FORTY-FIVE

It was dusk and nearing the end of visiting hours when the nephew of the sick man in the next bed arrived for a visit. A tall blond man with strong features, he plumped his uncle's pillows while telling all about his trip from Nebraska.

"I drove straight through so I could see you tonight. My partners already had left for California with the merchandise."

"Terrif!" exclaimed the sick man. His voice was remarkably strong for one operated on that afternoon.

Meanwhile, Staley was about ready to depart for the encampment. He held out a shaky hand to his wife. "My love, can you find a gurney for them to . . ."

"HIM!" yelled a Gypsy just coming into the room. All eyes turned to him, but he was pointing at the nephew of the sick man in the other bed. "HE'S THE CAR THIEF WHAT TOOK MY CADILLAC!"

Tucon Yonkovich never got to finish. Larry Ballard hit the doorway running, bursting through the gathered Gypsies like flood stage through a dam. Half a hundred Gypsies took out after him, shrieking their wrath. Even Staley, forgetting the iron-haired, iron-faced man in the other bed, hit the floor running to go see the fun.

328

"*Staley!*" yelled Lulu in warning.

He turned to stagger back to bed, but it was much too late.

"Remarkable recovery," said Dan Kearny with a hard-faced grin. "Almost miraculous."

Staley gave a little shrug—what could he do? He'd just forgotten himself after all those weeks in that goddamned bed.

"You too," he said.

Kearny nodded. "How you gonna keep the Gyppos from finding out you've been scamming them from the beginning?"

He was at the closet taking out his clothes. Staley made a gesture and Lulu went out, closing the door behind her.

"How indeed?" said Staley tentatively.

$$* \quad * \quad *$$

Larry Ballard was running for his life on the floor below, a corridor full of Gypsies in hot pursuit. He kept trying to slow them down by throwing anything he could find into their path—a waiting room lamp, an abandoned gurney, an unused Murphy stand without any plastic IV bottles, an empty laundry hamper.

But whoever he took out of the chase, there were fifty still in it. Seeking the emergency stairs, he skittered into a cross-corridor under the nose of a nurse wheeling an old gentleman in a wheelchair with a blanket across his knees. He'd hit full stride before he realized he'd turned the wrong direction. The stairs were the other way.

Rooms right and left, worse traps than the hallway, linen closet, ditto, rest rooms, ditto, the shouting throng was closing in on him, the dead-end wall loomed ahead.

With an open window. Ballard started to yell when he was ten feet from it, hit his stride like a hurdler, leaped out feet-first, ready to tuck and roll when he hit the ground below. Instead, with a bone-jarring impact, he landed right in the backseat of an open convertible tucked away behind the hospital.

"*OOOF!*"

The car leaped forward. Ballard could hear the diminishing yells of the Gyppos hanging out of the window behind him, even as he felt himself over for anything broken. The driver jerked around to stare wide-eyed over his shoulder at whatever had landed in his car. The driver was Rudolph Marino! The car was the pink Caddy! Recognition widened the eyes of both men.

"Bastard!" Marino yelped.

"Son of a bitch!" Ballard croaked.

Neither man got physical. Marino was too busy not using his lights while dodging hardwoods with nothing more than a dirt track to follow. Ballard was too breathless. The Eldorado went into a controlled skid, righted itself, CRASHED across a curb, squealed its tires in another skid, and was driving sedately along a back street of Stupidville.

"You stole my money and this car from me!"

"Yana's car. The hotel's money."

"My car now—I've just stolen it back again."

"Until I take it away again."

By the illumination of passing streetlights, Marino found Ballard's face in the rearview mirror.

"They'll tear you apart if they find you."

"I'll get by."

"No you won't. I'll have to disguise you to save your worthless butt, *gadjo*, until I am King and can protect you."

Why the hell not him as Gypsy King, come to think of it? Yana as Queen would be inaccessible, but if Rudolph were King . . .

"Maybe I can help you with that King thing," said Ballard.

*   *   *

The Elks Lodge was a big bare echoing room with stuffed deer heads on bare wooden walls, hardwood floors scarred and stained by countless years of Saturday night smokers, as well as the occasional holiday special events when the Elks could bring their Does to dance polkas.

At tonight's Town Meeting no one was dancing, or even drinking. Mix alcohol with emotion, Mayor Strohbach, presiding, said sententiously, and you could have vigilantism.

"Maybe we need a little vigilantism," said Himmler, the former nosetackle.

"They're corrupting our youth," asserted Mary Lonquist.

"They steal babies," said Noreen Degenhart, kindergarten teacher. "When I was a child—"

"We must be Christian men and women," said Reverend Tidmarsh. "There has been a great deal of stealing, but no one has been assaulted—"

32 Cadillacs

"Look what they did at the hospital today!" burst out Himmler, neck veins swelling dangerously. "I say, throw them out before they wreck the town!"

"They've already done that—"

"As Christians we can't condone—"

"I don't care, my children's safety—"

Mayor Strohbach pounded the table with a makeshift gavel, but no one listened. The Town Meeting was getting away from him.

* * *

Giselle had never known anything like it. The encampment suddenly was every Gypsy movie she had ever seen. Fires filled the night with the rich smell of roasting meat and fowl. The women were in traditional dress: long silks and bright scarves, great glittering golden hoop earrings swaying as they danced. Children and pets were everywhere, scooting underfoot, leaping over the campfires. Violins, tambourines, balalaikas.

Firelight across brown faces, strong bodies. Someone with a splendid sob in her alto voice was singing an old Romany song whose meaning Giselle could only guess at.

> *Kay hin m'ro vodyi?*
> *Ujes hin cavo,*
> *Ujes sar o kam,*
> *Ujes sar pani . . .*

But nowhere did she see Rudolph. The word was that the King had had some sort of miraculous recovery; when he arrived, surely Rudolph would also appear.

She cut through some bushes toward another part of the encampment, gnawing on a turkey leg, when there in front of her, gleaming like a polished rocket, was the pink Eldorado convertible! Top down, whitewalls glowing in the semi-dark . . .

If she could spirit away the car, she would control the succession for the dying King's crown! Her head whirled: was she repowoman, or a woman with a *rom* lover? Would she—

"HER!" shrieked a hate-filled voice. "THAT'S HER!" Giselle whirled to be impaled by flashlight beams. Sonia Lovari! No longer

Miwok Indian, now only *rom*. *"She's no newswoman, she's the repo bitch who stole my car in San Francisco!"*

"Repo bitch! Repo bitch!"

"Get her!"

Nonviolent Gypsies? Giselle fled through the woods, half a hundred screaming *rom* women after her. She leaped a campfire, ran down a row of trailers and campers, darted between them . . .

And came face-to-face with that same most beautiful woman she had ever seen. Yana!

"You!" they exclaimed together.

There was a frozen moment; then something passed between them. Something unspoken, some measurement of worth, some understanding between women who'd had to cut their own deals in a man's world on man's terms—and had survived. And prospered.

"Quickly, come, or they will tear you apart!"

Yana threw open the door of the nearest trailer and shoved her inside, tumbled in behind her. She pulled the door silently closed as the clamor of pursuit passed by outside.

"I must hide you, keep you alive until I am Queen."

Well, why not? thought Giselle. A Rudolph who was King would be totally inaccessible. But if Yana were Queen . . .

"I know where the pink Cadillac is," she said.

"Hidden behind the hospital."

"No."

An almost imperceptible pause, then: "I will disguise you so you can show me."

*   *   *

Staley Zlachi stood on an impromptu platform in the middle of the encampment, in the midst of his people, tears in his eyes. His loyal subjects! Still roaring with laughter from his tale of his complicated scam to take the insurance man for $75,000.

"Assembled people of Romany, you know of my recovery this day at the hospital—"

A mighty roar from five hundred throats.

"But though cured, I must ask if perhaps it is time to step aside for younger blood. But how to choose?" No shouts now—the throng was not taking the question as rhetorical. They wanted to know.

"Well, what is the Gypsy way? How can the contenders show they are better steeped in our Gypsy traditions than any other?"

He looked around the assembled throng. Oh, he had them in the palm of his hand!

"Since Christ our Savior hung on the shameful cross, it has been our way to steal from the *gadje*—who through the centuries have stolen from us our place in the sun, our very lives."

A great shout went up. Yes! To be a *rom* was to rip off the *gadje!* The one who did it best deserved to lead the *rom!*

"WHO CLAIMS MY THRONE?" yelled Staley.

Springing up on either side of him were Yana and Rudolph. Each in finest Gypsy dress. Across Staley's portly figure they exchanged looks, each triumphant. Staley took a hand of each.

"Now, my children, how do you honor your King?"

Almost in unison, they exclaimed, "With a pink nineteen fifty-eight Cadillac convertible like that in which you drove to your coronation."

"Wonderful!" exclaimed Staley, beaming upon them. "The kind of car I sought to be buried in." He looked from one to the other. "*Which* of you has brought me such a car?"

Each cried out in ringing tones, "I have!"

Again almost in unison, they both turned and gestured out into the crowd. Which parted. And the massive pink Cadillac rolled majestically forward into the cleared space in front of the platform.

But behind the wheel was no minion of either! Staley's wife, Lulu, was driving it!

Staley looked from one to the other in apparent amazement.

"You each claim this car as your gift, yet it is my wife who drives it?"

Yana and Rudolph looked at one another in confusion; both were sure they had secured the car and had subverted their own particular DKA lackey to bring it here on their signal.

Lulu stepped out with Queenly grace, letting all see the interior beauty of the car before shutting the door.

"*Who claims it now?*" thundered Staley.

There was silence.

CHAPTER
FORTY-SIX

At that exquisite moment a tall lean Gypsy lad dressed in tight leggings and a loose silk tunic with puff sleeves, a silk bandana knotted around his head, streaked through the crowd to vault lightly into the car, hit the horn and the accelerator, and ROAR it forward. It ran right through a cook fire, sending a big iron cauldron of soup spinning lazily off into the darkness, scattering Gypsies, kids, dogs, cats, and chickens—even a pig—in every direction.

Giselle in her boy's clothing spun the wheel, skidding on the grass, threading her way through cars, trailers, pickups, tents, cook fires . . .

Repowoman.

Seeing Rudolph up there with his own, she had suddenly known he was where he should be—trying to scam his way into power among his people. And she was where *she* should be—stealing his goddam car!

She shrieked and stood on the brakes as almost up in front of her popped an aged Gyspy crone in tattered silks, clanking metal coins and beads and hoops and ornaments, her head shawled in a bright scarf. But as the car slewed by almost sideways, she vaulted lightly into the rider's seat beside Giselle. The Caddy shot out of the encampment into the highway as they fought for control of it.

Behind them, everyone was scrambling for cars, trucks, campers, anything on wheels in which to give pursuit, but they were arrested by Staley's suddenly booming voice.

"LET IT GO!" Movement ceased, heads turned faces slack with confusion toward him. "*Let it go*, my children, I cannot now claim it, anyway. I have realized that *I* must remain King of the Gypsies until I die! I cannot give away this sacred power, for we now see that only I know how to wield it fully . . ."

Right into the outskirts of town the glorious finned monster roared, as the two apparent Gypsies battled for control of it. Half the time the car drove itself as they tried to shove each other, elbowed and cursed and . . .

The crone's clutching fingers tore Giselle's scarf from her head. Her lustrous blond hair tumbled out to blow about her face. The crone stopped fighting, staring at her openmouthed. Giselle, sensing advantage, tried to slam the crone's head against the dash. Instead, she stripped the silken shawl from around her shoulders and face.

Rather, Ballard's face.

No hand on the wheel, no foot on the accelerator, the pink Cadillac slowed to a halt half on and half off the road.

Of common accord, they leaped out to stagger around in the road like drunks, laughing, wiping the makeup from their faces, panting out their stories . . . Giselle was suddenly sober.

"Larry, what about Yana? If you love her—"

"When I saw her up there with Rudolph, Giselle, I suddenly realized . . . that's where she belongs . . ." He jerked his head at the pink Cadillac. "And here's where I belong. Stealing cars from the goddam Gyppos."

The last barrier was down. They hugged each other, delighted with their rediscovered friendship. And thus did not see the trunk lid pop up a few careful inches.

"The look on your face when I almost ran you down . . ."

"The look on yours when I jumped in and started fighting you for the wheel . . ."

With a ROAR the pink Cadillac fishtailed away from them, leaving them gaping in the middle of the road. They ran after it a few steps, then stopped. Hopeless.

They looked at one another, both started to speak, neither did. By common accord, they started trudging wearily down the road. The greatest sin in Dan Kearny's moral code was losing a repo once you had your hands on it. What the hell were they going to tell him when they got to their distant motel?

*　　*　　*

If they got there. Most of the townspeople, after their Town Meeting, had gone to their beds like good citizens. But a small group, led by Herr Himmler, had gone hunting along highways and byways with lanterns and clubs. They found no Gyppos, of course, because they were giving the encampment a wide berth. Out there, after all, were half a thousand Gypsies to their scant fifty. Where was the glory in that?

But God was good. God was just.

Walking down the road toward them were *two* Gypsies, all alone, one a tall old crone, the other a tall young man . . .

"There's two of the bastards!" yelled Himmler. He slapped his bat against his palm and started running toward them.

"Get 'em!" screamed Mary Lonquist, and tightened her grip on her short-handled garden hoe as she broke into a dainty run.

Yes, they would pet them with lead pipes, make them believers with baseball bats . . .

*　　*　　*

Coming at them in a sudden rush down the blacktop was a solid mass of local yokels with hoes, rakes, bats, lead pipes, scythes, their wildly bouncing lanterns illuminating their hate-distorted faces.

"Christ!" yelled Ballard, "it's the villagers, come to get us! We're in a goddam Frankenstein movie!"

They whirled and ran for their lives, but it had been a long day and a longer night, and the angry townspeople gained on them with every stride.

Ballard, chest heaving, said, "Keep going. Get help. I'll slow them down."

"No! I'll stand with you!"

But out of the darkness came snarling a great gleaming pink

beast. "GET IN! GET IN!" yelled the driver, already tromping on it even as they were tumbling into the backseat.

As Dan Kearny sent the car arrowing away from the angry, frustrated mob, Ballard said bitterly, "So it was *you* in the trunk! You stole this thing from us!"

"Yeah. Of course."

"But why . . ." Giselle was nonplussed.

"Why, for old Staley, of course." Kearny gestured with one hand while driving with the other. "He wants this car, but he couldn't keep it if he wasn't going to die, or at least surrender the crown. But if he could *steal* it back from a couple of *gadje* who stole it from him . . ."

"You *expected* one of us to grab it at the encampment."

"One or both of you, sure. I found it hidden in the bushes, had Lulu drive it while I hid in the trunk."

"So you're going to just turn it back to him? After—"

"Hell no!" Kearny swung the wheel to send the long sleek car up the road to the top of the bluff where O'B had come to grief the night before. "We'll let the village idiots go home before we do anything else."

He braked the car, killed the engine. They could hear wild music, voices, laughter, singing from the Gypsy encampment below, carried to them up the face of the bluff on the rising night air.

They walked to the edge and looked down at a hundred gleaming campfires that silhouetted cavorting figures in archaic costumes. Kearny mused, "What with this car and the insurance money and all the death gifts from the *rom*, I suppose old Staley'll clear a couple hundred grand from all this."

"And that doesn't bother you?" demanded Ballard savagely.

"Why should it, Larry? If fools get taken—"

Giselle said almost dreamily, "What about DKA's extra hundred-eighty grand? Does *that* bother you?"

"No. We're going to set up the Daniel Kearny Associates Foundation with that money," said Kearny airily.

"A foundation?" she said weakly. "To do what?"

"Help Gyppos who want to learn how to read and write."

Giselle didn't understand it, but was seeing it all now.

"And who better to tell us who wants an education than—"

"Who better indeed? Staley Zlachi."

Ballard said almost hoarsely, "King of the Gyppos? Are you nuts? Soft in the head? If he gets his hands on that money—"

"He won't. We pay the tuition directly to the school—he just advises." He shrugged. "Hell, maybe I'm just getting old."

They fell silent, still staring down at the scene below. Distance made it like a childhood dream of summer, a memory of something never known yet somehow recalled. It was, for that pure moment, a fairy tale brought to life. Dan Kearny sighed.

"Well, we'd better go pick up O'B at the motel. We still got ten Cal-Cit cars to get."

They walked back to the pink Cadillac, paused with the doors open.

"Okay, I'll bite," said Ballard. "Old Zlachi's gonna advise us on this foundation, but who's gonna advise us on where to find those Gyppo Cadillacs?"

"Zlachi already has. He gets back *this* car only *after* we get the other Cadillacs."

"You mean he's selling out his own people."

"That was the whole idea. To put him in the vise so—"

Giselle demanded, "Dan, when did you decide to—"

"Back in San Francisco, when you told me he wanted a pink Cadillac to be buried in. I figured that just *had* to be a scam on his own people. That's when I knew I could make a deal with the crooked old bastard."

Getting into the car, Giselle remembered what a nice old gentleman Staley looked while actually being slippery as a snake.

"If you sup with the devil, Dan'l, you better have a long spoon."

"I hope Zlachi's is long enough," said Dan Kearny.

He started the pink Cadillac. Larry Ballard and Giselle Marc fell into each other's arms in helpless laughter.